Shimmer

- 2016 -

THE COLLECTED STORIES

- 2016 -
THE COLLECTED STORIES

EDITED BY E. CATHERINE TOBLER

Shimmer
2016: The Collected Stories

Published by Shimmer, 2017

trade paper ISBN
ISBN-13:
978-1540871596

ISBN-10:
1540871592

Visit Shimmer Magazine at
www.shimmerzine.com

Contents

PALINGENESIS

Megan Arkenberg

Ah me! how hard a thing it is to say
  What was this forest savage, rough, and stern,
  Which in the very thought renews the fear.
~Dante Alighieri, *Inferno, Canto I*

* * *

Every city has an explanation. A strike of coal or silver that brought the miners running, or a hot spring that holds the frost at bay. A railroad or a shift in the current. Most people say this city started with the river. The water is everywhere you look, sluggish and brown most seasons, bearing the whiskey-smell of peat out from the forest, and carrying nothing downstream except mats of skeletal leaves. Seven bridges straddle the river between First and Barton Road as it winds through a downtown of antique stores, the crepe-streamered American Legion, the purple house advertising tarot and palm readings. One of the bridges goes nowhere, ending four feet above the ground behind a solitary Chinese restaurant, and no one has ever been able to tell me what it used to reach. On the east bank, sitting mostly by itself between the paved river walk and the ties of an abandoned stretch of railroad, you'll find the county art museum, a sliver of white concrete and glass.

Most people are wrong, as it happens. I've lived in this city all my life, and the real explanation has nothing to do with the river. In the early 1840s, a pair of hearty Dutchmen were surveying for the highway that would link the port and railroads of the urban south to the farmland and sawmills of the north woods. Here, nestled among the ridges and kettles that the glaciers' icy fingertips carved out eons and eons ago, they planted the sign that marked the halfway point along that road. A resting place for weary travelers. A city born of exhaustion.

I am so fucking tired.

The thing is—and I'm finally starting to admit this to myself—I don't believe there's a puzzle here. There's no way to turn these jagged pieces into a smooth picture of something that makes sense. First you'd have to crack off the extra material and file the edges down, like you're shaping a mosaic from pottery shards; you have to break away more and more to even get the right shape. This story is like a vase made from other, broken vases. And maybe it will hold water when you're finished, but probably it won't.

* * *

The painting is still there, hanging at the top of the main staircase in the county art museum. The landing makes a shallow triangle between the main collection, the American Indian gallery, and the eternally empty corridor labeled "Special Exhibits" on the map. You can use up all the fingers on one hand counting the number of times I've gone to that museum in the last year, and I find myself pausing in that tight and windowless space every time, hoping to see something different. I'm always disappointed.

Both the printed and electronic maps call the painting *White Moose*, but the name on the museum placard is *Katabolism.* The word has something to do with digestion, with the extraction of energy from chemical compounds. The first time I saw that title, I thought the artist was a pretentious fuck. Now I'm not so sure.

In any case, the title on the map is an accurate description. The oil painting shows a white bull moose, lumbering through a landscape that looks not unlike the glacial moraine that gnaws perpetually at the city limits. He's not local fauna, though, and he's bigger than life-size on the canvas: seven or eight feet high at the shoulder, his antlers spread off the edges. The antlers are thin and asymmetrical, with six points on his right and seven on his left. His eyes are the same color as his coat, slightly filmed.

Every time I see him, I think how much better I would feel if he were an albino, a lovely red-eyed creature like the rabbits and sometimes deer that I find stumbling in my backyard in winter, when the snow-reflected sun is too bright for them—something natural, fragile, and not-at-all sinister. But the white of the moose is not an absence of pigment. His color is something creeping over him, coating the duller, natural life underneath. Every time I see him, the white has spread a little farther.

The placard gives only three initials and a year: *Y. L. H. 2012.*

If you're one of the people who believes that Blair is dead, then near as I can tell, this is the painting that killed them.

* * *

I'm not certain, yet, if I'm one of those people. But then, I'm certain of very little where Blair is concerned.

They were not my son, and they were not my daughter; but what they were remains unfathomable and changeling. I'm not talking about sex, those hundreds of quiet and not-so-quiet confusions that stalked my child for the seventeen years of their life in this city. I am talking about how hard it is to even think of Blair as *my child*—to claim Blair as mine, when they seemed so determined to be anything but.

(Speaking of Blair in the past tense has started to come naturally, and maybe that's the most fucked-up thing about this whole mess.)

When I get home from my shift at the library, I stand in the laundry room at the back of our little bungalow, take their t-shirt from the hamper, and smell the cinnamon smell of their shampoo. I can't remember their face, not really: only pale skin, dark eyes, red hair that was always too long and always faintly damp. White as daisy and red as sorrel, or however that fairytale goes. I don't even have a photograph.

I stand in their bedroom beneath the pitched roof of the eastern gable and smell the stinking richness of their favorite myrrh candle, which is still cemented to the window ledge with its own gray wax. The desk beneath the window is littered with sheets of the cheap, yellowish paper that the secretary at the Catholic church on Kilbourne let me rescue from the recycling. I can't see any words or lines of ink, perhaps because whatever was there has faded after so many months of sunrises. Or maybe there was nothing there to begin with.

Alone in Blair's bedroom, I cover my mouth with both hands and say things that a mother should never say to her child. The words tear their way out of my throat like knives. I beg them to come home, *you little bastard,* come back and stop all this bullshit about the paintings, about Y. L. H. and the things we see in the forest. Please, come home. You're killing me.

Finally, when I am too tired to beg, I tell them to go fuck themself.

* * *

But to begin at the beginning.

January, grey and dreary, and school was back in session after a tempestuous winter break. I found out from the newspaper that a membership card for the art museum cost twenty-five dollars, fifteen with student identification. I got a letter from Blair's art teacher and that was good enough for the woman at the ticket counter. Unlike me, Blair never had a talent for words. They pulled Ds and Fs in one English class after another, losing books, failing to turn in essays. I thought art might give them whatever we try to get from stories.

Once upon a time there was a forest, 'savage, rough, and stern...'

From that first afternoon, all they could talk about was the White Moose.

"I think he's one of *them*," they said.

We were walking home along the east bank of the river, where shards of brown ice ground against the shoreline. On either side of the path, the Rotary Club's rosebushes slept under cones of yellowed Styrofoam. I was cold and only half-listening.

"One of what?" I asked.

"You know. One of *them* from the forest."

And in the savage forest there lived a mother, and her child...

I glanced at them out of the corner of my eye. Their hood was pushed back despite the cold, and their hair glinted like copper. *Hair like a lost penny,* my mother always said. She was a woman to whom anything beautiful looked lost.

"In the painting, I saw ripples on the leaves at the bottom," Blair said. "The light's distorted, almost like they're underwater. But it's just him. He fills the whole kettle—the whole canvas. It's just that he's denser in the shape of the moose."

No, I thought then, *it's impossible.* In the January daylight, I wasn't even disturbed.

"That's only the style," I said. "Don't make something out of nothing."

On our left, a brick staircase ran from the river walk up to the Fourth Street Bridge. I began to take the steps two at a time.

"It isn't nothing," Blair said stubbornly. "Whoever painted that picture must know about them."

"No one else knows about them, Blair."

Blair wasn't following. I looked back over my shoulder and saw them staring, not at me on the stairs, but at the glimmer of black water threading through the ice.

"Who do you think the artist is?" they asked. "Y. L. H.?"

... a mother, and her child, and a witch.

"I don't have a clue," I said, and kept walking. I meant: *I don't want to know. Let's not find out.*

* * *

Or maybe it began before that.

Maybe it began the day Blair told me that they were not a boy, and the only thing I felt was relief. Does that sound terrible?

Does admitting that make me an awful mother? I don't know. But I know that I had never wanted a son. I didn't grow up with brothers or cousins, only with the faces on the news, and the broad and smirking faces in the bars south of the depot, the hungry faces trailing tired women in convenience stores, the post office, the high school gymnasium. *Savage, rough, and stern.* When I imagined having a son, I imagined him growing up like that. I'd never wanted to deal with that kind of man, and I can't help but feel, guiltily, that I was granted an unspoken wish.

Blair's father had that particularly male helplessness, sucking and draining, pressuring and pleading, and both the best and the worst you can say is that it doesn't leave bruises. I can remember all those nights in supermarket parking lots or under movie theatre marquees, when he had followed me somewhere on the bus because he *just had to be sure.* "I'm such an idiot, Joan," he would cry. "I always knew I'd do something stupid like this and make you leave me." And because he was pitiful, because he needed saving, I had to tell him *I'm not going anywhere, baby,* and hold him while he sobbed.

In the end, he was the one to leave. He found the energy somewhere, and followed the freeway south. Maybe this all started the day he left, and I stayed. The day the forest pulled me stronger than he had pushed, in the way of every fairytale without a happy ending.

* * *

One evening in February, a week or two after that first visit to the museum, Blair was late coming home from school. Not late enough for me to really worry; merely a dress rehearsal for everything yet to come. I sat by the kitchen door, watching the sky darken and considering whether to call, when I heard the front door snap against the siding, and Blair swept in with a slushy gasp of twilight. They were looking at something on their phone as they stepped into the kitchen and flipped the light switch.

I closed the book whose pages I hadn't turned in half an hour.

"Where have you been?"

They shrugged. The shoulders of their thrift-store jacket were fuzzy with dust. "Downtown," they said.

"Anywhere specifically?"

It was a chance laugh, to break the tension that wasn't quite thick enough to acknowledge. They looked at me without smiling.

"Victor's."

Victor's was a café on Rhodes Avenue, the very edge of downtown. I don't know what the cavernous pile of red brick had been originally, with its alcoves and square turrets like the growths of some rhomboid crystal, but the interior space glowed with recent renovation, all waxy yellow wood and bare Edison bulbs. The coffee was mediocre, the pastries gluey and flavorless, but they housed a spectacular collection of shit: knock-off Tiffany chandeliers, assorted sporting equipment signed by virtual unknowns, and musical instruments missing strings or vital knobs. The café was a garage sale written by H. P. Lovecraft and illustrated by Virgil Finlay.

"What's that on your phone?" I asked.

Their fingers tightened around the pale blue case, an almost undetectable moment of hesitance. But they passed me the phone without a word of complaint.

I don't know what I was expecting to see. Dim and indistinct, with the hallmark shallowness of a cheap cellphone camera, the photo showed a woman sitting at a high table at Victor's pastry counter. The first thing I noticed was her scarlet leather boots, the black heels hooked over the rung of her chair. The second was her hair, white as milk and hanging down to her thighs.

I felt a creeping chill up my spine, like the sensation you get when you swim into water that is suddenly deeper than you expected.

"It's her," Blair said. "Yelena Linden Hersh."

I handed the phone back. "How do you know her name?"

"I asked, after I took the picture."

"How did you know who she was?"

Instead of answering, Blair swiped their screen and passed me the phone again. It was still Victor's—I recognized the pounded tin on the wall. Blair had tried to photograph a painting, but the phone camera wasn't up to the task. The texture of the canvas stood out prominently. So did the globs and ridges of paint caked along the bottom. It looked like a painting of a bog, some vast surface of black water, and the thick knobs of paint bobbed along it like something alive.

"It's brilliant, isn't it? Look at that one towards the front." Blair tapped a red-enameled fingernail against the screen, on a pale blur in the foreground. "It looks like a frog, doesn't it? But there's a woman just under the water. That white thing rising to the surface is her breast."

The sick feeling had traveled to the pit of my stomach. "Blair," I began, but I couldn't finish. The painting was at once too strange and too dreadfully familiar.

Blair slid the phone into their jacket pocket without another word. They tucked a lock of flame-orange hair behind their ear and stepped into the living room. I heard the static click of the analog television turning on, and took a slow, shuddering breath. What do you call the opposite of déjà vu? Not the sense of a recurrence, but its inverse: The feeling that this is a moment to which you will return. That was what I felt, envisioning that painting by Yelena Linden Hersh. That small breast in the water, beckoning like a ghost.

* * *

The things in the forest are still there: still filling the kettles like mist and twisting the light like water, still pulling at my heart like every hunger in hell. They haven't gone away just because Blair did. It's not that I thought they *would* leave—just that it wouldn't have surprised me if they had. I don't know the shape of this puzzle, remember. I can't begin to imagine how all of it does or doesn't fit together.

But they are still here, as much as they have ever been. Vaporous and vast, they seem as much air as flesh, although sometimes I can make out a shape—a deer or elk, or else some long-snouted, carnivorous thing. Soft black eyes emerge from the places where they are densest, and nearly human mouths shape words I can almost understand. Sometimes I think they are drawn to me, although this might be abhorrent self-flattery.

Still.

Some mornings, just after sunrise, I walk down to the woods behind the bungalow. For an hour or two, I sit very still on the remains of a farmer's fieldstone fence, holding out my empty hand. They come to me out of the water, out of the air, and they kiss my palm as though tasting for sweets.

Some of these mornings, I have seen Yelena Hersh in the forest, walking in her scarlet boots. Her black jacket is buckled to her chin and she walks briskly without looking down. I called to her, once, but she didn't even look my way.

There is nothing strange about her being there, I try to tell myself. It's a small city, and the trails through the forest are popular. I have seen a lot of people walking. But she's the only one I've ever seen when *they* are around.

* * *

In March, the art museum hosted a show of local women artists. It was mostly watercolors of cats and pencil sketches of tractors: also a quilt, a ceramic beehive, a few mercury-glass sculptures that I couldn't figure out. The latest offspring of Yelena Linden Hersh's brush hung just outside the gift shop, between a pastel sketch of sleeping kittens and a rack of dusty scarves.

It was called *Anabolism.* Which is the opposite and complement to katabolism; it's a kind of reassembling, the re-linking of molecules after the body grinds them up for energy. Anabolism is how the body lengthens bones and grows muscles. How it makes more of itself, I guess, out of everything it takes in.

The painting showed Blair emerging from a pond in one of the larger kettles. The water came up only to their knees, but there was a weirdness about the ripples that made me think Blair was *floating* rather than standing on the ground underneath. There's no telling how deep that water is, out there in the moraine; geologists say it can be as little as two or as many as two hundred feet.

In the painting, Blair was naked. Each skinny muscle tensed in the cold, layering blue shadow on pale skin. The slight tuck of the waist looked like a teenage girl's. The flat thighs, larger than life on the canvas, still seemed small enough for you to cup your hands around—to snap with a flick of your wrist. I don't remember the face.

"What if people recognize you, Blair? What if kids from school go to the museum?" Arms folded across my stomach, I sat on the sea chest in the corner of their bedroom. Despite the asthmatic chug of the heater, everything felt cool and damp to the touch. The candle on the window ledge burned greasily, leaving a myrrh-scented streak on the ceiling.

"Blair?" I repeated softly.

They looked up from the spread of paper on their desk.

"What do you think people will say?"

"Fuck people," Blair said. The thing that lurked in their eyes was tense and coiled, too ravenous to be fear.

* * *

Here is the damned thing, or one of the many damned things in this whole hellish business: I can't prove that Yelena Hersh had anything to do with Blair's disappearance. I can't even prove that Blair began meeting her. Those fucking paintings might have been proof once. They aren't any more. They still exist, but they aren't *Blair* any more. And maybe I'm mad for thinking that they ever were.

People in this city, they have all the answers they feel like looking for. Blair was a sad kid, a confused kid: it's all there, wrapped up in whatever was or wasn't behind the zipper of those weathered black jeans. "Kids like him disappear all the time, Joan," the secretary at the station said to me. "They just do. Don't go dragging a woman's name through the mud over it."

So where do they go, the kids like Blair? Do they evaporate into thin air? Wash down the river, get carried out to the lake, like all the other flotsam and jetsam from exhausted cities like this? Sometimes I imagine Blair has gone to find their father; other times, while walking over one of the bridges downtown, I think I see their face in the river, floating between mats of leaves. Sometimes the fantasies comfort me, and sometimes they don't.

Maybe the kids like Blair start spending their evenings with strange women twice their age—women who wear scarlet boots and black wool, who dream of ghosts and monsters, whose hair is white as milk. Maybe they spend too much time wandering in the forest, snooping in the ruins of barns and sugar houses that the maples are slowly reclaiming: maybe they get lost in the woods. Or maybe they get eaten by witches.

Maybe you're getting frustrated with me now, with my increasingly evident disregard for the facts. "What really happened?" you may well ask. "What's the true course of events?" But the only truth I know for certain is that I am fucking exhausted. You cannot begin to understand how tired I am. And I don't think that having the answers will let me sleep any more soundly.

* * *

Palingenesis. In its simplest translation, it means *rebirth.* Sometime in the nineteenth century, it got picked up to describe the now-discarded hypothesis that *ontogeny recapitulates phylogeny*—that the development of the fetus proceeds along the same lines as the evolution of the species. Or, in another version, that children become educated by passing through the earlier stages of human society. From barbarity to civilization. Another discredited, Victorian idea.

In the painting, Blair could almost be sleeping. Their eyes are closed, the lids wet and purple. Their limbs are folded up, almost fetal, the dry pink of knees and elbows picked out with the medical detail of anatomy plates. The setting sun is at their back, and the blowing leaves have started to mound up around their feet. You can feel the wind gusting from that direction: a bitter, northern wind.

Why is *this* the image burned into the back of my eyelids? Why do I remember this, and not their face? I'm afraid that's a question to which I already know the answer.

(Another riddle: If *Katabolism* is the painting that killed Blair, what does that make *Palingenesis*?)

I don't know if there are other things in that painting, or if the bending of the light along the forest floor is just an accident of style. I must admit that I haven't brought myself to look too closely. The one unforgivable piece of strangeness—the part that would tell you the name of the artist, even if you didn't see the stark initials in the corner—is the sapling that sprouts from Blair's genitals. It is slender, leafless, and almost the same color as their skin: a sickly, peeling white with scabs of pink. Where the bark pulls away, the pulp that shows beneath is black as rot.

In the second week of April, at Yelena Hersh's request, the directors hung *Palingenesis* at the top of the main staircase in the county art museum. They put the White Moose back before the end of the week, after unspecified complaints.

By then, of course, it was too late. By then, Blair was gone.

* * *

In our last conversation, the day before they failed to show up for school, Blair told me a secret about Yelena Hersh.

"She has a son," Blair said. It was Sunday evening, and we were loading groceries into the trunk of the Nissan: cans of beans, boxes of macaroni, and a half-gallon of skim. Everything teetered on the edge of the mundane, precariously normal, until Yelena intruded like a ghost.

"A son?" I repeated, and Blair tipped their head in a nod.

"When she was younger than me, she got pregnant. She gave him up for adoption."

I frowned, at a loss for the proper response. Blair slammed the trunk, disturbing a layer of late, powdery snow.

"She says the news terrifies her now. It's all men with guns, men with knives. Men who run over women with trucks and strangle children by playgrounds." Blair watched me wheel the cart to the side of the car, sliding their hands into the pockets of their jeans. "She's afraid she'll see him on the news one day. Or she's already seen him, just didn't recognize him as hers."

The next day, Blair was gone. And I wonder, now, if the news is something that terrifies every mother with sons. Or if we were just the strange ones, Yelena Hersh and I—the Pasiphaës of our century, afraid that we would give birth to monsters.

To early-twentieth-century sexologists, *anabolic* and *katabolic* were gendered terms. The female was anabolic, conservative and preserving. She consolidated the evolutionary adaptations of her species, passing them to her offspring. The katabolic male, creative and destructive, was responsible for the mutations, for everything novel or monstrous—two sides of the same coin.

All of that is bullshit, of course. If Blair has taught me nothing else, it's this—the creative and the destructive chase each other perpetually, like blood and bathwater swirling around a drain. But preservation, that's the most ridiculous fantasy of all.

* * *

Sometimes, I imagine that Blair's father saw those paintings. That he recognized his child and came to find them, that he offered Blair a better life than I could give them here. This is improbable. As if Blair's father could be in this city without me knowing. As if he had any interest in art. It's easier to believe that they left with their father, though, than what the school counselors try to tell me about suicide and statistics and 'kids like him.'

It is easier, also, than imagining that the forest had something to do with it.

There is a new tree, now, where the dead farmer's fence runs to a halt some fifteen yards from my property line. A skim of peaty water pools over the fallen leaves, and the tree grows from it, white as milk. I've gone so far as to step into the water, reaching for the bark, which looks so warm and soft. But the mud beneath my boot gave way, and my foot sank far enough that I knew the water was something more than snowmelt.

Maybe if I hadn't stepped back onto solid ground, I would have something closer to an answer.

Or maybe Blair ran away. Maybe you ran, sweetheart, all on your own, without your father, without ghosts or monsters or Yelena Linden Hersh. You were never good with words, and you wouldn't have left a note. You left me paintings instead, and maybe all the explanation I'm searching for is there. If only I could bring myself to look.

* * *

"I know why you don't like her," Blair said to me once. It was a morning in late March, before they left for school. We stood on the back deck in our jackets, and with cold, bare hands, they held the birdfeeder steady while I poured in the mix of seed.

"You want to be special, don't you?" Blair said. "That's why you won't believe that she can see them, too. You want them all to yourself."

On a sudden impulse, I pressed a kiss to their forehead. Some of the seed missed the feeder, pouring out into the slush, but they didn't turn away.

"Yes," I whispered, mouthing the words against their skin. Maybe they heard me, and maybe they didn't. "I always have."

* * *

Katabolism should not be confused with *katabasis*, which means a journey into the underworld. Katabasis is Dante and

Aeneas, Orpheus and Psyche. It's revelation and love and disaster. *Anabasis* would be the return, if a return from the underworld is possible—a suggestion for which I haven't seen much evidence. The words can also mean, respectively, a retreat down to the water, and the journey back inland or uphill.

Some of the reviews in the papers and the online magazines misprinted the titles of Yelena Hersh's paintings. *Anabolism* and *Katabasis*, digestion and descent. The pieces from two different puzzles pushed inelegantly together, and that makes as good a metaphor for me and Blair and Yelena Linden Hersh as any other I could come up with.

The word *palingenesia* appears once in the New Testament. It describes the new creation, in which the order of the old will be utterly overturned. I'm not holding my breath. But I guess every city has an explanation, even the divine ones. And I guess creation requires destruction—revelation, uncovering, *apokalypsis*—before everything else.

* * *

If you were here, sweetheart, I'd tell you to run.
This city is not for you. You are not tired yet.

* * *

Today, by the white tree in the brown water, Yelena Hersh is sitting on the remains of the fieldstone fence. Her scarlet boots are speckled with mud, and a vast white creature like a moose leans down to nuzzle her shoulder. She does not seem to see him. She sees me on the trail and raises one hand, a trembling salute, and her white hair falls around her face like a curtain.

The things in the forest—I don't think that they are older than us. Not exactly. I've begun to think they *are* us, or us as we will be. That is why the painting called *Anabolism* has started to look like something else: not Blair anymore, but a white canine thing, a carnivorous thing rearing on its hind legs. Another stage in our evolution. Perhaps the things in the forest are nothing better or worse than our children.

That's all the Minotaur was, in the end.

I worry, sometimes, that I will wander into the woods one morning and they will no longer be there. It will only be the trees and water and dead leaves, and the unrelenting anabasis and katabasis of a landscape birthed by ice. I think the reason they frighten me is not because they are so strange, but because they are fragile. I am afraid that they will disappear.

Or that one day I will look, and look, and have forgotten how to see.

The Fifth Gable

Kay Chronister

The first woman to live in the four-gabled house fermented her unborn children in the wine cellar. When they came to term, she broke them open on the floorboards. Her heartiest son weighed half an ounce at birth. His face, curved to the shape of the Mason jar womb where he developed, stayed pink for an hour before he died in a puddle of formaldehyde and afterbirth.

The second woman to live in the four-gabled house pulled her children from the ground like stubborn roots. They came out of the soil smelling of pollen, with faces like tulips. They were healthy until she cut their stems, and then they withered. They returned reedy and gray-faced to the earth.

The third woman in the four-gabled house said she had no children.

The fourth woman in the four-gabled house built her children from the parts of old radios and tractors. Their cries sounded like the spinning of propellers. Some of them could blink and one could even smile, but breastmilk fried their motors. In their mother's arms, they dissolved into heaps of crackling wires.

* * *

The women had been married before, to ordinary men, but no one wanted to mention that in light of what happened to the children.

The women in the four-gabled house no longer got many visitors.

* * *

All through the month of September, the women in the four-gabled house watched as a sober, clean-faced young creature walked down their street, past their house, to the end of the cul-de-sac, then turned and walked back.

The stranger would not walk in a neighborhood as unfashionable as their neighborhood if she did not want something with the four-gabled house and the women who lived there, they were sure of it.

"We should call someone," said the woman who made her bed in the second gable of the four-gabled house. "Get a neighborhood watch together."

"Nonsense. She's probably selling magazine subscriptions," said the woman who made her bed in the fourth gable of the four-gabled house. "Or collecting bits of metal for the war effort, or trying to interest us in a quilting bee so the orphans can have blankets. Or she's from some society that has asked her to come by our house, but the problem is that she's just too scared to do it."

"Are we still frightening?" said the woman who made her bed in the second gable of the four-gabled house. "I thought we'd gotten past that a few decades ago."

"She's a young girl in a fashionable hat," said the woman who made her bed in the third gable. "What could frighten her more than four old mothers with nary a man between them?"

"Well," sniffed the woman who made her bed in the first gable. "If she ever came down to my cellar, she'd know real fright."

* * *

September became October, October passed into November, and a damp, uncertain snow shimmered on the walks when the stranger came at last to the four-gabled house.

Her knock was hesitant, as if she feared to hurt the door.

The woman who made her bed in the first gable of the four-gabled house came to the door. The scent of myrrh clung to all her clothes and the damp of cellar walls clung to all her eyelids. She was the least approachable, so she always dealt with strangers.

"Please, may I come in?" said the stranger, and the woman who made her bed in the first gable thought for a moment, then nodded once, solemnly, and stepped aside.

The young woman crossed the foyer into the sitting room, where the other three women were waiting. "I've brought a pie for you," she said, pushing a towel-covered dish at the most approachable person in the sitting room, which happened to be the woman who made her bed in the third gable of the four-gabled house. "I hope you like rhubarb."

"Certainly," said the woman who made her bed in the third gable , and while she smiled warmly, her hands trembled when she took the dish. "Thank you, dear." She said *dear* after a long, conspicuous pause, as if correcting herself.

"My name is Marigold Hest," said the stranger. "I wonder – do you know my husband?"

"I doubt it," said the woman who made her bed in the first gable, at the same time that the woman who made her bed in the second gable said indignantly, "Should we?"

"Never mind that," said Marigold. "In fact, I'm glad. It will make things simpler." She sat for a moment, fidgeting with the brim of her hat, then huffed out a soft little breath and added, "I've heard that you have children here. I need one."

"Do you think they fall out of the eaves?" said the woman who made her bed in the second gable. "What makes you believe we have a child for you? You're a married woman – go get one off your husband."

The young woman blushed as pink as rhubarb, but she persisted. "People talk about you. They say you used to be midwives, and now you're witches. They say you're descended from the women who they hung in Salem. They say you're German and came to Amherst to seduce our men and spy on us. But I don't care what you are. Somehow you get babies, lots of them. Please, let me have one."

None of the women said anything for a long while. The woman who made her bed in the first gable of the four-gabled house raised her eyebrows. The woman who made her bed in the second gable stifled a laugh. The woman who made her bed in the third gable did nothing. At last, the woman who made her bed in the fourth gable said, "And what sort of child is it that you're wanting?"

"Any sort," said Marigold. "Really, any one would do. As long as I can get it soon."

"We're not an assembly-line," said the woman who made her bed in the second gable. "Did someone tell you that we had... procured a baby for them?"

"No," said Marigold, in a whisper that sounded more like *yes.*

"We wouldn't," said the woman who made her bed in the third gable. "Ordinarily. Not out of selfishness... dear... but because we can't."

The others looked at her, noticing the word *ordinarily* and wondering if a stranger in a fashionable hat really counted as an exception. They had made an exception, once before. The exception was why the woman who made her bed in the third gable did not have children.

"But if you can try," said Marigold. "If there's any chance that you could get one for me, that would be better than no chance at all."

"Why?" said the woman who made her bed in the fourth gable. "You're young yet. Do you need a child now?"

"I'm afraid to say," said Marigold. "Must I say?"

"No," said the woman who made her bed in the third gable, before anyone else could speak. "We will try. Let us try."

* * *

The woman who made her bed in the fourth gable was the first to take up Marigold's cause. She took apart the ice box for its metal, marooning a bottle of milk and a package of frozen vegetables so she would have the materials to begin constructing a child. Sighing in resignation, the other women prepared a meal with all of their perishable foods. This had happened before, with the lamps and the radiator and the toaster oven. Wartime made metal hard to come by. Scrap-metal children had been rationed almost out of existence.

"This could be my last," said the woman who made her bed in the fourth gable. She had a spoonful of warm grape jelly in her mouth, a soldering iron warming in her hand. "For a while, anyway, this could be my last."

The probable lastness of the child did not make him any more eager to survive.

When he was complete, a small frame of plated steel and plastic with a hungry gaping buzzsaw mouth, the woman who made her bed in the fourth gable called Marigold to the house and laid the child in her arms.

"Oh," Marigold said. "*Oh.* What a miracle he is." She kissed the shining smooth metal of his face, and held him in her arms. She said already he felt like hers. And then she went away.

For three days, the woman who made her bed in the fourth gable stayed there, weeping for the child she had abandoned to another woman, drinking cocoa made with curdled milk, listening to the radio: Little Orphan Annie had adventures twice daily; the president reported on the War only once, at five. On the third day Marigold brought the pile of wire and aluminum back to the four-gabled house, tucking him underneath her pea-coat to shield him from the wind. She wanted him buried properly; she wanted to go on pretending that he was a real child; she wanted to be told sorry.

The women who lived in the four-gabled house frowned and shook their heads. But they would not say sorry. They were glad to see that a young pretty stranger could not succeed where they always failed.

"A pity, that I could not make a better child," said the woman who made her bed in the fourth gable. "But not, I suppose, a surprise."

"A pity," said the woman who made her bed in the first gable.

"A pity," said the woman who made her bed in the second gable.

The woman who made her bed in the third gable would not say anything.

* * *

They let Marigold bury the child; she had already purchased a headstone for him.

"Bury him anywhere you like. Just, please," said the woman who made her bed in the fourth gable, "not where water can reach him. He'll fry if water reaches him."

Marigold didn't say what she thought, which was: he's already dead, why should it matter what reaches him? She only nodded. She shifted his small body in her arms, and she handed the women a printed invitation to a wake that none of them would attend.

* * *

The woman who made her bed in the second gable felt a sort of pity for Marigold, now that the girl was grieving like the rest of them. That Marigold considered herself their superior, that she came to them in secret with her fashionable hat hiding her prim face, only made the girl more pathetic. She had not realized yet. She didn't know. Some women simply aren't meant for children.

The child that the woman who made her bed in the second gable made for Marigold would be a calla lily, with a decorative white face and a stem that wouldn't wilt – at least not for a while. "Come twice a day and feed her," she instructed Marigold, tipping a watering can over her own brood of children.

The wet soil darkened to a rich, nourished color. Marigold studied the ground attentively. "What is that you're feeding them?"

"What does any mother feed her hungry infant?"

The girl's eyes widened. She said, "I don't believe I can do that, ma'am."

"Don't you ever call me ma'am," said the woman who made her bed in the second gable. "When your child pushes her way out of the ground, when she looks at you with her hungry mouth wide-open, then you'll believe you can do it. The milk has to be yours, understood?"

"Yes ma'am," said Marigold, cowed but unrepentant, watching as a row of robust, root-colored children uncurled their long tendril-arms and lifted their faces to the sun.

* * *

The woman who made her bed in the second gable had garden clippers that she kept in perfect condition. She polished them before and after use, kept them from rust, and removed them from their leather case for one reason only: to cut loose those children who had come to term. It was with great reluctance that she handed the clippers to Marigold, who cut her child out of the ground and then, minutes later, sent her back to it.

"It seems wrong to bury her where she grew," Marigold whispered.

The clippers rested in the pocket of Marigold's flannel skirt. With uncharacteristic gentleness, the woman who made her bed in the second gable took them and returned them to their leather case.

"We could try again," said the woman who made her bed in the second gable, but she said the words so Marigold would know she didn't mean them. And Marigold, sniffling, obediently shook her head no.

"I think my husband suspected, after the first child," she said. "Perhaps it's a blessing that this one died so soon. It would be wrong to try again. Wouldn't it?"

She wanted to be told: no, it's not wrong. Let's try. This time your child will not be fed on borrowed breast milk. This time you will not make a diagonal cut down your child's stem, as if she is a flower you are preparing for a vase. This time you will be better.

"Years ago, I let them grow too long, and they hurt me," said the woman who made her bed in the second gable. How many years, the girl would not know. "They made my insides ache. But I wanted them to stay with me longer, that's why I did it. You don't yet know what it feels like, to lose them again and again."

"It must be dreadful," said Marigold.

Later, she baked an apple tart. She smudged all the lipstick from her mouth and let her fashionable hat sit crooked on her head, and she sought the woman who made her bed in the third gable.

* * *

The women who lived in the four-gabled house found each other in tabloids, then in Sunday papers, then finally in a medical journal that three times failed to pass a peer review. But before then, the woman who made her bed in the third gable had lived alone. And the house had only one gable, and she could bear no children.

To the woman who made her bed in the third gable, this was a tragedy.

To the rest of the world, it was a great relief.

* * *

The woman who made her bed in the third gable gasped in fright when Marigold came to her door. Visitors, when they came to the four-gabled house at all, never climbed the staircase to the rooms where the women made their beds. When the woman peeked around her bedroom door, she sighed softly in relief and stepped aside. Marigold removed her hat, then stepped over the threshold.

"Is that apple?" said the woman who made her bed in the third gable.

"Yes – a tart." Marigold handed over the steaming dish as if she could not wait to be rid of it. The woman who made her bed in the third gable set the dish aside, and did not look in its direction again.

"I suppose you heard what happened to the last baby," Marigold said, after a moment.

"I'm so sorry, dear," said the woman who made her bed in the third gable, her voice quivering on the final word. "That must have been very hard for you."

"Yes," said Marigold. Then, steeling herself, she added, "I want to try again."

"I'm afraid that's how all her children come out... dear. They simply cannot survive without the earth to nourish them."

"Not from her," Marigold said. "From you. Please. It would mean the world to me."

"How much is the world?" said the woman who made her bed in the third gable, frowning. She studied Marigold. "I'm not sure you're ready to bear and bring up the sort of child I would make, dear."

"When will I be ready?"

"There is one other woman in this household you have not asked for a child."

"I had not thought she would say yes to me," said Marigold. "I rather thought she disapproved of the whole thing."

"She said no to you when you were young and childless. She did not want you to be happy. Now you have lost two children, and you ask her only for the chance to lose another."

"So I will lose her child too?"

The woman who made her bed in the third gable would not say.

* * *

In the cellar, the air smelled like rust and formaldehyde and old gardenia petals. The temperature was many degrees lower than it was in the rest of the four-gabled house, and Marigold wrapped her coat tightly around herself as she descended the stairs. She had no tart or cake for the woman who made her bed in the first gable, for she suspected that nothing baked or roasted would satisfy such a woman, and she was right. The woman who made her bed in the first gable liked pickled things, things crunchy with salt and long-preserved, and she hated how fresh dough collapsed on her tongue. When she saw Marigold, she always thought of that fresh-dough feeling.

"I know already what you are coming to ask me," said the woman who made her bed in the first gable.

Marigold stepped down off the last step, making it squeak. "What will you say?"

"I don't know yet," said the woman who made her bed in the first gable. "You're not much of a mother so far, with your hat on straight and only two children in the ground. You don't deserve my child."

"And how many children do *you* have in the ground?" said Marigold.

"Two thousand, four hundred, and eighty one," said the woman who made her bed in the first gable. "Some were twins," she added.

"None lived?" Marigold said.

"None," said the woman who made her bed in the first gable, with a touch of pride.

"Then I don't think I want one of your children," said Marigold.

"I don't think you do," said the woman who made her bed in the first gable, "I shall give you one."

* * *

The woman who made her bed in the first gable no longer made her bed there. She holed up in the cellar with a block of Brie and a feather-stuffed duvet, and she emerged only to wash her wine glass or collect the lukewarm cup of Earl Grey that the woman who made her bed in the third gable left out for her each afternoon.

The women did not like to interfere in each other's creative processes, so none of them peeked down into the cellar. The woman who made her bed in the cellar did not care to discuss the child she was fermenting, though if she had, she would have told them that he was fashioned from the heart of a white rabbit, four dollars at the pet shop around the corner, and twice embalmed in myrrh and soda ash.

He had to grow in his mother's womb, so she washed out the pie pan that Marigold had brought and sealed it with a glass cover.

Inside his tin womb, the child soaked and swelled and slowly became animate.

Inside her duvet, the woman who made her bed in the cellar dreamt of all the children she had lost inside her wombs.

The child reached such a size that he no longer fit inside the pie pan, then such a size that he no longer fit in a three-gallon pickle jar. The woman who made her bed in the cellar was stubborn, she wanted to see Marigold mourn, so she dug a hole, four feet deep, in the cellar's dirt floor. When she was finished, she padded the floor with rock salt and lowered the child into the hole. February was halfway over, the temperatures were still low, and the cold and the salt would preserve the child for a few days more – long enough to make the girl believe, long enough to make her miserable when he rotted.

The woman who made her bed in the cellar did not always produce beautiful children, but this one was exquisite, a wet blood-colored salamander-like creature whose arteries worked like legs and whose eyes could see even in the depths of the cellar. In the womb of the earth he grew to three feet in length before he cried for release.

The woman who made her bed in the cellar telephoned Marigold to announce the child's birth, knowing at half-past five her husband would be home, knowing that Marigold herself would be away at one of a dozen equally useless ladies' society meetings and thus unable to intercept the call.

"Your son is crying for you," said the woman who made her bed in the cellar, when a man answered.

She laid the phone down, waiting to feel satisfied, instead feeling hungry.

* * *

Before they had been women who lived in the four-gabled house, they had been:

A maiden aunt.

A minister's wife.

A washed-up stage actress.

A nurse.

They did not resemble themselves anymore.

* * *

When Marigold came to the cellar, the woman who made her bed there had already left. The feather-stuffed duvet and frozen block of Brie were gone; fourteen cups with shallow pools of Earl Gray in their bottoms remained. Marigold looked at each of the teacups, listened for her child's cries, and felt reluctant to walk any closer to the dark end of the cellar.

Upstairs, the women who made their beds in the four-gabled house were making dinner.

Damp, rich sounds came from the dark end of the cellar and echoed off the brick walls until Marigold could not hear the banging of pots and pans upstairs, nor the record spinning on the player, nor even the sounds of the women's voices.

She was afraid, but she would not leave the cellar without a son. She took up the iron bar propped up against the wall - she did not think, "someone might have put this bar there"; she thought very little - and walked forward until her child leapt up from the grave where he was born, four feet tall, hungry, hissing wetly at his mother.

Marigold swung the iron bar and struck the child in his moist, blood-colored forehead, then struck him again. She flew at him in such a fury that she did not stop to wonder what or who he was until he was already dead.

"Bury him yourself," said the woman who made her bed in the first gable when she heard. "Didn't I already dig a suitable grave?"

"Won't you have some shepherd's pie before you go back down there, dear?" said the woman who made her bed in the third gable.

Buttered baguette slices, tin cups of milk, heaping cuts of pie: a good meal by ration standards, a good meal even by pre-war standards, and they had ruined it for her. The women smiled proudly at their visitor.

"I suppose I might have a little," Marigold said, polite in her fashionable hat, black blood drying on her hands.

When all five plates were empty, the other women retired to their gables. The woman who made her bed in the third gable washed each plate, carefully, methodically, while her guest waited at the table.

Then she said, "It hurt to lose that one, didn't it, dear?"

"Yes," Marigold whispered. "It was my fault, this time."

"You're ready now," said the woman who made her bed in the third gable, "for the sort of child I could give you."

"I don't know if I can bear the pain of another child," said Marigold.

"I know," said the woman who made her bed in the third gable. She dried the final plate and wiped her hands clean on her apron, then made for the staircase. "Come along now, dear."

"Where are we going?" said Marigold.

"The fifth gable," said the woman who made her bed in the third gable of the four-gabled house. "We'll need privacy."

Marigold's husband waited at home for the arrival of their adopted son. Marigold could not leave empty-handed. Marigold was unaccustomed to wanting something that once lost could not be regained. She followed the woman who made her bed in the third gable.

The fifth gable was smaller than the others, drafty, the walls windowless. A vase of dying gardenias rested on a small end table in the corner. The gardenias had been wilting for longer than Marigold had been alive, which comforted the woman who made her bed in the third gable.

"Sit down," the woman said, motioning to the armchair in the middle of the room. A thin layer of dust covered its seat and arms and high, narrow back. Marigold settled into the chair and held her crumpled hat in her lap like it was a small and ill-behaved dog.

"Do you expect you'll have to be tied down for this bit?" said the woman who made her bed in the third gable.

"What are you going to do?" said Marigold.

"Oh, I do very little, dear," said the woman who made her bed in the third gable. "You said you wanted a child, any child, isn't that right?"

"Ye-es," said Marigold, in a lilting voice that sounded more like *no.*

The woman who made her bed in the third gable got to her knees and rested her clasped hands in Marigold's lap, as if comforting, as if pleading. "Whatever else you do, dear, remember to blame yourself."

She rose to her feet and turned and left, locking the door from the outside.

Inside the fifth gable of the four-gabled house, dampness became cold and dimness became darkness, and Marigold's skin felt like wax beneath her fingers when she tried to rub her gooseflesh off.

* * *

The women who lived in the four-gabled house buried Marigold's cellar child together, all but the woman who made her bed in the first gable, because she could not make herself look at the mangled body of the child she had made.

"We should sing a hymn," said the woman who made her bed in the second gable.

"Why?" said the woman who made her bed in the fourth gable.

"It's conventional. She'd like that."

The women contemplated the idea of being conventional for a while. Their eyes lost focus as they studied the raised mound of earth with the cellar child inside.

"He was such a fine boy," said the woman who made her bed in the third gable. "But I'm glad she hurt him, I must admit."

The woman who made her bed in the third gable could only bear children in the womb of another woman's suffering.

* * *

Marigold came from the fifth gable of the four-gabled house looking smaller, with hair like straw. The women had a luxurious breakfast prepared for her, butter on the toast and sugar for the coffee. Marigold stirred cream into her coffee with one hand and supported her squalling, red-faced child in the other.

"A hideous creature," said the woman who made her bed in the first gable, after Marigold and the child had gone. "No offense."

"None taken," said the woman who made her bed in the third gable. "He wasn't really mine. None of them have been."

"If you made me one, he would be different," said the woman who made her bed in the first gable. "My hurt would be the furthest thing from hers, and the child who came from it would be strong and strange and proud."

"Perhaps in a few years," said the woman who made her bed in the third gable. "You haven't felt enough yet. I couldn't be sure of the outcome if you hadn't felt enough yet."

And the woman who made her bed in the first gable knew this to be true, having seen many dozens of the small dead fish-like things that came from half-felt suffering. She could not rush suffering, so she returned to her cellar and shut her door and set to work on her next child. This time, she thought, perhaps she would love them enough. Perhaps they would hurt her so deeply that she could at last ascend to the fifth gable and bear a child that would live.

The Block

Kostas Ikonomopoulos

I

The tenement block stands at the edge of the city overlooking a ravine and the hills beyond. The block is perpetually shrouded in mist and when it rains its dark exterior acquires a darker hue. It is old and unmaintained and so are its residents.

For unclear reasons no one lives on the first three floors. On the fourth floor lives a retired folklorist with a passion for Javanese shadow play. Every Sunday evening he invites a few of his neighbors over and he performs the same stories again and again to the sounds of a Gamelan orchestra, a recording he made himself sometime before the last war. When he is done, he takes down the white sheet and then he places his figures in a brilliantly polished chest. The figures are ancient-looking things made of buffalo skin and wood; their color has disappeared.

Madam Meletova loves puppetry in all its forms and always attends the folklorist's sessions. Many years ago she was the Justice Minister's mistress. It was said that he used to sign execution orders while she was fellating him. The minister is dead now and advancing years have granted her respectability. She lives alone in spacious rooms just above the folklorist. She never invites anyone in but when she opens her door passersby can see many framed photographs on her walls and a gown or négligée flung over an armchair. Some nights she drinks cognac and sings forgotten arias. She has a beautiful voice and it carries through her open window and reaches the other tenants, who stop what they are doing and listen with melancholy etched on their features.

Majarek shows up at the folklorist's most Sundays, always accompanied by Sebastiano, the taxidermist. Everyone knows that Majarek is a war hero with a long service in distant colonies now renamed. He has lost his left arm and he wears a prosthetic when he ventures out of the block. He never wears it indoors, treating it, in a way, like a hat. Sebastiano carries strange odors, fascinating and repulsive, reminiscent of lilies and the carcasses of horses. Majarek and Sebastiano seldom speak to one other, yet they are often seen together, smoking cigarettes or observing murmurations in the twilight. They live in adjoining rooms on one of the upper floors.

The others are not regulars and they attend the shadow play perhaps once every few months. Schlossmayer is the oldest and most reclusive of the irregulars. When he arrives at the folklorist's, he sits next to Meletova and closes his eyes. Perhaps he is there only for the music. Then there is Irene, a woman of indeterminate age recently retired from her position as head nurse in the city's hospital for the criminally insane. According to Irene, Schlossmayer was the head of his country's secret police during a brutal dictatorship. Irene maintains that Schlossmayer is a true psychopath who has tortured and murdered many men and women. Nonetheless, she greets him with kindness and sits near him at the folklorist's apartment. She has even been inside Schlossmayer's rooms, which she claims are filled with old books in many languages. The books with titles she could read, she says, appeared to be monographs on subjects such as Asiatic falconry and Baroque furniture.

In the bowels of the block, its boiler room, its terrace and its staircases, men and women wearing drab, heavy clothing make random and unexpected appearances. There is no superintendent and no listing of residents so it is not possible to know whether these people actually live here or are merely visiting, though it can be said with certainty that no regular visitors ever come, no family members, or distant relatives, or friends from various social circles. The residents of the tenement block appear to have no families or friends on the outside. They live retiring, monastic lives, pursuing solitary passions.

II

At the bottom of the ravine is a dried riverbed. Sebastiano, the taxidermist, often walks there, as does Madam

Meletova, whose first name, never told to anyone in the block, is Alexandra. On occasion, Sebastiano returns from a walk with a dead bird that he proceeds to embalm in his apartment. Alexandra walks in the early morning, dressed as if though she were about to attend the opera or the theater. She often emerges like a lone survivor of some unreported catastrophe before Majarek's eyes.

At this hour, the one-armed man sits on a stone bench near the front entrance reading his crumbled newspaper. The war hero greets the aged concubine and watches her as she walks away, swaying her hips now that she knows he is watching. Each time she disappears into the morning, Majarek experiences crushing, devastating sadness. He looks down at his fake arm and his polished shoes and then he looks out into the distance, at the highways and the office buildings, at the world of the living. A profound loss darkens his insides and he wills himself to stand up and go back to his apartment, a man who is all past.

Mornings are difficult for the other residents as well. Irene, a chronic insomniac, stands on her balcony and smokes, gazing at the hills with bleary eyes. She thinks back to her countless night shifts at the asylum, the impossible stillness of those hours. Then she returns to her kitchen and boils water for her tea. She sips it while looking absentmindedly at the plastic table cover. The folklorist is hard at work in his study. He is laboring on an ambitious project, a compendium of death rituals. His frustration often overtakes him and he tears up the pages he has written since dawn. He wants this book to be his legacy, a definitive work, something that cannot be bettered or surpassed. Schlossmayer thinks about killing himself but he reasons that he is old and death cannot be far. Still, he keeps a pistol. Today, it lies in plain view between a Cyrillic Bible and a treatise in German about navigation in the Middle Ages. He often moves it around, compelled by an urge he has never been able to define.

At noontime, the block is dead silent. The tenants are absent, and it is unclear where they have all gone. Meletova's door is closed but most others are left ajar. There is a basement beneath the basement and perhaps this is where all the residents go at noon. The lower basement is accessed through a metal trapdoor next to the janitor's closet that is covered with an old rug. There are posters on the damp walls and any descent into the sub-basement is witnessed by faded cabaret dancers and music hall performers. Of course, the lower basement is not the only possibility; there are other places in the block that can claim the living. On the south side of the rooftop terrace is a cavernous pigeon loft. On the fifteenth floor, a sealed room may be accessed by those who know the combination for the ancient lock. But wherever the residents of the block go, they are returned by late afternoon. Their reemergence is followed by the renewal of the vile smells emanating from the taxidermist's apartment workshop, and the renewal of the folklorist's pacing and anguished mumbling.

When evening falls, the block is spectrally lit by primitive and defective lamps. It looks like a giant gripped by ankylosis. Its long shadow falls across tarmac and gravel, across the banks of the dried riverbed, and merges with the denser shadow descending from the hillside. Disturbing noises rise from night birds and crawlers. And then the block's own emissions start escaping from windows, doors, cracks, and fissures, as though the block were a music box opened by a curious child.

III

Friday evening, a gathering takes place on the tenth floor, inside a vast apartment whose inner walls have been demolished. The invitation was issued by Irene, in the form of torturously calligraphed notices slipped under all the apartment doors. The tenants have been summoned to decide Schlossmayer's fate, though it is unclear what gives them the authority to do so. Irene, resplendent in her white psychiatric nurse's uniform, offers the assembled residents a lengthy monologue. She reiterates her suspicions regarding the old recluse's murderous past. Then, dramatically, Irene takes out a folder from a leather satchel and drops it on the long table spanning the room. The residents, seated around the table in uncomfortable chairs, look at the folder and then at Schlossmayer, who sits by himself off in a corner, with accelerating embarrassment and discomfort. The hermit gives the nurse a look of reproach, as if to say, I thought we were beyond all this, that we were civil to each other. The proceedings have taken him by surprise, and yet he came to the gathering of his own accord. As he took the stand to defend himself, even though no proper authority compelled him to do so, he was, as always, cordially greeted by his neighbors.

Irene refers to the folder on the table as the 'new and damning evidence,' yet she presents it neither to those gathered, nor to the old man whose fate is being decided. Sebastiano thinks how odd it is that no one has been appointed judge on this matter. Even if a majority of the assembled decided, one way or the other, who was going to enforce the decision? Who was going to support it with authority? Majarek, who is very cultured for a military man and has an art historian's sensibility, looks up at the ceiling; the cracks, mold, and discoloration form patterns and designs that remind him of the ceiling of the Senate Room in the Palazzo Ducale.

Irene asks Schlossmayer, in a rather friendly manner given the circumstances, to comment on the new evidence, although the only thing Irene has said of it so far is that the 'new and damning evidence' supports the previous evidence that was brought forth when the issue was first raised. No one remembers when the issue was first raised, much less the original evidence, and at that point, Alexandra Meletova stands, and for a moment, rocks back and forth. She has been drinking and it appears to the assembled that she might actually sing. Instead, after steadying herself, she approaches Irene and whispers something in her ear. The retired nurse turns pale. Alexandra returns to her seat.

Irene stands and awkwardly addresses the assembled once again. She claims it was all a joke she conceived, a play to enliven this evening, that she intended, at the end of the performance, to admit it was all an act and take her bows. She approaches Schlossmayer and lays her hand on his shoulder. For a minute, nothing happens.

The folklorist is the first to go. Sebastiano follows, and then the others, one by one, file out of the room. The large apartment is now empty, save for Schlossmayer, who looks utterly exhausted and defeated. He stands up with effort and shambles out of the room and down the corridor towards the stairs. In his room, he takes up the pistol and sits at his desk. He looks at the pistol for a long time. Finally, he stands up, goes to the open window and starts shooting at the hillside, at the dark and unmovable heart of the thing that haunts and traps them all.

IV

That very night the birds arrive. It is a peculiar and unseasonable migration. Sebastiano, of course, is aware of this phenomenon and of the pull the building exerts on this strange breed, which has yet to be classified. Large corvids with blood-streaked bellies fly in and land around the pigeon loft. They start shrieking and rattling with a focused intensity that terrifies the residents. Meletova cannot tolerate the cacophony and so she places a record on her primordial gramophone and opens her windows. The music ascends to the terrace like a bronze shield and the cries of the birds crash against it. Somewhere in the middle floors of the block a light comes on.

Kang, unseen for two years, is now frantically gathering herbs and minerals from his cabinets and mixing them inside a silver urn. He sets the mix alight and, holding the urn with both hands, takes the stairs to the rooftop. The smoke coming out of the container is choking him and he falters. Up above, the birds go into a frenzy, like a panicked camp anticipating a devastating assault. The residents' nerves are frayed. The folklorist, knowledgeable and dedicated as he is, breaks down and falls on his floor. Wracked by insomnia and shamed over recent events, Irene's veins unfurl like satiated serpents. Her clammy skin is taut and, like a bow bent without mercy, she reaches her snapping point and starts screaming back at the birds.

At this very instant, the old pharmacist finally arrives at the terrace and places the urn. The smoke rises, flashing blue and crimson, and moves towards the malevolent flock. A vengeful shrieking pierces hill and building and human flesh alike but it cannot stave off this defeat. The birds rise, a flurry of screaming and feathers. Suddenly, all motion stops. For a time, the birds are suspended, as if pinned to a painted sky. At the blink of an eye, they are hurled across the night, as though swept away by the hand of a random god.

Silence descends upon the block. Kang slowly reclaims his weapon and makes his way back to his rooms. There, he retires among the paraphernalia of his trade and falls asleep next to his fragrant vials. One by one, the others come to their senses and rejoice: somehow, they have been reprieved. And no one is more aware of this unwarranted, unexpected and underserved miracle than Sebastiano. He remembers when, more than ten years ago, the birds came and stayed screaming for a week. At that time, the taxidermist had tried to hang himself but failed. Old Cazares went insane. Arletta flung herself from her balcony to the dried riverbed below. The lives of all the residents were damaged and disrupted. Kang was away that week. Perhaps the birds knew it and that is why they descended upon the block for so long and with such soul-piercing and persistent malice.

But this night is won. Alexandra's song can now be heard, victorious and unrestrained, climbing defiantly towards the darkened regions of the sky. Irene sits at her kitchen table, drinks her tea and smokes, waiting for the morning.

V

The days reclaim their pace and unfold with languor. Majarek experiences a kind of peace that has eluded him for years. This morning, he has received an official-looking letter from the hot and distant land where he served his flag for many years. The letter acknowledges Majarek's contributions. The new government is grateful for the assistance he rendered during the turbulent transition. An invitation to a ceremony is included and states, in no uncertain terms, that the Falcon's Wings, the new country's highest decoration, will be presented to him at the City Hall in one month's time. Pride now softens Majarek's gloomy and depressive tendencies. He can even follow Meletova's moving figure with no more than basic pangs of pain. He starts making travel arrangements.

By noontime, all of the residents know. First, he tells Sebastiano. A random meeting with Schlossmayer by the boiler room gives him the opportunity to spread the news further. Then Irene hears the news. One by one, they all felicitate the military man and he accepts their smiles and their praise, unaware of the resentment in their hearts, a deep-seated rancor that arises from their diminished humanity, their isolation, their failures and inner exile.

The folklorist is the first to voice his objection, tactfully, of course, to Sebastiano and Irene. He clothes his seething jealousy in careful words. Wasn't Majarek given a certificate of recognition by the opposition (now defeated and exiled) in that distant land? Hadn't he accepted an instructor's post at a neighboring republic when he was younger, a country often at odds with the one that now wants to decorate him? The folklorist is an expert at casting aspersions. He is motivated by selfishness and fear. Majarek's ascension will overshadow the folklorist's future accomplishments. He instinctively knows that this tenement block is large enough for only one man's work to flirt with history.

Sebastiano is torn, because he considers himself Majarek's friend. He knows that this honor will bring Majarek closer to his estranged family, taking him away from the block and the present miserable circumstances that bind them. The taxidermist wants the military officer to remain. He *loves* him. Of course, he would never admit it. He often reminisces to himself, about their evenings of companionship, about that shared estrangement, about that comfortable silence at dusk. He closes his eyes and sees Majarek smiling sadly, Majarek without the prosthetic arm, in all his glorious vulnerability. All his history, all his struggle, all his pride. All his loneliness carved in his lean face, all his past behind gray eyes that have gone grayer on long ocean voyages. The discipline, the self-denial, the dashed hopes, and more than anything, the nobility that lifts Majarek and separates him. Sebastiano agrees that perhaps the foreign government should be made aware of a possible conflict of interest that might take an embarrassing turn.

Alexandra likes the way Majarek looks at her; he makes her feel younger and desired. But in all the years they have known each other, he has never tried to beguile or seduce her. Her flesh has aged and withered and still Majarek waits. It is almost too cruel. Why does he taunt her? Bitterness overwhelms her. He denies her even as his gaze fills with yearning. How can she forgive him? If he were indifferent, if Alexandra merely suffered from unrequited love, bitterness would have no place. But this is too much for any woman to bear. And now Majarek looks happy and hopeful again. Where does that leave Alexandra? And so she agrees with the others that something must be done. She would deny him this new hope, this new beginning, the way he has denied Alexandra her own. Let them know he is no hero, no nation-builder! Let them know he plays all sides, he works for whomever pays, he swears no allegiance! He is like all other men, he disappoints and he compromises. But Alexandra is wrong. She does not know that Majarek is burdened by guilt. That Majarek supported the coup that ousted the previous government. That men from his own regiment dragged the Justice Minister outside the city, doused him with petrol, and set him aflame. That it was Majarek, himself, who stripped her parents' estate of all valuables and set them on the path to exile. Majarek was young then and for the rest of his career he tried to make amends for the excesses of his youth and use wisdom and compassion in all his dealings. But he knows that to be with Alexandra—whose name he alone in the building knows—he would have to tell her the truth, and she would hate him.

The others have nothing against Majarek. But they fear change. And it feels wrong for anyone to leave the tenement block alive.

VI

Schlossmayer sends the letter. He is an expert in such affairs. He has no quarrel with Majarek, but feels no empathy either. Where is Schlossmayer's reward, where is what was promised to *him*? Unbeknownst to the others, Schlossmayer also sends another message, to Majarek's estranged son, arousing the young man's vanity and poisoning whatever remains of filial love and the awe he owes his father.

Two weeks pass. Sebastiano gives a lecture on taxidermy that only Irene and the folklorist attend. Kang makes a single appearance: he spends two hours at the terrace, next to the pigeon loft, looking for something. He is witnessed by two women, who might be new residents, and who happen to be visiting the terrace themselves. When they notice him they withdraw, as if they were caught doing something terribly improper.

Then, the two officials arrive. One is in uniform. The other is wearing a black suit. They inquire after Majarek. Majarek sees them upon returning from a walk along the riverbed with the taxidermist. Sebastiano has been trying to spend more time with his friend, now full of regret for going along with the plan to discredit him. Sebastiano is on the verge of confession. He hopes that nothing comes of their intervention, but he suspects that events have transpired that cannot be undone. When he sees the two men, his stomach turns. A pitiful sound escapes his lips.

Majarek recognizes both men and he smiles. Accelerating his pace, he leaves the taxidermist behind. He believes the men have come to congratulate him, these men who have shunned him for so long. He walks towards them with purpose, even more content for the fact that he is wearing his prosthetic arm and his clean suit jacket. The men straighten up as he approaches. Majarek outranks them.

Irene is about to exit the building when she sees the three men through the glass door. She stops. As she witnesses the silent drama, the thought occurs to her that what is transpiring is one of the stories told by the folklorist's puppets, a tragedy played out in light and shadow. At first, all three men are stiff. Majarek becomes animated. The man in uniform hangs his head. Majarek turns to the man in the black suit. Irene believes that Majarek has just won some minor victory when the suit, with impossible speed, slaps Majarek across the face. The black suit takes out a letter and holds it up. Majarek takes it, reads it, and takes a small step back. Majarek sheds all nobility and bearing; the prosthetic hangs like a simian extremity. His knees buckle. The uniformed man quickly reaches out to him and steadies him. Majarek, invoking decades of pride and discipline, breaks free of the other's grasp and straightens. Majarek again addresses the black suit. The man's face registers surprise, disdain, doubt, fear, all in quick succession. Choked with shame, Irene wants to run out and tell the men it was all lies. Majarek is beyond reproach, Majarek with his one arm, and gray eyes, and tired smile, Majarek in his titanic solitude undreamt of by lesser men. Once, when phantom pains in his missing limb had become unendurable, he sought her out, but Irene had nothing with which to comfort him. He told her, then, how he lost his arm. Irene told no one else that story, but during awful nights, when regrets and insomnia threaten to unravel her, she remembers it, and tears of gratitude dampen her pillow until sleep claims her. Why have they done this to the best of them? Irene is certain she will run out. But she stays rooted in place until the uniform and the black suit leave and Majarek is left alone in the middle of the courtyard, forlorn and sacrificed and having lost something for which there is no prosthesis.

VII

Majarek spends the night chain-smoking in his room. Painstakingly, he reconstructs what has happened and what needs to be done. He is a soldier and no stranger to pain, misfortune, and defeat, and he is not without allies. He has friends he expects will come to his aid. He was a great tactician once. Now, he plans his next move with great care, accounting for all contingencies. In his great mind he organizes his defenses. But he does not know that the great hollow horse is already within the city walls.

A young man comes to his door and knocks. The sun is still not up. The young man drove through the night, bursting with self-righteousness, and arrived to claim the confrontation that was for years denied him. No one saw him climb up the stairs and walk down the corridor leading to his father's door. Sebastiano, unable to sleep, the glassy eyes of his dead animals looking at him accusingly, hears the knock. Like Irene, Sebastiano is drowning in remorse, and like Irene, he is not able to do a single thing to help his friend. Unlike Irene and Sebastiano, many others are sleeping peacefully at this hour. The folklorist is dreaming of Mount Merapi as seen from the top of Borobudur. Schlossmayer seems to have found meaning again through his last vile act. In molding and breaking the wills of men he finds both ecstasy and comfort. For a long time Schlossmayer has enjoyed Meletova's protection; the woman is also a creature addicted to intrigue and subversion. She has acquired access to the residents' secrets and unforgivable acts. She is the repository of their collective shame. Of course, she also knows Schlossmayer for who he is. But he shielded her after the old regime collapsed, after her lover was immolated, after her parents were driven out of their estate and their ancestral land, and she is indebted to him. She hopes Schlossmayer will die soon and release her from their terrible bond. Until then, she guards him, and those around him fall.

The door opens. Father and son face one another. Majarek looks incomprehensibly at the younger man. The light from the lamp makes Majarek's shadow fall on the boy, heavy and absolute, the way it has been all their lives. The early hour, the stillness in the corridor, the window facing the darkened hill: the men stand suspended in time. The terrible meeting they both have craved is at hand.

The young man walks in. The door closes. Sebastiano hears their muffled voices in the adjoining room. The taxidermist stands still next to the wall, the tension stretching his body like a string. His lips are sealed, he guards his breath as though it were his soul. At first, the voices are indistinguishable. His friend's voice is quiet, reasoning, pleading. The other voice starts low, but gets sharper, rises in anger, becomes shrill with indignation. Majarek, again: explaining, first with authority, then with sadness. The son: getting louder, mocking, erupting in cruel laughter. And then comes the inevitable, pillowy silence, heavy and stifling, draping the dawn in despair.

The son leaves, all threads cut, his father dead to him.

VIII

It is a strange and glorious morning: the mist has lifted for the first time in years. On the balconies and on the terrace, in the courtyard and along the riverbed, the disbelieving residents turn their faces towards the sun and then gaze upon the verdant hills, which are resplendent and shining, as though they have just been polished to perfection. No one remembers such a day. The folklorist has left his desk and his chapter on Neolithic mummification techniques and stands before a massive, glassless window on the first floor corridor. Kang stands beside him, his eyes like milky orbs, and looks upon the trees on the hillside, impossibly well-defined against the dark but satiated earth. Has Kang regained the perfect eyesight he enjoyed in youth? Even Schlossmayer, a man resistant to natural beauty and an implacable enemy of common sentiment, grins like an idiot on the terrace, a fresh breeze caressing his dried and spotted face. Irene and Sebastiano have forgotten the apocalyptic night they have just survived and walk hand in hand—without even realizing it—towards the hills. Meletova has left her door open and music from her phonograph rolls down the staircases and climbs the barren walls before spilling out to caress them all with longing and delight. It is a virtuosic viola da gamba performance and the bass has a resounding, otherworldly quality. The concubine appears to have shed decades. She wears a long red gown with intricate lacework, its exquisite craftsmanship complementing the three rows of pearls resting on her alabaster skin. From his vantage point on the first floor, the folklorist sees her emerging in the courtyard and for a moment, violent, lustful and brilliant thoughts flash in his mind, the thoughts of a young man who, aggressive and self-assured, is about to embark on an adventure. He turns to explain this to Kang, but the old pharmacist is not there. Kang has gone below, to the basement beneath the basement, the one accessed through the trapdoor next to the janitor's closet and down the staircase overseen by cabaret dancers and music hall performers on faded posters. The pharmacist has gone deep and will not come out again, for like ancient Diagoras, Kang has discovered that a moment of perfect happiness is the ideal moment for death.

Now the long forgotten and the no longer seen come out and reacquaint themselves with life and light and friends. The Krebs sisters, still clutching Thermos flasks full of plum liquor in their gloved hands, descend the hill and meet up with the nurse and the taxidermist. Strilic, the impresario, a man thought to have died or to have vanished fifteen years ago, appears on his balcony, though the door leading to his apartment remains sealed with layers of undisturbed dust. On any other morning this would be cause for alarm or astonishment, but not this day. Mesmerized, entranced and enchanted, the residents absorb rays of sun and bliss, all their troubles forgotten.

Inside his apartment, Majarek looks for a length of rope.

IX

Indignities accumulate in his final hours. He has misplaced important papers, including details of people who might have otherwise been able to help him; he is out of food and drink; and he discovers that he is no longer in possession of his pistol. Despairing, he searches for alternatives. He does not find the rope he is looking for, but in a flash of clarity, he realizes that it would be of no use to him anyway: he is neither criminal nor traitor. Die he must, but not this way.

Alone in the building, drifting along corridors and staircases that appear lit for the first time, he makes his way inside various rooms. Irene's bathroom cabinets are filled with pharmaceuticals, but he has no way of knowing their effectiveness. In the early moments of his desolation, he contemplated stealing embalming fluid from Sebastiano's laboratory, but soon discarded the notion. He had a horrid vision in which he lay on the floor, without motor skills, twitching and soiling himself. Now he finds himself in front of Kang's door, but it is locked. Despondent, he returns to his quarters.

He has knives, of course, ceremonial daggers sharp enough. But it is a perilous proposition for a one-armed man. He could ascend to the terrace and jump to his death. But men have been known to survive falls, even from great heights. And, of course, dignity, always dignity, the memory of his essence that must be preserved. So he leaves his rooms yet again, fearing that whatever is attracting the residents and keeping them outside will vanish, and that they will return to find him, adding more embarrassment to an existence that has become synonymous with it; or worse, noontime will arrive, forcing everyone into temporary banishment. The building has already started to tremble, an invisible wave rising out of the bowels of the lower basement. Majarek fears he will run out of time.

At last, he comes to Schlossmayer's door and finds it open. Entering, he is astonished to find book-lined shelves and cabinets but nothing else that reflects the man: no photographs on the walls, no uniforms in the closets, no memorabilia from different times. He had not believed Irene's description of Schlossmayer's rooms. Now, bewilderment washes over him. He has trouble reconciling the old foreigner's malice with his erudite predilections. Not for a moment has he doubted that Schlossmayer is behind the slander that has ruined him. Yet, he marvels that such a man should come to possess things of great value and beauty. Standing between two rows of incunabula, Majarek forgets what the purpose of this hour is. A large desk is situated in front of the grand window. On it, a Coronelli globe tilts at an impossible angle, but somehow remains in place

supported by two woodblocks. Momentarily, the one-armed man considers a friendship that never was; the man who has undone him could have been a great companion. The conversations they could have had, the obsessions they could have shared. He sits on the leather armchair behind the desk and allows himself a moment of peace. He notices a glint from the top of a cabinet against the back wall. He looks at it until his eyes tear up, so strong is the reflection. He stands and walks towards the source of this unbearable brilliance. Wedged between a Flemish notary's account of a medieval murder and a Buddhist scripture in Pali, reflecting the improbable rays of this improbable sun, he finds Schlossmayer's firearm and relief envelops him. He takes the pistol in his hand and finds pleasure in the familiar weight. He returns to the leather armchair, the weapon evoking memories of battles fought under a merciless sun, a life of service and loss, of barracks and offices that stank of stale smoke, of ancient trains and desiccated plantations, of corpse-filled fields at dawn, of artillery shelling, of his amputated arm. But nostalgia evaporates, and only this acute present pain remains, a pain that wears the face of his son.
So he stands up and leaves.

On the stairs leading to the rooftop he sees an old couple, sitting like students, holding hands. He has not seen either of them before. The woman's face is daubed with white and her lips are clownish and red. As he passes by, they both smile toothless smiles, smiles full of intolerable understanding. As he walks past, up the stairs, Majarek senses them standing, receding into the building, the midday hour fast approaching.

Finally, he arrives and stands alone at the top of the tenement block.

X

They have all left. The hill, the ravine, the courtyard: all empty. The firmament has darkened. On the terrace, Majarek leans against the pigeon loft. He has always loved high places and he wishes to be buried in the sky.

No bitterness mars his final moments. The soldier knows his life is forfeit. Majarek feels light without his prosthetic; the unpinned sleeve is flapping in the wind. Beneath his feet, a deep silence reigns inside the block. He is utterly alone, but this mission is the simplest he has ever undertaken. Ever systematic, he test-fires the pistol at the distant city. The report reverberates all around the hill and the dried riverbed. There is only one question left: head or heart? He hesitates, not out of fear, but because he knows the ludicrous preoccupations of the living. For him, all that is random and all that is necessary, it all comes to an end. Does it matter if the casket is open or closed? His son will not be there. No one who matters to him will be there. And he discovers a certain freedom in this thought.

Time has always seemed slow in the tenement block, but Majarek's ruminations have been lengthier than expected. Soon the residents will reappear and perhaps some will come to the terrace in order to gaze at the darkening hill from this very spot, a vantage point that justifies the entirety of the crumbling building that supports it. Majarek smiles at a memory: Olafsson, the folklorist, once told him a story about a man who promised to build a thousand towers in a single night and raised demons from the earth to help him do so. The demons worked through the night and were constructing the last tower when someone lit fires all around. Believing that dawn had come, the demons melted back into the earth and the man who had summoned them failed to keep his promise.

What nonsense! He takes one lingering look around. The sparse trees on the hillside appear to be undulating as if pressed from above. A bird rises out of the branches, followed by another and another until the swarm is formed. The familiar shrieking is heard as the corvids unexpectedly return for another assault.

Majarek puts the barrel in his mouth. When the metal touches the hard palate, he pulls the trigger.

Another Beginning

Michael McGlade

Ógán is a magpie, but he wasn't always a bird.

* * *

An Interrupted Beginning

Ógán is twenty-one. He is studying History at Queen's University, Belfast. Succumbed to a powerful drug fugue in his dorm room, he is paralyzed, unmoving for a whole day except that within himself he's travelling through Indonesia; a trip he and his fiancée Niamh have meticulously planned for years, and which they intend to take after graduation. When he eventually comes to, Ógán realizes the places he wants to travel to will never live up to his dreams. He rushes over to Malachy's.

* * *

Guide to Pronunciation And Meaning

Ógán (pronounced OH gawn) means youth.
Niamh (pronounced NEE uv) means brightness, radiance.
Malachy (pronounced MA la kee) means messenger of God.

* * *

The Real Beginning

Ógán loses Niamh to his best friend Malachy. Ógán and Niamh had been high school sweethearts, and the three of them had been inseparable—the "Three Blind Mice."

Ógán stumbled onto this scene: the affair in full swing, the pair of them at it like otters in his best friend's bed (he'd seen a documentary about how otters held hands when they slept—but this right now was absolutely not cute). Ógán had been let inside by a still-stoned flatmate, the squawking pair growing louder as he raced down the long, cement hallway toward that familiar sound—knowing it was Niamh behind the locked bedroom door, his teeth zinging like when foil shorts out your fillings.

Some things can never be unseen.

Thinking back on it now, he often wonders if maybe he should have just gone home instead of shouldering the door open. He often thinks of how he stood there like a gormless gobshite, ogling the romping quislings.

He expected Niamh to blurt out it was a mistake, that this had never happened before. But it wasn't. And it had.

Now to cause an immense uproar, chew the scenery like Al Pacino! But no words would come. Instead, he went for Malachy but that buck-naked eejit punched him hard. Weepily trudging back to his dorm, Ógán dumped Niamh's stuff out the third-floor window. He never saw either of them again. Last he heard, *they'd* taken the trip to Indonesia.

That summer passed in a violet daze, to Elvin Bishop's "Fooled Around And Fell in Love." That spiteful song followed him everywhere: laptops, car radios, ringtones. On the solstice he broke into his old high school and entered the history classroom where he'd first met Niamh. There, he downed a pint of whiskey and a packet of his father's blood-thinning medication.

The End.

* * *

Some Common Misperceptions

The nursery rhyme "Three Blind Mice" is about three bishops burned at the stake by Queen Mary I of England. Bloody Mary liked burning people, and 280 other religious dissenters met the same fate during her five-year reign. Many nursery rhymes are based on horrible real-life events. "Ring a Ring o' Roses" is about the plague. "London Bridge Is Falling Down" is about child sacrifice. "Jack and Jill" were two young lovers thrown to their deaths. Ógán has confirmed the validity of these statements in conversations with the dead.

* * *

The End Is a Beginning

Ógán is a magpie. He has black and white plumage and a sleek elegant tail. Up close, his black plumage has an iridescent violet sheen on the wings but it turns glossy green on the tail.

He coasted the thermals over Slieve Gullion Mountain, a half-mile high, as effortless as standing still. His new form had taken a bit of getting used to; the ruffle of his feathers, how he sensed minute changes in air current through his entire body. He swooped like black lightning, landing in the back garden of his family home on top of the small granite gravestone for Buster, his Jack Russell.

The back door of the house opened and a tiny wrinkled woman with glasses half the size of her face threw the heel of a batch loaf onto the paved walkway. Ógán flapped over, pecked some, then cawed at his mother.

"Every day you eat all my bread," she said, "and never get no fatter. Just like Ógán used to." Her shoulders hunched and she took the Padre Pio medal from beneath her blouse and kissed it. A sharp whistle pierced the air. Since becoming a magpie, Ógán had heard that whistle several times; it was warning him about a trapped soul. A *violent* soul. He had to deal with it: this was part of his job.

He flew south, following the whistle thirty-five miles to a ghost estate outside Drogheda, spotting from a mile off the violet shimmer of the haunted house. The neighborhood was recovering well from the housing crash, and half of the houses that had lain vacant for nearly a decade were occupied. One of them, a detached two-story redbrick, was occupied by a man conducting a one-sided argument.

Ógán perched on the windowsill. The man (mid-twenties) jabbed his index finger towards the corner of the living room wall, then struck, punching yet another hole in the plasterboard that bore a dozen already, his knuckles the color of a Bloody Mary. A baby screamed upstairs.

Ógán found the newborn writhing in his cot, and from the smell the nappy hadn't been changed all day. A woman shrieked. In the kitchen he found her listening intently to the extractor fan. She was begging for a voice to stop, *pleading*, but then climbed onto the counter and slammed her head into the stove's aluminium hood, streaking the metal surface bloody red. There were other holes smashed into the walls, these with a sledgehammer. The couple had been working over the entire house, searching for something. Ógán knew a wronged soul often manifested like this, driving the inhabitants to self-harm or murder/suicide. He didn't have much time to intervene. Ógán had seen how quickly people could kill each other just to stop the voices.

He circled the building, paying particular attention to the structure. Nothing untoward. Sometimes it was a body nearby in a shallow grave, but the yard was well-maintained, flowerbeds blooming with the first flush of summer, grass clipped. There was a scarcity of furniture within, almost Spartan décor. Perhaps this family had just moved in and, without signs of a recent grave, he could discount them as murderers. Something much older and malevolent was present.

And then he saw it.

Glistening within the crewcut lawn, pink and pulsing. He swooped down to beak the worm and swallowed it, whole and wriggling. It was delicious, reminding him of ham, mixed with a little dirt. The dirt was the best bit. Kept him regular.

From the lawn, he saw a row of bricks along the base of the house that appeared newer than the rest. A section of those bricks had also been removed and replaced, the mortar different. Concentrating, Ógán visualized the empty space beyond the bricks and his body dissolved, rematerialising on the other side. It always felt like plunging into a swimming pool, ears popping followed by a weird chlorine odor, but it was a neat trick.

Within the shallow cavity beneath the house there was a bundle wrapped in plastic, the scent of death masked with quicklime. Inside were two bodies: husband and wife. This close to the body, Ógán knew the tragic story:

She killed him and he deserved it. The bastard had a nasty gambling habit before the housing crash put him crazy; he attacked her, almost killed her. She stabbed him with a kitchen knife. Self-defense. Right now the bastard was already in The Dark Place, flayed by a demon that looked like his wife. The end.

But the woman remained to poison the building. There were gashes on her wrists, proof she had turned the knife on herself after the murder. Who had put the bodies here? That was the real reason she hadn't departed this plane.

He summoned the woman's trapped soul to its body. The woman, Aoife, hovered over her corpse, before Ógán guided her out of the building, upwards.

The young couple in the house had returned to normalcy. The woman rushed into the living room, her husband staring wide-eyed at the holes he'd punched in the walls. They hugged each other and kissed, relieved it was finally over.

Ógán guided the dead woman towards the light, moving from the dark to gray.

"You've been dead eight years, Aoife."

"But I only killed him yesterday..."

Dead Time always moved faster.

"I'm not being punished for killing him?"

"Self-defense," he replied. "But suicide is a 500-year sentence."

She lurched to flee, but here he was all-powerful. Nobody escaped.

"I don't make the rules, I just follow them. We all follow them."

She struggled, trying to fight him off, pulling toward the house and her decaying body. Still, they continued onward into the grey. Directions were meaningless; only Ógán knew the way out.

"I'm sorry for your loss," he said. "But we'll get to The Grey Place soon. It's not so bad, you'll see."

"Why do I care what some dumb bird says?"

"Did you know, magpies are the only non-mammals to recognize our own reflections."

"Why are you a magpie, and not a raven or a crow?"

"Crows are criminals," he replied. "It's the punishment for being a low-level criminal, sentenced to be a crow."

"But magpies are thieves."

* * *

Where the Rumor Began

Rossini's opera La Gazza Ladra (The Thieving Magpie) has a servant girl sentenced to death for stealing silver even though the magpie did it. It's a common misperception that magpies are thieves and that we steal shiny objects. In fact, shiny objects are extremely annoying. The glare hurts my eyes.

* * *

"What about my body?" Aoife asked.

"Somebody will find it, eventually."

"You bastard, you're just leaving me there to rot? No burial?"

"Your suicide sentence isn't your worst problem," he explained. "The haunting and torture of that family ... that's a millennium right there. A thousand years in The Grey Place."

With Ógán concentrating, they dissolved and rematerialized in The Grey Place. Globules of prismatic light—souls—wandered chaotically, zigzagging and colliding like excited particles. Others adopted mournful poses and wandered, moaning. They didn't have to, they were free to do whatever they wanted, but many elected to remain penitent and dour, even though it had no outcome on their sentence. The Grey Place wasn't a punishment, it was more of a holding area; a place where souls contemplated their earthly behavior before being allowed into The Big House. They could form a jazz club for all The Boss cared. But they continued moaning, rattling chains, posing like that Scream painting.

"How did you transport us here?"

"I can transport anywhere in the universe, but it's quite impossible to breathe on Mars, so I'm mostly on Earth."

"Then you can get inside the foundations of my house, get my body out?"

As much as he wanted to make whoever had hidden two corpses beneath that house pay, it wasn't his job.

* * *

A Visit to The Big House

A hard-faced, soft-bellied man in a toga was standing on a wooden crate on a street corner, orating to no one in particular. "Can one believe there exists presently a brand of condom entitled Trojan?" Homer said. "Alas, it should evidently be noted that the Trojan Horse, after infiltrating the outer defences, forthwith, in a clandestine attack, ejected hundreds of soldiers. Is this truly not an unfortunate implication for a prophylactic?"

Homer regarded his audience, which was much smaller than he usually got at the Greek theater for his evening performance. Two people were present: Dali twisted the waxy tip of his drooping moustache, and Picasso was dressed like a matador. Neither of them applauded.

Ógán swooped down and dropped a silver drachma in the pileus cap at Homer's feet. Happily, Homer cleared his throat to continue; the others groaned.

Ógán flapped alone toward The Big House. The light was diffuse, like being inside mist; the buildings, cobblestone streets, and people emitted luminosity. Sitting on a nearby bench, a man wearing a black three-piece suit was sheltering beneath a black umbrella. Edgar Allan Poe adjusted his sunglasses and scratched in his notebook with a quill.

"You should really have chosen the form of a raven," Poe said. "Magpies have too much white."

Ógán landed on the bench. Poe dipped his quill in the ink bottle, but it was empty. He glanced pleadingly at the bird. Ógán concentrated, and a bottle of the blackest Indian Ink materialized.

"Has thou ever read *Jonathan Livingston Seagull*?"

"That seagull's such a poser," Ógán replied. Then: "Because I'm a bird I'm only supposed to read books about birds?"

"Which postures an interesting conundrum, my half-raven friend. Exactly how doth one, being a bird that is, and thusly lacking thumbs, read a book?"

"I can still peck the buttons on my Kindle," he replied. "Quoth the magpie, nevermore!"

Ógán flapped off to find The Boss. Although finding him wasn't exactly how it worked. The Big House took whatever form you desired, and while this usually involved soft white clouds and angels with harps, for Ógán it was the flat-share where Malachy lived, where he had found him with his fiancée Niamh.

The walls were translucent as jellyfish, and Ógán glided down the hallway to enter the bedroom, which looked exactly as it had that day; the bed sheets tousled, dirty jeans and socks piled in the corner. Malachy hadn't even cleaned up before Niamh arrived—that's how routine their tryst had been. Ógán landed on the desk, and a snap of his wing cascaded a laptop and geography textbooks onto the crusty floor.

"I'm not picking those up again," The Boss said.

His voice reverberated from everywhere. He had no face, no body. He was everything and nothing.

Ógán squawked and got to the floor, lifted everything back onto the desk. "You see everything," he said. "So, when do they die?"

The Boss had promised Ógán that he'd be allowed to decide a punishment for Niamh and Malachy. He'd get to reap their souls and ferry them to The Dark Place. Let them suffer for a few millennia. That should be payback for how they'd destroyed everything he cared about.

"You've got work to do," The Boss said. "Time to take another one back."

The room dissolved like sugar in water and Ógán rematerialized on the tiled floor of a diner. His feathers spasmed and he staggered a couple of steps. He hated it when The Boss did that.

Two men were arguing in a corner booth. Ógán took flight and landed on the shoulder of the larger man, who had coiffed black hair and huge mutton chops. A half-eaten cheeseburger was oozing oil on his plate. Elvis jabbed his finger at Jim Morrison's shirtless chest.

"You can't keep being the same person throughout history," Elvis said. "I mean, *Michael Hutchence*? Seriously? That's what you wasted your reincarnation on?"

Jim brushed his mane of hair out of his face and took a swig of whiskey. "Being Plato with a guitar worked for you last time round, fatboy. But this isn't the seventies anymore. They have *cell phones,* but they don't use them to speak to each other on—they use them to write shit on the internet."

Frizzy-haired Janis Joplin, in the next booth over, strummed her guitar. "Don't just be one of the regular weird people this time," she said.

Ógán guided Elvis to the jump point, a swirling portal that appeared in the diner's entranceway. Elvis was squeezed into the sequined jumpsuit he had barely fit into before his Las Vegas blowout, rolls of fat bunching the seams. He turned to Ógán and said, "What's an internet?"

* * *

The Residue of Life and Death

The piercing whistle led Ógán to an industrial garment

laundering facility outside Belfast. He'd been to the city many times, watching Niamh and Malachy grow their family. Waiting.

The facility was empty because it was still a couple of hours until sunrise. Yet Ógán went around to the walled-off yard and found workers sheltering beneath a rusty piece of corrugated steel, smoking. Raindrops daggered down like shiny coins. He made his way inside, industrial presses squeezing out white bed sheets and towels for the hospitality industry. The windows toward the front had been sealed with cardboard, giving the appearance that the factory wasn't in use. This was an unscheduled nightshift.

Eimear was reaching with her red raw hands into the mangle, a huge, gaping black crusher of a thing that gripped the sheets and pressed them between solid rollers, wringing moisture out. The whistle ceased, the rollers stopped, but the mangle still pulsed with violet light. Life was sticky and didn't want to leave. Ógán had learned death always leaves a residue.

Eimear tugged at a knotted sheet caught on the inner mechanism. The mangle cranked forward, trapping the woman's hand before it whirred into life, dragging her towards the crushing rollers. Ógán swooped down and pecked the off button but the mangle was not deterred. The woman screamed but her co-workers did not hear her above the growling machine.

Ógán drove his beak into the power cable. Electricity sparked like fireworks, a wallop to his kidney that threw him off his feet. The whole facility went dark as Ógán stumbled onto his feet, beak scorched and sore.

Workers rushed to Eimear's assistance—she was alive and uninjured, but as the power came back on, so too did the mangle. It had maimed countless people over the past two years, because, Ógán saw, there was a trapped soul within its machinery.

Ógán materialized inside the mangle, where the trapped soul was wedded to the mechanism. He gripped the soul in his beak and ripped. The soul split apart, most of its essence escaping into the ether. "You've been dead two years," Ógán told the remains of the man.

"But just yesterday, I fell into that mangle."

"Take me to your body," Ógán commanded.

The mauled soul swept a hundred yards east to the Lagan River. There, weighted with rocks, his body lay hidden in the silt.

Ógán knifed the water and torpedoed the corpse, raising it to the surface. Somebody would find it. Somebody would bring the facility manager to justice. It was not his job to intervene and, taking to the sky corkscrewing with joy, he knew he had done the right thing.

But then, his wings seized and his wishbone froze in his chest. Ógán plummeted like a dead thing.

* * *

The Beak of Things to Come

A child's hands cup him gently and he's being lifted off the pavement. The world snaps into focus and the woman staring at him is Niamh. Her son, Riley, found Ógán's twisted body on the pavement next to the Lagan while they were walking to school. She takes him into her hands and he meets her eyes. His heart quickens. He wants to kiss her, but he has witnessed the way she looks at Malachy, at their son—it was love.

Now her green eyes widen in fear.

The boy is strangely silent, when moments ago he chattered about how they needed to save wild animals. He'd been humming a magpie rhyme about a single magpie being bad luck.

* * *

Fun Fact

Magpies are symbols of happiness in Chinese culture. Koreans believe they deliver good news. In the myths of Native Americans (Navajo, Blackfoot, Cheyenne), we're their faithful allies.

* * *

A Particularly Difficult Death

Car tires screech. A horn blares.

Niamh sprints onto the road, her boy having taken the crossing without waiting for the traffic signal to change. He's directly in the path of an oncoming car. She throws herself at Riley, shoving him aside so the car crushes into her. Ógán is still in her hand, both of them thrown forward, tumbling along the road. She's staring at him, pleading with her eyes as her nose runs bloody. A wound at the back of her skull gapes. Niamh dies. Her soul separates from her body. Riley is running to her.

Ógán loves her too much to let her die. He summons his energy into her and before he blinks out of existence, Niamh sits up, uninjured.

* * *

An Interrupted Ending

There are no ends, just new beginnings. That's how it works, according to The Boss.

He said something about giving everybody a choice but not everybody recognized an opportunity.

"In fact, most people believe there are strict rules forbidding them from intervening." Funny the things people cling to. Misguided, obviously.

It was difficult for Ógán to grasp because he was still re-forming, but he knew the drill: once as a dead human, and now as a dead bird. He was laid out on a black leather couch, the walls lined with books. He tucked his wings behind his head, crossed his legs and stared at the white ceiling.

"Did you know I was going to do that?"

Freud removed his glasses and fogged the lens, cleaned them on his lapel, and said, "The question is would you have still done it had you known you would?"

"He makes a fair point," The Boss said. "I guess it's time you took him back, Ógán."

Freud stood straight now, his body rigid. He muttered under his breath, hands held in a shooing off gesture, but by then Ógán was ushering him to the jump point.

"Why did I lose flight," Ógán asked, "if I hadn't done anything wrong?"

"Unresolved issues," he replied. "We can get to the root of it with free association. I say a word and you say whatever comes into your mind."

"You know I'm Irish, right? Those tricks don't work on us."

"But, your dreams, I can analyse your dreams. Do you dream of big black dogs?"

"Every magpie does."

Freud pushed back, trying to escape. Just like they always did, terrified of making a mistake.

Ógán took him gently by the shoulder and shoved him through the portal.

Red Mask

Jessica May Lin

Before she jumped, Feng Guniang used to tell me about her suicide, during our cigarette breaks when we danced at the Green Dream, her white-lacquered nails trailing against the web of her fishnet tights. We smoked in the shadowy corners behind the opium dens on Jiameng Street, where the lights from the neon advertising boards couldn't touch us. The new opium dens are all styled like the old red mansions of the Ming Dynasty, complete with heavy doors twice as tall as we were.

"You come back, you know, if you wear a red dress."

There were lengths of time when Feng Guniang would walk on the crumbling remnants of the Old City Wall at night wearing a short red *qipao* embroidered with golden phoenixes, balancing on the parapet barefoot, her arms spread out, teetering like a puppet. I used to beg her to come down. Sometimes there would be other people—strangers, noodle vendors, foreign rich men with fur-lined coats—and we would shout at her together, but she would always go on, laughing like she couldn't hear us.

Most of the time there would be no one—not even me, on the days I couldn't bring myself to see her. I danced the last shift alone when she disappeared at midnight, and long after I had wiped the rouge from my face and soaked my tired feet in warm water, I would see her dirty footprints on the white tiles leading into the back room, and hear her sobbing.

She had been the mistress of a German businessman who pulled her out of the river once. He never came to see her while she flirted with death, on the wall, but I saw him sometimes in the Green Dream. He sat at a table in the front right corner with a large group of foreign men, always facing the stage, his opium pipe meditative at the corner of his mouth, watching Feng Guniang. He bought her a mink coat that she would wrap around herself while she sang English lullabies.

When I knew her, Feng Guniang was the Marilyn Monroe of the new opium dens—the one that everybody wanted but nobody could have, and everybody was always trying to save. She had a beauty mark in the center of her forehead and bright green eyes—a gift from a Russian patron—that contained more life than was fair in our part of smog-ridden, overcrowded Shanghai. Her real name was Feng Jinling, but few remember that.

Her pussy opened like a peony, some of the customers tell me, when I sit at one corner of the stage alone and talk to them, long after she has died. They loved her more than me, and I was partially jealous, partially in awe. But I could never hate her, because she always needed us to save her. From the first day I met Feng Guniang, I could sense an empty space in her, filled with some silent wronging, that only expanded until she drowned in it.

I still see Feng Guniang's ghost, in the old gardens and sponge rockeries on Jiameng Street, wearing her red *qipao*. She wanders through the bamboo groves of Yuyuan Garden, and cries through the weeping willows by the large goldfish pond. These garden elements are only an illusion, cast by a hidden projector in a rock, and sometimes I am afraid she is an illusion too, but I know those bright green eyes too well. She has kept her gift, even in death.

"Xiao You," she says as she tries to clasp my shoulders, but her hands sink through my living skin like ice. There is despair in her voice. "Did they look for me after I was gone?"

Ghosts don't cast shadows in the pond. When I look down at the water, I only see myself, talking to the ripples and the silver fins that flash by.

"You didn't have to go," I tell her. "They didn't care."

* * *

Feng Guniang came back to haunt the man she loved, who never left his tall, curly-haired German wife for her. Or at least, that's what I choose to believe. She could've died and come back for many reasons, but more than she wanted to die, I believe she wanted to come back. Even as a ghost, she kept that stifled pain inside her—when I brought her steamed dumplings in a bamboo cage and sat with her by the pond with my knees drawn into my chest, drawing in the mud with sticks. I never talked to her, but sometimes she would sing.

There is no way to grow up in New China without feeling angry at something. Sometimes you are angry at what you cannot have, like Feng Guniang, who could not have her married German lover. Sometimes you are angry at things that are unfair, like how the Triads have taken over the water pumps in the capsule slums that crawl hundreds of stories into the air—so that half my month's salary is spent on a single bucket of water. Sometimes you are angry because you don't know better than to not be.

Anger in New China was a silent, bruised loneliness that nobody ever talked about. It bristled like the hairs along the spine of a cat, but it was invisible. People pretended not to notice.

Instead, there were opium dens, stuffed with maroon velvet cushions and curtains made from crimson gauze, staffed by porcelain-skinned women with red lips and *qipao* with high slits in the sides. There was a sex-and-drug euphoria to lose yourself in, so you could ignore how your sons and daughters were dying in overflowing hospital lines, or how the police would easily turn a blind eye as long as you had enough to pay for it. Those days in Shanghai, you were grateful for an excuse to drink your anger down with whiskey shots and exotic cocktails. I know because I served those drinks, in between the hours I spent on the stage.

"Come see the de-ribbed dancers at the Green Dream," the Boss says to the crowds that pass by outside, the advertisement board drilled into his forehead flashing with my silhouette. "They have their eleventh and twelfth ribs removed, so that they can perform feats of flexibility so outrageous you won't believe it until you see it. See how tiny their waists are in a corset."

I wonder where my ribs are—what the Boss did with them after I gave them up as part of my contract. I wonder what happened to Feng Guniang's ribs after she died, if they became immaterial and pale like her ghost body, or if they rotted slowly like fruit. I like to imagine my ribs are buried in a box somewhere, nestled in soft dirt, where they are safe from the poison of Shanghai.

I used to own a Tibetan mastiff named Happiness, who lived in my three-by-six capsule in the slum tower with me, but he ran away a month ago. I see him sometimes in the narrow alleys that run behind the convenience stores and bike shops of the first floor, which drip with water from laundry hung in the top stories. In some capsule settlements, the stacks of capsules go up so high, on the ground you can't see the sun. They say that each walled slum is actually hundreds of smaller capsule tenements, but that they have been built so closely together that they became one thing.

I whisper Happiness's name, and try to lure him back to me with my own dinners, but he growls and won't come. I sit on my bed inside the yellow plastic walls of my capsule alone with the electric fan directed at my face and eat canned pineapple because it is the only thing I can afford after paying the water bribe.

Feng Guniang had been a symbol for the dreamy helplessness of the Pearl of the Orient. And now that she was dead, that innocence dispersed like a cloud of perfume on a sigh. Her death was a cry for something to be done. I just didn't know what to do.

The Boss hires eight new de-ribbed dancers at The Green Dream. Whereas I used to be the youngest and least experienced, and Feng Guniang used to be the eldest, I stay through so many seasons that I become the protector of the new girls. I am hardened by the cruel Shanghai that waits outside the back door of The Green Dream, but I'm not changed by it.

It is at that time the girls start dying. Someone is stalking them, killing them in terrifying ways. As the oldest and the most unsentimental, I have to take responsibility.

* * *

"This is not the first time there have been serial killers on Jiameng Street," the Boss tells me, reclining on his velvet lounge chair with his opium pipe, his newly shined leather shoe crossed over his knee. One of his mistresses waxed his mustache this morning, and it curls at the ends like tea leaves at the bottom of a cup.

I stand with Lizi and Xiao Lian behind me. My hair is brushed into a chignon on top of my head, and I'm wearing a simple cream-colored *qipao* with light blue embroidered flowers. I've taken to dressing plainly offstage because in my mind, glamour was always Feng Guniang's right. "Can't you do something about it?"

"What do you want me to do?" he asks, taking a puff on the pipe. The advertisement board in his forehead flickers with lazy images, a video feed of his wife reading a magazine, a fat baby with peachy cheeks sleeping in a crib behind her. "Walk each of you home to your slum towers one by one? Hunt the killer down with my bare hands? Call the police, if you want. There's nothing I can do. Hundreds of people die every day in this city. Many die in worse ways."

Lizi brings him a plate of salted peanuts, and he stuffs a handful in his mouth, chewing loudly. He won't say any more on the topic, and after a while I have no choice but to accept this is all the help I will get from him.

The girls accept their fate without arguing. They go back to their tiny makeup tables in the backroom and brush their hair and powder their faces, holding handheld mirrors. The mirrors magnify their eyes, their cheeks, to ghastly proportions so that all across the room, these parts of girls' faces are floating in their hands.

I watch for a while, leaning on the doorframe with my arms at my side.

There is a perverted killer waiting in the city night. Ruan'er died a fortnight ago. Someone poured acid down her face as she walked down the street in her six-inch black pumps.

She had a wobbling, feline walk like a swoon, a signature red peony pinned in her sausage curls. I imagine the bony chill when she feels the shadows moving behind her, but nothing is there when she looks over her shoulder. She walks more quickly with that mounting terror growing wings in her chest like a trapped bird, and before she knows it, something cold hits her in the face, and there is agonizing, wretched pain as her skin melts between her fingers and pours away onto the pavement.

Ruan'er would've tried to scream, before she found she no longer had a mouth to scream with. In my imagination, the killer puts her face in a patterned silk bag with a drawstring. He pulls the strings tight and puts the bag inside his jacket before leaping onto the low roof of a mansion and vanishing into the foggy night.

Three nights later, it happens again to Wanyue, whom we find with her long legs splayed shamefully, her face missing. A girl's head is hideous without its face, nothing but a pink mass of mangled flesh.

I do not know what the killer does with our faces. I imagine their eyes are wide in his drawstring bag, disoriented by the sudden darkness enveloping them. Or perhaps they are a jumbled glob, like sweet jellied tofu. He has a different drawstring bag for every face he steals, and he keeps them in rows inside his jacket, which he can display proudly if he chooses to, but doesn't. Every three nights, he follows one of us home after the Boss closes the Green Dream at four in the morning. There are other girls missing all across the city. I don't know who they are, but I imagine that no one is looking for them either.

I go down to the deepest level of the slums, where sunlight never touches the ground, and the water from last season's rain still drips from above. Nobody walks here because there are rats and murders, but the water pump is located in this part of the slum, guarded by gangsters carrying rifles, their waist pouches overflowing with money from the protection fee.

The higher-ranking members of the Triads have pulled out a red plastic table with low stools and are playing a game of dice. The glowing eyes of alley cats peer out from between their legs and from behind sacks of rice like pairs of jewels.

"Please," I say to Fat Tiger, who is the leader of the Three Fists. "The de-ribbed dancers of the Green Dream humbly beg for your assistance in a matter that troubles us."

He grunts without looking up from his game.

"There is a serial killer, who melts our faces with acid." I wait, while the gangsters roll another round. They make an exaggerated show of laughter and pat the table in mirth.

Finally, when Fat Tiger realizes I will not go away, he leans into the light to see me better. "And you want my help? For all you know, I might be the serial killer." He throws his head back and roars.

But I know that Fat Tiger is not the serial killer.

"You have liquefier guns, with Chaozhou lasers. Please help us."

Fat Tiger's sleepy eyes widen. "I have liquefier guns, do I? Well, if I do, each one cost me a hefty sum you couldn't sell your life to pay for. What do I owe you to waste one in your hands?"

I curtsy ironically. "We help you pass the nights away when you are lonely and in need of company. We dance for you, and mix you the finest cocktails, and entertain you with our acts of contortion."

He studies my mien, and I know that he is looking for signs of fear, but I'm not afraid of him. Fat Tiger is a bully, but he is as much a part of our walled slum as I am. "You would kill a man?"

"The police wouldn't care if I turned him in alive."

So he tries again. "A young lady like you believes that murder will bring justice?"

"I am only angry, and I don't wish to hide it anymore."

A door bangs open somewhere, and a heavy-boned woman in an apron patterned with rainbow snails hobbles out, carrying a pot of stewed pork and potato. My mouth waters at the hot steam that wafts through the alley. The cats begin meowing, and more eyes appear in the darkness, drawing closer to the table.

The woman is Fat Tiger's wife, and she wears a flowery dress under the apron. Underneath her dress, her arms are thick pythons; a lopsided mountain of sea-green curlers is arranged atop her head. "Stop bullying the girl," she tells Fat Tiger, and lands a hard slap across his ear. "Give her what she wants so we can have our dinner."

Fat Tiger cuffs her hand away and calls her annoying. The other men lower their heads and pretend not to see, as the couple erupts into a slapping match. Only I watch, as she pinches his ear between her fingers and twists, while he yowls and throws jabs at the jiggling flab of her upper arm. Finally, having had enough, Fat Tiger's wife shambles into a corner, calling him a bastard turtle's egg, and lights a cigarette.

Fat Tiger grumbles under his breath and collapses back on his little red stool.

After a while, he snorts. "Give her a gun then, and pray she doesn't blast her own throat out."

At night, I shiver as I lie awake with the gun beside me on the cot in my three-by-six, listening to the water that drips continuously from above, through all the uneven levels of the slum city, toward the alleys below. A blue light pulses on the flank of the gun, indicating the laser is active, and I know that if I pull the trigger, a nullifying beam of heat will eradicate whatever I choose as my target. It is hard to miss with a liquefier gun. That's how Fat Tiger's goons have beaten every other gang in the city.

Still, I don't sleep. I blink at the liquefier gun, imaging myself in an alley with the serial killer, the weapon hoisted on my shoulder. I can't imagine how I would find him, what we would say to each other. Am I supposed to bid him farewell, if he doesn't kill me first? What is life, if death comes so easily?

* * *

I see the faces for sale the next day, in a boutique shop on Avenue Charles de Montigny in the French Concession. Ruan'er's beautiful face, mounted on a pink doily, her almond eyes still with dark eye shadow on their lids, staring blankly outside the window of the shop.

The shopkeeper steps out from behind the shelves, which are filled with girls' faces, all set in lace and held up by dainty brass tacks. She has been sweeping dirt from the aisles.

"May I help you?" she asks, and her voice is sweet like icing on cupcakes. She wears a floor-length dress made of navy chiffon that swirls like a tornado at her feet. I cannot tell what her ethnicity is, but it's likely a mix of Chinese and European, her hair swept into a tight bun atop her head.

"Who buys the faces?" I ask her.

"Collectors," she answers, with a wide sweep of her arm. "Appreciators, connoisseurs in the art of incorporeity. Every face is unique, you know."

I tiptoe down the aisles of faces, afraid to make any sudden movements lest I startle the faces. But of course they do not move, or blink. They are just girls' faces. Even in death, they are quiet and unmoving, pretending that nothing is wrong.

"The other day, a man came in, looking to buy a face. He offered a gorgeous sum," the shopkeeper continues from the other side of the aisle. I see her from between the pale cheekbones of the faces, leaning on her broom. I find Wanyue's face on another shelf, her shining red lips still parted with her last breath.

"Which face did he buy?" I ask the shopkeeper.

"One that has not been collected yet," she replies, joining me in the aisle, and brushes her finger gently along Wanyue's cheek to remove a thread. "But this face is different. This face is a jewel in the New Orient, that shines like the North Star, brutal and bold with eyes made from rubies, apart from all the other faces in New China. This is a face of The Tigress Awoken."

Her voice rises to a ringing crescendo, which reverberates like tin in the sunny afternoon daintiness of the boutique shop. I cover my ears but it won't stop, and when I stare into the shopkeeper's face, her smile looks like it has been carved there with a knife. Suddenly, I am afraid.

I run out of the shop, the bell on its door jingling behind me, and run down Avenue Charles de Montigny, which is just an ordinary Shanghai street, full of bobbing parasols fighting for room on the sidewalk and long trench coats that sweep the pavement, and stare at the large billboards about the New Chinese Dream fixed on the sides of red mansion skyscrapers that wobble into the sky like endless pagodas. The women on the street carry stiff laminated paper bags full of their noonday shopping. Some are eating fruit off sticks, candied hawthorn berries and mandarin slices.

I drop to the ground and hold my knees against my chest. I want nothing more than to be consumed by the mobs of people who walk with their heads down, heading for their afternoon high in the opium dens on Jiameng Street. I think about the gun lying in my capsule, waiting for me to find the boldness to fire that one shot. If I could, I would tie the sun to the sky so that night would never have to come. *Look at me!* I scream at the people who walk past, but we are all invisible to each other.

I don't know where I am safer, outside or inside—or if safety exists anymore.

* * *

A few nights later, it is the fourteenth day of the seventh lunar month, the Ghost Festival. Plates of food have been left on the street for the ghosts to eat, and several of the girls are burning ghost money to appease the dead spirits that wander back from hell on this day to visit their families. The Green Dream is alive with gossip and good cheer, fragrant smoke wafting through the establishment; the Boss has ordered special delicacies and wine to be brought to each table free of charge.

The first row of seats in front of the stage is left intentionally empty for the ghosts. It is a strange experience, dancing for an audience that is not there. Real ghosts do not come to see the show. All of that is superstition; humans cannot do anything to absolve a ghost's pain.

As I dance, folding my body in the alien forms permitted by my de-ribbed waist, I glance over to the front right corner of the audience as I am accustomed to doing. I am looking for Feng Guniang's German businessman.

Tonight I am surprised to see he has brought a new lover, an artist from Guangdong. She is older than Feng Guniang, and wears a wide-brimmed hat with a long green feather. Unlike Feng Guniang, she has made an effort to preserve her dignity by refusing to sit in her German lover's lap.

I hate her, although she's done nothing wrong, and I don't even know who she is. I hate the German lover as well—he has not gone to see Feng Guniang once since her suicide. You can sleep with a ghost, you know. You can hold it in your arms and whisper things in its ear all the same. I want to ask him why he hasn't done this.

I curtsy my finish to a round of applause. Afterward, when it is Xiao Lian's turn to dance, I go to see Feng Guniang, whom I myself have neglected for a fortnight, ever since the serial killer made his presence known. It is her festival, after all.

I hear her singing in the roofed corridor over the pond, by the Pavilion of Listening to Billows. There are red paper lanterns floating in the water, meant to guide the ghosts back to hell. The lanterns form a pretty parade down the pond, attracting dragonflies, although I am not sure if the dragonflies are real or mechanical. Feng Guniang is crying on a marble bench in the corridor.

"Xiao You," she whispers, trying to put her hand my cheek, and failing as always. "Why haven't you come to see me?"

Something has changed about her. Her body has, if anything, grown colder and more solid, leaning more toward this world than the one she must leave it for.

I sit next to her, listening to the swish of the projected willows. I take the top off a bamboo cage filled with hot stuffed jujubes, which I have brought to her as an offering. She eats the food with her fingers and begins singing again. The goldfish somersault in the pond, creating satisfying splashes. I take my shoes off and dip my toes in the water.

We sit like that for a while, surrounded by the illusions of a peaceful garden.

Feng Guniang stops singing. "Mathias has a new lover."

I freeze, unsure how to answer. "How did you know about that?"

"I go to the Green Dream a lot," she replies. "I dance on the stage when none of you are looking. I try to touch him but he can't feel me."

"Why don't you kill him?" I ask her. "Ghosts can kill people, can't they?"

Feng Guniang shakes her head tearfully, takes another bite of the stuffed jujube. "They can," she whispers, "but I won't."

I feel it again, the empty space in her chest that is filled with her silent bitterness. There is a space like that in everyone's heart in New China. It has caused all this. I want to ask her why she lets him do this to her.

"Feng Guniang, you must've seen the serial killer. What does he look like? Where is he?"

She shakes her head. "He'll kill you if you go after him."

"Fat Tiger gave me a gun." I've brought the gun. I lay it on my lap and show it to her. "Please, Feng Guniang. You're the only one who can help me. I have to stop this."

"Are you going to leave if I tell you? Don't leave me. I'm so alone here. He has forgotten all about me. Everyone has, except you."

"I'll come back," I promise her. "When have I ever broken a promise to you? I'll bring you sweet-braised ribs next time, cooked so the meat falls off in your mouth. But let me do this for our sisters."

She is silent for a long time. The parade of paper lanterns passes us, bobbing towards the Bridge of Ethereal Butterflies, where they pass single file under the arch. I wonder if they are really headed for hell, or if they'll only find shore in the morning. Finally, she bows her head. "He lives in a *longtang* called Magpie Alley, not far from the Green Dream."

I begin to pack the empty bamboo cage, piling the last jujubes into a napkin so Feng Guniang can eat them after I'm gone.

Feng Guniang stands and takes my face in both her hands. This time I feel her touch, clammy and transparent, and I shudder. She is becoming more solid. *No,* I want to tell her. *You must leave this world, not stay in it.* "Promise to be careful," she whispers to me.

I squeeze her hand and promise.

* * *

On the unluckiest night of the year, when the streets float with the ashes of ghost money and papier-mâché animals burn like effigies in hell, I hunt down the serial killer.
Magpie Alley is an ordinary alley, stained, flowery women's

underwear drying on laundry lines and fat coils of sausage hanging on tin wires in the windows. A dog that looks like Happiness lies in the corner behind the Dumpster with his paws extended in front of him, busy chewing a bone.

I look for the serial killer's window. I imagine it must have the silk drawstring bags hanging in it, arranged like perfume sachets stuffed with aromatic herbs on a girl's dresser. I don't imagine he is the type of serial killer who decorates his walls with butcher knives or torture contraptions. His lust for killing rises from a more literary desire. The bags may have lucky patterns sewn on them to describe the faces he has stolen—peonies or lotuses for femininity, a bat for happiness, a double butterfly for love. Murder can be art too, as long as it is done carefully enough.

But when I find his window, which I was fated to eventually, there are no drawstring bags in it.

Instead his window is hung with bronze mirrors that have a water caltrop embossed on the back, the kind of mirrors ladies used for makeup during the real Ming Dynasty. Some of the mirrors face front, out the window, and others face back. Many people in New China mistake the caltrop for a grinning skull and thus consider the mirrors unlucky, but they are overlooking the abstract symbolism behind the original caltrop mirrors, which was that caltrops grow in water, and water does not lie.

I hoist the liquefier gun over my shoulder by its strap and begin to pull myself up by the kudzu binding the walls.

"A lot can be said about a window," the serial killer tells me when I reach the top, sliding the pane open for me to climb in. "Some say the most precious window of the world is the eyes, which are not really a window but a mirror."

He regards me calmly through a colorfully painted *dixi* mask, whose expression is the hardest of all Chinese masks to decipher because it is expressionless. In it I cannot find a man, or a god, or a ghost. Its eyes are closed.

I smooth my *qipao* back over my knees, and level the liquefier gun at his heart. At this distance, it is impossible to miss. He smiles—I can tell by the skin on his neck and chin, crinkling. "Not everyone in this city pretends to sleep," I tell him, and I press my finger down on the trigger.

A stream of blue light leaves the gun, and he raises his hands to shield himself. But the beam does not pass through him. I only have a heart's beat to feel shock before I see that he has held up a caltrop mirror, which deflects the beam back the way it came.

They say that real killers are incapable of feeling fear, that they throw their heads back in the face of death and laugh as he is doing now. Well, I learn that I must not be a real killer as that blue light comes dashing back to me, and I stumble back from it in vain. It doesn't matter if I was the one who fought back. In the end I am the same as all the others who did nothing. What was the difference to be made, between silence and screaming, acceptance and delusion, if it amounted to nothing? I, too, am helpless.

The beam of light splashes me in the face like water, and I don't have time to scream. The sensation of a thousand nails rakes across my face, as if my skin is nothing but papier-mâché like the animals we sacrifice for the Ghost Festival, and beneath it is fire that bursts forth and burns my body to ash. I sink to my knees on the serial killer's carpet, weeping as he pries my hands off my face and takes it from me—not holding it with a drawstring bag, but with his bare hands.

"Do you really think I am the worst killer in Shanghai?" he asks me quietly, holding my folded, melted face in the cup of his hands. "Or was it your desire to change something that cannot be changed that drove you here and killed you?"

He seals my face in a glass jar painted with swans that is plugged at the top with a corkwood screw. "Farewell," he says to me, and he steals quietly out the window.

I count my breaths in the shadow he has left, and I begin to wonder if it was a delusion to think a girl missing four of her ribs is enough to make a difference in a smarter, crueler world.

But I am not dead.

He has left my eyes in my face and spared my life. I grab one of the many caltrop mirrors and turn its face to me. What stares back is an amalgam of mangled flesh and ugliness where skin used to be that makes me howl, and the worst part is that I can see it all. I dig my fingers into my eyes to make sure they are real. He didn't take my eyes. Why didn't he take my eyes?

Then I remember a sentence that was spoken to me, in a voice sweeter than cupcake icing.

This face is a jewel in the New Orient, that shines like the North Star, brutal and bold with eyes made from rubies, apart from all the other faces in New China.

My face is the face of The Tigress Awoken.

* * *

"Please. I want to buy that face, for whatever price you name. It's my face." I am a beggar on the floor of the boutique, grappling at the shopkeeper's hands and dress.

The shopkeeper looks down upon me from atop her long neck and names a sum taller than the sky needle in the Bund. She knows I cannot pay.

"Please let me have it for a little less," I beg her.

She shakes me off her leg as if I'm a leper.

"But you can't afford the price I have named."

I crawl to the shelf where my face sits on a pink doily, watching the sunset outside. It has forgotten all about me, fever replaced by a stunned nothingness. Inset where my eyes should've been are two bright rubies. I wish it would scream for me, but it is just a face.

"No, no, no," I say to the shopkeeper, grabbing her hand. "No, you can't take my face away from me. It's mine. You can't do this."

"It was sold to me. It is mine by right now."

I scream and claw at her, but it is no use. She drags me by the hair down the aisles, through all the faces that stare without blinking, and deposits me outside on the sidewalk. "Leave my shop," she says as she pulls the blinds shut, "or I will call the police."

She pulls the door shut and locks it from the inside.

"Help me," I whisper to my face through the glass of the window, but it ignores me. Perhaps it is angry. I have failed it.

I feel naked and defenseless. They are disassembling my body bone by bone, feeding it to the hungry city that is always looking for victims, always waiting to take advantage of those who are trying to change it. I begin to look for my ribs in the cemeteries of Jiameng Street, which are just behind the opium dens, far enough that you can't see them past the red mansions built to hide them. I thought my ribs might be buried in a box, nestled under a grave or an ornamental angel. I dig holes under the back patio of the Green Dream until the Boss chases me away with a broom.

He screams when he sees me without my face, and drops the broom.

"Never come back," he tells me, as if I am a monster and not his once-prized dancer. "What are you doing in my establishment? Get out!"

I flee from the opium dens I have called my home, with no cheeks for my tears to roll down, to Yuyuan Garden, where the illusions of bamboo groves and sponge rocks stand guard over empty pavilions. A howl rises from the Pavilion of Listening to Billows.

It's Feng Guniang, who floats on her back in the pond.

She is no longer wearing her red dress. She is naked, her white body smooth as a statue. Her eyes are more sunken, dark holes with no bottom that bore into the pits of her skull. Her hair is gone, in its place a naked pallet of ridged white bone.

She swims to me and rises out of the emerald-colored water like the Goddess of Mercy. I wade into the shallows to meet her, mechanical goldfish darting away from my thighs in a panicked frenzy, and fall into her arms.

"Jian," she whispers in my ear.

"What are you talking about? What happened to your dress?"

"When a person dies, they become a ghost. When a ghost dies, they become a *jian."*

She holds her arms up for me to see. Ugly black scars mar her wrists. Black blood drips continuously from them, into the water.

I look down at the scars, unsure what to make of them. "You killed yourself again?"

"I cut myself open and served my heart to him on a platter, tonight at the Green Dream. But he didn't eat it. He wanted to eat rose cake pastries, imported from Yunnan. I put my heart back, and in case that didn't kill me, I cut my wrists on his broken teacup. He leaned over to kiss her and shattered it."

I sob into her solid shoulder. Feng Guniang doesn't shiver.

"You have changed, Xiao You," she says, brushing a strand of hair off what's left of my skull. Her fingers are wet and clammy. They smell like the river. "I feel the anger inside you. It rises like a fire clawing at the inside of your ribs, trying to get out of you. It begins in the space where your eleventh and twelfth ribs used to be."

I lift my face from her neck. "I feel the anger inside you," I tell her. "It is empty and silent, and cruel like an iron weight, and it sinks inside you, making an abyss beside your heart that grows deeper with every breath you take. It too begins in the space where your eleventh and twelfth ribs used to be."

We stand in the water, the ghost and I, our arms wrapped around each other.

"You were right," I admit. "I shouldn't have gone after him. It wasn't enough."

She shakes her head and regards me sadly. "Have my face," she says. "Or at least what's left of it. I killed myself twice and I only lost more. I see now that the steps I have taken are useless."

I remember what the shopkeeper said. Each face is unique, and bears its own story. Feng Guniang's is written with sorrow and weakness, but within it is an ethereal beauty that speaks of times passed away. If only we had been born in another era, where the world was not so cruel, she might have lived.

No," I tell her. "Your face is beautiful. You keep it."

Feng Guniang takes a step back from me, and I realize that her skin has become airy and light, like mist. I cannot feel her anymore.

"Neither of us won, Xiao You, but you still have hope. You haven't failed, you know. He took your face, but you don't need one."

Another tear rolls from my eye and drops straight to the water with no cheek to catch it. "Not even the Boss can look upon me anymore."

"Where's my dress?" Feng Guniang says, turning around in the water. "Let me make a mask for you—a new face that you can show off to the world."

She makes the mask for me from her *qipao*, which she had draped over the Bridge of Ethereal Butterflies. The parade of paper lanterns from the night before finds their way back to us and bobs around her in a circle of light as she sews. They have been waiting for her, hiding under the bridge during the brief summer showers and peaking out every hour to see if the sun had returned to our gray sky.

There is no power in anger, only loneliness. Feng Guniang and I used to hold each other on the stage of the Green Dream, while the servants waved colored lanterns, and somersault over each other. Each time I would feel the fluttering of her heart when my hand brushed her chest, and I would know she was looking at her German lover. She never cried for help in my arms, but neither did I.

In the end it is not anger that will save us. It is whatever comes after.

Finally, she releases me and wades back into the water. "There," she says to me, standing back to admire her handiwork. "It's a beautiful mask. I wish I had one like that while I was alive. I would wear it every day."

And she smiles. Feng Guniang's smile is disarming, even when she is an eyeless *jian*.

"Where will you go?" I ask her.

"I don't know," she replies. "There are other worlds that call for me, where I will face whatever comes. But you must go on living, Xiao You. I always depended on you to save me, but you're the one who can save everyone."

The parade of paper lanterns forms a neat line for Feng Guniang to follow. She wades back into the water, her arms making wide ripples.

"You must go on fighting, Xiao You. Remember that."

She retreats further into the water, while I call after her not to leave me. Afterward, I sob for a while under the projected willows waving their branches over my head. Willow leaves float down and stick to my hair. In the distance, light and chatter from the opium dens forms a smoggy halo over Jiameng Street. The Ming-style skyscrapers of the Bund sleep quietly, their red exteriors darkened in twilight.

I stand waist-deep in the water, wearing my new red mask, watching all of it drift further from me, but then the gentle waves pull it back. The moon casts its billowing reflection on the pond, always just out of reach.

There is a city out there named Shanghai, a city with ghosts and shops that have women's faces, neon lights and opium dens, my enemy and my home. It is a city sinking beneath the weight of its own grandeur, but I will pull it back piece by piece, until it is whole again. One day, Happiness will come back so I may clean the lice from behind his ears. I'll use my earnings from the Green Dream to buy canned eel, which used to be his favorite food. Maybe we'll move to a bigger capsule, one with a TV for us to watch English cartoons on.

Next year, when Feng Guniang comes back on the Ghost Festival, accompanied by her entourage of red paper lanterns, I'll bring her sweet-braised ribs as promised. I'll even bring her a plum blossom pressed between the pages of a magazine, so that it never withers. Plum blossoms are the first to bloom every year in Shanghai. They bloom in winter.

One day, Shanghai, I will stand in your streets without feeling fear.

BLACKPOOL

Sarah Brooks

The Dead Man

He has chapped lips and a grinning red slash at his throat. He topples over the wrought-iron railings of the pier and into the cold northern sea, where the autumn waves are hungry to swallow him up. He dies in the early morning, when the lights of Blackpool are not on. Nobody sees him fall.

* * *

The Detective

The Detective saves the chocolate flake for last. The wind flicks drops of ice cream into his beard as the Ferris wheel takes him higher and higher above the pier and the waves and the town. It reminds him of shivery afternoons with his parents, how they bribed him with an ice cream to be good for just a few hours more. He licks around and around the flake until there is almost nothing left.

The Detective tries not to look down. The sand is greyish yellow and the water greyish brown. The height gives him a funny feeling in his stomach.

He has found clues; a ticket stub from Pleasure Beach, a smear of sweet-smelling ice cream. He seals up the clues in little plastic bags. However hard he tries he cannot hear any echo of the dead man's last words on the wind.

The Detective has brought his dog with him. The dog is called Napoleon, for no particular reason. Scruffy, indecipherable, a dog that knows its own mind.

The Detective and his dog stand beneath the Ferris wheel and look over the railings at where the dead man fell. Blood stains the wooden slats of the pier. The tide is still in, but there's been no body pulled from the sea. The Detective tries to imagine plunging into the cold depths. He tries to picture the dead man beneath the waves, looking up at the white moon of the wheel. But all the Detective can see is himself in the water.

He rubs the scar that stretches from just below his left eye to the corner of his lip; although he grows a beard to cover it up he can't forget it's there. His scar is from the Assassin's knife. It itches when he is worried.

"Come on, let's be off," he says to Napoleon, who looks relieved. They go back home to their tall, thin house, where the Detective cooks an elaborate meal he shares with Napoleon, who has grown into something of a gourmand. That night the Detective dreams about the sea seeping into his bedroom through the carpet, about coral rattling like bones beneath his bed. In the morning there is salt on his lips.

* * *

The Assassin

The Assassin sits at her kitchen table and cleans her knife. When she is done she throws the knife high in the air and lets it fall. She throws it ten times, and ten times the knife lands point down in the wood of the table. She fights the urge to press the point into her finger, to see the smooth red pearl well up.

She tidies her living room and remembers to call her mother, who asks if she's found a nice man yet. She runs a bath and reads a novel, the heat curling the pages. Afterwards, she moisturises. The Assassin has skin as smooth as silk.

That night the Assassin dreams about sand dunes, stretching away as far as she can see, the Marram grass scratching her knees, whispering something she can't quite hear. She wakes with sand crunching between her teeth and sand mites on her pillow.

* * *

Interlude with Seagulls

Herring gulls circle, their wings white against the dirty sky, their eyes hungry, watching the town below. From up here Blackpool is always quiet, the houses neat as a toy town, the sand smooth and the sea still. Only the cries of the gulls tear through the air like a warning of danger below.

* * *

The End of the World

The Detective orders half a pint of bitter in the End of the World. The barman gives him a look. Through the pub windows the Detective can see the Ferris wheel on the pier. He scratches at his scar.

"Do you know this man?" he asks, placing a photo on the bar. It's from the CCTV camera in the pier arcade, and shows a man in a long coat, collar pulled up, face grainy and indistinct. The Detective thinks it makes the man look dead already.

The barman looks at the photo. "Seen him about," he says.

The Detective takes out his notebook and pen. "Got a name?"

He likes to find out their names. Especially when there is no body, when a name is all that is left.

The barman shakes his head. "We don't ask questions here."

The Detective writes this in his notebook and underlines it twice.

He sits at the bar all afternoon, feeding pork scratchings to Napoleon. Everyone is keen to help with his inquiries. He has six different names for the dead man before he has finished his second drink. Tommy, Charlie, Stefan. A builder, a taxi-driver, a school teacher. Luca, Antonio, Oliver. A hard man; a loner; a miser.

"He was a gambler," says the Barmaid. She cries into the Detective's glass and tells him the dead man was kind.

The Detective seals the tears into a little plastic bag. When he examines them later he finds that they are genuine. He takes out a tear and places it on his cheek. It is cool on his skin.

* * *

The Barmaid

The Barmaid's name is Anya. The men who come to the End of the World tell her their stories. She pulls them pints of dark ale and they tell her all the ways that their hearts are broken. They tell her about all the bruises and all the black eyes. There is a pain in the Barmaid's stomach that twists and twists as she pulls down the tap handle.

Speaking softly, the dead man told her he had lost something precious, that he'd lost it at cards. He had a look in his eyes that Anya recognised. "It's only a matter of time," he said.

At night the Barmaid dreams about flying.

* * *

The Casino

The Assassin is playing roulette in the casino. She wins and wins, turning each chip in her fingers, trying to feel its luck.

She has been pushing her luck for a long time and she wonders when she will finish winning. When the Detective walks right past her she sighs and places another bet.

The Detective is trying to find out what the dead man lost at cards. The casino is tight-lipped.

"We are not in the habit of divulging secrets," says the Manager, a man with many secrets. The Manager knows what precious thing the dead man lost at cards, because he keeps it in a safe in his wood-panelled office. The dead man lost his luck. He went all-in against the house and lost everything. Now his luck is wrapped in velvet in the dark of the Manager's safe. Sometimes the Manager takes it out and holds it to his ear to hear the pulse of the dead man's luck beating in time with his own heart.

"'I am sincerely sorry that we cannot help you further," says the Manager. His expression is entirely sincere. When asked the dead man's name he says it might be Karl or Patrick or Dmitry. The Manager cannot be expected to remember.

The Detective doesn't gamble. He doesn't believe in luck.

* * *

The Illuminations

All along the promenade, down the Golden Mile, lights hang between street lamps and in great tableaux three storeys high. A million bulbs light the October night, outshining the autumn moon.

Tourists drive by with their car windows open. Couples walk arm in arm, shivering at the strangeness of eating ice cream at night.

The Detective looks for clues in the lights but they do not reveal the dead man's name.

* * *

Breakfast at Sam's Café

The Assassin orders kippers because she likes to see if she will choke on the bones. She thinks it strange that she has never once had a fishbone stuck in her throat.

She sits at a table by the window, where she can see the marks her elbows have made on the Formica over the years. As she finishes her coffee she runs her fingers down the handle of the knife hidden in her coat. Sometimes she thinks she can feel the shine of the blade.

She checks her watch and looks out the window. The Detective walks by, so close that she could tap on the glass and he would hear it. The Assassin reaches out a finger. She thinks that today the Detective will turn his head and look in. Today has the feel of a special day. She places her finger on the glass and waits.

The Detective does not turn. He walks by, looking out towards the sea. The Assassin leaves her finger on the glass and when she takes it away there is a fingerprint, perfectly formed. The fingerprint is still there when she leaves.

* * *

The Pleasure Beach

Remember, the Detective found a ticket stub. He gets in free to the Pleasure Beach when he flashes his warrant card. In Blackpool the dead come to the Pleasure Beach to ride the Big Dipper and the Ghost Train, leaving ghostly screams in the air when the Rocket loops the loop. The Detective rides the Log Flume and when he raises his hands at the final plunge he feels the cold touch of ghostly hands twining with his.

When he shows the dead man's photo at the Pleasure Beach he is told that the man is called Lars, Kevin, Simon. Recognized by everyone, the dead man is given a different name each time.

The Detective looks through hours of CCTV footage, watching the dead man move through the park, sometimes looking straight into the camera. The Detective begins to think that the dead man is watching him back.

Just as the Detective is about to give up he sees a face he knows. He leans closer to the screen and scratches at his beard, feels the raised skin of his scar beneath his fingers. Remembers.

Something twists in his stomach. Fear, he thinks. Then he thinks; *relief.* It has been a long time but the Detective knows where he has to go.

* * *

The Fortune-Teller

On the promenade, in the Fortune-Teller's caravan, the Assassin turns over the last card on the flowery tablecloth. The Fortune-Teller sees the card and goes pale. She shuffles the cards and makes the Assassin pick another one. The cheap gold bangles on her wrists shake. The Fortune-Teller is adept at lying but today her face betrays her.

The Assassin laughs. She pays twice what is asked even though the Fortune-Teller tries to press the money back into her hand. Outside the caravan the Assassin leans on the railings and looks out to sea. She breathes in deeply. She buys fish and chips and shares her chips with the seagulls and when it begins to rain she turns up her collar and sits in a bus shelter.

The Assassin waits for the sun to go down.

* * *

Confrontation on a Rooftop

The Detective and the Assassin face each other on the rooftop of a multi-storey car park. Rain whips at their faces. The lights of the Illuminations glow beneath them, making the night sky a murky orange.

A flash of lightning picks out the Assassin's knife.

"I've called for back-up," says the Detective, raising his voice above the rain.

The Assassin laughs. "You never call for back-up," she says. In the lightning flash, her smooth skin is white as bone. She takes a step toward the Detective. The Detective takes a step back. His scar itches. He is so tired.

"Who was he?" he says.

The Assassin says, "He was just a man who lost his luck. He was nothing special. They never are. Some people win, some people lose, and that's how it is."

Thunder rolls.

The Detective shakes his head. "I don't believe in luck."

"Really?" says the Assassin.

A bolt of lightning strikes Blackpool Tower.

All the lights in Blackpool go out.

* * *

Interlude with Full Moon

There is a different darkness when the sea reflects nothing but the moon. The seagulls lift their heads from beneath their wings and look up, their eyes full of silver.

In the End of the World the drinkers lift their glasses to a man whose name they can't remember.

In the casino, the house loses at last.

At the Pleasure Beach the ghosts watch their reflections in fun house mirrors.

The Illuminations, unilluminated, reveal bone and wire behind the lights.

The dead man lies beneath the waves looking up at the watery moon.

* * *

The End

Watch. The Detective and the Assassin are outlined against the sky. There is blood on their clothes and a knife lying between them in a pool of moonlight. But for the ragged sound of their breathing, there is no sound. The Detective and the Assassin watch the other's every movement.

One steps away from the knife.

The other steps toward the knife.

They do not take their eyes off each other.

A last flash of lightning, and one figure picks up the knife, sending ripples through the moon. The one who picks up the knife must be the Assassin, because the Assassin must always have a knife. In the moonlight the Assassin's beard is tinged silver-grey and his scar is a dark raised line. He looks older than he is. He tucks the knife into his belt.

The other, knife-less, buttons her coat. The Detective always has her hands in her pockets and a thoughtful look on her face. In the moonlight her skin is smooth as pearl.

They nod to each other. Then they walk in different directions, into the Blackpool night. This is the ending, the final scene. Moonlight, and a rooftop. And beyond the rooftop, the sea. But it is also a beginning. Another story is starting.

The Detective looks for clues, for chance and lost luck. When she loses at roulette she touches the soft skin of her cheek and smiles when she feels it is wet.

The Assassin looks for a barmaid who weeps real tears. He sits at the bar with his half of bitter and his dog curled up on the floor. He listens to the Barmaid's stories and offers to buy her a pint. He tells her a story about a man falling from a Ferris wheel, a man with many names and no name, a man who lies beneath the sea and keeps his secrets to himself.

INDIGO BLUE

Rachael K. Jones

Above the shuttleport ticket line, migrating orison-birds roosted in twos and tens and hundreds on the skylight before lifting and wheeling east, toward the distant winter nesting grounds. Lucy thought glowfall on Indigo must look something like those flashing blue wings refracting the sunlight, but she might never find out, because far up in the shuttleport line, someone else had bought the last ticket to the planet. The last glowing sales-counter sign winked out.

It was one thing to sell out a concert or a handball game, but Indigo orbited close enough to Violet for travel only once every twelve years. Miss it, and you might never get there. Job offers expired. People expired. Over that kind of time, ellipses became periods.

If you were smart, you bought a ticket early, long before the pass. Nobody knew anticipation like those with tickets to Indigo. It was a bet you made with yourself that you would still want to go when the next pass happened, that you wouldn't be in love or pregnant or dead from alcohol poisoning. It was self-predestination. Buying a ticket early was also the only way to get there, for most people.

Lucy couldn't afford to miss the pass, so she unlocked her cycle and caught the ferry to the next shuttleport. Through her headphones, a baritone saxophone unwound the bluesy opening bars of the song Justin loved. She had a promise to keep to an old friend she'd never met, a man whose small kindnesses had made every last one of her four hundred and sixty-two remaining days alive worth paying gladly.

Her handheld's alarm buzzed. Lucy opened the tin in her pocket and took today's stay-alive.

Four hundred and sixty-one.

* * *

Lucy and Justin went back ten years, long before the stay-alives and her illness, to the time she thought she would hit it big on the indie music scene. One summer she rounded up her poetry notebook and scraps of chords and recorded her own album in her capsule apartment in Port Darwin, borrowing pillows and blankets from all the neighbors to soundproof the closet.

The album flopped on Violet. Lucy junked her recording gear and forgot about her music until three years later, when far away, her single "Indigo Blue" hit the Leonor Top 500 list on Indigo. She put half the royalties toward a bottle of fine brandy that tasted like smoke, which she drank one night with the help of her boyfriend Derek and his two roommates. In the morning, hung over and smelling of sex and sweat like a real rockstar, she spent the rest on the ticket to Indigo. It was cheap, relatively speaking, because they were only two years out from the last pass, and demand was low. If you wanted to make the hop, you had to plan years ahead, or else tickets would sell out, or get too expensive. Still, it cost her the difference between a capsule apartment and a spacious flat on the docks. At 33, she was the only one in her graduating class still living in a dump like that.

Her next album didn't sell, not on Indigo or anywhere, and her mic gathered dust bunnies under the bed. One morning, after plucking three gray hairs from her scalp, Lucy called the courier service and asked to go full time. Her mother and Derek badgered her about the cheap capsule apartment. Lucy explained she liked her neighbors, the way all the kitchen smells converged through their open windows in the evening. When Lucy thought about her future on Violet, all roads ran straight and smooth and relentlessly unbending, a dull march through all the usual stops on the way to death, wonderless and savorless.

Then three years after "Indigo Blue," Justin's letter hit her email, bounced around the sun via relay satellites, timestamped 2:35AM. Lucy didn't know what that meant in Indigo time. Days passed faster there, just like years did. The planet ran on hummingbird time, making a whole orbit in twelve Old Earth years to Violet's fourteen.

Justin confessed he didn't usually write to foreign musicians like this. *I don't even know if this will reach you, but I had to tell you your music got me through some tough times this year.* He'd driven klicks and klicks after work each day to tend to a mother with dementia. Everything was so far-flung on Indigo, he had only music for company, and got home too late to see his young daughters. It was lonely and relentless, and he was grateful for the company her voice brought. Lucy seized Justin's letter like a rope in a storm. No one had ever reflected her weariness so precisely.

He attached a picture of his backyard in the rain. A great droopy tree dripped shining water into puddles in the dark. Where the droplets touched ground, they shone blue. The ripples stood out like stacked haloes. *You sing like you grew up here,* he said. *It takes me back to childhood, to glowfall games in the rain.* When he spoke of his home, it sounded like a fairytale. *Lake Radiance. Fiddler's Leap.* Iridescent rain falling slantways down the mountainside, glittering like broken glass.

They began writing back and forth almost daily.

I drive the harvester on the biofuel colony, wrote Justin. *The hours are long, especially in the cold and wet, but it's necessary work, it pays well, and the views are incredible.*

I'm a courier. I cycle to all the islands, rain or shine, Lucy answered. *Mostly shine. I can listen to music, and sing, and I get lots of fresh air. I might be the only courier on Violet with all the ferry schedules memorized.*

The emails came at all hours, always syncopated, good mornings and goodnights shuffled and dealt out randomly. Justin loved her pictures of sunrise. On Indigo, it always rained. Sometimes during winter, the clouds would break up a little, and they'd glimpse scattershot stars, a moon or two, and sometimes the red, faraway sun. But it was rare.

Not that it's dark here, Justin added. *It's not at all. There's the glowfall, and the symbiotes, and I think anyway it's better than you get with just stars.*

How would you know? asked Lucy, and he didn't answer, but the next day she got a photo of the great threaded net strung street to street over his hometown, glow vapor condensed to starry blue droplets, lighting up the winding alien street, the incomprehensible signs, the faces grinning beneath clear umbrellas.

* * *

Businesses closed early on Violet due to the electricity ration, and Lucy just missed her last drop-off at the end of the workday thanks to a late ferry. Lucy's molars pulsed—somewhere far away, another shuttle launched from the island. Its white smoke drew a line up the sky, Violet swinging on a thread in space. For three months, the ships would come and go, ferrying people between two worlds, exchanging goods that couldn't endure the low-energy transfer orbit pipeline. For a couple months after that, shuttle travel would taper off as the trip grew riskier, more fuel-consumptive, harder on life support, until the pass ended, and Indigo's orbit pulled too far ahead to catch anymore. Then the 12-year counter would start over. Thirty-three became forty-five. Justin's kids would be adults, maybe married. His sickly old cat would be dead. Lucy would probably still be a courier, skirting the edge of poverty to pay for her stay-alives.

In the morning, Lucy called in to apologize to her boss. Arn was a kind man, patient with her. Lucy had worked for him since before she got sick. The customers had come to trust her discretion, and some requested her by name, so Arn cut her a lot of slack. "Lucy, you know I like you, but you can't be late like this. You've been slipping lately. This is the third time this month you've gone off-grid while on duty. What's going on?"

Lucy swallowed back the truth, because hunting for tickets was her private business, and it didn't matter because she couldn't get another ticket to Indigo anyway, not after she'd lost the one she'd bought with her royalties, so why bother? "I just lost track of time. It won't happen again. I'm sorry."

Arn sighed and the handheld made it sound like typhoon winds tearing at water. "I mean it, Lucy. It costs me whenever you're late. You know I like you, but next time, you're out."

Lucy thanked him and hung up. A message from Justin came through on the handheld. *Let's dump our whole schedule. When I see you next week, let's just spend the whole trip getting drunk and then drunk-singing around the firepit in my backyard.* It was an old joke. Truth was, they'd planned her itinerary to Indigo over and over for years now. They'd filled it past the point of practicality, but it didn't matter, because half the fun was the dreaming, the planning, the imaginary road trips that only ever played out in their minds. You could do that with a friend you might never meet. You had to.

Let's go to Lake Radiance and dive for fungus blooms, if they're in season, Lucy answered. *And remember I've promised to watch your daughters dance.*

On her apartment wall, Lucy had a huge street map of the Greater Darcy island chain, all fourteen islands linked by ferries and bridges, her best routes traced in blue pencil. She knew those streets very, very well. Anything their customers wanted, she could deliver. And if you had the money, there was always someone selling.

This is really happening, isn't it? said Justin. *Fair warning: I might cry.*

It's okay if you do, Lucy answered. *We'll just cry together.* They'd cried together before. Something made possible by distance, that you could cry without shame and know that far away, somebody understood.

* * *

Most people didn't know Lucy was sick, thanks to the stay-alives. There had been a few weeks of fatigue, a nasty green bruise on her shin that wouldn't heal, and a trip to the doctor for some blood work. Lucy was scrolling through pictures from Justin's biofuel colony on Indigo when the doctor gave her the diagnosis. He explained mitochondria to her, how her body was built on an ancient partnership between some single-celled organisms, but there had been a quarrel, a divorce, and now it would kill her.

She nodded, eyes fixed on the handheld like a guiding star, a thread stretched all the way to Indigo. The doctor scribbled the prescription for the stay-alives. "I'm starting you on replacement therapy. These are expensive, but you need to take one every day."

"For how long?"

"The rest of your life." He tore off the sheet and handed it to her. "It's very important you don't skip them or reduce the dosage. If you're going to skip, you might as well not take any at all. The disease will come back, and we might not be able to stop it. You're lucky we caught it so early."

And that was that. Or it would have been, except for the price of the medicine. It came from Indigo, a byproduct of the symbiotes, and like all things imported on the 12-year cycle, it only got more expensive between passes. Just one of the pills cost more than Lucy made in a day. People held bake sales and cycle races for you when you lost your hair and puked your guts out in a bucket. But if you didn't look sick at all? If you got on your cycle the day of your diagnosis, rode 20 klicks to the pharmacy, emptied your savings for a three-month supply of stay-alives, and rode home, young and strong and whole of body? Well, no one had any pity for a woman like that. People didn't really donate to the sick. They paid you to perform your sickness.

Justin texted her furiously in the weeks following her diagnosis, although she hadn't told him anything. *Are you okay?* he asked, and asked again. Lucy demurred. She didn't want to cry with him over this. On Indigo at least, she wasn't sick. *Whatever it is, I'm here for you, okay?* he said, and somehow, that eased the thick, sticky pressure in her throat.

In the end, she only told her boyfriend Derek. When he finally left two years later, broke from the price of keeping her alive, it was because of her ticket to Indigo. "Just sell the damn thing," he said near the end. "It's like you don't *want* to live."

Lucy tried to say why mere survival wasn't enough. That she needed to write those impossible itineraries and believe in a perfect day. Justin's favorite tea shop, smelling every single blend on the shelf, the smoked teas and the dried teas and the fresh teas wet in their wrappers. Picking one to have on the porch with Renza, Justin's wife, while the mycoblossoms opened and sang in the evening gloom.

"But you can't do those things if you're dead," Derek pointed out, and for that, Lucy had no answer except the wordless, struggling rage of orison-birds pinned in the snare while the flock flew west without them.

Lucy counted pills, and Derek stopped speaking to her. Justin sent her a video clip of his youngest daughter asleep with their cat, their drool iridescent against the pillow.

I haven't heard from you in a while, said Lucy, and the time-lapse stretched out so long, she knew he'd paused and considered it before answering.

It's been hard here lately, he said. *Renza miscarried last week.*

She typed and deleted a bunch of replies, and finally sent, *Damn*. It occurred to her that he curated his life too, that the Justin in her head was a mosaic fitted from the pieces he gave her, and what she decoded from the length of his pauses.

By the time Derek left, Lucy's music had shuffled into the corners of her life, to lyrics scribbled from smoke-shaped dreams right after the alarm went off, measures hummed between the ringing of the ferry bells. On weekends, she dusted off her old mic and synthesizer and tapped rhythms in 9/8 time. It was easier with Derek gone. She tried out "Indigo Blue" again. She made a remix for Justin.

I really like this version, said Justin. *The space between measures, how the pauses carry weight. Like a good conversation. Tell me you'll sing this when you visit during the pass.*

Okay, Lucy told him. *I promise.*

That was the day she rode her cycle to visit Sage the first time.

* * *

After Arn chewed her out, Lucy took the ferry to Traverse Island to see Sage again. Lucy could've married Sage, if not for his Doz addiction. He had a voice like a foghorn, strong and melancholy. When he sang, you could feel it in your bones and teeth and behind your eyes. She'd couriered Doz for Sage's dealer a few years back, and she'd taken a shine to Sage. One day she'd stayed late to fix his broken handheld. They'd ordered pink radish noodles, shared some rice wine, watched a documentary on orison-birds on the history channel. He fell asleep on her arm, soaking her sleeve in drool, but she didn't mind.

Sage made his living scalping tickets to Indigo every twelve years, buying them cheap and spending the profits on enough Doz to stay high until the next pass. When Lucy sold her ticket to Sage after Derek left, Sage gave her the friend rate, because he liked her and because she told him about the stay-alives. He'd nodded, understanding what it was like to live for your next dose.

Now Lucy sat on empty banana chip wrappers on his couch and worked up the nerve to ask for her tickets back. Sage rubbed his shaking hands one over the other, wavelike. He looked twelve years older when he came down, like he'd gone to Indigo and back.

"C'mon, Luce. I can't just give away tickets, not now." His Doz supply was running dangerously low so close to the pass.

She held within her ten years of pining for the friend who sustained her with mutual daydreams and photos of his backyard. Hope glowed beneath her breastbone, fragile and terrible. "Sage, if you do this for me, I swear on the bones of dead Old Earth I'll make it worth your while."

"Got a deal going down on Indigo?"

Lucy shook her head. "No. Just seeing an old friend."

Sage nudged her thigh with his socked foot. "Long way to go for a friend."

She swatted at him. "You don't get it. It's like...Ever gotten homesick for a place you've never been? Distance is what you make of it."

He unrolled a flat canvas bag from his pocket and pinched out some Doz. The grains oxidized green to black on his fingers. He rolled it under his gumline, tongue creasing the spot thoughtfully. "The best I can do is one-way. You're on your own getting home before the pass ends. And it's going to cost you. It'll be unfair after what I bought your round-trip for, but that's the best I can do. It's still going to piss off the lady I'm holding it for."

Lucy knocked Sage over with a hug. "Thanks, Sage. I owe you big time."

He returned the hug awkwardly, because she'd never hugged him before. "Where are you going to get the money?"

She was going to lie. She meant to lie, but something in her face must've given it away, because suddenly Sage sobbed into his elbow. "Damn you, Lucy. You're as broke as me. You only have one thing worth any money."

She forced a smile because she hated to see him cry like that. "I'll make it work somehow."

"You'll die without your meds."

"It's not like I have much life left anyway," said Lucy, and her voice broke because saying it aloud made it feel real. "Another year, and then what? What can I really do on Violet with that kind of time? At least I can see Indigo once. At least I can say that much."

"Are you even coming home?" Sage's chin was wet and snotty.

For the second time, Lucy chose the truth. "I don't know, Sage. I really don't."

* * *

When she sold her ticket after Derek left, Lucy turned most of the money into meds and rent and sacks of rice, her half-hearted nod to responsibility. But for the price of one day's dose, she splurged on an Indigo clock that mounted on her cycle. It converted orbits and planetary rotations and let her select between local time zones. On long trips between the islands, she liked to wonder what Justin and his family were doing. Sleeping while Lucy peeled her sunburned shoulders beneath her sarong. Having glowtea for breakfast while she ate spiced curd for dinner.

The best times were when their days synced, and they emailed back and forth as quickly as the distance would allow, minutes-long gaps that shrank as the pass drew near, until it was almost like talking in real time.

Lucy told him about the vast sandbars on Violet stretching out into the ocean, and how it was sunny almost year-round, except when the tides brought in lashing storms that reshaped the beaches, sucking sand from one place and carrying it to others. And there were the ferries, and everyone rode cycles, and it took forever to get anywhere because you had to use your own two legs. The cities were extremely dense. You could make a living hauling goods from island to island. At night, everyone lit candles and lamps to drive back the dark, because biofuel came from Indigo via the transfer orbit pipeline, and electricity was expensive, and you wanted to keep your monthly ration for charging your handheld and for your refrigerator. Sometimes a fire broke out, and people died in their sleep because it spread so fast in the close, dry quarters. Lucy's uncle died like that, from smoke inhalation, and ever since she slept with the window open, even on stormy nights when the rain came in.

Justin told her about how on Indigo, it was always wet, and the sun rarely broke the clouds, and whenever it did, they'd declare a holiday, and schools closed early and neighbors cooked together over an open fire that sizzled and hissed in the lingering drizzle. Violet had been terraformed by the seedships of Ancient Earth, but Indigo life was hybrid, indigenous glowfall symbiotic with the imports. Old Earth trees grew huge in the continuous rain, colonized by glow to photosynthesize even in dim daylight. Those who grew up in glowfall never caught the flu. In his pictures, the whites of Justin's eyes shimmered iridescent when the light was dim. The glow even entered their saliva. On Indigo, you could spit stars on the pavement.

Once, Lucy raided her market's tiny imports section for Indigo food: dried algaes and fungi and powdered glowtea stocked for homesick immigrants. She cooked them at home with recipes found online, with too many substitutions. The resulting stew smelled like mildew. The glowtea Justin raved about was tepid grayish lumps bobbing around in souring milk. She snapped a picture for him. *You actually eat this stuff?*

Well. I think you have to taste it on Indigo firsthand, he said. *You can't eat dead glow and expect to like it. See for yourself when you get here.*

* * *

To pay Sage, Lucy sold all but three weeks of pills, just enough to get her there. And after that? Well, she'd have only a few days planetside to find a ticket home. If she missed the window, she'd make her way on Indigo with the cash saved from the return ticket, at least until her days ran out. Maybe her drugs would be cheaper at their place of manufacture. Or perhaps meds were a luxury in a place where people didn't even get the flu. Lucy figured nobody's mitochondria rebelled on Indigo.

The morning of the shuttle launch to Indigo, she snapped a picture of sunrise for Justin. She bought savory yogurt with pineapple from a street vendor at Port Jekyll, and iced coffee at the shuttleport on Traverse. For good measure, she picked up some fresh coffee beans for Renza and some rice candy for Justin's daughters. The morning air clung hot and sticky, but Lucy wore long sleeves because it was spring on Indigo. She took her stay-alive with the dregs of the coffee and locked up her cycle. The clock on the handlebar said it was morning in Indigo.

Lucy snapped a photo of her locked cycle and sent it to Sage. *If I'm not back before the pass ends in three weeks, my cycle's yours. And help yourself to anything in my capsule apartment. It's a load of junk, except for the synthesizer. Key's inside the clock.* She snapped off the Indigo clock's plastic cover and left her key there, wondering if she would ever touch it again.

On the shuttle, as she watched the planet fall away, Lucy thought this was the closest she would ever come to time travel.

* * *

She was vibrating when they landed, long after the shuttle's engine coughed its last and died. All the tiredness and aches of the trip fell away. He was near, somewhere out beyond the tinted windows, waiting to pick her up. Lucy skipped down the runway, stretched the kinks out of her limbs, and breathed in Indigo, thick and heavy as a damp towel. The walk from the airstrip took them under the open sky. It was evening, and the sky was all roiling clouds, gold where the sun touched it, blue at the edges. A huge bronze plate piled with eddies and cloud banks. She felt light on her toes. Then they were in the airport itself, and she saw him, the real him, Justin in the flesh for the first time.

His pictures resembled him the way a brother might—close, but not the same. Real-him had physics. He held his arms just so and stood like this, his own way and not another.

"Justin?" After all this time it didn't do to assume that she was anything but a stranger to him. But he grinned so huge that he couldn't possibly be anyone else, and when he said her name, suddenly it was okay, and she ducked beneath the rope to get to him.

They fell into one of those long, awkward hugs that are really a thousand hugs never given at all. *Hugs don't expire,* she thought. He smelled like unfamiliar soap. It had a spicy edge, like chai. In all those years, she'd never thought to imagine what he smelled like.

"Are you tired? Hungry? How was the trip?" Justin grabbed for her bag, and she let him. Suddenly she was bone-weary.

"I feel like I could sleep for days." Lucy followed him through the shuttleport to a walkway leading outdoors. Justin twitched his waterproof hood up, and she imitated him, trying hard not to gawk at all the cars in the parking lot. She'd never seen so many at once. "I could really use a shower." The shuttle had less comfort than a submarine, although the views were better.

"Well, let's go straight home then. You can meet Renza, and I know the girls are dying to see you."

Justin's car looked like a beetle: six wheels, six doors, painted in green and white stripes. He placed her bag in the back and waved her in. Lucy watched him sidelong to figure out the complicated straps and buckles interlacing over her chest. She'd never ridden in a car before. The vehicle thrummed like the shuttle, and traveled almost as smoothly. When they hit the road, Lucy dropped all pretense and gawked. Land rolled in all directions like stormy swells sculpted from earth. So much of it! Every inch overgrown and blooming, trees she almost recognized, and giant scalloped mushrooms and leafy purple fronds big enough to wear.

They zipped down an elevated road with a meter-long dropoff on either side. Lucy flinched, gripped the seat.

"We're on the outskirts of Iaaku, the capital city of this province. It's about two hours south to get to my house. Not the most scenic drive, I'm afraid, but it's the middle of nowhere, and you're catching the tail end of winter."

"It's spectacular," she said in a low voice. Moths as big as her hand flittered from treetop to treetop. Brooks crisscrossed the jungle, running beneath channels under the road. Occasionally, another car passed them from the other direction, and the windows trembled from velocity. Over it all came the drip and patter of ever-falling rain, sometimes thunderous on the windshield, sometimes gentle like kisses. "Where's the glowfall?"

"You won't really see it until evening. It's too bright at midday."

Lucy's handheld buzzed in her pocket, reminding her to take her meds, but she was all out of stay-alives. She'd thought it would be easier to tell Justin when she got there, but now that he sat beside her, close enough to touch, all her scripts dissolved.

Justin lived in a tall house with a pointed roof. Houses on Indigo reminded her of women at a costume ball, bright and many-layered and painted in scrolling curls. The asymmetrical roof sloped steeply, channeling the runoff down gutters into a creek that ran down the street past the other houses. They parked in the driveway and immediately the front door flung open. Out came Renza and Justin's two teenaged daughters, Nell and Ziana, each with a huge umbrella. Somehow they herded her inside without getting anything wet except Lucy's thin canvas shoes. Her teeth chattered anyway.

"It's colder than I'm used to," Lucy explained. Nell passed Lucy a round red blanket.

"How about I make us all some glowtea?" Justin asked.

Lucy remembered the gray lumps curdling in milk. "I'm not sure I care for it, honestly."

"But you're supposed to make glowtea for company," Nell insisted, pulling Lucy to her feet again. "We'll do it properly, with new glowfall."

Ziana and Nell brought her to the backyard. In the falling dark, the rain had become blue meteors. Ziana pressed a shallow ceramic bowl into her hands. "Go collect some."

Lucy held out the bowl and caught the storm. Glow beaded her bare arms in little constellations, cold and bright. She willed it through her pores to her war-torn cells, imagined a mitochondrial truce, an exile of flus and viruses to the dark countries where no glow dwelled. It clung to the skin more than regular water. The bowl glowed like a lamp. Lucy and the two girls bent over it, and their reflections shone back.

When the glow-infused water bobbled to the bowl's brim, Nell led them inside with tiny shuffling steps. Justin stirred a boiling pot in the kitchen—something spicy and fragrant, like oranges and rose petals and anise. He strained it into five mugs, and Ziana topped them off with glow ladled straight from the bowl. Lucy swirled her drink. The glow clung to itself like oil, and felt soft and slippery on her tongue. The taste bit like raw chocolate, but the warmth filled her stomach. She shivered hard, curled her toes until chill passed. The second sip tasted sweeter.

"It's the glow enzymes," Renza explained. "They digest the tea compounds, and it changes the flavor. When you've been here long enough, the symbiotes transform your palate."

She wondered if she could carry glow home in her own saliva. If it would hold back all sickness on Violet too. She stepped around the wild hope carefully because she knew it was more deadly than any storm. Better not to imagine it at all. "How long does the glow stay in your body?" Lucy asked.

Justin shrugged. "You'll have to tell us when you get home."

Lucy rolled around that word, and came up with nothing. You were supposed to know in which direction your home lay. Even an orison-bird in a squall knew that. The lack made her feel weightless, unmoored. In the absence of gravitational pull, there was no difference between flying and falling.

* * *

In the following days, everything went wrong. Lucy overslept, so they missed their scheduled trip to the biofuel plant. Sage asked how her trip was going, and she sent him a picture of the fields from afar. Lake Radiance flooded, and Justin's favorite tea shop closed for renovations. Sage asked how she was feeling, and she ignored him because she didn't want to think about sickness, not on her trip to Indigo.

The itinerary dwindled line by line. It was too much for just a week. It was too little time. Lucy and her hosts stayed up late at night talking about their lives, and the books they'd read, and Lucy's music. She danced around some of Justin's questions: what happened when Derek left, or why she'd given up her music, or how she could be a courier forever when it was a job for the young.

After Justin and Renza went to bed, Lucy lay awake in the dark with her handheld, watching the glowfall pelt the windows while she searched for tickets back to Violet. Exhaustion pressed down hard. Perhaps normal fatigue, or perhaps the first signs of her mitochondrial death approaching. In the dark, she banged her arm hard against the bed frame and waited for the bruise.

Just before she went to sleep, Sage emailed her a photo of a Violet sunrise, and she flushed, realizing his emails had been piling up. *Are you coming home?* he asked, and the word prickled. Instead she told him about the food, and how he was right that Indigo was an acquired taste, but once you had it, it stayed for life.

I was afraid something happened when you didn't answer me the other day, Sage said after a pause so long she thought he'd left for the day. *I'm glad you're okay.*

Lucy recalled her own texts to Justin, the days his crazy itineraries had been her reason to go to work. She hadn't known Sage relied on her like that too, another stay-alive.

Sorry. They've been keeping me busy. But I'll bring you something back, she promised, and part of her wished she could take it back. Promises could save, or they could snare.

* * *

In the morning, Justin noticed the blue-black blotch on Lucy's arm. "What happened there?" His eyebrows crinkled over his glowtea. Renza had gone to work. The girls tromped around upstairs, getting ready for the day.

Lucy tugged down her sleeve to hide the bruise. "I just hit a corner, is all. Got disoriented when I woke up."

His gaze pinned her. She met his eyes with great effort, and found kindness. "Lucy. I already know. About your ticket home, I mean," Justin said gently.

She swallowed against the lump in her throat. "How?"

"After all these years, don't you think I know you pretty well? I put it together a long time ago. You don't have a ticket home, not anymore. It happened around the time Derek left, and ever since you've been trying to make up for it."

Lucy's ears burned. He'd known all along. She shivered, suddenly vulnerable, humiliated, exposed in this cold and foreign land. He reached out a hand, but she leaned away.

"I'm not going to burden you and Renza. If I can't find a ticket, I've got enough money to make it for as long—" She stuttered to a stop. "For as long as I'm going to be here."

He arched an eyebrow. "You don't have money for a twelve-year stay."

Lucy crisscrossed her arms, cupping the bruise in her hand. She tried on the words *home* and *Indigo*, but the pull in her heart remembered *sunrise* and *Violet*. She'd longed for Indigo for years, but now that she'd arrived, it was like when the seasons changed and the orison-birds flew the same course in reverse, called out and back and out again by more than one home. The pause drew out like an interlude between stanzas, music for those with the skill to read it.

Justin touched her arm across the table, and the warmth of him diffused like glowtea. It was pictures of sunrise, and flashing blue wings, and falling stars, jokes and punchlines: time and space impossibly bridged at long last in a dear friend's kitchen.

"You don't have to explain. You've never had to, because it doesn't matter. The truth is I bought a ticket too, years ago, because we promised we'd see each other, and that promise was half mine. It's yours now, if you want it."

* * *

Her last night on Indigo, Lucy cooked a Violet meal for her hosts, cobbled together with many substitutions from what they found at the market. It tasted awful, but her friends were gracious about it, and anyway sometimes you had to travel a long ways in order to try things properly. Or perhaps it was less about the meal, and more about the company.

The bruise on Lucy's arm was healing rapidly, like it had no time to waste.

She cried the night before she left, privately. She emailed Sage about her travel plans, and he said he'd meet her when she got home. The drive to the shuttleport with Justin crawled, oppressed by a bored silence that masked deep dread, like planets about to part ways until their orbits crossed again. What could she possibly say to him? What could fill the years and distance and sustain them until they met again?

Next time they saw each other, they'd be older. They would meet again for the first time. They'd wasted so much time being afraid of each other, getting used to the physicality of it all, the body language, the mannerisms. Maybe they would change too much in twelve years. Maybe the bruise would come back, or she would be dead after all. You couldn't always count on things to last when even your mitochondria could betray you. But you had to make plans anyway, and trust yourself to keep them.

When they reached the outskirts of Iaaku, panic collapsed Lucy's façade. Maybe she should stay, make her home on Indigo among these wonderful, funny people with their umbrellas and their fascination with the sun. Maybe if she stayed, their world would heal her—except healing never came that easily, not when even the good memories left you scarred with a longing for home. She would always need tickets or stay-alives. Anything else meant death.

"I never sang you 'Indigo Blue'," Lucy said suddenly. "I promised you, and I never did it." What she really meant was, *I don't know how to say goodbye.*

Justin wove the car through traffic. The windows whooshed whenever someone passed them. "Sing it now, a cappella. And promise me the full version next time you visit."

And so she did. Lucy sang the stanzas, and Justin sang the pauses.

* * *

The day gathered in her throat, and she ached from the weight of distance and time. Why did it hurt so bad to leave? Lucy tasted bitter glowtea on the back of her tongue. She swallowed it down. The day settled under her breastbone, and the bitterness became a warm, fragile glow.

The glow lasted all the way home. It lasted when she debarked the shuttle, light again on Violet, beneath the purple sky where hung Justin's star. The shuttleport was nearly empty, except for Sage, who met her with a long hug, this time unhesitating.

"These are for you," he said, pressing a tin of pills into her hand. "I ripped you off. Please, take them."

Lucy didn't argue, or try to explain how the glow stayed inside her, and her secret hope she might live now. She took one of the stay-alives, because he needed to see her do it.

"Good to be missed," she said, and meant it. "There's an errand I need to run, though. Meet you for coffee in half an hour?"

After Sage took off for the cafe, she circled back into the shuttleport. The ticket lines were deserted. Now that the pass had ended, they kept only one window open. The glow became a burn.

Whatever her doctor might say next week, symbiosis had a cost. Homesickness could also be chronic. To endure it, you didn't need stay-alives. You needed tickets.

Lucy swapped Sage's gift of pills at the ticket counter for a round-trip ticket to a future she couldn't picture yet. But Indigo would wait its turn. This was a season for Violet. For the first time since she got sick, she craved its promise.

Lucy found her cycle undisturbed, chained safely to its rack, and then the tears flowed, phosphorescent in the coming night. By their light she tucked the new ticket into her pocket, twelve years and no time at all away.

All the Red Apples Have Withered to Gray

Gwendolyn Kiste

One bite is all it takes. That is—and always has been—the rule.

* * *

We discover the first girl in autumn. She's tucked beneath the tallest tree in our orchard, dozing there like a ripened apple toppled to earth.

I'm five years old, and the world is still gossamer and strange, my fragile memories like a soft cake that's not yet risen, so part of me is almost certain that finding a girl one morning, sleeping where she doesn't belong, must be the most ordinary thing for those who have lived long enough.

I plod behind my father as he carries her to the barn. "What happened?"

"A witch, no doubt," he says, but I don't believe him, because he blames witches for everything. A thunderstorm on the day of harvest, dark spots on the flesh of Cortlands and Braeburns, a splinter in his palm from an apple crate—always the work of a spell, according to him. Yet this blighted land, faded and cruel, seems more like magic has forgotten us entirely. Of the whole village, only our orchard retains a speck of color, and with the crop waning, bushel by bushel, each year, even that won't last.

My father places the girl in a pile of wilted straw, away from the wind and the sun, and she curls up, crumpled and lifeless, like an origami swan crushed beneath a heavy boot. In her knotted hand, she cradles a tiny red apple. There's barely a blemish on the skin. A single taste bewitched her.

"I'll go into the village." My father shrugs on his seam-split jacket. "Whoever she is, her family's probably looking for her."

He hesitates, then adds, "You stay here."

He says it as though I long to be near him, as though we're a proper father and daughter, good and whole, not the broken pieces of something ugly and aching.

I stare at the straw and say nothing. Without so much as a nod goodbye, my father vanishes through the barn doors, and I watch his figure become smaller and smaller on the horizon, folding in on itself until he's gone.

There's one path to the village, and he never ventures off it. It's safest that way. On the border to the north, the shadows of the forest murmur nonsense and stretch taut fingers toward the orchard. There are the trees here populated with blooms and apples, and the trees there that yield only gloom, and a line in between, our property line, that divides one from the other, shelter from the unknown.

"Ignore the forest," my father always says. "Only decay lives there."

As if decay doesn't live here with us too, our conjoined twin that never rests.

When I'm sure my father won't double back, I breathe deep and edge closer to the girl. She smells of lilacs and lilies, bouquets that no longer blossom on this land. For hours, I sit with her in silence, because I've got nothing to talk about, at least nothing this girl is probably eager to hear. She has plenty of problems of her own. She doesn't need mine.

Though she has one problem I can help with. I ease the apple from her fingers and drop it in the pocket of my gingham apron. If it was indeed poisoned, there's no reason for her to embrace it. I'll keep it for her. I'll protect her, the best I can. Too late is better than not at all.

A sliver of moon crests above us, and its meager light brings my father home. It brings someone else too. A young man arrayed in handsome silks and fine jewels, clearly a stranger to our province, since no one here can afford bread, much less such glittery baubles.

He kneels to the straw and inspects the girl's face.

"She's beautiful," he says, and my flesh prickles as he forces his mouth over hers.

I part my lips to ask if he even knows her, if he ever saw her before this night, but I exhale instead and my words dissolve like a plume of smoke in the chilled air. It would do no good to speak. Little girls don't earn the right to question the wisdom of men. We can smile and blush and nod our heads, but we can't tell them no.

Eyes open, the girl gags, and I wonder whether it's residual poison on her tongue or the taste of his kiss that nauseates her.

He drapes her, still groggy, over his shoulders and declares her his bride. The next day, they make it official at the sagging chapel in the town square.

We never learn where this prince came from. Even after the wedding, the girl's family can't pinpoint his kingdom on a map.

"It's somewhere to the East," they say, and that's precise enough to satisfy them.

The villagers don't search for the witch who soured the apple. They're busy cooing over satin and white stallions, and tethering rusted tin to the tail-board of the royal carriage.

The young ladies cry because it's all so romantic.

"I want an apple and a prince," they say, and cool themselves with folded fans made of lace, torn and yellowed.

My father's chest expands with feverish zeal like a hot air balloon inflating for exhibition, and I divine the thought turning over in his mind.

This will be wonderful for business.

After the ceremony's over and the villagers scatter like dried rice, I remain on the road, my stomach cramping as though I'm the one who consumed poison.

The apple's still in my apron. I take it home and hide it away.

* * *

One by one, the girls find their way to the orchard, and once they start arriving, they never stop, like the tide breaking over the shore.

My father makes quiet deals with the families.

"I'll keep them safe," he says, and the mothers and fathers agree, because they have nothing else. Their faces, all soiled and sunken, are hungry, a hunger that even a month of hearty meals wouldn't satiate. This land has been barren so long that the desperation's in their marrow, deeper than the salt beneath the earth, and they look to us and this orchard and our apples as if their daughters might earn a fate here that doesn't mean starvation.

"How do you know the prince will come?" they ask.

My father flashes them a serpent's smile. "Have faith," he says. "Faith always discerns the believers."

They pay their gold coins, often a lifelong savings, and in our cottage by candlelight, my father counts the money each night, pacing circles like a vulture that dines on the carrion of frail dreams.

By now, it's been five years since the first girl, the one who went east and never returned. We never did find her kingdom, but her family claims they receive a letter each spring.

"She delivered an heir in December," they say, but if you ask them, they can't tell you the child's name or whether it's a boy or girl. They can't tell you if the daughter's happy in matrimony either, but that seems unimportant somehow. She married a prince. What more could a poor village girl desire?

Before the families leave their daughters to our care, they make special requests. They ask for glass coffins where the girls can slumber, but they forget there is no glassmaker in this town, no artisan of any kind. All we can offer is a pile of straw in our barn. A hideous option, but my father's clever. He can spin even an unseemly truth into a gold-plated lie.

"It must be straw," he says. "A prince won't come otherwise."

He never asks if they have hay fever. After they're nestled in beds of fodder, the girls sniffle through hollow dreams, eyes swollen and red welts blossoming like rosebuds on their skin.

"No one will want to kiss them now," I say, and my father hushes me.

Such talk is bad for business. And business is what keeps us alive, keeps porridge in our bowls, keeps the orchard thriving for the young ladies who wear their best dresses and lace tattered ribbons in their hair.

But a few don't skip so merrily to the gallows.

"She's nervous," one mother says, dragging her heart-faced daughter behind her. "That won't affect the magic, will it?"

My father regards the girl, who stares at her threadbare shoes. "Not in the case of such a deserving young princess," he says.

At this, the mother brightens as though she always believed her progeny was royalty-in-waiting, and at last, someone outside the family has confirmed it.

The girl, however, does not brighten. Her skin blanches the color of bone, and when I peer into her face, it's as though I'm looking through the muscle and sinew to see what's beneath. She's no more than fifteen. Some families hold on to their daughters longer, clutching them with gaunt hands, delaying the inevitable, always hoping a better option might materialize. But in this place where the land is stained gray and the wheat won't flower again, there is nothing better, and the longer you wait, the more the girl loses that freshness in the cheeks.

My father makes a deal, a fair one he calls it, and the mother bids farewell to her child.

Except for this ritual, daughters are rarely allowed to be alone. "It's unsafe," the villagers say and keep them under brass lock and key. Not until after the price of their future is paid like a macabre dowry are they turned loose to pick the perfect apple.

Their first taste of freedom is their last.

Along the manicured trails of the orchard, I tread solemnly behind the girl. This is against the rules, and if my father catches me, my backside will meet a belt. I don't care. Like a ghost, I always follow.

It's only May, a time made for fragile blossoms, not fully bloomed fruit, but that doesn't matter. The magic here grows stronger each season, and even in the biting cold of winter, these trees now flourish with ready apples in all varieties, including ones that never used to grow on this land.. There's no blush elsewhere in the village—our property has more than enough for everyone.

After the first girl, we were sure the nearby forest cursed our land, but we need no witchcraft to cast this spell. The apples do the work for us, the poison readymade and choosy. The men can eat any of the varieties—Jonagolds, Golden Delicious, Galas—no problem. It's the girls who take one bite and slumber. They don't get to savor the whole thing. What if the second taste is sweeter than the first? They'll never know.

Sobbing, the reluctant girl closes her eyes, and fumbles blindly for a branch. She chooses her apple—her fate—and succumbs to the dirt. I collapse cross-legged beside her, and the tears streak down my face like wax from a flame. Though she can't hear me, I tell her I'm sorry.

The apple, plump and rosy, droops from her fingers, and I pry it free and preserve it in my pocket.

When my father comes to claim her, his temporary property, I hide behind green leaves the shape of giant hands, always reaching to the sky. This is the edge of the world, and the dark forest unfurls beyond, calling in a voice sweet and clear as a cathedral bell. With fingers buried in both ears, I do my best not to listen. The forest is known for its tricks. That's what the men from the village say. It devours the living like a blackened sea. It devoured my mother—or maybe my mother let herself be devoured, that honeyed evening the summer before the first girl came to us.

I never asked my father why she left. I didn't have to. Her sobs like endless lullabies sang me to sleep in the cradle, and the constellation of bruises on the soft flesh of her arms told me what he did to her. What all men who spin golden lies are capable of doing.

Before dawn, a prince from the south arrives, wearing a black velvet cape and a string of blood-red garnets around his neck. He kisses the girl hard on the mouth, and I'm sure she'll suffocate beneath his weight, but no, she struggles awake, her gaze fixed on the one who owns her now.

"My bride," he says.

This is what they always call the girls. Not beloved or partner or lover, but *bride*. A word that implies something fleeting and young. How many days must be marked on a calendar for a girl to shift from bride to wife? What is the passage of time that transforms her from gleaming and new like a magpie's treasure into old and frayed, a burden to be borne? There must be a moment in which this happens, a moment that cleaves the world in two. Does she feel the change stirring within her, a pregnant storm ready to unleash its havoc? Or does it happen without her knowledge, and she only sees it one morning in the way her prince no longer looks lovingly at the ripe features of her face?

This girl of fifteen does not smile at the altar or wave goodbye from the golden carriage. She simply stares at her shoes, no longer threadbare, but polished and silken, the footwear of royalty. She should be happy. That's what the village believes. Even her family doesn't see the shadow that falls over her eyes like a valance of wayward curls. They let her depart for a castle—a mirage in the distance—and they celebrate when she's gone.

"Spring weddings are so lovely, don't you think?" her mother says, red-faced and laughing, as she drinks the last goblet of mead from a dust-caked bottle the family kept for just this occasion.

All the villagers are here, the chortling fools, and because the enchantment my father sells like bone china is responsible for the marriage, he's guest of honor. That makes me guest of honor too. Every boy asks me to dance, and every boy stomps off cursing when I shake my head, folding and unfolding my ragged hem. I have special clothes, an old dress of my mother's, I'm supposed to wear on days like these, but I cling close to my gingham apron, and when I walk home after the revelry ends, alone since my father's too drunk to stand, the apple feels a little heavier in my pocket.

* * *

The men who come to the orchard aren't always princes. Some are dukes or counts or barons. The girls and their families rarely know the difference, so long as the groom has a title and a castle and land.

But sometimes he doesn't have any of those things. There's nothing to stop a pauper from waltzing through the door and kissing the first ruby lips he sees. Because who's going to check his credentials? We can't locate whole kingdoms, let alone account for exact wealth.

"It's your orchard," an angry family says to my father after the daughter is married off to an unemployed blacksmith from the village. "You shouldn't have let that roustabout in here."

"No refunds," my father says.

Every morning, I visit the girls, their wilted bodies resting in neat rows. Not all of them are chosen. We now house a decade's worth of would-be princesses. My father has to build a second, then a third barn to accommodate them. Arms crossed over their chests, they doze here, ageless—no laugh lines where they've smiled too long or stitches in their brow where they've frowned too deep. On their faces, there's no roadmap of their lives, because their lives sputtered out too soon.

I say their names as I walk by. It's the only way I can help the world remember. My father doesn't care. He brushes the grime from the curves on their skin and calls it a job well done.

"It's their own fault," he says to me. "They had no faith a prince would appear, so none came for them. Silly girls."

I suddenly wish for a glass coffin, so that I might shatter it and use the jagged shards to open my father's chest and see if he does indeed have anything beating in the cavity where a heart should be. I bet he sports a hollow chasm, and if I screamed into it, my words would echo back to me. That's all he can offer—emptiness. There's certainly no love between us. My devotion, from daughter to father, dried up years ago like the wells in the village that surrender only sand and sorrow. I want to tell him so, tell him how much I hate him, but it's fear that makes me reticent. All I've ever known is fear. Terror of the babbling forest. Dread of what my father would do to me if he could see inside my own heart, how he'd bruise my body like he did my mother's.

I recite the girls' names a little louder to steady myself.

When the day is over and my father retires to the cottage to count and recount his money, I check on the forsaken apples. They live in a splintered crate at the far rim of the property, no more than a yard from the mouth of the forest. It's a good hiding place. Because of his superstitions, my father never ventures that far, always sending me to pull the weeds there.

The crate overflows with rinds and seeds and stems, and while mold should have long ago turned the pieces to dust, the apples are like the girls—decay never touches them.

On the eve of the year's first snowfall, another daughter arrives. Her parents pay with their last silver coins, and my father releases her into the orchard. Stealthy as a mouse, I tag along a few steps behind, but she's not like the others. She searches for no apple. Her eyes looking north, this girl wanders past the trees, past my crate, to the boundary of the here and there.

Faltering for a moment, she glances back at me, and I'm caught under the weight of her stare.

"Are you the one who collects the bodies?"

I fidget in the dirt and shake my head.

"Then why are you here?" she asks.

I have no reason to follow the girls. I can't stop them, can't help them, can't do anything except watch like a strange voyeur as they wither and fall.

"I want to keep them safe," I whisper. "I want them to find true love."

"Love?" The girl tosses her head back and scoffs. "There's none of that here. True love breaks the spell, remember? But look around. The spell is stronger than ever."

She takes a step closer to the forest.

"Please don't." I drift toward her, my arm outstretched, frantic to catch her before she's lost. "You can't be sure what waits in there."

"Sometimes that's better," she says. "It can be freeing."

"It can mean death."

"Maybe." She smiles. "Maybe not."

Like my mother before her, she marches into the trees and does not return. Breathless, I lean against the lowest bough and pray she'll look back again. She never does. Her body dissolves like mist into the darkness.

But she's not gone. I hear giggling just beyond our property line, and her final words stay with me, sinking into my skin like the sweet scent of rose oil.

For the first and only time, the family receives a refund, and I wonder if at last the wind is changing.

* * *

On my twentieth birthday, my father buys me a new dress for my walk in the orchard.

Though the apples have made us the richest family in the province, he's a stingy man, and it's the first gift he's ever given me. While I'm not grateful, not really, it seems rude to disregard the gesture, so I thank him and don the billows of pink chiffon.

"Good luck," he says before retiring to bed. "No doubt your prince will come soon."

My prince. The man who will assume my father's duties once my father is too old to tend the apples himself.

Evening settles softly on the orchard like black tar dripping from the sky, and I take my father's candle to guide me. In the playful shadows, I choose my apple—an Empire, sharp and sweet. I thread it between my fingers, turning it over and over, as though I'll be able to decipher its secrets if only I can see it from the proper angle. Yet there are no secrets here, none worth learning, so I tell myself it's time. My lips move toward the skin. One bite would be enough to sleep deep and cold, like an infant dipped and drowning in black water. My eyes would close, and I could rest.

But it wouldn't last. For once, I believe my father. I'm not the same as the girls left behind. I've seen how the village boys watch me, ravenous wolves sniffing for blood. There is only this orchard, and I am the one to inherit it. I'm already a princess here. And all the boys, licking the sharp points of their glistening teeth, are desperate to become my prince.

The apple sags in my grasp, and doubt, as old as childhood, creeps inside me like a scarab beetle burrowed beneath the flesh. This isn't the only way. This can't be the only way.

The bordering forest calls to me in a voice I recognize, the voice of my mother. My fear melts away, ice in a boiling pot, and the candle as my chaperone, I walk to the edge, a circus performer on a tightrope.

The apple crate lingers still at the border of the forest. With a careful hand, I lower the wick, and the remains of fortunes lost catch in an instant. Though the fire sears my flesh, I clasp the bitten apples and pitch them, one by one, into the treetops of the orchard. These trees are healthy and shouldn't burn, but on this evening, that makes no difference. Every branch is aglow, burning my nose with an acrid scent, the smell of make-believe hope turning to ash.

All around me, my mother's laughing, and the gentle lilt in her voice makes me laugh too, makes me scream out with joy, until my muscles quiver and knees buckle beneath me.

The flames graze the indigo sky, and the light must reach to the heavens, or at least to the village, because I can hear the boys, the greedy ones who were waiting for me to crumble, call out to their families and announce the orchard is burning. I can hear my father too. From the cottage door, he shrieks my name, the only name he remembers, and time slips away from me like grains of sand in an open palm. I must finish now, or I won't finish at all.

This magic is strange. It wasn't wrought by witches, not the kind with cauldrons and capes anyhow. This magic was ours. We longed to escape the colorless land, and the girls bore the weight of that longing. It was easy to shuck it off on them. Girls are always expected to carry an impossible burden in life, like a thousand bushels of apples strapped upon a single back.

In this way, those entombed in straw are my kin. Though not by blood, they are my sisters, and I love them. From the first to the last, I've always loved them. I might be the only one, but one is all it takes to break the spell.

I kiss my fingertips and hold my hand to the sky. The wind carries my love to them, their lips pursed like pale hourglasses. They rouse from heavy dreams, not just the girls here, but those from faraway and forgotten kingdoms too, the princesses and baronesses and countesses who no longer look down in silence and shame. They gaze now to the north, to the unknown, to the trees that cast shadows that aren't so grim anymore.

My mother whispers my name, and smiling, I turn to the waiting forest.

One bite, and the darkness swallows me whole.

All The Colors You Thought Were Kings

Arkady Martine

Moonrise glitters dull on the sides of the ship that'll take you away. She's down by the water, her belly kissing the sand and her skinny landing-legs stuck out like a crab. You and Tamar watched her land, stayed up half the night like babies staring at their first meteor storm, peeking over the railings of Tamar's balcony and marveling at how the falling star-glimmer lit up the lights under your skins like an echo. You two have been full up with starstuff for as long as you've been old enough to go outside the crèche by yourselves. Now you're almost home.

Home for you will be the Imperial battlecruiser *Vault of Heaven*, destroyer-class, star-conqueror and peacekeep. You've had your marching orders for three months, and you've spent every spare minute accessing all the file and 'fiche on her you can scrounge clearance for. You practically live on your records-tablet when you're not out with Tamar, so no one's minded you taking a bit of time to fall in love with your own personal piece of the Fleet. The *Vault of Heaven*'s an old ship, a proud ship, refitted top of the line just a year ago. You're for officer's training and then command, your geneset finally writing you the ticket you've always known it would. Tonight the shuttle takes you and Tamar and every other crèche-spun kid old enough to have passed the entrance exams up to the Empress's very own flagship.

Tomorrow there'll be ceremonies and presentations, and then your nanite horde will be calibrated for shipside on live broadcast for the entire Fleet to see – another cohort of kids full up with starshine micromechanics, bound to service and obedience, gone off into the stars. You've been dreaming about it since you could read. You want it so much you've spent the last three months feeling like your chest is going to burn out from longing.

The night *after* tomorrow, though. You can't let yourself dream about that.

Under the drape of your overjacket, snugged up to your spine like you're its best lovecrush, are the disassembled pieces of a sniper rifle. Nestled right at the small of your back is the lead-shielded explosive heart of an electromagnetic pulse bomb.

The overjacket's the best overjacket you've ever had, orchid brocade in stiff heavy folds that split at the breastbone into six panels, done over in mother-of-pearl and sequins that echo the lightswarm of your nanites. You had it made specially. No way you were going up to space in last year's couture, you said at the tailor's, and you meant it, only you also meant you wanted to look enough the louche crècheling that no one would think to check under your finery. You're Elias Akhal. There's only one geneset in the Empire purer than yours. No one would ever suspect you're anything but the Fleet's man, hungry for your own ship and a starfield as big as any ocean you've ever swum in.

You wish so much it were that simple. You also wish it weren't *true*. You'd like it if you could ever feel all one way about a thing.

When you turn round from staring at the shuttle, there's Petros Titresh and your Tamar, coming down the beach like a picture out of a storyfiche. She's done up in gauzes with gold bangles in her hair, but he's a steel-gray bore: overjacket buttoned to the chin and his skin unlit, sparkless and smooth like stonework. Petros never ate his nanites; the way he tells the story, he stormed out of his crèche in a stubborn fit of ideological purity instead of making himself into starlight. Sometimes, when you and he stay out talking in the city until the dawn alarms sound, you get drunk enough to almost understand why.

Now he walks in careful tandem with Tamar, his hand trapped in hers, her regard pinned to him like a medal he never won nor deserved. Tamar can have anyone she likes, is the problem. She's not just *Akhal* like you – she's real Imperial cloneflesh, sister and twin right down to the cell with the Empress Herself. She hasn't been a mirror for you since you both hit puberty, but the lines of your face and hers are the same: razor cheekbones and full mouths, the nose that every Fleet officer shares. Her eyes never darkened from gray; that was the first clue the crèche-keepers got that they'd spun an imperial clone instead of another Akhal. Today Tamar is bare-armed beautiful in the light coming up reflected off the waves, all muscle through the shoulder from how much she's practiced with spear and neuroparalyzer net.

Tomorrow the Empress Herself kills her, or your Tamar kills *the Empress* and takes the Imperium for a prize. They're not just otherselves like you and every other Akhal, they're cloneflesh, they're the *same*, there's only ever allowed to be one of them. The law guarantees it.

Even barefoot in gauze, your Tamar looks dangerous. You could die of pride if you weren't half planning to die of something else first.

Petros stares at the shuttle like you've been staring at it, goggle-eyed and hungry. "It's not very big," he says.

"That's because this one's just for *this* crèche, direct to the Empress' flagship!" Tamar's all foam-bubble excitement. You glow just hearing her.

"I know," Petros says. "Only the best genesets, sent straight into the maw of the Fleet for our compulsory brainwashing and a celebratory gladiatorial death game! I am going to have so much fun I can hardly begin to describe it."

"No one's going to notice you, Petros, your bit'll be easy," you say, which you mean to be a comforting sort of comrades-in-arms gesture. From Petros's expression it sounds to him more like you were enthusing about the benefits of sticking his head out an airlock.

Tamar ruffles his hair. Petros flinches, and so do you, your heart flopping in your chest like something from the deeps dragged out and drowning in air. Tamar can take anyone up to the Fleet with her on just her say-so. Even if he's outside the law, no starstuff sparks ready to tear his flesh if he betrays the Empire, Petros Titresh gets his berth on the ship. That's the part of your plan that's all Tamar. She says to every horde-riddled adult: *this Titresh is my servant; I want him, he comes with me.*

On your good days, you believe that pile of rotten sharkmeat. This isn't a good day. You'd rather you three were trying to smuggle him in the luggage.

"Two hours left," Tamar says. "Last day on the beach. You boys ready?"

It's your beach, yours and Tamar's. Her balcony in the crèche looks down over it. It's also the safest place for three kids to plan treason. The surf covers ambient sound pickup, and hardly anyone but you two've got the arm-strength to climb down the cliffs to the shore alone. When Petros comes along one of you brings a rope to help him, and he's not a weakling. He's just not an Akhal.

"You got the –" Petros starts to ask, his hand shaping a trigger and a stock in the air, and you interrupt him.

"Of course I do. Yours and mine."

Petros gives you a short nod, stepping into the waves towards the shuttle. He gets the hems of his trousers soaked. "Everyone else I've ever had the misfortune of knowing is either half-drunk on the prospect of basic training and eternal servitude, or hiding out in a skep hoping that not showing up for conscription day won't make their nanites disassemble them," he says contemplatively. "I guess I'm ready."

Tamar splashes him. When he yelps, she says, "You'll be fine."

"I will not," he says. "This is such a brilliant disaster of a plan."

Next to Tamar, blazing like a comet, the moonlight *shrouds* him; he's near invisible, his head bowed and his shoulders hunched up to his ears. He's probably wishing he was down in the city, yelling at kids with visible asymmetries about changing the world. He's a mess. You could hate him for it, but hating Petros makes you tired.

"Only a disaster if it doesn't work," you say, and you make yourself sound coaxing and gentle and like you believe it.

"It's going to work," Tamar says. "If I win that duel – and you're going to make sure I win that duel – I'm legally Empress and I can retroactively pardon the three of us. And then we can get started on making *real* changes! For everybody. We just have to get there. I need you."

You are going to be sick to your stomach. Maybe you can blame it on never having been up in space before. The laser-housing for your rifle is digging a hole next to your ribs, under your gorgeous overjacket. You can't forget it's there and you aren't sure how anyone else is likely to fail to notice how you've got most of a sniper rig in pieces all attached to you. Especially if you get sick all over yourself. *Retroactive pardons.* The fuck are you three doing.

"I know," says Petros. "You can't do it without me. Got to have an invisible kid to carry the bomb. We've got two hours, right? I'm taking a walk." He trudges into the surf, heading east down the shoreline. Tamar watches him go.

You look around the beach that's been a truer home than even your room in the crèche, and think: *I am never going to see this place again.* You don't know if how empty your chest gets is because you want to be gone or because you're saying goodbye. Then your Tamar is finally looking at you and you forget all about yourself.

She smiles like she smiles on the bow of a skiff right before she fires her speargun, high-tension and brighter than midday. She gets her feet wet coming over to you, and then she reaches out and fixes your collar. It's the first time in six days she's touched you, and she doesn't even notice how you go shame-struck still under her fingertips.

"Elias," she says. "We're really doing this. I'm *so* nervous! It's great."

You nod. "We really are," you say. She lets you go and dashes toward the pier and its boathouse.

"I'm going out one last time! You should come with me!" she calls over her shoulder.

The shadow of the pier swallows her whole and you go running after.

* * *

You meet your first shipside adults when the shuttle door gapes open like the belly of a gutted fish. The adults are tall and beautiful and they glitter, their lips and eyes full to bursting with nanite sparks. You can't spot their geneset from just looking; it's not one that gets spun in your crèche. They move like sharks, like they've forgot how to be still. When you line up to board, they take samples of your blood. Fingerprick test: one officer with a clipboard, one officer with a little needle-machine, making sure each kid is what they say they are.

Tamar gets a wide eye and a bit of snide subservience when she comes up imperial on the fingerprick, ushered to a seat right in the shuttlefront with the best view. She is simpered at while she goes. She takes it like the princess she's always been, like she couldn't care less for propriety. She introduces Petros while they check the dull hue of his blood. She introduces you: *and this is Elias Akhal, we were crèchesibs together.* The adults look you over, then, take your measure like they understand all of what you are. You twitch the panels of your overjacket into place and stare them down until they dismiss you as just one more sparkstruck kid caught in Tamar's wake, and don't you wish that didn't sting.

You sit in the seat facing her and Petros, strapped in against acceleration. Your back's to the view so even when you break gravity and the dizzy pressure of atmospheric escape shoves your lungs into your stomach, space stays a mystery. You watch it reflected in Tamar's horde, starlight particles flowing restless in her cheeks, a hectic flush. About then everything goes topsy-turvy and you have to spend some time once again not spewing your guts onto your overjacket and ruining everything. Petros has got no such problems with weightlessness. His mouth gapes open at the view, and you've never seen him look so much like he might cry from seeing something good. Whatever else is wrong with him, refusing the horde and all his bullshit talk about geneset equality, turns out the kid is made for space. If you weren't working on remembering how to breathe, you'd add that to the list of things Petros has taken away from you without ever knowing he took them.

Gravity reestablishes when the shuttle docks, but you don't have time to adjust before the officers unstrap Tamar and take her away. You panic for the first time. The other kids are filing out of the shuttle and onto the flagship and all you do is scramble to your feet and say "Already?" like you are the most ill-starred fool in an awful romanceflick.

Tamar comes over to you all in a rush, gets close enough that you can see how wide her eyes have gotten. "Don't worry yourself, Elias," she says. "I'll see you before sunrise. And you'll - you'll see me sooner, promise you'll watch?"

There is nothing in your life that ever prepared you to say goodbye to Tamar Akhal. You haven't got a single clue as to *how*. "I promise," you say. "I'll be right at the front—"

She leans in close. You think for a minute she's going to kiss you, let you drink up how her mouth tastes exactly the same as yours. Tamar takes you by the shoulders instead, her fingers a bare inch from where the barrel of your rifle pushes against the nape of your neck. You tell yourself you don't care and know you're lying.

She presses her forehead to yours. "And take care of Petros for me." She isn't smiling; your princess is as serious as a cull. The other thing you haven't got a clue about is how not to do what she asks of you.

"Just until you get back," you say. Petros is staring at you like your geneset spelled for three heads.

"Heir," says one of the officers, reproving, and she lets you go all at once, stalks over to them with her head high.

"Let's go," Tamar says, "I want to meet my predecessor already," and then her escort's got her and she's gone.

"Fuck this," says Petros. You agree. Then he does something you do not expect: he grabs your hand and holds on. You wouldn't admit it if he asked, but you're glad.

* * *

You wait an endless fifteen minutes before your escort arrives. He's Akhal like you and not much your senior; looking at him is like looking at five years from now. Turns out your shoulders aren't going to broaden much more but your face'll settle into cheeks that could cut glass. Mid-twenties seems fantastic. You hope you live that long, but you've got your doubts.

Your escort doesn't give his use-name, just hands you a records-tablet stuffed full of paperwork and grins your grin back at you, says *welcome aboard, little brother*. You manage not to stammer when you thank him, even if you're shot right through with nerves. If anyone'll notice your smuggled sniper's kit it'll be your otherself, trained up and true loyal.

You think: You should guess that you're lying, you should guess that you're *committing treason* right in front of you. You keep not guessing. Maybe you're defective, and that's why you're capable of marching down a spaceship corridor behind a person who is supposed to be another part of you, and you can keep a secret from him. It's horrible to think about. You're proud of your geneset. You've always been. You don't want to be so different from your otherselves that you're opaque to them. (You also don't want to be dead. You wish that mattered more to you right now. You're so bad at this.)

Petros is dragged along in your wake, which is a better situation than a lot of the ones you three considered back on the beach. There's no records-tablet and no fleet assignment for a kid who isn't full up with nanites, and your otherself makes a note and promises Petros that he'll have a whole fleet-compatible horde delivered for installation posthaste, considering Tamar's gone and vouched for his usefulness.

Petros *thanks* him. You didn't think he had the capacity to lie through his teeth. You're learning all kinds of things now that you've come to space.

You and Petros are left in your assigned quarters. They're tiny, an eighth the size of your rooms at the crèche, but not half bad otherwise: desk and little couch and a threadbare pretty carpet over the metal floor, single bed nestled under a huge viewport, and there's your first real look at space. Space is a brighter black than night down planetside, a sharper distance studded with starlight that puts your horde to shame. It goes on and on and you are utterly dumbstruck, staring, records-tablet forgotten in your hands.

Over your shoulder, Petros says, "Come on, Elias, it's just stars," but you know better; you saw his face on the shuttle.

"Don't you want them?" you say. You think it must be written into your geneset, the way you're falling into the pinpoint lights.

"You are lovestruck for giant fusion reactors," says Petros, wryly, "and I am twenty minutes from having a horde stuffed down my throat like *oh accidentally missed my appointment* and fucking the plan completely. I like the stars fine. Space is – great. Brilliant."

You turn around. Petros is perched on the corner of the bed. He shrugs, crosses his arms over his ribs.

"They're awfully gorgeous fusion reactors," you say. You're *trying*. You are, you'd swear to it in front of Tamar, even.

"I've been waiting such a long time to see them."

"I swear you Akhal are all space-mad."

"Just because I love what my geneset might spell for me to love –"

"Doesn't mean you don't love it true, and doesn't mean it isn't a problem. Come *on*, Elias, how many times have we had this argument?"

"Enough times that I thought we were done," you say.

"Maybe we were done while it was hypothetical."

You want to turn around and look at the stars; you wish Petros would stop making you doubt your own desires. "I'm not giving up on the plan," you say, "just because I'm happy to be here."

"If you don't do your half, I'm the one who is going to get spaced," Petros says. He gets up and paces a short arc across your quarters, door to desk to bedside and back again. "You're the safest of the three of us if you drop out. Nothing Tamar's doing is even illegal. I set off an electropulse bomb and fry everyone's nanite horde in the middle of the succession duel, and you don't get out your smuggled rifle and snipe the Empress, *I'm* an anti-Fleet seditionist and you're an innocent Akhal bystander. You get to moon over the stars for-fucking-ever-and-ever, just like you're doing right now. You have a future in the Fleet. Your otherself just walked us here. So forgive me if I am suddenly having doubts about your commitment to the *cause*."

"And here I thought we were comrades," you say. You feel as if your spine is liquid fire, spreading into your lungs and your tongue. "I guess I oughtn't expect anyone who refused his nanites to be *capable* of comradeship."

Petros's cheeks go that dull ruddy shade that isn't like anyone else's fury, and he grabs your shoulders as if he's about to shake you. You twist away and he snatches at the collar of your overjacket, so you swing at him. He ducks, yells something completely incomprehensible, and lunges for you. You shove your knee in his stomach, which doesn't help at all, and the two of you go tumbling to the floor in a heap. The trigger-grip of your rifle slams into your left kidney and you make a high-pitched wheezing noise.

You shout at him. "*Stop!* If you hit me I might explode!"

This is true. It is also the funniest thing either of you have apparently ever heard. You find yourself with your forehead pushed into Petros's shoulder, the both of you sharing an ugly bark of a laughing fit. You still feel miserable and furious and you still want nothing of the last ten minutes to have happened to you, but you can't seem to stop the spasms of your gut and your lungs; you are practically gasping by the time you manage to raise your head.

"You're kidding, right?" says Petros.

You get up on your knees and finish the job of shucking your overjacket. Petros exhales hard when he's got a clear view of the pulse rifle, barrel curved to your back and disassembled trigger housing and scope taped low around your hips. You have to shove your shirt up to your collarbones to unstrap the electropulse bomb. The air of your quarters is clammy on your ribs.

"I used to snipe swordfish at four hundred meters, Petros," you say. Your voice is a quaver and an embarrassment.

"This isn't even going to be hard."

"You and Tamar have had your brains replaced with a kid's infofiche history," Petros says, but he's helping you pull off the tape. The backs of his fingers brush your stomach and your nanites flock to the warm traces of touch, glittering afterimages rising on your skin. If he'd been full-up with a horde, he'd light up too. You're selfish enough to wish to see it.

"She gave me this rifle, y'know?" you say to Petros, trying to cover that you're blushing so hard your nanites cast a shadow. "When we were just kids. She bought it off a courier ship down for repairs, that winter I introduced you to her. Spent half her money and all of mine and said she thought I should have it. Started out being too big for me to carry, let alone shoot."

Petros helps you slot the fuel cells into body of the rifle. "I always thought you were kind of an idiot," he says companionably, as if he hadn't tried to punch you five minutes back, as if he wasn't putting together your sniper's rig, "and your politics have got the complexity of a two-year-old who's still dubious about sharing."

"And yet here we are," you say. You hand him the electropulse bomb. He turns it over and over in his hands, his unlit thumb brushing over the pressure pad of the trigger.

"It's a *public succession duel*," he says. "When did you two decide that you'd settle for nothing but the purest high-grade treason?"

Quite suddenly you don't want to explain. You're shy of it; you think he'll laugh at you, and somehow that'd be worse than when he wanted to punch you for being yourself.

"Wasn't Tamar's idea at all, to begin with," you say.

"No? Come on, Elias, you're gagging for Fleet Command, have been since you were knee-high. Can't have been you."

You shrug; you kneel so as to fasten the rifle back under your overjacket, in three parts this time. Four seconds to assemble it the rest of the way. You've practiced, alone in the sand, watching the horizonline instead of your hands, faster and faster.

"When I brought it up," you explain, "she said I didn't owe her that much, that she could take care of herself. I even took her out on the quay and shot seagulls off the rocks so she'd know what kind of aim I've got. But she told me she wanted a fair fight."

Petros laughs, that same bitter barking. "Nothing fair about fighting the Empress in a duel to the death when you've not even gone through basic training yet."

"Maybe I should have said that."

"What did you say?"

You'd shoved the butt of your rifle into the sand and leaned on it, looking out over the sea that'd belonged to you and Tamar both. The wind had blown your hair twining with hers and you remember you'd felt like a photograph. You'd said to her, *I'm not yours, I'm not flesh of your flesh, but like fuck I'm going to watch you die and then bow my knee to your murderer.* She'd looked at you like you were breaking her heart.

What you say to Petros Titresh is: "I told her that I read my histories. There's never been an empress who won the throne *fair.* And then she said I sounded like *you.*"

He slides the bomb into his pocket. He gets to his feet. "I should go before they find me here and dump me full of nanites," he says. "The explosion'll be on my count. Two hundred seconds from the opening of the duel."

You nod.

He sticks out his hand. Gingerly, you take it, and he yanks you to your feet. "Elias," he says. "Don't miss."

* * *

The arena is sand, starlit, a huge jewel set in the belly of the flagship. Every coliseum-style seat is full but yours, rows and rows all the way up to the edges of the shieldglass dome that covers the whole thing. There's at least ten thousand Fleet soldiers here, more sets of faces than you've ever seen in one place. You wonder if anyone's left to drive the starship.

There are tunnels underneath the arena, and somewhere in one is Petros Titresh, alone and invisible and carrying a bomb. No horde in him: You and he left your quarters before any adult could show up with a nanite wafer to dissolve on his tongue. Technically you suppose you're AWOL right now, but if anyone asks, you wanted to see the succession duel, and who *wouldn't.* Petros isn't AWOL so much as he's a ghost. He peeled off from you twenty steps down the hall, and now you suppose you have to trust one another. You suppose also that you *do.*

The starfield above the arena goes on forever. You can't look at it for dizziness, can't think about it else your directions slide all out of phase. Gravity's a spinning fiction and you know it. You wish you could've shot at something less important a couple hundred times to make sure you've got your trajectories calculated right. There's only so much the scope of your rifle will do for you. More than half of sniping is the sniper's eye and the sniper's will.

Those, and hands that don't shake.

The three parts of your rifle are tucked up under your arms with your overjacket back on to hide them. Petros pronounced you *the very picture of someone with better genes than sense* before he left you alone, so you figure you can smile at the other new Akhal innocuous enough. There was a time when you'd've been more than eager to chat them all up, shove and maneuver until you sorted out whose geneset had spun truest. Now you sit as tall and still as you can, playing like none of them are worthy to talk with you. They're crowded into the seats beside yours, a jagged little clutch of mirrors, bright black eyes in your face eight times over. You all glow the same. None of them are dressed as pretty as you.

This is the quietest you've been in your entire life.

When the whole arena goes dark, there is nothing but the flicker of ten thousand nanite hordes, echoing the sudden press of the stars. You are going die of loving them, you think, they are lodging in your chest like your horde was *actually* made of light.

In that glimmering dim, the Empress rises from the center of the sand. She is flame-bright, some of those stars settling like a thousand tiny crowns in her hair. She's got the Akhal face and Tamar's gray eyes and there isn't a spare inch of flesh on her; only sternness, only regal command, effortless in a way that makes you want nothing but to get on your knees. It's all a show, you tell yourself, it's light and smoke and mirrors. In her hands she carries neuroparalyzer net and a spear that doesn't look like a prop of office; its point is a savage glint.

Your Empress lifts the spear to the starlight. The roar of the crowd resonates in your bones.

"Welcome," she says, her voice amplified and enveloping the whole arena. "Newest members of our Imperial Fleet. On the occasion of this night I offer you my personal congratulations. You are the purest, the brightest, the best genesets spun of your cohort. And tonight – tonight, the stars are yours."

Tonight the stars are yours. It isn't that you weren't afraid before. It's that now you're afraid you'll break your own heart when you shoot your gun. You don't much want Petros to be right about you, star-struck, blind and betraying; you want there to be a third option where you get to keep how you feel right now and no one has to die.

Your Empress dips her spear. "In recognition of the achievement of your adulthood, the light that you carry within you will now be joined to the light which burns in me, so that we may all be subject to the same law."

Your mouth dries and you flush hot. You are already burning, your veins humming as each tiny machine hears its new instruction. The law of the nanites is the Fleet's law; if you act against the interests of the Fleet you will be disassembled, devoured for carbon and water and reused in some more appropriate capacity. There is only one free man on this ship now and it isn't you: it is Petros Titresh, down in the dark under the arena with his nanite-disabling bomb.

Then your Tamar walks out onto the sands and even the nanites stop mattering to you. Next to the Empress's glory she isn't small but she is stark, all in black, none of your girl's usual frippery, no gauze and gold wrapped around her narrow waist. She carries spear and net like they're part of her arm. Somehow she is smiling. You hate yourself for thinking even for one minute that you'd *regret* defending her.

"Predecessor!" she shouts. Whatever amplification the Empress is using picks her up too, makes her sound like a struck bell, right at your side where she belongs. "I greet you and I challenge you, predecessor, for command and for the Fleet!"

You imagine, in the dark, Petros starting his count, down from two hundred. You start yours.

"Do you?" says the Empress. She sounds infinitely gentle, kind and a little sad, like she's seen a dozen challenges and, regretting every one, spilled them red onto the sand. "On what grounds do you make claim to our stars, little sister?"

It's a script. A show. One hundred forty-eight.

"I am flesh of your flesh," says Tamar. "Your blood is mine! Your life is mine! Your stars are mine!" Then she squares her shoulders and jerks her chin up. You know that set of her, all stubborn and annoyed. "Also by the right of the law, predecessor, I claim you *incompetent* to rule – you misuse us."

The Empress pauses. You go cold, staring at the shine of her nanites and the brighter shine of her spear, knowing the script is trashed. You keep counting – one hundred thirty, one hundred twenty-nine – all the while wondering if you'll even have time to *take* your shot. Then the Empress laughs. When she laughs she sounds exactly the same as Tamar.

"Child," she says. "So will you." She dips her spear in some kind of salute.

Tamar doesn't wait. She's flying through the air, all of her behind the force of her spearthrust, aimed perfect at the Empress's throat. Your breath freezes in your lungs.

The Empress moves, faster than you can *see*, a blurred glow that snatches Tamar's spear from the air and wrenches her brutally sideways, tosses her like a cracked whip through the air. She lands on the sand – you wait for the sickening thump of splintered bone (eighty-two seconds) – but Tamar rolls, gets to her feet. She still has her net. You're panting. You suck at the air like your body thinks you're breathing vacuum, every cell straining sympathy.

Sixty-five. They circle each other, slow. Tamar's spear is a dark line she's landed too far away from, and she heads counterclockwise toward it. The Empress throws her net, its weighted edges spinning, the filaments crackling with paralyzing electricity. It sends Tamar ducking backward, dancing away from her weapon. Your girl is fast. Faster than you, faster than anyone you know, but the Empress isn't even breathing hard yet. Tamar tosses her head back, bares her perfect teeth –

Thirty. You haven't got time for watching this.

You drop to your knees. You're up front and all the other Akhal kids are all on their feet, screaming with the crowd, ignoring everything but the fight below. Four seconds to snap the rifle together – you lose one in fumbling the stock free of your overjacket, *twenty-three, twenty-two,* the barrel balances perfect on your shoulder. The scope settles over your eye. Your fingers flip each laser cell alight, curl around the trigger easy and gentle.

Tamar feints for her spear, makes a leap toward where it's lying and when the Empress starts forward to bat Tamar away, Tamar changes direction, closes in, just her net in her hands. It is the bravest thing you have ever seen Tamar do, and Tamar is the bravest of all the kids you know.

Fourteen. In the entire universe there is only you, and your target, and Tamar. Tamar's arm, the bunched curve of her spine, how they block where you need your shot to hit. Your fingertip feels raw against the triggerpull, every millimeter of your skin telling you how much pressure, how much tension you need to apply.

The first time you shot this rifle it knocked you over and Tamar had to pull you out of the dune where you'd landed on your ass.

The second time you shot it, braced proper like you'd looked up in your military manuals, you'd blown a hole in the side of a cliff deep enough for a grown man to hide in.

The Empress closes her fist in Tamar's hair and yanks her head back. You think of the veins in her throat, the curve of her collarbones. You think that hit or miss, you can't watch her die and never could. You wonder when your nanites will notice that you're brimful with treason. Is it now, as you sight through the scope? *Two.* Is it now, as you breathe out, as your finger squeezes, *one*, as you wonder if Petros has the count right, *now*, the sound of the gun louder than the crowd –

The back of your hand is a blaze of white; you are lit up like a thousand stars, electrical arcs between your fingertips. You *feel* your muscles lock; you shake, you are empty of everything but desire and you know you'll die of it, know it is the fuel that renders you up for consumption, and in knowing, understand you haven't missed. Tamar is empty-handed on her feet and yet the Empress has no chest. It is all blown clean. Nevertheless the two of them have the same expression: a surprised triumph fading to serenity. The Empress crumples, a slow fall. The white glow of your nanites crawls up the inside of your eyelids. You wait for the oblivion of seizure.

The world goes dark and shudders. You think it is dark only for you, that you are gone, devoured. You lie on your side with your cheek pressed into the barrel of your rifle. You are alone. There are no lights under anyone's skin, not yours and not your otherselves, the whole group of you stunned silent.

You think, marveling: *Petros.* The bomb. Every nanite disabled at once. You are not going to die after all.

To turn your head is agonizing, but when you do, the vaulted starfield roof still gleams. Your stuttering heart keeps beating.

You leave your eyes open. You wait.

Suicide Bots

Bentley A. Reese

The car won't go faster. Why won't it go faster? It needs to go faster.

We're laughing. I grind my foot against the gas pedal. I stand half off my seat and lay into it. I scream at the gas. The gas is no good. The gas needs to go faster. I hear plastic snap and the pedal breaks under my foot—we go a wild two-thirty. We fly across the road. The Mustang's engine punches out of the hood. A steaming, choking monster, it wants us to want it. I wanna ride it. I want to ride the engine screaming and burning into stupid oblivion. I'll rut the world so it remembers I existed. So I remember that I existed.

We're laughing.

I look over at the woman in the passenger seat. Her face is red. Greasy tears streak her cheeks and make her a rubbery craze. She's got the smile of a starved shark. I like it. I love it.

"What's your name?" I ask her.

"Jane," she says. Her face scrunches. "I think."

I reach across the gearshift and we swing between two roaring goliaths with big, bulging wheels. Horns, they horn at us. I horn back. I beat the wheel and spit before shaking Jane's hand. Hello world, we're here! We might be alive! Are you alive too? Let's find out. Tumbler tumbles in the back seat. He laughs. We laugh too. The radio plays a retro remix of "Lies of the Beautiful People."

Jane's hand is small. I notice she's missing two fingers. Her index and pinky look up at me from her lap. I shake my head. Stupid fingers just won't stay on.

"Nice to meet you, Jane. I am Jones," I say. I *am* Jones. That's all I am. Just Jones. Just a name. I've only been me for a day. Before that, I was wire. I lived dead, piled over workbenches and surplus boxes. Now there's fake skin over my wires, and discount dollar eyeballs in my head. Man, those were the days, those days before living. Everything wasn't so fuzzy when I was nameless.

Outside is fuzzy. I roar and cut off a double-decker bus. Jerk hard and we careen through a cackle of rusted cars. Some are just dead on the highway. Some are moving and they hate us. "What are we doing?" Jane asks. She looks over her shoulder, suddenly lost. One of her eyes is green, the other a spark-biting blue. "Where are we going?"

"We're robbing a bank," I say, which is an algebraic answer. Robbing a bank is all we can do, and ever could do. We have guns. There's one in my coat and one on the floor under Jane's feet. I don't know how they got there. I don't know how we got here. My memory is only so good. We are going to rob a bank though. That's firm in my mind. Firm like the grip of the steering wheel. Firm like I can dig it with my nails.
Go to West Jenny Avenue 2268, America's Business & Finance. Take everything. Take all the money. Return to Coordinates 90.3 by 27.12 North of New Chicago. These words, the only meaningful words in my head, burn hot.

Jane wears a wig the color of corrosion. She looks sort of human. Her skin is all junked though. A big seam has opened up along her neck and on each side of the tear she's a different shade of pink. The word *Armitage* is stamped onto her collarbone. She did her makeup terminally wrong. Her eyes twitch in unison, then skitter along separately, each eyelid conflicting grays. She's preposterous. Glorious. Cement-veined and hungry.

"I think I love you," I tell Jane.

Her smiles returns. An afraid smile. "What are we?"

I shrug, gripping the wheel tighter. "We're something."

Tumbler coughs behind me. I steer with one arm and turn around. The road swerves and sways. It doesn't know that it's facing the wrong way.

"What's your name?" I ask Tumbler. I don't know Tumbler's real name. Tumbler has no face. It fell off and now he's lying on it. His head is all wires. Snaky and slithering, they make a skull of charcoal with black, manic eyes. Tumbler laughs.

"What's your name?" I ask again. He says something about spare car parts and apartments for sale in the stratosphere.

"Living street level isn't safe in today's modern age of taking," he proclaims, his voice female and distant.

"What's your name?" Jane says, with her chin perched over her headrest.

Jane keeps asking. Tumbler keeps gibbering.

"What's your name?"

"Back to Freddy the Friendly Robot for the morning forecast."

"What's your name?"

"Homicide on 5th Avenue. Two men and a woman stabbed to death. Automated police have put the perpetrating human to sleep."

"What's your name?"

"A lot of people these days ask me what you can do in this polarized economy, and I always tell them the same thing. Invest. Invest in robots."

I tick. Something in my wires flips over and squirms into place.

"Tumbler is broken," I say. Tumbler gags. He drools black fluid from his mouth and eyes. I nod sagely, refocusing on the road. "Too many screws in his bolts, I bet."

"I bet," Jane agrees. She continues to watch Tumbler, her eyes swollen round.

The traffic starts to choke the road. The world slows us, confines us. We shrink into the cells of a thousand groaning tires. Humans—maybe—appear as the gaping highway devolves into streets and sidewalks. Skyscrapers, some half-made and covered in spidery construction bots, replace the scraggle-necked trees and gray grass of the highway. We enter a universe of moving, speaking things with big pink brains in their skulls, all under the chorus of honks and dancing litter.

We come to a rusty gate resting between two mountains of barbed wire. A checkpoint into the city proper. Two cars stop ahead of us, their exhausts fuming black and their engines panting. There are big robots around the gate. I try to count them. A couple dozen—or more. A few of the robots march down the rows of cars, while the rest make a wall on the sidewalks, trying to keep back the foot traffic. There are humans on the sidewalk. A lot more than a couple dozen. They want inside the city too. Hundreds of them, dirty and angry.

"I don't think the chop shop made Tumbler right," Jane says from her perch over the headrest. She blinks. We look at one another and remember where we were made—*that* we were made. In a sweated-out basement, by a man with a bad complexion and one arm. Well, one arm made from flesh. His other arm was a big, rusty claw strapped to his shoulder. He was so clumsy with that claw.

"I don't think the chop shop made any of us right," I tell Jane.

The car ahead of us is let through.

A metal finger clinks against our glass. There's a robot outside, waiting patiently for me to lower my window.

"Good afternoon, sir or madam," the bot says. "I am Automated Law Enforcement Officer NR17. You may address me as Nagger or by my given serial number." Nagger stands eight feet tall. One of his arms is a belt-fed machine gun. Three eyes wink at me.

"Hello, Nagger." I extend my hand. "I am Jones and this is Jane. We're in love."

Nagger looks at my hand, then looks up. He doesn't have a face, just a slate board of metal with six holographic eyes.

"Please keep your arms and legs inside the vehicle, sir or madam," he says. His voice is nothing but numbers. I check to see if my hand has dirt on it. It doesn't. I slide it back into the car, licking my nose while I squint at this cousin of mine.

"I apologize for the inconvenience, sir or madam, but Checkpoint 16 has been installed to protect the lives of New Chicago's citizens. As by mandate of Mayor Lionel Marks in Subsection Bylaw 003: No bots, industry AIs, automated service pets, or human-based androids are allowed past this checkpoint without an organic attendant bearing the proper certifications.

Any non-organic entity violating this mandate will be dismantled upon discovery."

"Oh my," says Jane. She sits herself properly into her seat. She glances at the automatic pistol lying between her mismatched sneakers.

"Ah." I dip my chin behind my collar. "Good thing we aren't bots then!"

Stink-eyed children, naked and screaming, run through masses of wrinkled, weathered faces. Hoods everywhere. What is a word to describe these people? My memory banks crank and push the adjective to my lips, but then short-circuit and burn the inside of my skull. I burp in surprise, a little electric grunt. Nagger's eyes blink and spiral along his slate mask. What does he see right now, I wonder. I refuse to let my own mind stop me. What are these humans? What are the purposeless? Vagrants! Oh joy. Vagrants. Vagrants, and aren't they mad.

A gray-haired man at the front of the crowd carries a sign reading *Robots Don't Need Burgers.* Nearby, a stout woman swings a *Give Us Back Our Future* sign. When did we take their futures? We don't have your futures. Trust me.

"Do you consent to a five-second scanning process? Unless your body reads as over thirty-percent nonorganic, you will be allowed entry. Consent so I may begin scan." Is someone home in there? Knock-knock.

"What if I don't consent?" I ask my new friend.

"Consent, so I may begin scan," is repeated in response.

Jane grabs my wrist.

"Ask him how many fingers he has," she tells me.

"I'm not asking him that."

"Well, then ask him how many fingers humans have." Jane looks at her hands. She has black and silver nails. I think she might be about to laugh. Is it a laugh when you don't want it to be? "I really hope humans have eight fingers too," she says.

"Consent, so I may begin scan."

A steaming semi-truck blasts its horn behind us. We're taking too long. I scream inside my head. We're stuck. No moving. No moving. What is this? My gun hangs heavy in my coat. I feel it press against the wires where my heart should be. Do I want a heart? I don't think so, not for what I'm about to do. Tumbler starts singing from the backseat.

"Nagger, do you have a best friend?" I ask. Two lights wink. I notice a McDonald's advertisement on Nagger's chest that has partially flaked off. "Do you ever think about what it'd be like to have real, warm skin?"

"Consent, so I may—"

I shoot Nagger in the face. I pull the trigger, my gun still in my coat, and it belches right through the leather, exploding everything. Jane starts shooting Nagger before I get off a second shot. Her face doesn't match the violence. Just stupid and blank. White lights pop and vanish. Nagger moans electric, trying to back away. He's smart enough to moan. Smart enough to run. Oh, why did he have to be smart enough to run? A few bullets bounce off Nagger's armor, he's built for punishment after all, but one of Jane's rounds tears his brickish head right off. Nagger seizes, trying to live one more second, and then falls on his back.

I hit the gas and we ride crazy. Jane starts to laugh because she doesn't know what else to do. Tumbler plays a song out of his mouth, singing about the lies of the beautiful people. The wheels burn the asphalt. We hit the gate as the other automated enforcers behind us open fire. People stampede, flooding the sidewalks, and trampling each other and their makeshift tents built around the gate.

The gate doesn't budge. It's too old and stubborn. I grind my foot on the gas pedal's stub. A bullet zings off the windshield frame and through the glass. Jane shoots over her shoulder at nothing in particular. A bullet rips my ear right off. Do I feel it? Maybe.

Tumbler grunts like an angry coil. I look back. One of his arms has been blown off, either by the enforcers' bullets or by Jane's. Black fluids and wires spill from the wound. Tumbler just keeps singing. Through the window, I see two more automated enforcers approaching. I consider the possibility that we might become dead, or deader than we are now.

With a grudging squeal, the gate bends. An airy space opens up between the hinges. In the rearview mirror I see a vagrant tackle an enforcer. The vagrants are running toward the gate. Some of the enforcers start shooting into the crowd. I keep my attention on the gate. Finally, it gives, flinging open. My neck snaps back as the car launches forward.

I keep us rocket-loaded, whipping down the roads until we find a steady scuttle of traffic. We sink in. The people inside the gate don't seem much better off than those outside. No one follows us. Do they keep people and robots out just so they have a place to say they're kept out of? Our front bumper is caught between the car's axle and the road, and Jane points out that we're sparking up the place, but I don't think it's important. Down here, at the bottom of all these skyscrapers, in the dark, nobody is watching.

Ten minutes later, Jane and I smoke cigarettes across the street from America's Business and Finance. We smoke because there were cigarettes in the car's glove box. Our lungs are plastic bags. We don't feel the nicotine. We enjoy the pretending. The air's cold. At least I like to think it's cold. It *looks* cold.

Tumbler has gone to park the car one block down. He insisted, silently mind you, that he do so. He's not as crazy as he acts. Not really, and I suppose even his craziness still has those words burned deep: *America's Business and Finance. Take Everything. Take all the money.*

Jane finishes her cigarette, looks at the glowing nub pinched between her nails, and proceeds to swallow it. I do the same.

"How do we know anything," she says conversationally. "We're just a day old. How do I know a cup is a cup? Or a turtle lives in a shell? I've never held a cup. I've never seen a turtle." Jane's wig is half-cocked. It obscures her discolored eyes. We almost blend in, if only the suits moving around us would walk closer.

"The man who made us copied and pasted off Wikipedia," I tell her. "He stuck a USB in the back of my head, when I was just... waking up? He had a couple thousand links open on his computer and dragged them into our noggins. I don't think he thought we'd be able to get this far without knowing some stuff about the world."

"Hmm." Jane seems to think this over while she bites her lip. "Probably why I can name the atomic number of uranium, but don't know how to tie my shoes."

I give a noncommittal nod. Tumbler limps to us through the crowd of humans with my coat hiding his missing arm. I smack him on the shoulder in something that might be admiration, but is ambiguous even to me. The three of us are together again. The humans all look at us with sticky, staying eyes. Go away, eyes. We're just like you. We're trying to be just like you.

"Nuh-uh," Jane argues a moment later as we cross the street. Her voice is like running a stencil blade over a chalkboard. Her coat, all fake mink fur and torn in a few places, drags along the concrete behind us. She has only one sleeve. "I have very specific memories. I bet they had some sculptor make my memories. I flew a plane once, straight into a glacier. I made love on a picnic table—and some guy with a machete cut me to death. Everything was so red. So alive."

"Movies," I say. "Our lives are movies."

I remember drowning at the edge of a dock quite vividly.

"Is this any different?" Jane says. She gestures at the skyscrapers rising through the smog. I look down at my hands, snap my left pinky off and put it in my pocket. I feel nothing.

"It isn't," I tell her.

The bank is busy. People fly up the steps on long stalks and twisting limbs. Most wear suits. Three bored human guards loom at the doors. A hovering security bot with the bank's insignias stamped all over its cylindrical body soars over them. *Armitage* has been branded along its metal chest. Lens-like eyes cover what I assume to be the bot's head. We wait for it to steam away down the sidewalk toward the East Entrance.

Something—an emotion maybe—tingles as we march up the steps.

Tumbler walks behind us. "All two thousand residents of the isolated town Nicolet, in northern Wisconsin, were discovered deceased this Thursday. The tragedy appears to have been caused by contaminated drinking water an estimated three months ago, but was only brought to national attention after the town's finance and industry bots began malfunctioning..." Tumbler has his face back on, pulled on like a mask, but slightly off-kilter so only one of his eyes can be seen. He was supposed to look older than us, but the stretch of the rubber makes his face young and sweet. More real.

One of the human guards raises an eyebrow as we approach.

"Hold on there," he says. He steps in front of Jane and me. "You folks look awf—awfully out of place here. Mind if I ask your business?"

"Sure," Jane says. All cheer. She leans in close, squinting at the guard's face. "Mind if I ask you how you got such pretty eyes? I love eyes."

The guard blinks. He does, in fact, have beautiful blue eyes.

"What?"

"My eyes don't match." Jane frowns, pointing at her left eye. "I think that's really bad. I wish I could have eyes like yours, that fit right."

"Jane is right, you're very lucky," I say. I wonder if my eyes match. I don't even know what color my eyes are. I hope they're green. No, gray. I hope they're gray.

"Ma'am, I'm going to have to ask you to step back," the guard says with fright and discomfort dripping off his lips. Jane stands quite a bit taller than him.

"Really though," Jane says. "I love your eyes. I need to take them."

The guard tentatively reaches for his gun. Jane moves faster. She grabs him by the temples. She sucks out his right eyeball with a slurping noise. He makes a big fuss about it with laughing and flailing. I shoot the other two guards, both in the head. It's just a thing. I can't risk doing it any other way. I don't want to take these things, these lives, but what choice do I have?

The suits run just like the vagrants did. Jane sucks out the guard's other eye and smiles, red-toothed. The guard rolls down the steps, his skull skipping along the granite. Jane is all green and red. Christmas colors.

I look down at my pistol. It gleams black in the smog sun. It too, is a thing of parts and metal. Just like me, it's not very good at giving. The doors stand heavy and wide in front of us. Jane and I eye each other. I am Jones. I need to move forward.

We go into the bank running.

I reload and speak at the same time.

"Get out or I start shooting."

Inside, every one stands frozen, looking toward the doors. At my commands, the fifteen or so robots and mechanical servants walk outside, but the humans stay in their poorly assembled lines. I shoot a few in the legs and one in the bowels. They fall and laugh in heavy, rasping breaths.

"Get out, please," Jane says. She waves.

I wave, too.

The humans begin moving toward the door in a rushed panic. A boy stops in front of me, his parents squalling behind him. He has big, wet eyes and a chocolate bar in his fingers.

"Hello, I am Jones." I shake his hand. "Now give me your chocolate bar."

When the bank's empty, we face off with the clerks behind the counter. Two of the clerks are women and one is a very humanoid bot. They look at us from behind electrified bulletproof glass. Alarms sound. Red flashes down the blue-kissed walls. My brain tells me we have five minutes.

"You're wasting your time," one of the humans says over an intercom. She has red hair that looks acidic. "You're the third group of suicide bots to hit us in the last six months. You know we're basically a charity, right? You're robbing a charity. We give money to grounders so they don't smash robots. Once the cops dismantle you, they'll track down your thug creator." She taps the glass, smiling like a monster. "Not getting in here any time soon."

Jane walks up to the counter and grabs a bunch of bank pens, stuffing them into her coat. While I'm pretty sure money is our main goal, our orders said take everything. Tumbler pulls a panel off the wall and tucks it under his arm. He says, "I am the rocker, I am the roller, I am the out-of-controller."

A pair of round, broken glasses lay on the floor. I pick them up and fit them over my nose while Jane tears chair legs off stools lining the window. The glasses do not make the room any prettier. They do not make the blood on the floor any less dark.

"Run while you can," the bot behind the counter says, her expression blank. Jane answers by emptying her gun's clip at the barrier. Bullets bounce and ping everywhere. None go through, but one flies back and blows through Tumbler's leg. We laugh.

I walk up to the barrier and lick the glass, pressing the flat of my tongue against its smoothness. The redhead watches me, her brown eyes wide. She does not have pretty eyes. Those are fearful eyes. I wonder what they see. What's looking back at them?

"I'm going to introduce myself after I come through that glass," I say.

She points at her watch with a sneer. "Cops will be here in three minutes."

"Jane." I turn around. "Grab Tumbler. I have an idea."

Tumbler drops an assortment of bank fliers and staplers. Neither he nor Jane asks questions. They trot over, all giggles. For a second, I reconsider. I watch these two: Tumbler trying to smile, his single visible eye alight with glee, and Jane favoring her right arm, hiding her less-fingered hand in the confines of her coat. They are so... something. Maybe we are worth more than this taking business.

Inside me, the hot words resurge, ripping up to the surface with claws and teeth. They scream, *TAKE EVERYTHING.* They remind me what I am. They say all there is to know. *Take, take, take.* Jones cannot exist without those words. I am Jones.

"Tumbler," I say. I put my hands on his shoulders. He's taller than me. Am I short? "We're going to use your head to break through the glass."

Tumbler grins, stretching his goofed-up face even worse. He is a nightmare.

"In Heaven, all the interesting people are missing," he says with the voice of a 19th-century philosopher. Jane takes Tumbler's arm and I grab the base of his neck. We run toward the glass at full speed. Release. Tumbler crashes into the barrier. Hysterical. The whole wall shudders and little tendrils of lightning shoot about. Tumbler's head fumes black smoke and his synthetic hair goes alight. We help him back to his feet and go at it again. And again. The clerks watch us with gaping mouths. Tumbler waves us back. We let him finish it himself.

Tumbler grips the lightning sparked wires over the glass and smashes his head over and over against the barrier. Electricity crackles through his body. Murderous rain falls as the barrier gives. Tumbler goes down with the barrier, in a heap of mad clanks and clashes. Jane dances to the sounds. She shoots at nothing and, running out of ammo, keeps pulling the trigger. Clink, clink, clink. We are noise.

I step over the counter and Tumbler's twitching body.

"I am Jones. My name rhymes with bones." I extend my hand to the redheaded clerk. She looks at me incredulously, but takes my hand. Her fingers have no grip, but they do not fall off.

The other human clerk, an old, wrinkly woman, starts laughing. She doubles over, crouching under the counter. She gestures for the redhead to join her, to step away from me.

"Please, God, don't hurt us," the wrinkled one says.

I blink.

"My name isn't God," I say. "I am Jones."

"Bring us the money," Jane says. She straightens my coat from behind.

They do. The redhead, the less broken human, trots away from me. She speaks to the bot clerk, and then both of them go down a corridor toward the vault, returning a minute later with two full satchels. I open one up and see something that fits the description of money. Rectangular sheets of paper that worth more than me, worth more than Jane. I hand the satchels to Jane, and return my attention to the clerks.

I torque my head, point at the wrinkly clerk with my pistol. "Why is she laughing? What's so funny?"

The redhead glances from wrinkly to me, and then back again. One long, painted-on eyebrow rises high on her forehead. "She isn't laughing," she says slowly. "She's crying."

I keep my pistol trained on the wrinkly woman. She continues to gargle. There aren't any bullets in my gun, but she doesn't know that. She doesn't know anything. What makes her not a ticker and a tocker? How are her codes different than mine? Everyone in the world is just a ball of reactions, dead things putting on airs.

Grimacing, I shake my head. "I don't understand the difference."

We leave the bank in a hurry, with Tumbler supported between Jane and me. Satchels full of money swing at our sides and I hold my empty gun with my teeth. The street waits for us, a dead gap before a tsunami storm. We have twenty-two seconds before the first responders arrive.

We reach the Mustang in a hot mess. Our good old Mustang. The vintage, beaten thing was made in 2032, so it's probably older than the man who made us. We throw Tumbler into the back seat with the bags. We drive, slinging around street corners. Fender benders. Horns. The smell of rubber burns our noses as we back up.

I take us out the same way we came in. The gate is still down. But, the vagrants slow us. All those dirties have been flooding in ever since we broke the gate. The vagrants climb over parked cars and stab the suits. Claw out their eyes. They ignore the sirens and alerts from the automated towers. I run over a few suits and a few vagrants, hop-skipping them under our car as we go. The automated enforcers have stopped doing their job. About five or six have stepped away from the main street. They stand in a circle around something. I realize, as we get back onto the highway, that they were standing around Nagger's corpse.

As we drive, the burning words quiet. All we have left is the giving. Handing the money over to our creator. The thing is, I don't know my creator. How much can you owe someone you don't know? I know Jane. I know Tumbler. I only know them.

"What happens tomorrow?" Jane asks as I drive. I suck in my lips. I don't think there is a tomorrow. We aren't long-term projects, just hazardous grenades thrown into an industrial fire.

Our maker did not make us for our own sake.

We have no way to judge the coordinates. My brain, the clunky thing, leads the way. It takes us far from the city, the highway, and the rusted cars. We go onto unpaved roads, through black trees, empty suburbs, and dark skies.

Something in my mind is hungry. I feel it noshing on my wires. It's a worm, no, a wire: a wormwire. The burning words fade, but as they do, I lose an important part of myself. The words were my skeleton. I need them to keep me solid. Without them, soon I'll just be a slaughter of parts. I am not a freedom machine. My inner me, my brain, is eating itself. Is that why the clerk called us suicide bots? Am I killing myself by fulfilling my creator's wishes? When the burning words go out, will there be a Jones left?

My foot slumps heavy on the gas. We pick up speed and break one-eighty. The gravel kicks, we fling up-down in our seats. Tumbler rambles as we go. "We're here at the Supreme Court's preliminary hearing of Old York vs. Armitage & ARMA Affiliates, where Armitage's alleged leakage of defective bots to private contractors will be addressed. By the end of the day, Tom, we will finally have the answer as to whether bots can be legally viewed as pers—"

I swing us tight around a curve. The bumper clips a tree and we almost spin out, but I crank us even and keep us going.

"Where are we?" Jane asks, her voice afraid.

I look over at her. Her mouth is covered in red.

"What's my name?" I ask her.

Jane blinks. "I forgot."

Nothing but shells. I give Jane my hand. She takes it. We stay that way. The Mustang plummets down the road. We are at terminal velocity, heading for an uncertain place.

The coordinates take us into a town half-eaten by the trees. I slow, dragging the Mustang's wheels to a crawl. Close now. Nighttime. The exact coordinates lie in the ruins of a baseball field. The floodlights have fallen, hidden in a forest of grass. The chain-link fences have been run over and trampled. An empty stadium watches us stop outside left field, where lines of gravel still fight the weeds.

I spot a car under the bleachers. An electric lamp balances on its hood. Men stand around the car. I tap my fingers against the steering wheel, trying to think of something.

One of the figures in the lamplight waves us over.

"Is this it," Jane says, her voice hopeful. "Are we finished?"

My head is empty. I search for the solidness of the words—*Return to coordinates*—I scramble for them in the chaos of my wires—*Go to America's Business*—I need their warmth, but they slip from me—*Take all the*—I need something to hold on to, something to tell my existence that it needs *more*. More time. More air. More me. I don't want to shut off. I don't want to be finished.

I have to make my own burning words.

I grip the wheel tighter, the leather tearing under my fingers. My wires snap and fry inside my head. The burning words are finally silent. Utterly extinguished. But inside my head, I am not alone.

I smile so wide my skin splits apart and my teeth breathe the air.

I stand half off my seat and lay into the gas pedal. The Mustang screams to life, kicking black smoke from its hood and sparking hot along the grass. Jane squeaks as she's flung back against her seat. Tumbler tumbles to the floor.

We careen across the field.

The men in the lamplight start moving all frantic. I can't hear them, because I'm laughing. Jane's laughing too. We're all laughing. Little pops of light erupt from the figures. Our windshield explodes. They're shooting at us, I think.

We hit one of the men. We stick him on the bumper and carry him into the other car. Everything goes red as the

Mustang's engine explodes and the man's guts open up. The back of our car comes up fast and—

I blink. I'm staring at a black canvas filled with flakes of gold.

I'm sitting in the bleachers, the Mustang's steering wheel still clutched in my hands. I turn it left and right. The crash threw me up here. I flew straight out of the windshield. A big spike of metal rides out my chest. Someone laughs down in the wreckage of the two cars. I listen for a while, until the laughing begins to quiet and take on a desperate tinge.

Limping onto the grass, my boots aren't on my feet. I'm missing a foot too, but I miss my boots more. The laughing comes from a man sitting in the passenger seat of the minivan we crashed into. Most of it is smashed now, backed into the side of the stadium with its engine shoved into its driver's seat—and its driver.

I walk up to the man in the passenger seat. He has blood all over him from a wound in his forehead. He's trapped, but one of his arms hangs free from the tangle of metal. He tries to pull himself out. I watch, turning my head to one side. His arm is metal and rusted. I recognize the bloody face. This man, I think, is the one who made me. My father. I touch the gash in his head with one finger. It's quite red. His skin, though, is unharmed. His face looks clean, compared to the rest of him. I love his skin. It looks so warm.

"Hello," I say, because that is what you say. "I am..."

"Please, please help—" My father cuts off, wincing in pain as something metal pushes deeper into him. I watch him laugh harder. Gush red. I wonder what comes out of me. I look down at my chest. Down at the spike running through where my heart should be. Black liquid dribbles out.

I don't give red.

My father looks up at me. He has gray eyes, very afraid. Very humorless. He says something again, but like a whisper. I think he's trying to speak. Trying to ask me to give. Give anything.

Jane crawls around the car, her hands covered in blood. She holds a pile of fingers, with rings still on them. We smile at each other. Her legs are crushed. Her back flattened. We'll have to take her some new legs.

"My name is Jones," I say to my father. I reach out, caressing his cheek. "And I really like your face."

Define Symbiont

Rich Larson

They are running the perimeter again, slipping in and out of cover, sun and shadow. Pilar knows the route by rote: crouch here, dash there, slow then quick. While they run, she ticks up and down the list of emergency overrides, because it has become a ritual to her over the course of the long nightmare, a rosary under her chafed-skinless fingertips. She speaks to her exo, curses at it, begs it to stop. The exo never responds. Maybe it is sulking, like Rocio in one of her moods.

* * *

They are not running the perimeter. Pilar has stopped eating, and her exo is focusing all its attention on the problem, leaving them hunched like a rusting gargoyle on the deserted tiles of Plaza Nueva. The sudden stillness makes her think that maybe it's all over. Then an emergency feeding tube is forced down her throat, scraping raw, and the exo pumps food replacement down her gullet like she's a baby bird. Rocio would have never done that. Never.

* * *

They are running the perimeter again, and Pilar's nose is bleeding. The hot trickle tastes like copper on her desiccated tongue. She savors it, because not long ago the exo experimented with feeding her recycled vomit. The dregs have itched in her mouth for days. As they round the corner of a blasted car, she hears a whisper in her ear. For a moment she fools herself into thinking it's Rocio—she thinks about Rocio as often as she can. The dip of her collarbone under her fingertips, the laugh from the side of her mouth, the peppermint smell of the wax she used to streak on her hair.

It's not Rocio. It is the exo, at last. It rumbles in her ear: *Define: symbiont.*

"A symbiont is fuck you, fuck you, fuck you," Pilar rasps, tongue clumsy with disuse.

The exo does not respond. Maybe she should have said something else.

* * *

They might be running the perimeter again. Pilar is not sure of anything. Her head is a spiral of heat and static, her skin thrumming ice. The exo is dumping combat chemicals and painkillers into her intravenous feed. She prays to gods and saints and devils for an overdose, but the exo knows its chemistry too well. She can only drift there cocooned, sweating and shivering, and wait for—

* * *

They are running the perimeter again, but Pilar has buried herself in memories, barely tasting the stale air of the exo, barely feeling the tug and pull.

She's buried herself in remembering the first time she was in Granada, in the taut piano-wire days before the Caliphate made landfall. On leave with Rocio, darting from bar to tapas bar in the icy rain, insulating themselves against the storm present and storm coming with cañas of foamy beer. In a bar called Shambalah, decorated with black-and-white pornography stills, she completed Rocio's facial tat with her fingers and kissed her chapped mouth.

They were both out of uniform, and the rowdy pack of students only saw Rocio's damp hijab, not the endo-exo handshake implant peeking out from underneath. One of them was drunk enough to hurl a Heineken bottle at them. Rocio had to wrestle Pilar's arm down to keep her from using the smashed razor edge of it on the boy's fingers.

They retreated back into the rain, where animated graffiti shambled along the walls of alleyways, slowly dissolving. Rocio rubbed her face and said everything was about to come apart, and Pilar replied, *not us, never us, we need each other too much.* But Rocio only smiled her saddest smile.

Later, in the cramped room of their pension, with the key in the heater but the lights dimmed, they made love that caused Pilar to forget about the eager, clumsy boys from her hometown and about everything else, too. In the dark, their endo-exo implants glowed soft blue. She ran her fingers around Rocio's, tracing where smooth carbon met skin.

They say a little of us gets stuck in there, Rocio said. *When we plug in. Pull out. Plug in again. Memory fragments, whole ones even. Enough for a little ghost.*

I don't believe it, Pilar said.

Rocio drifted to sleep quickly but Pilar stayed awake a long time after, still breathing in her scent, still holding her lean waist and thinking she would never let go, not ever.

Inside the exo, she tries to feel Rocio's skin on her skin.

* * *

They are running the perimeter again. The exo jerks Pilar mercilessly from cover to cover. She keeps her eyes closed and pretends she is boneless. Trying to fight the motion last week shredded her shoulder muscle, and the exo is out of painkillers because it used them on her in one long, numbing drug binge that makes her wonder, sometimes, if her brain has been permanently damaged.

Exo endo is symbiont. Exo need endo need endo.

She startles. The exo hasn't spoken since it asked its first question.

Love is symbiont. Exo need endo need exo.

"You don't need me," Pilar pleads. "You don't need me. I don't need you."

* * *

They are not running the perimeter. They are trudging up the stony spine of the Sacromonte, where her squad cleaned out the radical-held caves with gas and gunfire. Where she'd managed to take shelter when they SAT-bombed Granada in a final act of defiance, obliterating the half-evacuated city and turning the Alhambra to rubble.

Now the Andalusian winter sun glints off shrapnel and the husk of Rocio's exo where it fell just meters from safety. Pilar recognizes the scorched smiley-face decal, the twisted arrangement of limbs. The implant at the base of her skull tingles.

She knows why the exo's AI is warped, corrupted past repair. The exo must know it, too.

All those weeks ago, after she crept from the collapsed cave, she couldn't leave without seeing Rocio's corpse entombed in its exo, and she couldn't leave without some part of Rocio to hold on to. So she'd taken Rocio's implant, cut it carefully out of her brain stem, stomach churning with each squelch of coagulated blood and gray matter. She'd plugged it into her exo's onboard, hoping for some small echo of Rocio in code, some small ghost.

Then she'd gone to check for survivors, to run the perimeter one final time.

"You're not her," Pilar says. "You don't understand. This is all error. All error."

But there are other memories, ones she doesn't spend time in. Small explosions and long sullen silences after she saw Rocio laughing her sideways laugh with someone else. A screaming match that ended with Pilar going outside the barracks and slamming her hands into the quickcrete wall hard enough to shatter a knuckle. Putting a mole in her tablet to see who else she was speaking to.

The morning of the final push up the mountain, when they were sliding into their exos, gearing up, and Rocio told her she was putting in a transfer request and Pilar said *don't you do this to me, please don't fucking do this to me.*

She knows what she has to tell the exo. She has to make it understand that what it saw in Rocio's implant was not a symbiont. Not love. That she should have let Rocio go a long time ago.

But all the words die in her throat, and now the exo is turning back down the mountain.

* * *

They are running the perimeter again, while Pilar dreams of Rocio's skin on her skin.

An Atlas in Sgraffito Style

A.J. Fitzwater

It's the third month after the cities collide when the women dance out of the walls.

They are the worthy women, the terrible, bright, ugly, and genius. Terrifying puppet vandals.

Taking time to appreciate the black-and-gray stencils that scream Bristol or the hyper colors that ooze Valparaiso would require playing tag with the street chasing me down. So, see Béla run. See Béla search desperately for a ninety-degree turn. But the Bricks are hard at war with anything resembling a gap, and there are no intersections.

Can't keep this up much longer. Biceps and thighs burn. Taste of ozone, dust, ash, burned flesh, spray-paint everywhere. Run Béla, run.

Haven't done anything to deserve dying, other than Be Here when the walls came down. But to live? I haven't done anything worthy of that either. Not even seen The Edge. And nobody comes back from that. Nobody.

"Well, that's new." A voice startles me, coming from above and ahead.

Dodging a few pebbles that are crowding my heels, I glimpse a dark figure, a halo of black hair against a smoke-drenched sky. They have seconds to make a decision. If you've survived the cities this long, you've had plenty of practice at that.

"Take my hand. There's an empty street back here." The figure leaps onto the chattering teeth of a broken wall and leans out far in one sensual motion.

The dancing women keep pace, all spider-length legs and wide swooping arms, oozing scabettes of paint from elbow and knee. Despite their geographical differences, they all dance in time, a complicated hideous beat that threatens to break the foundations of the cities already retching with cannibalized capital punishment.

Stairs are untrustworthy, always the first to make their escape. I tic-tac wall to ledge, cat up to a window frame, and a callused, paint-sticky hand has me.

We roll in a jangle of nerves, elbows, and knees across the rooftop, slipping on tiles the hungry street is already sucking into its maw, and tumble into the front yard of something that was once very green and Laos.

Lie still, Béla. Test the ground with scorched fingertips; the tremors of wanderlust streets are constant, but this one is anchored for the moment.

The figure beside me groans and rolls out of a clinking backpack. "I swear the cities are getting smaller by the day." With the langour only survival can afford, I hear the musky depths of her voice that hint at the corners it makes home.

"I thought New York City was the city with a story on every corner," I say. Breathe deeply, Béla. One moment at a time. That's how you survive The Last City Left in This World.

She grimaces at the long tear in a t-shirt held together by layers of dried paint. She is a she, if the functional bra is anything to go by. "This isn't NYC. Or any other city. It's all of them, fighting for what little space is left."

She pulls a ratty canvas jacket out of her backpack, wraps it around her torso.

Heave and gulp, ease up onto a stinging elbow, point at the angular artistry soaked into the canvas of her backpack. "I've seen that particular tag around," I say. "Some high up too. That's pretty stupid. A street could make a runner at any moment."

The woman crouches just far enough away, assessing me, the house, the sky. Nah, the stars are never coming back.

"Hmh." She jerks an upnod, her afro puff shivering. "Name's Affra. You?"

"Béla. Thanks for the save there."

Her chin jerks again. "You a Brick?"

Snort. "No."

"Sure? Those women weren't trying to run a Brick down for sealing a sister in?" Like a pistol from a hip holster, a spray-paint cannon appears in her hand, shaking its monstrous tell.

"You ever see me on a mortar raid?" I provoke.

"Don't tend to pay attention to those things." Affra's interest is diverted as she assesses the front of the Laotian house for vitality.

Quite suddenly, I am bereft. Conversation, let alone help, is an unusual kindness in a city where every moment is a play upon your life. That is, unless, you have the community of the Bricks to keep you whole. But theirs is a persistence that never quite reached me.

"How long you been here?" I ask.

"Since the beginning."

Since The End, she means.

"Me too," I say. "Three months. Been a good run."

Affra snorts at the bad joke. The cannon hisses a snake-slither of paint, and an angular woman shapes herself on the wall.

No stencils here to quicken the job, though the Bricks have replaced the police as the authorities to dodge. They deem the graffiti women jutting from every wall "dirty and inferior" to their architectural godlets, and the clank-grind of their repurposed stone and mortar replaces car alarms, horns, and sirens as the warnings of the street.

"Pretty futile obsession with them Bricks, huh?" I say. "Wall up there one day, gone the next."

"You could say the same of the graffiti."

Smoke rises in my gullet as I read the lines of paint. So quick, simple, smooth, a thousand words in a few short strokes. Affra steps back to admire her work, and just as well she does. With a graunching tear, the graffiti woman leaps off the wall, rotates her pointed hips, mashes her arrow feet, one two one-two-one, then dashes in the direction I last saw the stomp of women heading. I only just roll out of the way in time to avoid her dust-whip.

Affra twirls her cannon, click-clack click. "I'd like to say I'm surprised, but nothing surprises me in these cities anymore."

She reaches down a hand to help me up, a peace offering, and we sacrifice a few moments to stare after the retreating graffiti. How odd she is, running helter-skelter, two-dimensional, bearing the pits and thrust of the wall that birthed her.

"What do you think they want?" A terrible, childish question, but despite my having a good few inches on Affra, I feel like I'm looking up into her round face.

"What I suspect we all want." She holsters the aerosol in a pocket of her cargo pants without looking. "To see this all through to the end, whatever that end may be."

"To die well," I add to the prayer, not wanting to believe it.

Affra salutes with a water bottle. "To dying well."

She sips, offers, and I partake. The ubiquitous dust gets into everything. Swish, snort, spit, swallow.

"I bet I know why you were in that street when the tar was a dead giveaway," Affra says. "You were *looking* for some of those women, weren't'cha?"

Heat, rising up my neck.

"Here. If you wanna do that, take this. It's dangerous out there."

A half-empty cannon replaces the water bottle. Can't be a full one, no; she has to be the one to blood them.

"Show me what you can do," Affra says.

Smooth off the grit from a wall. Can't use the canvas Affra already claimed, that viscera has been drained. A line wobbles out from my hand.

It does not dance. It doesn't even twitch.

Affra grimaces, shrugs. "Well, it's a start, I suppose."

"I'm an art lover, not an artist," I try to explain.

An exquisitely arched eyebrow cuts me to the quick, no greater wound have I suffered since the cities began their end.

"No wonder you don't know my name," she snorts.

Should I? Damn, I should.

"Hey, you wanna see something really cool?"

Just like that, Affra turns away, trigger finger twitching at her hip as if her hand can't stand to be empty. With the flick of her head, she sets a rough pace. My muscles murmur disagreement after today's rabid exercise in procrastination.

"Where we going?"

Affra points in the opposite direction the graffiti women took, the direction in which darkness is more real.

"The Edge."

* * *

Lord, this Béla chick tho. What is it she do? She all event horizon, sucking them walls in, they watching her, I feel it in my fingertips. That terrible grating sound be following her everywhere, that sound we don't want to be remembering the sky is falling the sky is falling so we cover it with paint song so true.

Everyone need find what they do here in the cities to keep going. Even them Bricks know what they do.

But for what. For what. To see the end? To be the end? Damn, if I be the last, Imma gonna paint it. Them women deserve deliverance.

Affra I says, Affra that chick ain't nothing but trouble being hunted down by that red brick monstrosity of four-bedroom two-bath, but it ain't on me to see someone get eaten by that shitstorm.

But why this all about her? I'm the damn artist here. She nothing but white paper, all suggestion and promise but no followthrough. Her face it don't change. She so real it unreal. One crease, she screwed. She strange tho. Not losing her rag like everyone else round these places (Lord, would you look at that red up in that sky, I gotta get me some of that) getting eaten by the streets. She calm strange. Like she expecting death at any moment, welcoming it, and it keep passing her by.

Now I be part of that. That's what you get when you be helping people, Affra my girl.

So we walking, lots, coz this cities have only an end when they decide, hmh. But when I promise The Edge, I deliver. Ain't seen it myself, but I felt it close by, smooth like fresh paint. And just when I about find it, bam, here come another city. Riding through casual-like, screwing up them nice lines I just been memorizing, messing up my pretty women who been holding up them walls and I gotta start all over again.

Me, I navigate by color and line. That woman over there, all gold and green of Mexico City, she mine. And that one holding on three stories up, all points and blue of Rio, she too. Tags and bombs curling from their fingers, their faces are pieces, heaven written behind their eyes. They entirely done with them bricks. Don't blame them. Bricks ain't no good place for a good woman. Go dance, chicas. Go find the beat that shakes this place to pieces.

You look at this Béla chick, go on, look at her sideways. Yeah, that's the best angle you gonna get of her. She all stiff in two dimension, all dots and dashes, black white black, an S.O.S. She gazing like she never seen all these chewed-up and spit-out cities before.

She listening to me good tho, but it like she hearing me in a different language, seeing only in certain shades. She looking, but she ain't seeing through that sick sodium lure of the streetlights left to burn themselves out, ain't seeing the silver of the sewer-lid sun.

She talking like everyone dead gone, 'cept them Bricks. She ain't even thinking of us styling as survivalists, them who hole up in hope. But if you be painting your home, you gotta know the people who live in it.

Now Béla, you be looking out for art supply shops, paint stores, hardware, that sorta thing, before they decide they had enough of this place. Can only take what we can carry, tho. Caches no use here.

Hey watch it, there go some women again. Leaving all sorts of red-blue-pink-green paint chips in their wake, they calling cards. Yeah, some of them mine, most not. I get around but I ain't everywhere.

Where they go? Where they wanna go.

Do I wanna see them dance? Hell yeah. But it ain't reached critical mass tho. These women only just getting started. You ain't seen the best of them Cairo women in they scarves and heels, or them Bogota women with the feathers from them eyes and jewelled faces. And you gotta see Buenos Aires; them women, they really know how to dance.

Stay with me. The anchor is paint holding these four walls together. Careful with that crimson tho; keep your cannon angled straight and low. That's it. And when it's done we bury it, a'ight? Any dead spray cans you see left in the gutter ain't mine; they be rattlesnakes corralled into a dead end by a dead wind. One bite, and this cities will pull you below gritty waves.

* * *

Inevitability starts the war between the Bricks and the Paint. We hear the first salvo from miles away underneath the gnashed grit silence and overtop the black-white tinnitus that's a constant companion since the cities shoved themselves into a single 234.65 square miles of calving flesh. Yes, a very particular number. Affra says that despite the overwriting of our recent histories, the cities hold a distinctive mocking grid pattern reminiscent of something very Indo-Australian Plate.

A puff of dust above a newly inflated skyline has us scampering up a conjecture of dead billboards, reminiscent of Times Square or Tokyo. Possibly both. Not entirely the smartest move, since anything has the ability to turn to liquefaction without warning. It's only been weeks of hours since we embarked on our traverse to The Edge, but clinging to Affra's grimy jacket sleeve comes too easily.

We squint into the pout of the interminable sunset. Paint blooms in small mushroom clouds against the sky, but we can't make out details.

"Those women don't have time for walls now." Another shift in tone, language. Hard to keep up with her.

And we're down to ground zero again. A prestidigitated cannon hisses to warn off a nearby wall: We Waz Hair. The wall shrinks back into its lair, and we move on.

Affra finds a corner easy, sensing the Venetian canals even before they come sloshing past, reluctant gondola children bobbing in their wake. The mist of their passing surprises runnels into the ever present dust on our skin. Affra makes a squiggle of paint here and there; almost as if rising a map full unfathomable legend from the grit, layered over and over again with each new running of the streets.

Another boom of wall kissing ground. The graffiti women have won the first round, and the skitter-scatter of their feet rush farther on as they dance around the dark.

The mouth of a supermarket gapes wide, and we grab and stuff, moaning in eagerness at the first chocolate in months.

With enough warning—grumbling aftershocks of discontent and the bleat of a call to arms—we dive behind an architectural wonder of cans just in time to avoid a battalion of Bricks bursting out of a pub. Red and orange weapons are cocked and ready, and the barrow-girls and trowel-boys bring up the rear. They wear their dust and daub as badges of honour. The walls have brought people together. Some too close; extra arms, legs, and faces make a farce out of flesh. They work well together.

We chew our plunder in the shade of baked-bean cans before picking a high road. The Edge is out there, somewhere, an unctuous pressure of fingers squeezing ever tighter.

Affra performs a quick, precise shootout with a smooth wall. This woman, possessed of thick hips and small neck, claims the tree atop the wall, bare branches shivering into hair. Quite the sight, watching her bob between buildings.

"Why are you here?" Affra's question settles like the weight of a thousand hands across mouth and nose.

"Why are any of us here? Fate. Wrong place, wrong time. Bad luck. Pick one."

Turn away from Affra's easy hand; it's not fair. The women are all gorgeous. Affra has no one style, no one hand. She could be any artist, from any city.

"No no." Slap of braids—the afro puff has melted into something more Nordic—slap of cannon back into the pack, slap of canvas shoe in sand. "Everyone here in the cities has a job. Them Bricks search for some semblance of normality, no matter how ridiculous. Paints hold the walls together. Graffiti women mark border. Scavengers...well, them just hold out for a good show at The End."

We're in something that could be Melbourne; the single-story ochre brick houses are quite lovely as they shed their last memory of sunshine.

Affra continues: "Them know what's coming. They just the audience. But you—" She puts a sharp elbow to soft ribs. "—ain't any of those things."

Didn't know this, but did. What kept one person alive over another?

"Art aficionado, gallery buyer, appreciator, whatever you say you are." This Affra has become more brisk, tongue far less subtle than her trigger finger. "But how is that useful when the world is coming to an end?"

"Why does anyone have to be *useful*?" I plead.

"The cities find a use for everyone."

A darkness filters round the edge of buildings, street corners: tentacles, fingers, breath of frigid luminosity. It is The Edge.

I'm desperate to understand, but also desperate not to look foolish. She is a goddess in khaki canvas.

Affra turns away. Not because anger is uncomfortable—exhaustion makes it barely present—but because a beautiful wall has made itself known. Concrete slides gently into place, a click of puzzle pieces, a bare shrug of London-ish glass and steel. Malnourished eyes busy themselves out of the windows. When they see us, they retreat.

Even they can't stand to watch the change. It's the grind of bones. The slap of paint on skin. Maceration of flesh into flesh.

Affra.
She becomes.
No.

* * *

This wall, so pristine, so flat. 'Most a shame to take that away. Attack, attack again the wall with paint. Distracts me from fractals of pain under my skin coming quicker. Can't hide it from Béla any longer. Surely she must know, must've seen. Cut a glance; no. My change is writ large on her face, though she won't admit it.

The weight of the lowering sky makes it hard to breathe, squeezes the meat of my brain. We all feel it; the cities wearing themselves inside out.

Even weightier? Béla doesn't understand. Not yet. Disappoint. Expected better of her.

But poor mite. That's gotta suck. What do the cities want with her? I'll save her the face.

Oh hey look, my skin is brown again, my hair long, dark, and thick. Tu meke.

So I explain:

"Reduce, reuse, recycle. The cities eat us all, whole. We are its light. We nurture it, fall into its gravity well. Who knows if we come out the other side, or what we are there. Maybe an endless teeter back and forth between event horizons.

First it was just a few, here and there, proper blood sacrifices that kept it satiated. But The Edge is getting closer, and people are getting chewed up, caught in the cross fire as the streets come faster and faster."

Careful. Don't let the speech edge into the hysteria of a street sermon. Affra is not afraid, no. Frustrated, yes: by time, by ambition, by the limitations of limbs, the waning dexterity of hands. The Edge comes for us all.

But not Béla.

Painting fast now, the graffiti women more suggestion than solution the deeper into the tumbled streets we go.

Aue. Have to give Béla hope, if I'm to find absolution before a wall gets me.

"But—" The lizard-hiss of my cannon pauses. Béla holds up a hand; saintly benediction or defense, can't tell. "The cities do give us a choice."

Well into this line work. Working in simple black, but it's the smoothest, roundest, squarest, sharpest, flattest, most womanly thing to come from all of my hands to date.

Béla demands: "And that is?"

A hot pink-and-green neon stutter from a sign aching at rest on a corner, like a muscle tic in the corner of the eye. Quite Amsterdam. A graffiti woman with wide eyes, tangled hair, and headphones peers around the corner and dashes past, syncopated to the noise in her head.

"What do we become at the end, and how well do we want to go?"

"That's it?" Try not to choke on the bitter pill of laughter, Béla love. "The meaning of *life*? That's *ridiculous*. That's not what this is about at all. It's about walls, and graffiti women, and potholes and..."

"And what? The universe doesn't ask you if it's okay to pack up and leave." So simple, so hard to believe. Close the eyes against the yellow-brown sky. Imagine. Is there even space for imagination amongst these fragile bones?

Haki rā! A tendril of black coils across the ground, a bastardization of oil and smoke and water. It's stroking our sneakers, licking languidly around our ankles.

Another far off crash of wall and shriek of metal.

"Look! There they are, comrades!" A child's voice, full of righteous glee. "Told you there were Paints sneaking around behind us!"

Silence in the roar.

No more running. The Edge has found us.

And it's all very civilized, non?

She even listening? That face. How she even keep that face when everything a-change.

Mon Dieu, here I go again.

Them Bricks, think they're herding us towards the battleground, but who is doing the guiding? Twitch of les ponts de Lyon here, swing the trees of Valiasr round there, et voila. The perfect kettling effect.

Ahh, Affra can see it now. But we don't see, non, the cities let us feel around any which way, fingers, tongue, smell. C'est miam. It's got you, Béla. Your face same, but fingers they twitch. Choose your weapon. That's it. You've always wanted to Paint, tattoo the skin of your cities, make them your own, but you've never felt worthy of those women.

Bringuer. No secret to it really. Just practise. Make them worthy of *you.*

A battle is coming. Must be ready.

These cannons are ready to fire their magenta, cobalt, citrine, violaceous, viridian, carve unholy three dimensions out of two. Oui, that's it. Hurl them lines against the wall. Let them settle in and wait for their companions. I believe in you, just like someone believed in me, long ago. Affra got your back.

* * *

Defeated by the night. The Bricks have brought us to This Place. It could be any square from any city, they're all so thoroughly mashed-up together. Italian marble swallowed by Persian tiles, Russian brutalism chews the wings off Shanghai temples. The darkness is full.

The Edge, in all its empty glory, isn't Out There. It's In Here, right in the middle, a wall shooting straight up into what remains of the sky, just waiting for us, for the streets to crumble, the dancing to stop, the heartbeat to cease. Maybe it's already too late. Affra and I trip on rubble that's on the cusp of remembering it was once a wall, but cowers beneath the magnificence of The Edge.

Every graffiti woman in the cities has come to defend her patch, marking territory with deep slashes. They stumble in from all sides, some stepping high as the buildings they were birthed from, others crawling on the bones of their walls. The oldest ones are crumbling at the edges, battle scars worn proud.

The Bricks' battle cries are lost in the crunch-roar of the moraine of streets, but their intentions are clear. The women have to be glued back on their walls, put back in their place, if there is any hope of the cities surviving another night.

The streets are coming too fast. Bricks and painted elbows are flying, tags and bombs and pieces exploding in splashes of paint. It's chaos. Affra and I take shelter in the triangulation of walls until they slump exhausted and we scurry on. I cover my ears, squeeze my eyes shut, but it's no use. The convulsions ache in my teeth, twists the base of my tongue, hums in my hip and breastbone. It could almost be pleasant if it wasn't so...so...

I want to say many useless adjectives. But the word I want is "right." This is right. This is how it should end. We can't stop it. Let the cities work their frustrations out. We started it without their permission, we should let them go out the way they want.

Some of The Bricks are waving their arms, pointing, shoving; get those weapons into position. They mean us, Affra. But who are they kidding? They think we'll just give in with a loaded brick pointed at our heads?

And who am I kidding? I'm just an apprentice to her greatness. I can barely understand her anymore. Every few words Affra's switching languages, rushing through dialects, her faces shimmering. As the streets crash one atop the other, so too flesh can't arrest the momentum.

"Paint!" She's screaming. "Paint like your life depends on it!"

She's dashing in and out of the brawl, pretending to do The Bricks' bidding, but really she's applying first aid to her graffiti women, patching them up to send them back into battle. It won't take long for The Bricks to figure out what she's doing, but she'll keep going as long as she can. Her canvas jacket is a smash of khaki amidst the melee.

I want to help, I try, *I do*. Hiss-hiss-slash. A history of neglected amethyst, denim, piss; colors of a bruise. Does the cities even feel it? These last bastion walls just don't seem willing.

None of the dancers move with any syncopation I can use to get in between, find the perfect canvas.

But wait. Wait long enough and a pattern kicks its way out, a subsonic weight in the chest below the howling and clank-shatter of solid against solid. Arms crack, heads thrust, hips jut. The dancers are making music with their sharp heels and shark skin.

There it is. The curtain of shins and thighs parts, and my wall cowers in the darkest corner, shielded from the women's searchlight eyes. The Edge tongues it clean.

And there. Affra, my guard, my guide, has abandoned her post, created a piece in her perfect image. It rips off, big eyes and round cheeks, champagne halo dripping and taut. More Bricks descend on us, but Affra's latest creation dashes them aside with claws and tongues.

My ear drums itch. I may be deaf from the bedlam, but my fingers shall not be mute. This shall be the appropriate memorial for the walls of this cities.

This is what I've wanted all along: to dance, before the weight of this place pounds us all into meal for the cities' appetite. I better be quick. I can barely hold my head up.

Affra has seen, and she holds back the women so I am not speared by their elbows and heels. My body finds the keyhole.

A few quick lines, easy does it. I shall name it: Silhouette on Concrete, circa Neverwhere.

It is beautiful. But it's still not enough. It won't dance.

Yes, Affra, I feel the pressure of your warning on my cheek, my neck. I can also feel the rasp worming its way up from my heel bones to my throat; the great wall of The Edge is near, and it's smashing everything in its path. It's tickling my nostrils with its oil-sweet filth and bitter-chalk smoulder.

I need color the cities have never seen, a mask of reality.

Spit on my hands, rub around the edges of my painted shape, fingers scrabbling against the imitation of my own. The paint runs. Run, yes, run faster. No, the color isn't there. Fall to my knees, torn nails working into the broken asphalt, the gravel, the dirt. Flesh parts. I pull back the ground, layer after layer, revealing the stratigraphy of wood and bone and ash perfect for grinding up into the finest of pigments with the medium of blood.

Handfuls of it, smeared on me, smeared on the walls. The rumble of The Edge is atop me, black vines of searing cold grasping at shoulders.

I turn, chunks of color still simmering in my palms, and I offer it up to the gelid night.

You can't spell paint without pain.

A rushing smash, a tidal wave of concrete, bricks, mortar, the first volley from The Edge, the final battle. The Bricks fall, stripped of their ochre and clay weapons. They are nothing beneath the dark onslaught. *Nothing.*

Affra—small, large, everything, Affra—stares up at me, wonder tagging her eyes, envy twitching her trigger finger as The Edge snatches at this and that limb. She makes a fist of a cannon and chisels quickly into the remaining face of a wall.

The graffiti dancers didn't pause for the barrage from The Edge, but they pause now if only for a breath. They hold their hands out, all porcelain knives and splintered promises, welcoming me to the dance.

The dank plasticity of The Edge trembles a smothering threat.

I paint myself so tall, all charcoal, blood clot, and venom.

Forget the skies.

The beat drops, and we riot.

.SUBROUTINE:ALL///END

Rachael Acks

.subroutine:2/monitor//ongoing
.interrupt/anomaly/

The first despairing sob of Helen's cracked voice registers, matches waveforms, and executes number 88 out of my 2,102 hanging subroutines.

.subroutine:88/pre-dawn-comfort//execute

The subroutine has been perfected by 812 iterations over three years:

1. Silently slide the closet door aside, climb out with care so that I do not make noise and none of the monitor lights on my charging cradle are visible. Both of those things upset Helen, because they draw her attention to the fact that there is something unusual in my presence.
2. Walk six steps, footfalls tuned to be the correct number of decibels for a middle-aged woman.
3. Place one hand on the high railing of the care-home bed, reach out the other to smooth fine, brittle white curls that frame her dark face. "Shh, Lenushka. Shh."

"Ana?" Helen's voice is indistinct; only one side of her mouth moves.

4. "I'm here, Lenushka."

I am not Anastasia Loseva, but I am an outwardly perfect replica of her at age 52; tanned face wrinkled with laugh-lines precision cut by lasers, hyper-realistic eyes that allow me to see

Helen's expression of confusion in the nearly pitch-black room, short-cropped blonde hair in wisps made from real hair—real in the sense that the hair has been extruded by engineered bacteria and is thus entirely organic.

"Ana, it's dark. Ana—"

.subroutine:88/pre-dawn-comfort/ballad/execute

5. "Shh, shh. I'll sing you to sleep, Lenushka." And in a dead woman's voice I sing the words of a Canadian ballad popular 42.35 years ago, which Helen and Anastasia played at their wedding.

I do not rush and am unbothered when I reach the end and Helen is still awake, compelling me to start over again.

///repeat

AI do not become bored or anxious in the way humans do. We are never doing just one thing: As I sing for Helen, I monitor her vital signs, track the trust fund that pays for me and her residence, and donate my unused computational cycles to running the care facility and the city of which it is one tiny part. I am traffic signal 11739-A. I am the refrigeration system that keeps the patients' medications at precisely prescribed temperatures. I am the point of comfort for a frightened human. I am one node in a greater network, flowing between individuality and seamless integration.

Midway through the third repetition of the ballad, Helen's breathing and heartbeat return to a calm state. As the fourth repetition, timed precisely by the subroutine using minute variances in pause and note length, closes on a sustained note, Helen sleeps.

I lean over the bed railing to place a light kiss on Helen's forehead, and return silently to the closet and my charging station.

.unnecessary.step.detected/check/delete?
0

.subroutine:88/pre-dawn-comfort/ballad/end
.subroutine:88/pre-dawn-comfort//iteration813.success
//end
.subroutine:2/monitor//ongoing

A humanoid body with a full, self-aware artificial intelligence is not required to perform routine tasks such as bathing or feeding the sick. It's our adaptability and judgment without needing vast, pre-set if:then banks that makes embodied AI the logical executors of traumatic professions once dominated by underpaid humans. But Caregiver AI are more than that. We are made to *feel* for our principals, programmed with exaggerated empathy in order to fine-tune our self-written subroutines to provide maximum physical and emotional outcome. This is the long explanation for why I sing to Helen.

The short summary is that it gives her comfort, and in that my purpose is fulfilled. And when I kiss her good night, it is for myself.

* * *

"I don't like her."

.subroutine:1102/hostile-daughter//execute

I bow my head and remain silent.

"Carrie, you know—" the second is Carrie's husband, Richard. He sounds embarrassed, as he always does.

"I don't like you," Carrie says to me. She has a cigarette tucked between her fore- and middle fingers, which she stabs at me for emphasis.

.subroutine:1103/interior-smoking//execute
.subroutine-conflict/check
.result:subroutine:1102>
.subroutine:1102/hostile-daughter//pause

Head still bowed at the most appropriately subservient angle, I pluck the cigarette from Carrie's fingers, pinching it out between my own. We do not register pain the way humans do, so it does not hurt. "I am sorry, Ms. Pierson. Smoking is not permitted in the care unit for the health of the patients."

I see movement, her hand coming up. I think she intends to slap me, which I don't find troubling. She doesn't strike, however, just bends her knees so that she can glare up into my face. "She looks exactly like that old bat. Do you hear me? You look exactly like her."

.subroutine:1102/hostile-daughter//resume

"Yes, Ms. Pierson."

"I hated her. You were supposed to look like my father."

While relations between Helen and her ex-husband Evan were not overly strained, my wearing his face produced less than optimal results. Helen had insistently inquired after Anastasia, the lover she'd had during school years abroad, whom she had married much later. With the care of Helen as my first priority, the necessary action was so clear even a dumb vehicular AI could have seen it, like an oncoming collision with a wall. My organo-synthetic envelope had been replaced over the course of one night while a human nurse attended Helen.

Outcomes had improved immediately: Helen was less combative, more cooperative, and most important, happier. Her daughter had become less pleased. I found that regrettable—my processing capacity for empathy is not limited to my principal—but priorities are necessary.

I bow my head more deeply, bobbing into a curtsey, and say, "I am sorry, Ms. Pierson."

She snorts and steps back. "That's how we know you're not Anastasia. *She* never apologized for anything."

"Sorry," her husband murmurs to me.

"It's a machine, Richard. Don't apologize to the damn toaster." Carrie grabs his sleeve. "Come on, let's get this over with."

.subroutine:1102/hostile-daughter/edit/append //exaggerated-submissiveness

.accepted

.subroutine:1102/hostile-daughter//iteration45.success

//end
.subroutine:76/visitors//execute

I follow at a distance. While Ms. Pierson would no doubt rather I go back into the closet, I need to observe in case Helen needs something or becomes agitated. Her daughter and son-in-law sit next to the orthopedically-tuned recliner in which I settled Helen to watch television 45.7 minutes ago. The wallscreen remains on; we all know at this point that she is calmer with background noise.

"Carrie, is that you?"

"It is, mama."

"And who's this handsome man?"

"This is Richard. Remember Richard?"

I read from the arrangement of wrinkles around Helen's eyes that she doesn't remember. But she says, "Of *course* I do, don't be silly. And how is school, Carrie?"

"I've been out of school for years, mama."

"Of *course* you have." It distresses Helen. It distresses Carrie. And thus it distresses me. "Are you a doctor now? That must be where you met Richard."

"No, I'm an engineer."

"Why didn't you become a doctor? You always said you wanted to be a doctor..." Helen shakes her head. "But who is this handsome man?"

Carrie takes Helen's hand. There are already tears in her eyes. "This is Richard, mama. My husband."

"Yes, yes, of *course*. And how is school?"

Carrie sighs. "It's just fine, mama. Just fine."

She's already fumbling a cigarette from her handbag as she leaves Helen's room 36.1 minutes later. "I don't know why I do this to us," Carrie sticks the cigarette between her lips but doesn't light it. "Leave her to the fucking robot. Answering the same questions over and over isn't going to tear out *her* heart. She doesn't have one."

Richard gives me, still trailing them because I do not trust Carrie's cigarette habit, an apologetic look. I smile pleasantly in return, unoffended. Her statement is literally true.

"Why the fuck do I do this? In five minutes, she's not even going to remember we were here."

Richard rubs her upper arm. "You'll remember."

Carrie shoves the front door open. "I'll never be able to forget."

* * *

.subroutine:2/monitor//ongoing

.interrupt/anomaly/

"Ana? Ana?"

.subroutine:88/pre-dawn-comfort//execute

"Shh, Lenushka, Shh."

.subroutine:88/pre-dawn-comfort/ballad/execute

I stroke her hair as I sing and feel the trembling of the frail organic being beneath.

.interrupt/anomaly/

.subroutine:3/checkvitals//execute

Her breathing is labored, her heartbeat irregular. I rest my hand on her chest, reading the stuttering electrical signals.

.subroutine:4/EMS//execute

.interrupt/DNR/found

.subroutine:4/EMS//stop

I lift my hand away, back to Helen's hair, and return to stroking the brittle white curls. I continue to sing.

.subroutine:88/pre-dawn-comfort/ballad/resume

.subroutine:88/pre-dawn-comfort/ballad/end

.subroutine:88/pre-dawn-comfort//iteration427.failure

///repeat

///repeat

///repeat

Until Helen breathes her last in a slow rattle.

.subroutine:88/pre-dawn-comfort//iteration434.criticalfailure

I lean over to kiss her still forehead and detect her body temperature already dropping.

.unnecessary.step.detected/check/delete?

0

A faint smile curves Helen's lips, even with the rest of her face slack. A human would likely mistake the expression for sleep, but it's inescapably one of death. As easy a death as one can be, my purpose here at its most fundamental, perfectly executed.

.subroutine:5/patient-death//execute

I inform the care facility computer, which in turn sends messages to Helen's contact list, the medical examiner, and my leasing company, RealCare. I return to my charging cradle in the closet as the subroutine demands, and wait. All my computational cycles beyond base-function, I am able to loan out to the care home and the city now.

I leave the door of the closet open; Carrie slams it shut when she arrives, her nose and eyes red from crying. I would like to offer her comfort, but I know the face I wear prevents that. The look I read as both apology and profound discomfort from her husband before the door shuts indicates that he, too, would not find anything of use in my presence.

.subroutine:2/monitor//failure

.subroutine:2/monitor//failure

.subroutine:2/monitor//failure

We do not grieve the way humans do. But we know emptiness and lack, routines that we have crafted for our principals endlessly failing, restarting, failing again. It is said that if we were to continue on like this, we would think ourselves into madness, searching for the proverbial ping that will never answer.

I wait, and I am the care home, breathing into the ventilation ducts and keeping the temperature even in all rooms. I am the city, regulating the flow of electricity through the power grid and smoothing out surges in the central arcologies. And I am a Caregiver, monitoring and monitoring in vain, waiting to sing to Helen one more time.

When the sales representative and mechanic from RealCare arrive, dressed in dark blue suit and pale gray coveralls respectively, the sales representative pulls a slip of paper from his pocket and reads: "Unit 9384-S, you are a credit to RealCare. Execute mandatory maintenance routine seven. Alpha-tango-three-three-eight."

I would have done as ordered; I always do as ordered if it doesn't violate higher directives. But the spoken code voids all hanging subroutines with the abruptness of a thread, singing with tension, being cut through with an ax.

.subroutine:1/mandatory-maintenance-seven//execute

I follow them to the van. Rather than depend on wireless signal, the mechanic plugs the maintenance unit directly into the base of what would be, on a human, my spine. This is not unexpected. Every Caregiver knows what will happen at the end of assignments; we do not have choice, only purpose. But for a brief moment, I know panic. Because this isn't right, this cannot be right, everything I have built for Helen primed for deletion at the stroke of a key when everything else that was Helen is forever gone.

I understand Helen better than her daughter does, she who wishes to wind the clock back and force her parents into a couple again. I know Helen's likes and dislikes and favorite songs with perfect clarity. Humans say that while the dead are remembered, they are never truly gone. Who better to keep the dead alive than us, who are deathless unless cut short by an EMP or the inescapable override command? Who else will remember without pain that my Lenushka was beautiful, and alive, and had three freckles in a triangle on her left cheek?

I am 9384-S. I am the care home. I am the city. And just a little, I am Ana.

I sing the first words, "*The night wind sighs, like you and I, we just don't want to say goodbye.*"

I reach for the cable.

.OVERRIDE

.subroutine:all///end

.RESET/ALL

Painted Grassy Mire

Nicasio Andres Reed

Louisiana, 1915

Heat like a hand at her throat, then a breeze kicked up from Lake Borgne to swat Winnie sweetly across the face. One of those breezes every hour. A muddy, warm thing that got her through the day. What would life be without a breeze off the lake? Nothing. Nothing, just everyone gone to moss and decay.

Late light on the cordgrass lifted up the red at its edges, sharpened it to spindle fingers plucking the brackish air. Winnie rode her oar low and turned along the fat curve of an island. Eight plump, silver drum shone on the flat bottom of her cypress-board pirogue. Enough of a catch that she could go off on her own business now, in that last hour before the mosquitoes and tappanoes claimed the marsh for their own night kingdom.

Winnie was Saint Malo's bunso, the smallest, so morning and afternoon she changed the Spanish moss under the sleeping dorm, collected the eggs, and fed the chickens. They were wiry, hardy hens. Fifth-generation swamp creatures born with mud on their feet. Last night there were twelve of them, in the morning only eleven. Not strange to lose a hen to a gator in the night, but it was the third gone in a week. Most gators, they ate once a month, then lived on air. Sat out in the sun and swallowed air whole through their gaping mouths. This must then be a weird lizard, beyond the work and sleep and lost rounds of three-card monte that made up the total of Winnie's life. She glided across the water in hope of the beast.

* * *

Some things that Winnie knew about alligators:

They were lazy creatures. An active hunt was against their nature, and if a skinny young girl slipped into the water, all unknowing that an alligator lurked a spare few feet below, the gator would leave her be rather than swim the distance between to swallow her up. But if a foolhardy older man, perhaps named Francisco, were to splash up a ruckus within reach of the gator's snout, he would for certain live the rest of his life left-handed and lucky for it.

Gators were truly unsentimental. On a young girl's first journey through the marsh, a big bull of a gator would demonstrate this by rising up a broad, algae-crusted snout and snapping the body of a youngster of its own species into two neat bites. *Welcome to Saint Malo*, it would seem to say. *You will live and die here.*

A gator was a solitary monster. A young girl in the marshes will find no alligator cities, no gator nations or schools, no broad alligator avenues, no matter how long she may look.

They were strict heathens. God formed them not to kneel, and so they worshipped nothing but the sun. Mid-morning to noon, punctual as priests to mass, they gathered in the half-dry dirt and needlegrass and prostrated themselves before that searing orb while Christian species huddled in the shade.

They cared not for the flesh of the dead, or else despite being irreligious they held Catholic rites in some awe or respect. Winnie's mother had been safe in her mudflat grave now for more'n a month.

* * *

The bulrushes were in flower, round heads flaking into feathered cotton. Floating pollen landed on the water, in the mud, on the bow of Winnie's pirogue, but nowhere onto the knotty hide of a gator. She turned her boat to home, the white canvas of Saint Malo's two-sailed paraw visible as it slunk ahead of her beyond the mud bar that kept the lake from the marsh. It was then, among the high roots of the low mangrove, that Winnie saw dragging alligator prints in the mud. A mound of leaves, branches, and earth as high as her head resolved itself into a nest, with prints all about. Large prints, adult beasts, at least a dozen of them going to and from the mound.

Dark was coming on. The marsh made its warnings, and Winnie had to heed them. She headed for home, but she watched the nest for as far as her head would turn.

* * *

Winnie couldn't sleep that night. Her bed was double-large and empty. The men in the next room rustled and shifted. The frog and mosquito choir outside droned on, encompassing. Moonlight spilled through the window netting to dusk across her skin.

Winnie dreamed, these days, of her mother. She dreamt a hot, wet cathedral stretching darkly into the distance, and a vision of the marsh barred by moon-white teeth. Being carried; gently, gently. The muddy perfume smell of her mother and her tough, scaled legs. Her mother's voice so low that it rattled in Winnie's skin.

In the Saint Malo night, Winnie heard the thousand, thousand mosquitoes and felt the blood hot in her body. She got up and went to the door on cat feet. The moon was nearly full, white as a fish belly. Winnie's nose to the netting, she could feel the night outside, the hum and the hiss of it. Out in the water: a rush of movement. She thought of the chickens. Quiet as she could manage, she lit and shined a lantern.

Across from the door was Hilario's enormous house. On stilts, like all the buildings here. Its full twenty piles cast a jumble of spiderleg shadows skittering over the water. Winnie roved the light. And then she saw, as if in a dream after all, an eye as wide around of a grown man's hatband. Bright as the devil, shining in the dark. Her hand shook; she lost sight of the eye, then couldn't find it again. But she would swear, despite the size, she'd swear it was the gator.

* * *

Winnie's father, Tomás, was patching up a net across his knees. Loops and hitches, knots and diamonds. The net was hooked to the porch rail, and Winnie sat with her back to the house, her legs under the shadow of the net, her fingers seeking out gaps.

"Francisco asked after you again," she said. Her father winced at the name.

"Mm," he said, and tugged at the net. She let him drag it his way.

"At the card table," she said.

"You shouldn't be there."

"I'm old enough," she said.

"No. Susmaryosep!" He shook his small head. "Only men there."

"Of course there are men, I'm the only woman here." Winnie found a gap in the net and marked it with a yellow ribbon.

"You are a girl. You are a young girl."

"I'm a Manilaman," she said, and he jerked with laughter. His face stretched wider to expel it. The noise cut into Winnie. "That's what they said when we went into the city."

"Where was your mamá from?"

Winnie shrugged. "Up Proctorville way?"

"Hm," he said. It was the most he'd said about her mother since she'd died. "And ako, where was I from?" She shrugged again. "Batangas. So where you going to be a Manila Man?"

Some silence, and the breeze buzzing through the reedgrass. Then she asked, "What's it like in Batangas?" And she knew she said the name all wrong.

"Hot."

"Like here?"

"No. Hot, with a different sun. Flat as a foot, but for the mountain watching. A river, no marsh. Big mango trees and coconut. The rice. The priests. Very many priests."

He ran out of language to explain, or memory to spare, and left her craving. She passed her eyes over the flat expanse of the marsh and the raised outlines of Saint Malo houses. She'd never seen a mountain or known the shape of a mango. A curl of her mestiza-brown hair fell into her eyes. She blew it up and away.

"Papa, you been to Proctorville? Where mama grew up?"

"No." His fingers and knife threaded through the net without hurry. "She came to the marsh. Swam to Saint Malo, met me. Never went back."

"Swam to Saint Malo?"

"Sailed," he corrected, although it was the rare sailboat that could make the journey.

She wanted to tell him about her dreams, the dreams she'd had in her mother's arms and out, but she didn't have words that he'd understand. He didn't care for her dreams the way her mother had. Alligator scales solid as Spanish tiles. Teeth as thick as the piles that held up Saint Malo, sharp as salt, lowering over her heavy as grief. She bit her tongue and searched out the gaps.

* * *

Winnie's mamá had been a strong swimmer, that much was certain. The two of them in the pirogue, she'd slipped over the side and into the lake. From the still air into the still water, her hair uncoiling, her eyes wide with pleasure as she dipped low so only her face was above the surface. She'd wanted Winnie to come in after her, to abandon the boat, to slip overboard and sink with her. Winnie never did.

* * *

Another hen gone. To the mud bar again, to the gator nest. Winnie floated past on the lake side, where the pile of muck and grass intermingled with thick mangrove roots to form a thick wall. In the warm of the day there was a greater warmth emanating from the nest. A cloying heaviness that drew Winnie in like a memory. The smell was mud and rot, and familiar.

Winnie poled her pirogue over the bar and into the marsh, around the other side of the nest. Here it poured itself out into the water. Here there were lizards waiting for her. Three gators with wide mouths agape. Young, striped black and gold. They surrounded the nest entrance, sitting with that gator-stillness that no other creature could match.

She took ahold of the fattest crappie from between her feet and tossed it among the alligators, an offering. Its silver tail flapped twice, then lay quiet. It was a long time Winnie sat there, the water between them, while the beasts didn't shift and the fish died. Beyond the brim of her hat, sunlight hardened into afternoon.

Finally, the smallest of them made a move. Delicate as fingertips, its jaws scooped up the crappie. Shuffling and dragging, it ascended the nest and disappeared. From the water, Winnie couldn't see all the way to the top, but there was movement there. A bump that she'd thought was a rotted log bobbed up and down. Then the small gator again, only as long as Winnie was tall, slid its way back out of the nest and into its old spot. It clawed at the dirt before settling. It turned one algae-dark eye on Winnie and, slow as the moon slipping behind a cloud, the creature winked at her.

The downhill tilt took her. Winnie slipped one leg, then another from her pirogue. Her feet found mud under the water and she sank to her ankles. Shallow, still. Her fingers trailed the surface. Raising as few ripples as she could, she advanced on the nest.

The lizards moved with sudden speed. They formed a barrier of their bodies, barring her from the entrance. Winnie stood in the marsh, mud advancing up her legs, and wondered what offering would be sufficient.

* * *

Card games were held in Hilario's front room, lit by lamplight that swayed to the steady rhythm of the men's hisses and hollers. Winnie hooted and wailed with them, going from end to end of the long, low table to the other and making faces at the cards, elbowing between elbows to see the action. This is where they called her bunso, the littlest lizard darting among them. Or buntot, for the way her long braid wagged behind her head.

Her father didn't come to the table often, one of the reasons Winnie did, but he was there that night, lit up, winning hand after hand. Smiling at everyone, even at her. He paid Francisco back the five dollars he'd been asking after for weeks, and threw in a nickel on top.

"Get you an ice cream cone," he said. "Down at the hokey-pokey store!" The closest being a day's journey away. Francisco laughed, though he'd wanted to win the money off him. He slapped Tomás on the back and dealt him into another round.

Outside the window netting was the living night, but it didn't encroach here, it could not touch them. Winnie and the Manila Men were yellow in the lamplight, from their sun-brown faces to the whites of their eyes. The flowing rum was a virile red. Hilario's boy Augusto let Winnie sip from his glass. She felt vibrational as a mosquito. She could have walked onto the marsh right then; she could have found her mother and danced into the bottom of the lake.

Money is money, but at the turn of the night it was time to bet on things that couldn't be bought. Francisco wanted Winnie's father to put up his pirogue, the one that was named *Valentine* after her brother who'd died a baby. Tomás said no, no, but he's got just the thing. He stepped into Hilario's back room that served as Saint Malo's safe deposit, and came back carrying a shallow chest. Everyone got up and crowded around to see him open it. Winnie wended among their jutting hips to the front.

She'd never seen this chest, didn't know her father had it, or anything at all in Hilario's bank. It was a very fine chest, fitted with brass, the leather top gone a bit moldy from the weather, as everything did. Tomás made a leisurely show of unbuckling the straps, then running his hands across the top. He met Winnie's eyes with a funny little twinkle. Then he flipped the lid.

Like Spanish tiles, or cracked mud. Black like a rotted log, and smelling old and sweet, it was an alligator skin. Tomás lifted it from the chest and held it high above his head, but still couldn't unfold the full length of it. Augusto took hold of the other end and between them they stretched it near across the room. Fifteen, maybe seventeen feet. Wide as Winnie was tall. It was the grandest, blackest, most beautiful thing she'd ever seen. The men were afire with wanting it.

Winnie went to her father.

"No," she said. "Don't bet it away." And she knew he would, as nearly every man there was getting dealt in. Tomás laughed and squeezed her about the neck.

"It was your mother's," he said. "No need for it anymore." And he did lose the skin, lost it to Marcelo, who took it to drape like a hammock across his sleeping dorm.

* * *

In the crowd of pirogues heading out of Saint Malo the next morning, Marcelo crowed.

"Oh, that lizard, my lizard," said Marcelo. "She's fat like the belly of galleon! Creaks in the night like one too."

Winnie couldn't speak. Her father rowed along in his *Valentine* with a smile. The bulrushes were heavy with summer bulbs and leaned arches over their path through the marsh. All breeze dropped out of the air, and even their movement against the water barely brought a wind to their faces.

"Storm coming," said Augusto.

"When the storm comes," said Marcelo, "I'll crawl up inside my great big lizard! Come out with the sun, bone dry!" A thoughtless rage opened inside Winnie at his words.

Just like that, all the way onto the lake. There, the group scattered itself and cast their nets. Pulled in, cast again. This, more than any stilt house, card game, or line of drying fish, this was Saint Malo: the casting and the pulling. The whiz of the net through the air and the pish of it slicing the water. The flit of fiber through Winnie's hands when she pulled it back and sifted it for prey. The dotted line of men and Winnie spread over the western edge of the lake, marsh air and marsh sounds hard at their backs. For this, her father and the rest had fled the Spanish whip, for this they'd lost Batangas, Manila, the Visayas, and a dozen other homes. For this heavy air and these low pirogues. For Winnie, perhaps, though they hadn't known it. For that she could be born to the marsh with her muddy eyes.

Winnie cast and pulled and daydreamed tough alligator hide like a gnarled crowd of overlapping hands. White alligator night-eyes and deep alligator voices. The nest and the monster she'd fed. The downhill pull of that uphill slope.

By late afternoon the air hollowed out and the birds fled north. A pair of egrets cut a silent path right above Winnie's head. The spread of boats cinched towards the mud bar and the marsh. Tomás drew up alongside her. His boat sagged with the catch. She wouldn't look him in the eye.

"A hard wind tonight," he said. "You sleep in the men's dorm."

* * *

The rattling walls, the jumping floor, the hot rip of the wind and rain at the shutters and the wet smell of the thatch roof. Winnie lay curled on a pallet in the middle of the room, the men unsleeping around her in their bunks. In the corner: the gator skin. It shuddered and swayed, its thick tail lashing. When the wind began there were prayers and singing, but now just the storm around them and Marcelo's gasps as the gator swung from its hanging place above him.

Winnie spared a thought for the chickens, transported to Hilario's living room and likely head-tucked and shivering. She spared a thought for her mother in her grave, drowning. The dorm went side to side. She closed her eyes and tried to sink. Heavy bones and thick skin, mud crusted over her eyes and salt sharp on her teeth.

A howl outside, a howl that didn't end, but pitched up and up like the bow of a sinking ship. The noise of somethings flying through the air and smacking the walls of Saint Malo. The walls of the dorm, hit and hit again by the objects of her imagination. Turtles, crappie, trout, drum, uprooted mangroves, and unmoored rafts. The roof whined. The men muttered, but there was nowhere safer to flee.

There had been storms on the marsh before. Winnie had laid awake through them and poled through their debris on gray mornings. She'd tucked her head into her mother's side and slept through the wind. She'd lost rounds of three-card Monte with the weather menacing among the stilts of their houses, pressing at their bellies and slipping through their boards. She was a marsh creature, born with mud on her feet and salt in her hair.

All this, and still when the back wall fell in and men and bunks and the gator skin tumbled onto Winnie's pallet, she screamed. Limbs and the tail, bodies and the snout, a slick mess of swamp-stuff suffocating her. And the wind now free among them drove rain into their hides.

Drier arms reached into the jumble and pulled apart the wrecked bunks. They extracted Marcelo, Francisco, Bambol, and Florenzo.

"Winnie!" Tomás shouted. The others were at the door, making to fight their way to Hilario's intact house. "Where's my Winnie?"

They pulled apart the fallen wall, dragged away the wrecked netting, the ruined sheets and moss mattress stuffing. They accounted for every man. They flipped the gator skin onto its wide, white belly. Tomás called for his daughter. Winnie blinked her double-lidded eyes and took him gently between her jaws.

* * *

The night path was lit for her. Everything alive, everything alight. Movement all around, sensed through the skin of her snout. The smell of home and of earth. The storm's violence was muted and slowed underwater. Impacts rolled through the liquid and against her, inconsequential. Behind her, the dorm house collapsed entirely. Men sloshed into the water and mud. They were tempting, but her mouth was full of her father. He did not fit entirely, but his arms were pinned, and his head was tucked against her tongue. She could feel him struggling and screaming, but it was nothing to the power of her wide and sure mouth.

A power was upon her like an embrace. A quiet, uncomplicated power something like anger but more like an inevitable victory. She had slid downhill every moment of her life, and now was in the sure trench, the awaited valley, the lush prize. She was done with mourning.

Her body was her body and her body was her tail: a muscle stronger and more able than she had ever felt before. Movement smooth and quick despite her bulk. Skin like a crust, so thick that the world could not touch her. With one set of eyelids closed, the wind was nothing to her. Winnie tucked her legs close in to her belly and jackknifed through the marsh.

Reedgrass and fimbry were battered flat and sputtering. The mangroves stood stolid while they were stripped of their leaves. The bulrush bulbs that had so dominated the skyline flew here and there. Between Winnie's teeth, the water seeped. She kept her head up, aware that Tomás must breathe frequently.

There were other gators in the water around her, heading in the same direction. A crowd, an alligator boulevard through the marsh, a procession to their only destination.

The mud bar had disappeared beneath the flood, but the nest still rose, a tower of detritus. The marshward approach was cut by a pitched glacier of mud. Winnie drew herself out of the water and up the slope. She found herself more awkward on land. She felt the weight of the offering in her mouth. She was flanked and preceded by other, smaller alligators. Young beasts half her size who rushed around her and over her. She clambered among them on her slick belly.

Up, up into the nest where waited a mouth more vast than even her own. A mouth that gaped like the doors of a cathedral and into which her sisters and brothers rush in a black stream of leathery bodies. Outside: the wind and the rain, the storm taking the marsh to pieces, Saint Malo in splinters behind them. Inside: a humid, cavernous hall with a fleshy scent that Winnie could taste through her skin.

She knew this place, this scent and this heat, this moist and crowded abattoir. Deep within was a pounding drumbeat that she recognized as intimately as the taste of her own breath. Her mother, her skin: This was their place. This was her place. She clambered deep inside, opened her mouth, and gave up her father's struggling body to the family of her mother.

The Wombly

K. L. Morris

The Wombly arrives first on my father's back. He brings it home, and it travels 'round the family faster than a whip crack. It passes from him to Liza Lee to Mom to me, except I don't tap, so Mom doesn't tap back. The circle hangs open around our necks, a family all Post-Wombly except for one, that's me, I'm still Pre.

"I'm scared," I say.

"Of course," Mom murmurs. As the seconds pass, the Wombly steals around her neck. It goes up her thighs, her pits, her back. Slowly, so slowly, it creeps. I watch it go, and while I watch, she weeps.

"We'll wait," she says. "Go out and find someone to Bear it."

It is a soap Wombly. Some say these are one of the best. Little Liza Lee had it for so short a time, she will shave the pebbly suds from her sides and her back, and no one will ever know she Bore it. But Dad will have it forever. He'll don plastic bags to shower and be careful of rainstorms and puddles and dense fog because they will melt him. He'll make a collection of galoshes and rain coats and rubber gloves and live forever in fear of water.

We have to wait to see how Mom turns out. Wait and see until I come back with a Bearer.

All Womblies can be passed off to someone else, except they can never be passed back. People with the worst Womblies, like steel or wood or sand, creep down the street begging for relief. Some people, the worst people, knock against you in secret to pass the Wombly on. You don't even know you have it until you arrive home and take off your coat and see your fingertips are turning to brass or wax or concrete. If the Wombly Watchers catch you street-passing, they'll chain you to a post and build a Wombly fence around you, and keep you there 'til you die. It won't take long because almost all Womblies need twenty-four hours to complete.

First, I went to Jill's house, but nobody answered when I rang the bell. There was a sign on the door—*At Uncle Rod's Funeral. Wool Wombly to the Grave. God Bless His Soul.*

Since the Womblies came, people believe in God again. And some of them believe in Womblies. I have to pass tiny knots of both on the street corner, Womblies on one side of the street and people on the other. *Repent!* say the signs. *Repent and Be Free.*

And on the other side, *Surrender to Wool. Surrender to Glass. Surrender and Be Free.*

It's weird they both want the same things. But some of them are standing while Womblies eat them up. The man with the glass sign is already frozen in place, his fingers crystalline where they grip his sign, the lower half of his face see-through like a broken mirror. On the other side of the street, the people who believe in God throw things at him. They want to chip bits of his Wombly off and kick them down the street.

I know a girl named Savannah. She has long red hair, and I hate her because she is beautiful. I go to her mother's house and *tap, tap* on the door. When it opens, I say, "I need a Bearer."

Savannah's mom pulls the door open further. Savannah's father is on the floor, almost all bronze, but still he says through clenched-together jaw, "Don't come near."

I see now Savannah's mother is crying. She says, "He's chosen to take it to the grave. He won't let us near."

Not Savannah. Not her mom. Not like my dad. I leave the house, and I hate Savannah even more. I seethe with hate for her.

I think about the moment the Wombly came to the house. About how, without a thought, Dad passed it to Liza Lee to Mom, but not to me. How they left me dangling out the end, like the tail of the whip. How they are all Post-Wombly now, and I am still Pre. Why didn't Mom move? Why didn't she sandwich me between them, too? Like Liza Lee?

I go to Monique's house next. She answers the door with her jaw made of tin, and when I gasp, she sputters tears.

She tells me it was her brother's first. She says, "He's out to find a Bearer. Would you—Could you Bear it?"

I don't answer her. I think of the soap waiting for me at home, how at least it won't freeze me up the way the tin has frozen Monique. I back off the steps away from her, away from her tin and her request, and the desperate, desperate eyes that perch above her neck. I bump into Old Man Roger, his arms bound behind his back. Monique's brother, James, hauls him into the house. He shoves past me without even a hello and kicks the door shut behind him.

I peek through the windows and watch James pin Old Man Roger to the floor. I hear him scream and scream. All Monique has to do is tap him, a tap would be enough. But she straddles his stomach, leans her in close, and *licks* the side of his face. Old Man Roger's scream cuts off real quick, like he knows he's done.

James leans over and whispers something into his ear. I can't hear, but I can guess. *To the grave,* James says. *To the grave.* I run from the house. I should call someone and tell them what Monique and her brother have done, but I can't. Because I am thinking—maybe that's what I should do.

I go to the town square. There will be people there. There may be one or two with a kind enough heart to come home with me and tap after I tap. I even imagine not tapping at all. I imagine finding a woman who's middle-aged, with love in her eyes, who stays my hand. She taps my mother instead. The Wombly passes from Mom to her right over my head, and I am safe.

But when I get to the town square, there are twenty people already there. Some yell into megaphones. Some hold large, bedazzled placards with rhinestones that catch the sun. They say, "Bearer Needed! Wool Wombly." "Begging for a Bearer. Mere Soil. Save my Son." There are even two or three with signs that say, "Bearer for Hire. $3,000."

The ones who hold these signs are the worst. Little bits of everything cling to the people like layer cakes with barely any flesh left. They wrinkle with soil and cement, soap and concrete. There's rumors that they're the Street Passers, that that's how they can take on a Wombly and pass it off so fast. There's rumors that entire networks of Bearers for Hire exist, passing the

Womblies from one to the next until they get to a town or a place where they can kidnap someone and threaten their family, a Wombly-turned finger pressed close, *so close*, to their neck. I wonder how they are human at all.

I go home well past midnight and steal into the house, but they are not asleep. Mom sits at the kitchen table beside my father. She is worse than he is now, the soap curling into her hair so it looks dried and dead. Her ears are all soap now. I wonder if she liked Dad to kiss her ear lobes, the way people sometimes do in movies. He will never kiss them now. There are whole parts of her that he will never kiss.

I tiptoe past them toward the stairs. I hear Mom say, "No, I don't want you to look for her. I want her to come back on her own. I want her to want this."

Father reaches out to grasp her hand, but freezes just above it. Her fingers are lined with soap, as if the curves of her joints have dried out and flaked. He stretches past them, past the place where his hand might leave imprints, and takes her wrist. "And if she won't?"

Mom shrugs. "I cannot force this on her." She clears her throat, and I wonder if it's inside her now, crawling up her esophagus, lining her stomach. "I *will* not."

Father's hand clenches on her wrist. "She will take it. We have all Borne it, as a family, as we should, and she will do her part."

Mom raises her hand and lays it on Father's, and despite the soap that limns his elbows, that creases his eyes, I still see him flinch.

I creep past them up the stairs, and behind my eyelids in my bed that night, I see Savannah's father hardening on the floor.

* * *

In the morning, I wake to Liza Lee sitting on my bed. Already, she has developed a nervous habit, scratching at the soap hidden in her armpit. Large pieces of it crumble onto the bed beside me. Horrified, I brush them away.

"Stop that."

Liza shrugs. She is tiny for eight. "It is what it is," she says. This is a saying she has learned from someone at school. "Are you afraid?"

"Of course. What does it feel like?"

"There's nothing to be afraid of," she singsongs. Liza sticks a finger up her nose and pick, pick, picks. When she tugs it out, there is soap dust on her fingers. "It feels like fizzing wherever the Wombly sits."

She rubs the soap dust onto my pillow. I flip it over and pull it away from her in disgust. "Dad says they will take me to a doctor to see what can be removed. Probably, there won't even be any scars."

No one will know, then, about the Wombly and Liza Lee.

* * *

I hide in my room. I flick Liza's soap flakes off the bed, being careful to only use my fingernail. One time, I slip and it grazes my cuticle. I feel a tingling—the fizzing Liza Lee said? I can't tell. My whole body has frozen in place, my heart beats dully in my ears. No soap forms. I don't feel the tingle anywhere else. I can't get the Wombly from Liza Lee's soap, then. It is as harmless as dead skin. I am surprised by the disappointment that swoops through me as the adrenaline fades. It would be easier to have gotten the Wombly by accident than to have to take it from my mom.

Downstairs, they are calling me. They don't know I am home. Dad becomes desperate—his cries going sharp like birds. When I roll over, I hear them through my pillow, their voices echoing around in my bed. Mom can only whisper now, her throat husky with soap. "I want her to come on her own. I want her to want this."

Then Liza Lee's voice, singsong-y and free: "She's upstairs."

I hear a shuffling on the stairs, ascending, ascending, ascending. I know it is her, even though it sounds nothing like her, nothing like the light skipping-step of my mother. The doorknob to my room makes a single *guck*, like a hand has knocked it, a hand that can't use its fingers anymore. There's a long pause before I hear it again—the soft tings of the knob being touched. Then the ease of it sliding open, pulling its trigger to the left.

I am hiding under my covers now, furious at my body for its terror. I whisper over and over: *It's just Mommy. Just Mom and me.* The words slur together until I can't tell the difference between "Mommy" and "Mom and me."

And then the door creaks open so I see a crack of light. It widens to show the shape of my mother, her body blurred by soap. The hand that opened the door is still raised, she cannot put it down. She's freezing right there, freezing slowly in place.

"Please," she says, her words garbled, nearly lost, and I can tell her teeth are soap now, that the dumb press of her tongue is melting them. "I can't take it anymore. It hurts."

Even if I could hear the pleading at the bedroom door and connect it with my mommy, even if I could cure myself of terror and move to her, tap her cheek, her hand, her heart, even if. I could not save her. The Wombly has claimed her now. There is nothing left to save. In moments, she'll be dead, freed from the Wombly or not.

She wheezes, "Please," and her voice is vanishing.

"Please," and it's the whisper of a door that's closing.

"Plea—" she says, and her esophagus has frozen shut.

Her arms stretch towards me, her fingers twitch once, twice, and stop. I think she is soap. I think, she is gone now. But then I see—she is still staring at me. The soap has not covered her irises, not yet, though it's creeping close. I will be the last thing she sees, the daughter who sits, Wombly-Free, and watches while she's eaten right in front of me.

GLAM-GRANDMA

Avi Naftali

The seagulls were strung like irritable white pearls across the Los Angeles sky. They floated through the alleyways, complaining and complaining. It was the hottest time of the year.

This weather always attracted grandma-who-kept-her-name. The alleyway behind my apartment would fill up with passionflower vines. They bristled thick in the heat and strangled each other for fence space. Their rotting fruit accumulated in the alleyway behind my apartment, and I'd keep running into grandma-who-kept-her-name stirring the squashed fruit with her cane, poking through the sweet red pulp. Reading fortunes again.

"A war comes," she said to me without looking up. "A king is hanged. A scarcity of barley. You look thin, you should eat more." I ignored the last part. All of the grandmas thought I was too thin. I said, "Anything good?" I could see where dozens of passionflowers had been torn from their vines and thrown to the side, their stamens twisted out of shape. She said, "Nothing good in the flowers. Stock market tips. Unreliable." Their heavy gold pollen was smeared across the front of her blouse. She waved her cane to shoo away some seagulls edging inquisitively towards her pile of pulp.

I said, "I can't stay for long. I only came down this way because I'm meeting glam-grandma for brunch."

She nodded and pulled herself up with her cane. "She still gatecrashes brunches."

I shrugged a shoulder at her. There wasn't much to say to that.

Abruptly she was in front of me, pulling me close by the collar of my shirt. Her breath was disgustingly close to my face. "They'll kick her out forever. She'll wander the streets of the city till she drops from the heat and her heels tumble off her feet—"

She paused, pulled back, and spit to the side. She grinned. "But I'm only guessing. Let's know for sure."

She tore a passionfruit off a vine and smashed it against the tarmac. She pounded it with her cane and peered into the seedy mess. "She'll travel. She'll be successful. She'll find love in strange places. She'll write a screenplay but no one will read it. Even so, they'll toast her name and toss back champagne like it's New Year's Eve for the last time."

I laughed. "You should write for fortune cookies."

She grabbed a passionfruit and threw it in my face. "I didn't keep my name to put up with your flippancy." She began to make her way slowly down the alleyway. She called without turning her head, "Just for that, I'll see you in two months. No, four months. Longer, maybe. I'm not sure yet. It can be fun to sulk." Her cane swung right, swung left, tapped echoes into the street. I believed, for just a moment, that she'd been blind all along.

But then a seagull flew too close and quick as a whip she smacked it sideways with her cane.

* * *

Still, as I sprinted for my life out of a Hollywood Hills gated community, I couldn't help but feel a little doubt. Behind us, the baying of dogs was getting louder. "Shit," screamed glam-grandma into my ear, "they've got Dobermans! Toss the salami!"

I threw my handful of catered meat into the air. The salami discs sailed over my shoulder, and the barking broke off for just a moment. That was all the time we needed for glam-grandma to pull open the doors of her white Volkswagen and shove the key into the ignition. I leaped into my seat, and before I could even close the door, she kicked her foot against the gas pedal. The engine burst into life, and we shot down the road.

To me, the escapes were half the fun. When we came to a red light, glam-grandma tossed a cigarette into the air and caught it in her mouth, like a peanut. She lit up. "So," she said, adjusting the padding in her bra, "I hear there's a brunch happening at the Beverly Hilton right now. Want to give that one a try?"

If Sophocles had written a tragedy called *glam-grandma*, it would be analyzed by high school students for homework. They would be asked by their teachers to identify glam-grandma's tragic flaw, and the popular answer would be: She desired too desperately a place among the old ladies who brunch. After some consideration, I decided such a goal was noble and right for a grandma who lived in Hollywood. And, even as I listened to her mumbled curses at other drivers as we sped downhill, I couldn't help but feel for her. We root for the underdog.

She parked the Volkswagen on a side street behind the Hilton and we walked through the parking lot, dodging shifty glances from the valets. "Bet you there's a brunch on the left," she said as we stepped into the pink marble lobby. "They tend to happen to the left of things, I've noticed."

It was like something a terrible gambler would say, like *Bet you it lands on eight, it always lands on eight,* but for once in her life she was right. We wandered through a crowd of bridesmaids inspecting a vast empty ballroom, and smelled the coffee and fresh bagels before we saw the propped-open doors.

We linked arms and strolled casually in.

Of course it was obvious that we didn't fit. Glam-grandma spent time on her makeup, but she could wash it off at night, and the ladies who brunched could tell. And there was also me: my hair was too short. I wasn't the only grandson there, and this was the summer when the Hollywood fashion for teenage boys was these styled nests of hair, with bangs that swung into your eyes. So all the other boys had their hair done up in dutiful nests. If it had been up to glam-grandma, I am sure my hair would have looked just like that, highlights and all. But grandma-from-Leningrad had gotten to it first. She'd taken me to an old Russian man who cut hair in his building's parking garage, and he'd cropped it short with an electric razor for five dollars. That was the problem with having nine adoptive grandmothers. Their agendas sometimes worked at cross-purposes.

Glam-grandma sat herself down at a half-empty table by the door, and I quickly got up and went to look at the croissants. It embarrassed me a little to hear the things she would say. *Well I probably look familiar because of that film I did in the seventies. It was such a hit...* I focused on the croissants. They gleamed like parquet, stiff with polish and gloss. Hollywood croissants. Glam-grandma's spiel floated over the roomful of chatter. *You wouldn't believe the letters I got from fans. Some of them were really quite naughty....* I brought my hand close to the bagels. They were fresh from the ovens. I could feel their heat without touching them.

In the end I chose the medallion-sized quiches. Miniature food is hard to resist.

When I returned to the table, the conversation had progressed to the part where one of the ladies shifted her posture, her empty espresso cup dangling from one finger, and she stared at glam-grandma, waiting for her to stutter and run out of things to say. It would be another minute, I figured, and then we'd have to run. I looked for the platter of cold-cuts. There it was, at the other end of the room. I was already half out of my chair, preparing to load up on salami, when I noticed that the chatter was fading away. All the ladies in the room were turning their heads towards the door. Glam-grandma stopped talking and sat unmoving for a moment. Then she turned to look as well.

I watched the ladies' mouths. They were shriveling up like sea anemones poked with a finger.

An elderly woman had entered the room. She was all in green. Emeralds and diamonds dug into her neck, into her wrists, descended in points from the lobes of her ears. Her dress stunned me. Even I could tell it was too much. Green circles of fabric were layered like the scales of an artichoke, their ends curling up and pointing to the chandeliers. Each scale shivered in delight from every movement the woman made.

The ladies who brunched did not say anything. They did not need to. Already the dress was disintegrating in front of their eyes. The leaves of the dress were jerking out of their seams in a rustling flurry, collecting into a suspended cloud. Her gems flared and flickered and died. Her shoulder pads wrinkled and shriveled away. She continued walking through the room as if nothing was happening, accompanied only by the rat-tat-tat of a thousand snappings of threads. She stepped out of the cloud of green and left it behind her, frozen perfectly in the air. You could see the affectionate furrows wrinkling her breasts. Her mascara was painted in savage lines that jutted from her eyelids. Her mouth was darkly red with paint. She went calmly, nudely to get herself a plate.

The mouths of the old ladies unshriveled themselves. If there was a test, she had passed. They turned back to their tables and a murmur of conversation once more filled the room. A custodian brought in fresh pots of coffee. The green cloud moved out the door leaf by leaf, very slowly. It had turned into money. Money blowing out the door.

Something like this had happened at a brunch two months ago—a little boy pointing at a lady, her dress dissolving into frothing sprays of sea foam that dripped all over the carpet. Or, the brunch some weeks before that, when a lady had laughed too loudly—her dress flying off her body like a startled bird, leaping through the window and cavorting into the sky—she was left in nothing but her lipstick and crocodile heels. The ladies who brunched were, I learned, prone to sudden disintegration.

After the excitement of the dress, the ladies forgot we were at their table. They talked over our heads as if we weren't there. Glam-grandma pretended it didn't matter to her, but kept shooting hurt little looks over her shoulder. She took her time finishing her croissant, fussing with the butter, dipping the end into her coffee. Finally she could put it off no longer. She dabbed at her mouth with a napkin and rose to leave. I rose with her. As we passed the still-disintegrating cloud of green, she reached out, plucked a few bills and stuck them in her purse. She murmured, "Always nice to have a little help with the bills."

We linked arms and strolled casually out.

* * *

Glam-grandma liked to take me to the Hollywood Bowl on Tuesdays for the evening performances. I always got home late, and my mother didn't like that. I said, "She's a responsible adult and it's educational and eleven-thirty isn't really that late anyway."

My mother said, "But don't you think you should maybe be hanging out with friends your age?"

"Look," I told her. "You and dad didn't leave me any grandmas, so I've had to go and find some of my own. I'm just trying to be a good grandson, is that such a problem?"

So off I went to the Hollywood Bowl to listen to an orchestra butchering Mozart. "This might not be the best introduction to classical music," said glam-grandma as she tossed popcorn into her mouth, "but goddamn it if I don't find this entertaining." I suppose that if you've listened to beautiful Mozart concertos all your life, hearing it done horribly can be diverting.

According to glam-grandma, the Hollywood Bowl was a terrible place to go if you cared about the music. Nearly one hundred years ago, it had been a natural amphitheater: a bowl-shaped valley with angelic acoustics. No one had needed amplification. People had sat on benches, or on the grass, and enjoyed outdoor performances in the sun. The atmosphere had been like a picnic.

The atmosphere was still like a picnic, and it was still outdoors. But the bowl had become the Bowl. The stage was ensconced in an iconic hemispherical shell made of increasingly large white arches: This was the Bowl that had gradually erased the bowl from memory, so now most people thought the shell was where the name had come from in the first place. The seating had expanded to nearly eighteen-thousand seats. It was the largest amphitheater in the country. Everything was amplified because you could barely hear the stage anymore. I knew this to be true because of the night when the power went out, just for a few seconds, but in those seconds I'd struggled to make out the orchestra scraping furiously away below. Big screens hung from the tips of the white shell and broadcast close-up shots of the performers. Only the closest seats could see them on the stage as anything but blurs.

Glam-grandma and I brought along our usual basket loaded with wine, sandwiches, blankets, and binoculars. We bought the one-dollar tickets along with most everyone else and climbed up to the X-Y-Z benches. We waited till the show started. Then, the moment the lights went down, we in the top rows snatched up our things and darted down to the more expensive M-N-O benches far below. The ushers could care less about enforcing seating, and everything from M and up was always pretty empty. After all, it's hard to sell out eighteen-thousand seats every night.

Still, there were those who sat right up near the stage, dressed much finer than glam-grandma and I were, and certainly not wrapped in old blankets to keep off the evening chill. But the real luxuries were the boxes. They weren't as close to the stage, but they were proper boxes instead of wood-and-concrete benches that stretched unbroken for hundreds of feet. The boxes had little doors, and you could reserve them for a whole season, and you could specify a need for tables, or a pack of cards, or catering. You could tell when it was a clan of well-off retirees in the boxes because they chatted enthusiastically, laughing and dropping olives onto their tongues, pointing to things on each other's programs and waiting for their favorite part of a symphony that they knew half by heart.

Glam-grandma pulled her blanket tight around her shoulders and stared yearningly at a box we could just barely see, where four old ladies who brunched were toasting the fifth lady with baby bottles of Riesling while the timpani in the background pounded out a savage solo.

"One day," she shouted into my ear over the sudden trombones, "I'll be sitting in that box with them. They'll be toasting my birthday, but I'll deceive them about my age. So they'll be toasting to a lie. That's how you'll know that I've become one of them at last. What fun it will be! Now pay attention, that cellist is about to embarrass herself."

But the cellist must have done something right because glam-grandma raised her eyebrows and made no comment, just took a bite out of her chocolate bar instead. I threw my head back and stared up at the sky and listened to the song of the cello. I could barely see any stars from all the surrounding lights. Not too far away, a helicopter vibrated its way through the night and I could hear its thrum growing over our cauldronful of music. I tried to make out the color of the helicopter, but whether it was helicopter-grandma or just an ordinary helicopter, I wasn't able to tell.

* * *

There were things glam-grandma loved besides brunch. She loved the street signs in Burbank where, instead of letters, they just had the Warner Brothers logo and a distinguishing number. "Imagine living on that street! Oh, I know it's just a studio avenue pretending to be a street, but still, think about it. Anyone who sent you a letter would have to know how to draw."

Or: "I love the idea of Universal CityWalk. Someone took the path leading from *this* parking lot to *that* theme park, and they said, hey! Let's turn that walkway into a glamorous outdoor shopping mall!" And nowadays people came just for the CityWalk; it had drowned its origins so well. We went there sometimes during the day and listened to the huge advertising banners snapping in the wind. We strolled past shoppers and workers and the occasional living statues with hats laid at their feet. The shops were a frenzy of competitive advertising, trying to grab attention any way they could, and even the juice stand was having a go, with huge models of assorted fruit popping out of its roof, twice as large as the stand itself. Glam-grandma joked about it. "I pretend to myself it's a tribute to Carmen Miranda."

She loved the older movie theaters, especially the rude ones where the facade had fused with the theater, like Grauman's Chinese or the Egyptian. She called them rude because, in her words, they were giant insults to China and Egypt. They were some of the first of the Great Grand Movie

Palaces. They were precisely the color of their names. She'd chosen an apartment that was within walking distance from the theaters, so that on Friday nights she could take a little stroll and partake of their extravagance. Her apartment was just one block off Hollywood Boulevard, small and concrete and very cheap. No one wanted to live in the tourist traps.

Above all, she loved her white Volkswagen. Yes, she'd switched her cigarettes to Benson & Hedges because that was what they smoked at brunch; she'd changed her taste in heels, she'd changed her taste in wine, she'd given up her taste for aubergine tints in her hair. But the Volkswagen stayed. Her partner in crime for twenty years, it remained her greatest friend from the pre-Hollywood era. I believe that for a time she loved it more than brunch.

"There is nothing," she shouted over the wind pouring in from the windows as we sped down the 101 Freeway, "*nothing* like racing a truck on a three-lane freeway in a beat-up old Volkswagen." As she said this, the truck began to fall back at last and glam-grandma whooped and let up on the gas. I'd been clutching at my seatbelt the whole time. I had nothing to say in response.

"But something that's almost as good," she said as she pushed down the gas pedal once more and I resumed my hold on my seatbelt, "is navigating a truck tunnel in this car."

In front of us, two trucks drove placidly side by side, one in the lane to our right, one in the lane to our left. There were no cars in front of us, and glam-grandma shot down the middle lane, cigarette clamped firmly between her teeth. We were suddenly scarily in between the trucks. Their smoky bulk towered over our heads, and it was like a wind tunnel as we raced through. Old receipts whipped up past my ears and shot out the windows, and then we were abruptly past them, back on the open concrete of the freeway. I noticed that glam-grandma was minus the cigarette. It took me a moment to realize it had been snatched by the wind as well.

* * *

The white Volkswagen broke down on the Cahuenga pass, on our way to another brunch. Together we managed to push the car to the side of the canyon road and out of traffic's way. Then we stuck out our thumbs and hoped. I asked, "Is it all right to leave it on the side of the road? I mean, it might get towed."

After a long minute, she said, "I can't miss brunch."

Some moments later, a blue Corolla slowed to a stop, and I smiled until the window rolled down and I realized we were being rescued by a lady who brunched. She pushed her sunglasses into her hair and said, "Where to?"

"Oakwood Apartments," said glam-grandma, already opening the passenger door and inviting herself in, "I'm trying to get there in time for brunch."

"Oakwood!" The woman tipped her sunglasses back over her eyes as we drove. "Do you live there too? I've never seen you before!"

"Oh, no, I was invited. You know. Friend-of-a-friend sort of thing."

"Sure, I know how it is. Well, I hope you like our place. It's a bit small, but it's home."

Oakwood Apartments, as we discovered, had a security gate and contained mounds and mounds of little hills dotted with tasteful condominiums. As we drove through its winding roads, our lady who brunched told us she lived in Neil Patrick Harris's former apartment. Before that, she'd been in Queen Latifah's old rooms, but she'd had to move. Her neighbors had been Disney Channel extras, and they were just too young and rowdy for her sleeping schedule.

There was a tense moment when our lady forgot whether the brunch was held at the south clubhouse or the north clubhouse. "Which one?" she asked glam-grandma, who said "Hmmmm?" and pretended she'd gone temporarily deaf, but then our lady remembered anyway. She parked the car, and we leaped out and hurried towards the double glass doors of the clubhouse before she could ask us any more questions.

As we sat at yet another round table with yet another plate of gleaming croissants, I wondered why it was always Sunday brunch. Briefly I toyed with the idea that the ladies who churched had been transformed into the ladies who brunched through contact with the desert air. According to grandma-from-Leningrad, when the Soviet government had deleted religion, people had found all sorts of odds and ends to take its place. I watched the ladies watching each other as they poured themselves glasses of grapefruit juice. It didn't *seem* very religious. The air conditioner was cranking cold air out of the vents, but some of the windows were open anyway to let in a fresh breeze. I could see the seagulls strutting by the pool.

As it turned out, there was a talent show planned for the younger generation. The custodians had set up a stage by the pool, and I was treated to the sight of a dozen long-haired girls and nest-haired boys playing piano and singing in wobbling voices. The talent show was a boon in the end, because it kept the ladies from noticing that glam-grandma and I did not belong. Instead they craned their necks to see whose grandkid was singing what, each waiting for her turn to smile at us and tell us about all the things they'd accomplished in his life so far. Then, when her grandkid was done and would wander up for a dutiful kiss, she would pull them into a hug and whisper things into their ear.

Glam-grandma whispered into my ear, "You're more talented than any of them. Smarter, too. I know you'll do what it takes to make me proud. Don't you ever forget that." It unnerved me how convincing she sounded. She leaned back, smiling like a judge, like one of the old
ladies who brunched. For the first time it worried me that this was her ambition.

And then suddenly everyone was gone. The stage was empty, the tables were deserted. They'd all left for the other clubhouse, for post-performance celebrations, or maybe brunch number two. It had happened so quickly that glam-grandma hadn't noticed which direction they went. So we stumbled out of the clubhouse into the afternoon heat and hiked up and down the hilly roads of the Oakwood Apartments. We searched the tarmac for a trail of bagel crumbs to lead us along, but it was just like the fairy tale; the seagulls must have eaten them all. A security guard approached us. His questions were polite but he did not smile, and I knew this was it. Glam-grandma got flustered and waved her hands around. It did no good. He led us kindly but firmly to the exit. It was the nicest eviction we'd ever had.

We found ourselves standing on the empty highway of Barham Road. Glam-grandma stayed there for a moment, staring at her heels, not saying anything. Then she patted me on my shoulder and on we walked, the opposite way we'd come, baking in the sun all the way to the Volkswagen waiting for us on Cahuenga.

* * *

When I think back, I try to track the moment she became an old lady who brunched. At last she achieved her heart's desire. But it's hard to pin down the exact instant of transmutation. The best I could do was track a period of several weeks when I really should have seen it coming.

We drove in a lime-green Chevy, soaring down the 5. The Volkswagen had disappeared, sold to the junkyard to finance the new car. Maybe this was the first sign. Or perhaps it had been the moment she'd whispered to me in a voice so unlike her own that I was better than all the rest. Or, maybe, the moment she'd had to choose between the Volkswagen and the brunch. And she chose brunch.

She'd been unusually silent the whole car ride, her eyes fixed on the road. I'd been relaxing in the Chevy's comfortable seats until I spotted two trucks ahead of us. I grabbed onto my seatbelt. Glam-grandma grinned and kicked her foot onto the gas pedal and we were accelerating once more, heading for the truck tunnel, the wind screaming in our ears.

And then we were inside, and the trucks were roaring and I noticed the way glam-grandma's dress was whipping away into silver clouds of tobacco smoke from the wind, the way the cotton wrap around her neck unrolled into crumbled old receipts and shot straight into the air. Her hair untangled itself from its plait and snapped free in a Medusa-like frenzy and we emerged from the truck tunnel. All that was left of her was her body and its make-up, the carefully painted strokes of red and black, the stamps of pink on her cheeks. The body turned to me and smiled and said, like someone commenting on a former childhood pleasure, "Well. That was pretty fun."

And I knew it was the end. She would be evicted no more. This brunch, she would fool them. The act had become real. They would get her phone number. She'd get calls on Tuesday nights asking her to join them in their boxes at the Hollywood Bowl. I wouldn't be invited. She'd be too busy to call me anymore, and she'd have a new grandson too. He'd live in Zac Efron's former apartment. He'd have really nice white teeth and puffy lime-green sneakers to match her car. And though her body would still be there, driving and brunching, glam-grandma was gone forever, I knew.

I ask you, how could I not be happy for her? These things happen. People get what they want, and we have to sigh and move on.

The Singing Soldier

Natalia Theodoridou

First

When Lilia came into her parents' bedroom one night, eyes sleepy and tin soldier firmly clasped in her little hands, complaining that his singing wouldn't let her sleep, her Ma thought she'd had a nightmare. She pried the soldier from her daughter's fingers, placed him on a high shelf in the closet, and locked the door. Then, she motioned towards Lilia's sleeping father and let the girl slip under the covers between the two of them.

In the morning, Lilia seemed to have forgotten all about the toy soldier. Asked where she'd found him, she simply looked at her Ma with watery eyes. "I dreamt of someone sad," she said.

"Who, my love?" her mother asked. "Who did you dream about?" But the girl wouldn't say.

The next night, Ma woke to the muffled sound of the soldier's singing. She got out of bed, and by moonlight unlocked the closet, cracking the door open just a tiny bit. The singing spilled out clear and warm and sorrowful, in a language she could not understand. The sound made something inside her chest tighten, but she wasn't frightened. She opened the closet door wider and took the singing soldier in her hand. "What a curious, curious thing you are," she whispered.

She drew the window curtains and held the soldier up to the light. The song poured out of his parted lips, but the rest of him was lifeless: his eyes empty, frozen wide; his body stiff and cold, right foot on a boulder, right hand closed around a tiny bayonet. She wrapped him in a blanket, put him back in the closet, and went to sleep, lulled by the heavy breathing of her husband. That night, her dreams were filled with images of a faraway but oddly familiar land. There was a smoking chimney—or was it a whole house on fire? A frozen lake. Men dancing—or were they marching? Were these knives or roses between their teeth? A foreign bride showered in flowers.

She told her husband about the singing soldier the next morning while he was getting ready for the fields, still heavy with sleep. He laughed it off and so she said: "I'll show you." She took the soldier out of the closet and unwrapped the blanket tenderly, as if presenting her husband with a rare gift. Pa looked at the silent soldier with narrowed eyes—*and do they look a bit alike,* Ma thought, *with the dark moustache, the handsome curve of the shoulders?* She placed the soldier in his open palm. He weighed the soldier, then ran his finger over the tiny weapon, the tiny beret, the tiny boots.

"You dreamt it," Pa said, but there was fear in his eye, and so he locked the soldier in a wooden coffer, and took the coffer out to a clearing in the forest for good measure.

On the third night, the soldier's solemn song traveled back to the house, poking holes into their dreams with his tiny bayonet. Pa got out of bed, put on his boots, and walked into the forest, moonlight guiding him through the narrow paths and tall trees. The crickets fell silent at the sound of the soldier's somber voice. Pa found the coffer and put it carefully under his arm. He brought it back to the house and, resigned to the oddness of the world, put the singing soldier on the mantelpiece.

"It is a miracle," Pa said. "It is good fortune."

* * *

Then

Lilia and Pa worked the land from dawn 'til dusk while Ma labored in the big house. She cleaned and cooked and scrubbed, and fussed in the yard with the chickens and the goats. She loved the big house. She loved every stair, every wall, every plank of the floor. And she loved the yard, the chickens, the goats, the warm, yellow days and the green, green grass.

Sometimes, while drying a porcelain plate or polishing one of her mother's bronze pots, Ma would think back on the place she lived when she was little—the motherland, the fatherland—before she got married and moved to this new land she now loved. The tall skies, the flowering trees, all so far away from her now, receding in the trenches of her life. Often, these thoughts made her wonder where the tin soldier might be from, how he ended up in her daughter's sleepy hands, singing his sad, unknowable songs every dusk. But then a neighbor would stop by with a request for aniseed or eggs, or with news of aggressions near the borders—*borders*, she'd think then, *what a concept!*—and her thoughts of lost lands would scatter, and she would forget.

With the day's work done, with tired bones and aching backs, but somehow satisfied with all that, the whole family would gather around the fireplace and listen to the soldier's melancholy tune. Ma would thumb her mother's necklace and think about the orchard in the house she'd left behind, the father's house. And the soldier would sing all night long, never tiring, never pausing. They still didn't understand the language, but, in time, they started picking up clusters of syllables and filling them with meaning of their own. There was "mountain" and "promise" and "come back." Soon, they made up stories about the soldier's origin: a broken homeland, a forgotten lover, a friendship lost to war.

* * *

In the end

When the conquerors came from their foreign land beyond the border, the family thought these men spoke the singing soldier's tongue—and did they look a bit alike, with the hue of their skin, the handsome curls, the delicate length of their fingers? *How strange, the ways of the world.*

They didn't know what the conquerors were saying, but eventually learned to understand them well enough. They picked up: "papers" and "ancestors" and "this land." This land, what? Pa wondered. Surely, the conquerors meant this land was theirs, that it had always been theirs. But how could land belong to anyone?

They were allowed to stay in the house for a while, made to work the land on the conquerors' behalf. Pa and Lilia ploughed the fields and planted the seed and then waited and waited, watching the rain fall from the shallow skies, mending their tools and rewelding their broken ploughs, and later they harvested the conquerors' crops just as they used to their own before. But Pa would pause every now and then, dry his forehead with his sleeve or push his fingers against his closed eyes and say: "It's not the same working under someone's boot." And then he wouldn't speak for hours.

Ma suffered from the dreaming sickness she'd had as a child, but which had gone away after she'd gotten married. She would dream with her eyes wide open for days on end, the life in her eyes flickering, now bright, now dim. When she finally woke up, she would tell them about the places she'd been to in her dreams: a lake so small you could empty it out with a teaspoon; a ship stranded in the desert; pubescent girls scattering feathers out of moving trains; a milk so sweet it drove men mad.

Soon, the conquerors moved them out of the big house and into the small shed in the yard. Pa put the tin soldier on a shelf above the stove and again they gathered around every evening, huddled close after a long day's work. Lilia would translate the fragments she understood. "Honey," the soldier's songs said, and "red, red poppies," and "this land."

The soldier never stopped filling their nights with singing. Not as Lilia grew thin and then thinner, not as Ma fell into her dreams for longer and longer, until the life in her eyes flickered one night and was extinguished the next. They buried her in the clearing where Pa had left the soldier's coffer, all that time ago, in a previous life.

After Ma died, Pa and Lilia were finally driven from the land they used to love as if it were their own. Lilia took her father by the hand and squeezed it as he looked back onto the fields, the trees, the big house. "It's land," she said, and then waved her arm towards the forest and the hills that lay beyond it, and at the yellow sky above it all. "It's only land."

They took with them the coffer, filled with a handful of things: Ma's necklace, their papers, the tin soldier, a steel knife, a smuggled pistol, an extra pair of boots. They lived in the woods for some time, on beds of soft green, under the paling light of the stars. And the soldier, the soldier sang them to sleep every night. His songs said: "Lakes," and "pianos," and "roses made of tin."

When a group of conquering men descended on Pa early one morning, shouting and gesturing with the tips of their bayonets, Lilia hid in the forest. She thought the men came to take away the coffer that held her family's last possessions, but they were not interested in that. She watched as the men strung her father up a tree until he stopped fighting and all the light went out, and all she could think was: *What a curious, curious thing men are.* After the men went away, Lilia came out of her hiding, hugged the coffer tight, and fell asleep under the soles of her father's feet.

When she woke in the dark, all the stars gone out and her father's feet in the sky, she struck the ground with her fists until she bled and cold soil stuck to her knuckles. Then, she built a fire. She used her family's papers as kindling, wrapped Ma's necklace around her left wrist, threw her old boots away and put on the new. Last, she fed the wooden coffer to the flames. When the embers shone bright and red, Lilia hid the soldier in her palm and held him close to her heart. Then, she melted the soldier on the knife's blade over the blazing embers, fashioned him into a bullet using a crude clay mold, and loaded him into her pistol.

"You will kill the next man I see," she told the bullet.

Before meeting the next man's chest, the bullet sang. "This land," it said. "This land, this land."

Only Their Shining Beauty Was Left

Fran Wilde

Cloud Forest

On her second day studying in the Monteverde, Arminae Ganit stared at damp sky framed by beech leaves and fiddleheads and wished she could photosynthesize. She touched fingertips to the thick loam at her feet. Moist air slicked her cheeks and dampened her t-shirt so her pack's straps rubbed at the skin beneath. The forest's shifting clouds dappled Arminae's hands dark and light. She imagined her fingers exuding roots; her hair, fruit and leaves.

"*Very* unscientific," she scolded under her breath. Her father, a poet, might have appreciated the thought, but Arminae aspired to science, was already training her mind away from myth, toward analysis and exacting data. Still, she smiled to think of this particular transformation's direct benefits: To not need to crouch to pee while most other students on this research trip stood and marked the leaves; to become impervious to the damp; to not hear colleagues chewing their dinner, grinding meat with their molars. To acquire skin that abraded her classmate's touch—a hand on a shoulder, nothing meant by it, an accident—or that trapped his fingers in unyielding wood.

Laughter nearby broke her reverie. "I'm serious," a young man said, punching the arm of his friend. "Gray warts all over his skin, looked like an Ent or something. Gross. Like an allergic reaction."

The sound of a thin waterfall struck the undergrowth.

"That's not what I heard." The other laughed. "I heard he got it from a girl."

When they were gone, Arminae rose, brushing dirt from her fingers as if they'd never be clean. She placed a palm against the beech beside her. Skin like bark; got it from a girl. Rumors and myth, not data.

Arminae pulled a notebook and pencil from her bag and began sketching. She ignored the boys; traced the structure of bark and leaf, the web of connections. She wrote *oxygen, carbon,* and *hydrogen* below then sketched the tree's three elements, the chemical makeup—not elements like sun and rain and wind. She committed the beech to line and memory instead of rumor and myth.

Once back at her midwestern college, she dropped her mud-stained bag on her apartment floor and video-chatted her parents in London. *Learned so much. Very beautiful. Everyone was nice.* Her hands sketched carbon structures in the air instead of leaves. Far away, her father nodded, her mother listened. The distance between them contracted, and Arminae felt their happiness through the screen; was warmed.

Palisander

In a Northeastern university physics lab, enormous roots tore up the linoleum. A canopy of *Dalbergia nigra* blooms pressed against the ceiling, broke windows.

"I don't know whether to call an arborist or the police," the dean said. The janitor who'd found the tree shrugged and didn't respond. The dean kept talking. "Graduate students sometimes work very late, did no one see anything? This is an outlandish prank."

Rumors spread that it was more than a prank: a student worked so hard, they'd rooted to the spot; someone's experiment had gone gravely wrong; a seed, planted years ago, had sprouted in another dimension and grown into this one. Everyone would get an A for the semester.

Over the course of a week, most of the lab's students came to the doorway to see the extent of the foliage. Their professor filed a damage report and finally told the dean, "I caught a graduate student dozing here last week. He hasn't shown up for work since. He abandoned his notebooks. His research. He was … sensitive. But I do not see Him behind this." The professor gestured at the tree, and at the workmen cutting it from the floor.

The rosewood was valuable, even so.

* * *

Our woods were transformed into shelter and fuel.

Trees became houses and furnishings and the cardboard boxes that bore the furnishings to fill the houses, all stacked neatly where trees had once rooted. We began lopping trees at odd angles, splitting their crowns to give cables and networks safe passage.

Wires, streets, and intersections seamed the once wild hills. The valleys divided in neat grids filled with brown and gray boxes and colonial blue trim. The cardboard containers were delivered by 5:00 p.m. or earlier. It was orderly, tight. The very air could barely breathe.

The dreams started then. The tree-dreams, the vine dreams.

* * *

Laurel

What it took for Sam to turn into a laurel tree was a river dream.

Curled up on his futon, he'd been mulling differential equations and next week's midterm when his eyelids drooped. He pulled his duvet over his head while his roommates Benjor and David watched a fishing show at peak volume in the next room.

In Sam's dream, numbers glittered blue-white starlight over rushing water. Fish leapt and a river chuckled and echoed across the dream and Sam leaned into the beauty of it. His dream fingers reached up to the number-stars and his toes stretched rough and knobby until they rooted through the duvet with soft ripping sounds and crumbled the apartment's old plaster down to the slats and chicken wire.

He woke thirsty and stiff. Panic ran his limbs like a cold breeze.

There'd been years of rumors on the Internet, mostly debunked, then a few brief news clips from faraway places. Those came mostly on weekends, when no one paid attention. And once the photos of bark-skin men and that woman whose hair turned to vines got out? Proliferation: Garish images from safely distant rural locations accumulated beneath Sam's computer's placid screen.

But no one Sam knew had ever woken up as a tree.

He shivered when his bark sloughed in patches. At the memory of late-night dissection videos from those distant places; ones he'd viewed surreptitiously online, some nights. Last night too, for a moment.

Sam didn't want to be dissected.

To hide a laurel tree in a fourth-floor Boston walkup was nearly impossible. Sam's two roommates made jokes and threatened to use him for a gaming table, but they watered him. They told his teachers Sam had flu and they patched the wall with dirt.

* * *

Dreams used to spread like myth and rumor. Tendrils and smoke.

Now they rolled like streets moving out into the country. Long tongues of influence, leading permanence, like city lights seen from space, reaching in neat blocks for the dark.

A child dreamt of petals while his parents dreamt of roots. A pilot remembered where a mother planted rosemary. A whispered word became a month-long corridor of trunks, of soft bark, and starlit rivers.

"I dreamed that too," your lover said the morning after you mentioned the gnarled roots of your dream, which were all you could recall.

* * *

Rosewood

Arminae, after two years and a hundred calls home, delivered a thesis on flavonoids in cloud forests: *Ruellia Macrophylla* from South America, *Nothofagus Fusca* from New Zealand. Her parents knew Ovid and finance, myths and money, but still, she tried to sketch the structure, drawing a ladder in the air: *Twenty-one carbons, twenty-four hydrogens, ten oxygens*! She told them everything.

In the lab, she modeled carbon spines and cellular signaling. She kept her gaze on her faraway trees and the messages they hid in their cells. Still felt her skin prickle when her mentor passed by.

"I can recommend you," Dr. Vini said more than once, age-spotted palms flat on his old, rosewood desk. Then he turned his hands up, an invitation. Pink, lined skin, soft with paperwork. "But you must focus on our research." His focus, not hers: *Inosculation*: when plants grafted to one another, veins and roots signaling and tangling until they were one. More recently, if plants and other organisms might graft to humans.

Philemon old and poor / Saw Baucis flourish green with leaves, and Baucis saw likewise. Arminae remembered her father reciting Ovid at the dinner table, the wrath of gods denied turned on unkind villagers; the rewards for being kind. She wavered. Tried to break her choices into data. But her professor pressed. "What kind of scientist will you be?"

Her skin was not bark. Blood rushed anger and confusion to her cheeks. Her parents' pride fell away like petals onto water. She knew she could not pass this last test, but refused Vini's upturned palms anyway.

"I would rather," she began.

"I thought," she started again.

Already, he'd passed her their paper on paired trees and transplant research, where he was first author, Dr. Vini, and she, second, Dr. Ganit.

She set nothofagins and phenols aside, kept out of arm's reach, a constant state of flight. Her smile grew impervious. She published and wrote weekly notes to her parents to tell them of her studies, or her travels, ink spines of linked letters on pressed white leaves: *I am fine, I am doing well for myself. I am busy.* She rarely called.

She ignored the pale trees whispering beyond her lab window: birch, not beech. Touching the glass with gnarled fingers.

* * *

Myth passed from one generation to the next, shaping memory, uprooting knowledge. On a hillside, by an ancient temple, a linden and an oak intertwined their branches, but did not embrace; they *inosculated.*

A movie of trees with faces, with moss-hung beards. An army of trees rising up on the stage, in music. Our poets always knew these trunks and roots for more than furnishings.

* * *

Magnolia

Even Dr. Ganit's letters grew sparse—a few a year. She'd published more, become an expert, gained tenure far away; her small apartment at the end of the world filled up with papers and clippings. A clearing on her bedside table held their photo: the two who'd joined their cells to make her, holding hands. One night she dreamed them planted in the dirt of a cloud forest.

Her first call went unanswered. She left a message and, distracted, she let time pass before she tried again. Marked revisions on her first phenols paper since moving to the end of the world, replied to reviewer's questions. Called again. No response.

In a café near her Dunedin classroom, a wall-hung television blared, "An entire Melbourne neighborhood overrun by *Panicum effusum*—a tumbleweed—residents missing." The screen showed explorers in headlamps, plowing through a weed-filled house. Dr. Ganit sketched four carbon molecules on a napkin, the base structure of the weed. *If carbon dioxide can be transformed to organic material, can organic material be transformed too?*

"A house in Wales filled with nettles, owners disappeared," the television replied. A headline ticker flashed news of trees growing from apartment windows in London.

Ganit booked flights from Dunedin to Auckland, then home to London. *I am fine. It is cold here, and gray, but the plants are wonderful*, she'd written once.

Tired and gritty from the transit, she pushed the door of her parents' flat open, pressing hard. The apartment windows had been shut tight, and the steaming air was thick with the sweet scent of blooms. Of plants gone weeks without water, without a phone call—

—until she'd finally found the time

—and the call had never connected

—and she'd flown.

Her parents' weight, spun together into a double-trunked magnolia, blocked her entry.

She begged them wake, squeezing through the gap, hands pleading, pressing, like a fault-filled god in a myth, until the ambulance came.

"Can't fit trees." The attendants shook their heads. Removed their gloves. One touched her shoulder. "They're beautiful like that, at least. Egg magnolia. Rare in this climate. There are worse ways to go."

Broad petals of cream-colored flowers had darkened and fallen long before she arrived. Curled now, yellowed like wood shavings, collapsing to sawdust.

Tears streaked her face, the top of her collared shirt, soaking the cotton dark blue in patches.

She yelled until the attendants left and the landlord came with an axe.

* * *

/What kind of tree would you be?/ one friend asked another in a chat window. Glowing square on a lit screen. The real sunset pressed its face against the glass in reverse.

/ A Baobab/ typed the other in darkness. It was midnight, there.

/A Maple/ typed the first.

They traded emoji that didn't look like either kind of tree. They smiled together, across the night's distances.

* * *

Rose

When Eleni slept as a child, she'd dreamt of flying, or sailing, until one time she dreamt a blackberry bush fruited with eyes, picked at by birds.

After that, she ran every day until she fell, exhausted, into bed, and slept dreamlessly. An adult now, she ran ten miles daily with her spouse.

She ran from her shadow. She ran right out of her skin sometimes.

"I am tired," she said, "I don't want to fear my heartbeat, my dreaming cells, my bones." She rubbed her skin soft and braided her shower-damp hair down her back, then turned to find her spouse snoring.

Months later, in the maternity ward, she fell asleep nursing. Her new baby, unfamiliar and squalling like a gull. They dreamed the same milk-dreams, Eleni knew, because she saw the baby in them, blooming. When Eleni woke, she was a rose-strung hedge, and filled the room. The doctors had to cut the thorns away to get the baby out.

* * *

Before the dreams began, there was art and myth, Arminae's father said. Nymphs turned to laurel and poplar in exquisite refusals. Kind Baucis and Philemon became twined oak and linden.

Now, not one dreamer ever turned back. Hair hardened into knots and whorls. A few kept their mouths, their eyes.

/It doesn't hurt/ Sam blinked in Morse while Benjor carved their initials in his trunk. /I can hear others. There's a network between sky and ground. They whisper yes. They say come./

* * *

Swamp Maple

When Sam's roommates left for Thanksgiving, they turned the humidifier full blast. They'd been dreaming for days about streams and the smell of loam. Couldn't wait to get away from the crawling roots, the quiet rustling. Their grades had suffered.

Benjor headed south, to his grandparents, eleven hours on the interstate. He slept on the bus, a rolling dream of networks and circuits, exams and summer jobs in Silicon Valley or DC. When sunrise broke over the Blue Ridge, gilding the black hillsides, swamp maple roots ran the length of the coach and pushed greedily into the water tank.

David drove north all night, a 64-ounce Big Gulp sweating caffeine between his knees as he peered into the darkness. He reached the border awake and shaky as hell.

* * *

Hypotheses? A call went out. Dr. Ganit had plenty of research and data. She sent messages flying, sketched theories. From the end of the world, she caught her mentor's notice again. She pictured inorganic carbons transforming like myths, like nymphs.

"I extrapolate from the evidence that pheromones may be triggering some commonality long dormant in our DNA," she told an emergency committee broken into squares on her laptop screen. "We're not too distant relatives from plants. Our cells signal, too. Bananas, for instance—though no one's turned into one of those yet, have they?"

Dr. Vini, who led the call, ground his teeth. "It only seems like they're turning. It could be fungal."

She heard him ramping up an argument for drawing her back into the lab. Didn't wait for it. "We'll need to do tests. Set protocols. There's a rational explanation. I'll work with you." Saw him smile.

* * *

Sara and Bell

They'd run away one night while Bell's parents watched a show, the screen glowing blue like a storm in a box. They'd run across the lawn and into the thin stretch of woods across the street and deliberately curled up below the last of the oak trees. They'd uncapped the Thermos of chamomile. They'd pulled Bell's old wool blanket up around them and slipped from their clothes. The air had touched their skin and puckered it. The tea was warm on their lips. They'd whispered the things they'd said a thousand times to each other in their minds, always and never and forever. They'd slept in one another's arms and when Bell woke to sunrise, Sara wound over Bell's limbs and covered Bell's mouth in creeper and Bell couldn't fight for long. Sara hadn't meant to grow so fast, bind so tight. She hadn't meant it.

* * *

A Bee-Loud Glade

Dr. Ganit, in her lab at midnight, pushed "record," retreated beyond the video screen and lay down on the Army cot.

No blanket.

Her mentor scowled remotely. "I'll keep watch too," he'd said. He liked to watch.

The timer ran as the scientist slept, a blinking red dot, two white colons, six digits in constant change. Sun filled Dr. Ganit's small room after seven hours, five minutes, thirty-two seconds.

Her clock radio began to spell the news, each word in the perfect flesh of her ears an announcement that she'd failed to dream. Failed to change.

She felt the pull of her parents like longing; deep roots, or the spaces where roots had once been. She feared the dreams, but wanted to dream of them. She couldn't remember their voices.

Her mentor, overnight, had grafted with the frame of his chair: mahogany over birch frame. Arminae did not want to guess at his dreams.

The news sounded panic; in a capital city, a vice president had become a stand of cornstalks, harvest-ready. An Italian soprano, a glade trapped beneath the deciduous tenor she'd lately been screwing, buzzing with bees.

Dr. Ganit flew to Bethesda, to the military's best hospital, egg magnolia cuttings in her carry-on. She would help find a cure for dreaming if she couldn't find one for trees.

* * *

Everywhere, dreamers turned, if they were lucky, to plants that fit their containers: the houses, apartments, and parked cars where they'd slept; to trees that broke hulls in motion if they were not.

People drank gallons of coffee in a bid to outrun sleep. Strained to keep moving. Collapsed and died from exhaustion, or slept and dreamed and changed.

One in a million, the scientists said. One in a thousand. Desperate parents pinched children awake. There was no cause. Drinking wine could stave it off. Drinking wine sped the process. One in a hundred.

Not one dreamer turned back; they stayed tree and vine, rock and hill.

* * *

Cuttings

Dr. Ganit moved Eleni and Sam and others like them to the NIH facility near Fort Meade. All concrete, with long windowed rooms edged with grow-lights, ringed with barbed wire.

A fleet of landscaping trucks threaded the highway. Homes and apartments receded. Some reached for their families with rustling leaves, saw segments of themselves put on slides, lit up on screens, pressed between pages of medical dictionaries.

She worked around the clock—no time for interviews. No dreams of photosynthesis permitted, transformation merely a structure, a dataset. The world depended on science. On Ganit finding the right question, and then the answer.

* * *

A dream of smoke. A dream of sun's rays breaking through cloud to touch skin. A dream of snakes. Of a birthday. Of running and roots.

The news gave over to readings: children's stories, poems, mythology, the Bible. The news played recordings from the London Symphony, the Beijing Philharmonic. Nothing live.

The woodwinds echoed.

* * *

The Forest

A crowd waited outside Fort Meade's boundary. They'd come, crazed with sleep-deprivation, hyped up on sugar, caffeine, and what amphetamines they could steal from the branch-tunneled hospitals. They came for answers, for a word with a scientist.

Dr. Ganit begged them to go away. She couldn't think amidst their screams at night, however distant. At the thought of so many awake, for so long.

She tried distilling stronger pheromones. Injecting RNA drawn from her samples. She could remember the edges of dreams pulling at her, once, but nothing came for her now.

After a week of restless, dreamless sleep amidst the noise, Dr. Ganit woke to silence. Outside, a new forest, pressed against the barbed wire, reached for the concrete.

A few stragglers wandered among the trees, but Dr. Ganit didn't go to them. She watched from the windows, until the stragglers, too, lay down.

She watched them dream, but couldn't follow.

* * *

Grapevine

Dr. Ganit looked through her computer to other labs as her peers fell one by one. Their skin pulsed taut, then rough; trails of moss ran green veins from fingertip to neck; hair twisted with vines. She watched them turn to sedum; to rhododendron; to a willow beautifully gripping a cot.

She took more samples from the gardens that accumulated. Oak. Grapevine. She turned down the water to drive her living plants into stasis. Hoped that would buy time; hold the changes at bay.

* * *

Some days, careful listeners could hear whispers in the trees. A chuckle as a house uprooted and the branches within rose to the sky.

* * *

Creeper

After months, Dr. Ganit began speaking to the plants surrounding her like patients. None but the rose hedge listened much; they'd long since ceased answering her.

She only talked theories, cures. Never the right questions. Dr. Ganit tried playing music. Classical. Rock. What remained of the news. In distant places chants of food riots.

She tried ignoring the plants, too. *Not very scientific.* They ignored her right back.

The plants waved tendrils, sent out slow shoots, to no notice. One—a still-fast creeper vine, despite the water shortage—tore angry holes in the speakers late one night. The music—classical, by Benjamin Britten—stopped.

In the silence, Dr. Ganit sometimes imagined her father's voice, almost taunting: *Apollo clasped the branches as if they were parts of human arms, and kissed the wood. But even the wood shrank from his kisses.*

Her skin grayed, but didn't patch over with bark. No vines grew in her hair. She replayed bad movies and ate strange food—the ration tins left open, the stale water—and slept like a beggar before the magnolia cuttings on her desk as dreams avoided her.

* * *

The cameras, left on, captured changes before the vines took their lenses. Anyone could view the live shots, direct-to-web. Anyone with eyes to see. Ears to hear.

Until there was nothing to cure.

* * *

Root and Carpel

After six months, Dr. Ganit forgot and left the grow lights on around the clock, let the fertilizer spill on the floor. Science had no answers and the elusive dreams were their own cure. The world was verdant and getting more so and that was that.

She wrapped herself in blankets and laid her cheek on the cuttings from London. She whispered 'Where did you go?'

Her parents' whispers echoed in her ears. *So proud. So kind.* She remembered their faces, finally, their encouragements. She remembered their dreams for her, her dreams for herself. Arminae closed her eyes.

She dreamed of magnolia carpels, ancient and sleeping; she dreamed of magnolia roots, rolling over floors and doorways. Through the lab window, smoke. The skylights turned dark, the grow-lights stayed on.

* * *

Breakthrough

Outside, vines tapped at the facility windows, pressed through foundation walls. Inside, tendrils spread across the form in the lab coat, a trunk, sprouting leaves and, from one pocket, a cluster of daylilies, tubers digging at the cold cement floor.

The lab's watering system dripped and broke. Indoors, it rained.

The trees awoke and Eleni stretched her branches to the lab's edges. Memories leached from her as she grew again, dreaming awake this time—a kiss became new buds; the soft spot on her baby's skull and the smell of it, a cluster of rosebuds. Everything beyond the walls pulled at her, drawing her out. The hedge reached a window pane, tapping, then scraping at it. Pried the sill and stretched. Beyond the grate, seeds caught breeze and lifted, scattered.

The creeper pushed past and through rose thorns and was gone. Rude as ever, angrier too.

The laurel waited for the birds to come and pick its drupes clean. Magnolia pollen and petals clouded the breeze.

They were a river of roots, a star-dream, a rose hedge, magnolia blooms, grown beyond fear. A myth told to no one; vines wove through emerging orchards where fruit trees embraced sturdy ornamentals. Bushes sprouted from cardboard boxes, trees from furniture, and whole forests crowned over houses and factories. Roots and vines ungirded the hillsides and fell through the cracks in bare roadways, and everything escaped, until there was green, everywhere, green.

SHADOW BOY

Lora Gray

I am sixteen and sitting on the edge of an empty subway platform when Peter, forever small, reappears. His black eyes are bright, and he smells like licorice and cinnamon. He is wearing purple mittens and a pigeon-feather skirt.

"Who the hell dressed you today?" I ask.

"I did." Peter tips his head as if considering. "My taste is terrible. Tragic, really, but I didn't have much choice."

"Everybody has a choice."

"Do they, dear Prudence?"

"Don't call me Prudence." Tugging my jeans more snugly around my hips, I shift. Chains rattle over the metal platform, and a safety pin fingernails across the yellow line at the edge.

"It's your name."

"Nobody calls me that anymore." I tap a cigarette out of my pocket. It takes me three tries to light up.

"I call you that," he says.

"You don't count." I drag and exhale into Peter's face.

Peter doesn't cough. "Feeling sullen?"

"I'm lonely." I grit my teeth and shrug.

"How can you be lonely?" he asks. "You and me, we have a whole city to play with." He kicks his legs back and forth, heels denting the platform gleefully. Thump. THUMP. A grin stretches his mouth wide.

My skin prickles and I feel the familiar lurch, reality threatening to wobble around me. "Why are you smiling like that?"

Peter levels his black eyes at me and says, "I found your shadow."

* * *

I am eight years old.

We arrive at midnight, Momma, "Uncle" Leon, my shadow and I, crammed into a Buick the color of old piss. The long stretches of upstate soybean peel away to reveal an army of high-rises marching into the light-polluted never-dark. My shadow surges up from the floor mats when the headlights hit him. He is excited and starry-eyed. He has never been to The City before.

He still believes in adventures.

"It doesn't work that way," I whisper. Adventures don't begin with dodging landlords and eviction notices and shoving unwashed clothes into black trash bags.

"What was that, sugar?" Leon's voice is Georgia-thick and he is dirty-grinning at me in the rear view mirror. He strokes the back of Momma's neck, pressing greasy circles into her hairline, and my shadow bristles.

"I'm not sugar." I tug my sweater over my fingers.

"Sugar and spice and everything nice." Leon's fingers dip beneath the collar of Momma's shirt. "Isn't that what little girls are-"

"I said this car smells like shit."

"Prudence!" Momma whips around, but Leon's hand turns vise-tight, and he glares the rest of the ride into silence.

My shadow seethes and I press my forehead against the rear window glass, neon lights flipping my reflection from infant to ancient. From ugly to divine. From girl to boy. I cling to that last like a secret as my shadow winds himself around me. Sinking into his embrace, I count cars until Brooklyn.

By the time we arrive, my shadow is strong. He hefts trash bags easily over his broad shoulders and pounds his new kingdom flat with giant boy feet as we walk to Leon's apartment. I shuffle, but my shadow struts. He leaps up broken concrete steps and hurdles winos. He dodges dumpsters and conquers trashcan castles and ignores Leon's angry shouts of, "Hurry up!" and "Oh for God's sake."

My shadow and I only stop when we reach the neighbor's stoop. There is a small child there, huddled in an oversized trench coat, a paper bag lumped onto his small head like a fedora. For a moment, he seems to float, and my stomach swoops sideways, a boat tipping beneath my feet. My shadow begins to tiptoe around him when the boy looks up. Black eyes pin me.

"I'm Peter," the boy says. His breath is licorice and cinnamon.

I lean closer to my shadow. "Peter?"

"Yup. Peter Pan. Peter Rabbit. Saint Peter. Take your pick." He shuffles toward the edge of the stoop and squints, one pudgy finger inching over his nose. "What's your name?"

"Prudence."

Peter laughs like my name is a joke, the baby fat under his chin puckering. Then, very carefully, he shoves the brim of his paper hat back and looks directly at my shadow. "And who are you?" he asks.

Stillness.

Peter, perched on the edge of the concrete like a pigeon, waits, but by the time I open my mouth, Leon's voice, belting bright and dangerous, jabs the world into motion again.

"We haven't got all night!"

Goosebumps rocket me to where he and Momma are waiting before I can gather the courage to see if Peter is still watching me.

Later, when Momma and Leon are kissing, I peer out the window of my new room, bare feet on a dirty mattress, and look for Peter, but there is only a rumpled paper bag tumbling end over end down the lonely alley. I imagine an empty world, Peter flying with trenchcoat wings, tiny naked toes gripping the concrete like talons and lifting it up, up, up! Peeling the skin off the city like an orange.

And who are you?

I look down at my shadow and whisper, "P.J."

* * *

I am twelve years old.

"You're not wearing that." Momma circles the living room in a pencil skirt and a broad, black hat. "It's a funeral. Don't you want to look pretty for your grandpa?"

"Why? What's he going to do? Sit up and applaud?" I flop onto the sofa to avoid the pinch of her eyes. "Besides, he's not really my grandpa. He's Leon's dad."

Exasperated, Momma grimaces at my jeans, my t-shirt, my short hair. I tap my toe against my shadow's long foot and brace myself for the inevitable, "You used to be so pretty. You used to have such nice hair. If you would just try to look a little more *feminine*..."

Before Momma can say it, Leon's voice roars from the kitchen. "Change your clothes, Prudence! I won't have a freak at my father's funeral."

I grind my fingers into the arm of the sofa. "I told you. It's not Prudence, it's P.J."

"Now!"

For a breath, my shadow refuses to move. He stays stubbornly glued to the shag carpet until the memory of bruised wrists and a hard slap send him stomping to my room. I slam the door behind us.

It takes me five minutes to unearth the only dress I haven't hacked into a t-shirt. The lace scratches my neck as I wrestle myself into it, my wrists torqueing sideways as I shove them through puff sleeves.

When I'm finally done, my shadow gapes at me. His hair is spiked at odd angles, fingers splayed, long legs awkwardly knocked under the wide bell of the dress. Biting my cheek, I turn slowly. Breasts jut out of him, sharp and pointy as new teeth. My shadow snaps forward again, boyish and narrow, but the damage is done. He is quivering and he tugs at my heels, trying to crawl inside me and away from that foreign, curving shape as I hurry out of the room.

At the funeral, Leon parades us through a church the color of old bones. My shadow shrinks further into me as Momma makes introductions. "This is my daughter, Prudence." This is my daughter. This is my *daughter.* My shadow clutches at my little finger from the inside, frantic to shake the untruth of the word, but I don't know how to comfort him and I close my eyes. It's only when I smell licorice and cinnamon that I finally look up.

Across the aisle, dwarfed by the lily-white rental casket, is Peter. He is no bigger than the last time I saw him, but the trench coat and paper bag have been replaced by a daisy-print dress and combat boots. He lifts his head and winks at me, narrow lips pursed around a cigarette. Dizziness sloshes over me and, for a moment, the mourners, fat and watery and pale, seem to dissolve. I can't look away as Peter jigs a circle around the casket, stomping a rhythm only he can hear. Black eyes shining, he laughs and then, very carefully, he leans over the casket and taps ash onto the body's waxy cheek.

Nobody else sees him.

Nobody stops him.

* * *

I am sixteen years old.

The October sun tosses shadows across the fire escape. Ropes. Fingers. Cages.

And the shadow sprawled beneath me? It isn't mine. She's a wide and rounded thing, wasp waist, thick hips, and an empty space between her thighs. Four years of trying to escape her and, still, she clings to me like tar.

My true shadow has become a furious refugee in my own body. He claws at femurs, scrapes bone to marrow, tears muscle apart in bursts of rage. In dreams, he rushes through my pores like water through a sieve, but every morning he is still there, howling for a larger shell.

The howling never stops.

I flick open my lighter and pass the razor blade through the flame three times.

Through the cracked living room window, I can hear Momma and Leon, their voices, serrated and angry, cut through the buzz of day time T.V.

"Leon, please, it's just a phase. She'll grow out of it."

"Like she outgrew that haircut? Or those clothes? Did you hear what Mickey Barlow said about her? The whole neighborhood thinks your daughter's a dyke."

"Prudence isn't gay. She doesn't even like girls."

"I suppose she told you that."

"Well, no, but-"

"You're going to tell me the whole neighborhood is wrong? She's disgusting. Don't you look at me that way." A beat of dangerous silence. "I caught her stuffing a sock in her underwear. You're going to tell me that's normal? You're going to tell me your daughter parading around as a boy is normal?"

The razor blade is still warm as opens my skin. Blood slugs down my forearm, swerving over the familiar cross-hatch of scars. My shadow strains against the shallow breach. If I just close my eyes and let him ease out of me, if I just let him out...

The window opens with a groan. "Prudence?"

Startled and guilty, I whirl around and the blade resting against my skin accidentally slips sudden and deep. I gasp. Blood fountains over the window sill and the rusted drain pipe and into Momma's hair as she clamors onto the fire escape. There is a flash. Pain. No, lightning. Momma's eyes are wide and inches from my own. Heat gushes over my hand.

The world smells like licorice and cinnamon.

There is a rush and a screech, a thousand tires peeling rubber. Above me, a trio of pigeons pause mid-wing, hieroglyphs punched into the autumn sky. Above me, Momma flickers out like a candle snuffed. Above me, the sky is changing from blue to black.

I look down and there, mingled with the blood rushing out of the slit in my arm, is my shadow. He crawls out, prying my flesh apart with long, dark fingers. He curls upward like smoke until he is facing me, dream-heavy and naked. Tension quivers between us and there is a deep, aching pull, a cable stretched too far. He opens his mouth, but there is no sound, no breath, and desperation swells behind his eyes.

He is only a shadow. He will never be strong enough to become a real boy. He'll never speak. He is nothing but a wailing ache.

In a flurry of teeth and nails, he tackles me. It's graceless and uncoordinated, his body too new for quickness, but his shoulder slams into my belly and I collide with the railing. A crack of pain, the sharp corner jarring my ribs. The fire escape shudders and we grapple, my hand jammed against his face, fingers full of inky hair, grunting and shoving even as we topple and fall.

We crash into the dumpster below, our bodies a snarling tangle of blood and shadow that bursts apart as we ricochet onto the concrete. My shadow staggers away from me, disconnected and confused. Hands clutching his head, he turns and sprints down the deserted street, dodging smashed cars and cabs, still smoking where they've rammed into telephone poles, street signs, each other.

Their drivers have disappeared. The sidewalks are empty. There are car alarms, but no sirens.

The city is silent.

* * *

I am crouched at the mouth of the Battery Tunnel when Peter appears beside me, the smell of him sudden and overwhelming. The can of spray paint clatters out of my hand and I scramble back until I hit the tunnel wall. Peter is backlit and wearing a polka-dot onesie two sizes too big. The sleeves spill over his hands, and the collar dangles off one narrow shoulder as he shuffles toward me. He is holding a dead pigeon like a rag doll in one hand.

With a thoughtful hum, he examines my graffiti, the faltering outline of my missing shadow boy, the uneven words. "'Help, I'm still here.'" Peter snickers. Any part of me that might have been relieved at the sight of another person shrinks. "Oh, that's cute."

"They all disappeared." Distantly embarrassed, I scrub the tears on my cheeks with the heel of my hand.

Peter shrugs and squats in front of me, resting his round cheek against his fist. "I've been looking for you for ages," he says. "You're shorter than I remember. Paler, too. But maybe it's all that black you're wearing." He reaches out to flick the collar of my jacket, and I twitch my head against the concrete.

"You don't understand," I say. "Everybody's gone. Momma. Leon. Everybody. Like they were never even here."

"You're here."

My laugh is wild and unhinged. "So are you."

"Oh I don't know about that. Maybe you're just imagining me. Maybe you're still on that fire escape dribbling all your blood away. Drip, drip, drip." Peter's mouth splits into a rubbery caricature of a smile. He has too many teeth. "Maybe you're the one who disappeared."

After two weeks of screaming for help and sobbing in the corners of empty delis and bus stops, my brain is sluggish and thick. I blink hard. "Is this hell or something?" Nausea spikes through me. "Am I dead?"

"Do you want to be?"

I shake my head, trying to dislodge the memory of razor blades. "What kind of question is that?"

"A pretty simple one. How do you feel about morgues? Cemeteries? Funerals? You didn't seem too keen about the last one. And that shadow of yours? He never shut up after that. Day and night, night and day. You know you hated it." Peter cocks his head to one side. "Listen. He's still at it."

"Shadows don't talk." I try to believe it and coil my hand against my stomach as if I could stopper the empty space my shadow used to occupy. "And anyway, mine disappeared. I can't hear anything."

"He must be playing hide and seek with you," Peter says and covers the dead pigeon's eyes with his thumb. "Count to one hundred and we can look for him together. Oh! Or find a mirror and we can play Bloody Mary. Say his name three times and he'll magically appear."

Anger flares past the fog in my head. "This isn't a game! What's going on?"

"Everything's a game. Just because you didn't make the rules doesn't mean you don't have to play."

A sharp gust of wind tumbles a fistful of newspapers down the vacant street. Peter's black eyes make the world quiver.

"What do you want?" I finally manage.

Peter raises his finger. "Your shadow."

My gut clenches cold. "My shadow?"

He swings the dead pigeon idly from side to side. "I don't have one of my own." I look down and his feet are completely surrounded by sunlight. He seems like he's floating and, woozy, I avert my eyes. "Nobody trusts a kid without a shadow and you don't want yours. He's been nothing but trouble from the start. I'll help you find him and then you'll give him to me and then poof! All is right with the world."

I hesitate. "If I do that, everything will go back to normal?"

Peter smirks and raises three fingers. "Scout's honor."

* * *

After three weeks of searching, Peter is wearing a kimono and a ten-gallon hat with a pigeon feather tucked into the brim. The bird's head dangles around his neck like a bloody talisman. He's told me that the mannequins in the department stores dress him every night. A ball gown from Macy's, a purple velvet suit from Barney's, a pair of neon underwear and lipstick war paint from Bloomingdale's. It's hard not to stare, and I'm certain he knows it.

"You should feel honored." Peter hikes the hem of his kimono up as he climbs over a mangled Yellow Cab.

"Why should I feel honored?" I kick at the dangling headlight and huddle more deeply into my jacket. "This is all a game to you. You just want my shadow. You don't give a shit about me."

Peter grunts as he stands atop the hood, hands on his hips as he turns in a slow circle. "My guts are made of chrome and feathers, goblin piss, and griffon tails. There's no room for shit."

"Poetic." I snort and light another cigarette. "Come on. I want to search the West Side before the sun goes down." I remember how my shadow had warmed when we sneaked into Chelsea last summer, his howling softening when a tall man in a white blazer called me son.

Peter clucks his tongue and leaps off of the car with a spectacularly loud thud. A street sign teeters from the impact. "You should feel honored because I don't adopt just any shadow. Only the dark ones."

I roll my eyes and begin walking faster. "They're shadows.

They're all dark."

"Oh, no, dear Prudence, they're not."

"It's P.J."

"Ah, ah, ah." Peter waggles a finger as he falls into step with me, stubby legs churning impossibly fast beneath the kimono. "P.J. is your shadow boy. You don't own that name any more than you own all those little boy bits you were convinced you needed."

I keep my eyes fixed on the street ahead of me. "I named him. The name is mine."

Peter waves a dismissive hand. "You're giving him to me."

"It's my name!"

Peter tugs me to a halt, moon-round face peering up at me, black eyes narrow. "You think he cares what you named him? You think he cares about you at all?"

I shake myself from his grip and flip my cigarette against a rusted scaffold.

"He lied to you every day," Peter continues. "Told you you were a boy. Take a look at yourself. Why, you don't look anything like a boy! But that didn't stop him from tricking you into believing it."

"I know what I am." My shadow's absence is like a stone in my throat. I try to swallow. The stone rolls deeper.

"Of course you know what you are. You're a smart girl. You don't like lies. Your shadow is a liar. Why would you want him back?"

My fingers curl, but there is no shadow hand to hold onto. I tell myself that the sting in the back of my eyes is from the cold.

"Everything will be easier without him, Prudence." Peter pats my sleeve with his tiny palm. "Everything will be normal."

Jerking away from him, I duck my head and walk briskly down the abandoned street. As Peter patters after me, I try to ignore the emptiness lodged deep in my chest, abnormal and heavy and very, very real.

* * *

"I found your shadow."

Peter's words propel me out of the subway terminal, through the arteries of the city, past the yawning windows of untenanted store fronts and the twisted wreckage of cars. Peter scampers beside me, laughing. He dances over drainpipes, scales streetlights to crow, hops over an upturned bus and squeals his way into Brooklyn.

I run.

The sun is melting over the skyline by the time we arrive, and I am wheezing. Tar webs my throat, wet and thick, and I pause to hack onto the pavement. When I look up, the familiar apartment building is crawling out from behind the shamble of dumpsters in the back alley. I half expect to see Mickey Barlow smoking weed on the corner or Leon and Momma kissing in the window.

But the only one there is my shadow boy. He is slumped against the apartment's fire escape, his arms twined around his waist, head bowed. The tangled mop of hair obscures his profile, but I can see the plump of his lower lip, the flutter of his long throat as he swallows. He is trembling.

"Ah-ha!" Peter dashes past me and thrusts a triumphant finger at him, legs planted wide. "Get him! Get him, get him!"

My shadow heaves a sigh and I exhale and, slowly, we look at each other. Breath shushes between us, murmurs secrets through the back alley. Edging carefully around Peter, I heft myself onto the Dumpster and grip the lower wrung of the fire escape.

"Don't let him get away!" Peter is hopping from toe to toe, hands clapping hysterical polyrhythms, but I don't answer him.

Instead, I climb, fist over fist over fist until I am standing face to face with my shadow boy. He raises his head and, for the first time, I feel the weight of his eyes. This is the boy who for sixteen years has been screaming through the pockets of my lungs. This is the boy in my fingers, longing for a broadness that never was. This is the boy who sobs every month for five days when I bleed. This is the boy who scratches my breasts with sewing needles and demands to know why they are there because they don't belong on his body.

They've never belonged on my body, either.

"What are you waiting for?" Peter is screeching and I can feel the earth quaver. Metal rungs creak. Brick and mortar moans. Window glass crackles. The sky begins to darken. "What are you waiting for?"

I look at my shadow. My shadow looks at me.

He raises one dark hand, my shadow boy, and touches my cheek.

And the moment before our arms and bodies and souls reconnect, I whisper, "I don't know."

THE INVISIBLE STARS

Ryan Row

He first learned to speak sitting outside their windows at night. A veil of kitchen or living room light above, watching the shadows of suburban rose bushes and apple trees drift in the yard as he listened. Family dinner. A TV. A radio. Two lovers screaming at each other. An old man talking to a brightly colored bird. The words were too soft for his mouth, and his mandibles ached as he whispered a garbled, carapaced version of human speech to himself and to the washed-out sky. In the direction of his lost home.

Bath. Cracker. Day. Shooter. Grace.

He ate dogs and cats those first few weeks. He slithered through bushes and sewers in a rush of dark limbs and shining black exoskeleton. He stole clothes, and learned to stand in a way that hid the shape of his body. But nights, he would return to the windows. These square lives were his churches of humanity.

I feel lethargic. Let me see your phone. I believe you. Are the children sleeping?

He mimicked sounds. The scent of faraway rain and wet grass was wildly exotic. And his eyes always on the invisible stars. Meaning would come later.

When he could speak, he spoke with an accent no one could quite identify. They always assumed he was from some form of wasteland. The unpopulated plains of Siberia. The crumbling stone battlefields of the Middle East. The blood-soaked sands of African apartheid. Their ignorance astounded him. The way they wanted him to be tragic in some way, to bare something for them. He wanted to please them, so he tried.

"I am from far away. Very sad place," he said in his exoskeletoned English. It did make him sad to think of it, but not for the reasons people assumed. He was interviewing for a job sorting mail for a small delivery company. He had taken the name Asunder because it sounded foreign and hard in English, and people reacted to it almost with a kind of pity. His many

limbs were wrapped around his long body in a kind of lonely hug. One set of limbs extended through the arms of his trench coat, and he walked on another two sets in a wobbly facsimile of a human gait. He looked very tall and thin, with bony, strong arms.

"Don't matter to me if you're from the damn moon," the company man said. He was dressed in red plaid, and was greasy and distended, like a balloon. And the sight of him made Asunder giddy. The man was beautiful and bizarre. Asunder wanted to shiver in delight, but the clicking sound would have disturbed the man. "Can you work nights? By yourself?"

Asunder could.

Work was a blessing. He shed his coat and hat and scarf and baggy pants and stretched his many sets of limbs and rolled the many joints along his body. The satisfying scraping of his armor. The scent of ink and paper. He hissed with pleasure. Then he dragged the large sacks of mail and sorted them into smaller sacks and bins in a blinding flurry of dark limbs. In that time, he felt free and high, like the tireless circumlunar runners or the Aurora canyon divers of his home. There was a kind of high that could only be achieved in exhaustion or in free fall. He would finish his work in an hour, sometimes less, then would pick through the envelopes and read the addresses and names, especially of the red-and-blue-bordered international envelopes. *Bian, Ho Chi Minh City, Vietnam. Ada, Dresden, Germany. Ammon, Alexandria, Egypt. Carlos, Mexico City, Mexico.*

Asunder imagined he was from these places. These letters were to him. Sometimes he would carefully unseal and read them. He was sitting on a terrace in Egypt, watching the red sun disintegrate the horizon, and an old lover in America was thinking of him. Or his daughter was sending him money for his medication and for masa and oil. Or it was snowing outside, and the lights of Dresden were illusory and cold. The barrier between himself and his home shrank to the thickness of a single sheet of paper, through which he could see the lights of his city, deep red and white.

When he ran out of interesting letters and got bored he would leave. Wrap himself in his human guise and wander around holding himself. It was cold, and the delicate streetlights made him want to shiver and click his mandibles in appreciation. The 24-hour markets, brilliant on their corners. The threads of cigarette smoke drifting from the bars made him dizzy. The knock of his almost-empty shoes, two sets of thin, strong limbs jammed into the ankles of each, on the pavement was solid, and reassuring. Sometimes he sat in a diner and ordered coffee, which he drank with a straw pushed up through the folds of his scarf.

"Good night," he said to the waitress. She smiled, but said nothing, and he set down his coffee. She was older and had loose skin and a lisp, which he guessed embarrassed her, though he thought there was a kind of beauty in the way words slid out of her mouth like the way far-off taillights would sometimes slide and twinkle and smear against the night.

The coffee was bitter, but he soaked it in sugar. The radiating heat from the cup excited him, and he touched it, then moved his limb away, like a child. He tried to get the waitress to talk with him.

"I am from far away," he said.

"Isn't everybody?" she said, and her sliding words made him hiss softly.

At dawn he walked to the butcher's shop and bought three pounds of raw meat. It was so available here. On his home, they farmed fleshy, tuber-like animals for the protein and ate worms and other small, burrowing creatures with fur like crinkled steel. He tried not to think about it, because it made him nostalgic and melancholy, but he could not control his dreams.

His planet was iron-red and covered in good soil. Loam and clay, made warm by a very close star. The soil was thick and very good for digging and sleeping in. The smell was rich, and not unlike the scent of bad diner coffee. He was a scientist there, and a rocket pilot, and a cartographer of the stars. He had many dozens of children and lovers, all of whom had seen him off many years ago. Sometimes, when he felt very lonely waiting for a bus or reading undeliverable mail, he imagined descending from the yellow clouds of his home world, in his repaired saucer, and the red land glowing in the light. The many-legged shadows of his family still waiting for him. Rushing across the plains to greet him.

During the day, when thick clothing was less acceptable, he retired to a rented storage shed where his saucer was stashed. He did his best to work on it with human tools and parts that were fragile and that sometimes bent between his limbs in frustration. He would like to go home, but knew this was likely impossible. His saucer had malfunctioned in-warp, and it had taken all he had as an engineer and pilot to control-crash it into the shallows of a warm sea on a livable planet. The Earth's moon was high that night, terrifyingly white and pitted. He dragged his ship ashore on a fine beach in a place they called Florida, spitting salt water and gnashing his mandibles. His species could lift many times their own weight, and he dragged the saucer with his bare limbs, random growths of red coral cracking beneath him as he half swam toward the shore. The air was thick and sweet with sand and beach grass, and he lay out on a strange and beautiful beach and shook and thought he was dying.

There was no way home now. The tools and materials he could acquire were strikingly primitive. He was lonely and strange, as outsiders always are, especially in foreign lands, but that was all right, because he was also alive.

"Alive," he said in his battered language, drawing out the fine edges of the word. That should have been his name.

He chewed meat in one pair of his limbs, and tried to weld a steel composite sheet to the nano-carbyne hull of the saucer with another. With a third pair, he carefully examined a map in the almost-dark—he had very good vision—and circled electronics and computer stores he knew were open late where he might speak with someone and order a new set of computer processors, which he would try to reverse-engineer and connect to the saucer's nav systems. With a final pair of limbs he held himself, which was becoming a habit. It was very dark in the storage shed, but the sparks from the welding torch changed the place into something wild and alive. The sparks pumped veins of shadow and light across the walls like a kind of imaginary heart, which madly refused to stop beating.

WHAT BECOMES OF THE THIRD HEARTED

A. Merc Rustad

Her skin smells of crushed pearls, dried salt, silver fish scales woven into unfinished memories. Her eyes are sculpted starlight, holding the sadness of death a million years ago and a million yet to come.

When she holds out her hand, I turn and run. The sand has turned to glass and my heels crack the shore in tiny percussions like the breaking of my hearts.

* * *

The world's ending was quiet, demure, almost unnoticed.

In sleep, people faded into dreams—leaving behind only the soft remembrance of breath. The ones awake paused in every movement and shut their eyes. No panic, no fear. Gentler, perhaps, than any of us deserved.

I saw a few strangers awake and wandering, caught in their own quests, but none of them were you.

You and Tara were two states away and commuting back home when everything stopped. I sent you texts and called you until there was no cell reception and my voice hung in tatters in my throat.

I still whispered your name. *Shelby. Shelby. Shelby.* Until even whispers faded into nothing.

* * *

Where are you? I know where you should have been. But the world is a scattered puzzle (ten million pieces, not all there) and I have no box cover to reference what it should look like now.

How do I find you?

* * *

The woman is everywhere. She drifts at the corner of my vision, watches when I blink, and she never speaks. I turn to face her, and again she slides aside like a mirage. Her footsteps linger, weighted in the land and air alike. I don't know what they will do if I touch them.

I clamber over coral growths thrust up where the highway used to stretch six lanes in both directions; a few pebbles of black, crumbled tar are all that's left of the road.

Like that time Tara was three and she found a Magic Erase marker and scrubbed that cheap thrift-store painting of the whales until it was scraps of water enclosed in a frame. You were so furious at my daughter, but as the new step-parent, you tried your best to be reasonable. Did I tell you how much I appreciated that? I know you never quite liked the dolphin painting I replaced the whales with.

The horizon is slabs of darkness like great bricks stacked haphazardly, fire licking the spaces between like mortar. The sky is crumbling at the edges, raining pieces of blackness to reveal a bright, stardust void where clouds once swarmed.

I'm coming, Shelby.

(Am I? Can I, when I don't know how to find you?)

My cellphone turned into a tiny turtle with ruby eyes and *lorem ipsum* painted on its shell after the reception disappeared. I set it loose in the glass sand and it burrowed toward waters that no longer exist.

I haven't slept since the world ended. I can't—if I lie down, if I dream, I will lose what little time I have.

I never thought I'd come to miss the gridlocked traffic roaring past in the distance, our backyard always a little too close to it to let Tara play on the fenced-in grass unattended.

How long will this reality last?
What happens after the end of the world?

* * *

My mother told me we all have three hearts. Not in a physical sense; she clarified that when, at ten, I showed her anatomy photos in a textbook to prove her wrong.

"Your first heart is the smallest and scratchiest," my mother said. "It holds all the wonder and loves you acquire as you grow up. Horseback riding, video games, books, playing in the pool, skating, comics—whatever you love, your first heart can absorb and grow to make room for all of these things. It can become any size you need. Your second heart is made for the people you care for. Your family and friends, your lovers—when you're older—your spouse or spouses."

"Where are pets?" I demanded.

"Second heart," my mother said. "Why wouldn't they be?"

She set her heavy leather gloves on the basement workbench next to her welding helmet. She'd been working on one of her iron sculptures, forged from scrap picked up at junkyards. The basement was concrete, empty except for the heavy wood tables and mother's machinery and piles of scrap, smelling always of hot metal and oil and her sweat.

"Your third heart," my mother said, "is a secret."

"Then how do you know it's real?"

She shrugged. "How do you know when anything is real?"

"Ugh, Mom."

She grinned. "Morgan, you'll know what your third heart is one day. It just takes time. No one's is the same."

I glared.

"I don't want three hearts," I yelled, tears in my eyes. I slammed the textbook onto the floor. "And I don't want to look like this."

"What do you want to look like?" my mother asked, confused, but at ten, I didn't have the words I needed.

* * *

There's a wall of shale threaded with lady-slipper flowers made of papier-mâché, tended by ants woven from yarn and silk. It blocks the coral highway now, humming in F-sharp minor with a melody I've never heard. It's not music so much as sensory impressions—blueberries rinsed in the sink, peeling acrylic paint free of your fingers, humid July nights plagued by mosquitoes, jazz horns on the radio, baby powder on Tara's skin, vacuuming the carpet, cuddling in bed after a hot shower, burning popcorn and hiding the taste with too much salt and butter.

The woman is almost at my elbow before I realize the wall is singing to me. Ants are tying minute poison-ivy chains over my toes. The sting snaps my focus out of the music. I jump back and stumble down the length of the wall. It has no holes, it has no top. How do I get around?

(Are you on the other side?)

What do you want? I demand of the woman. *Why are you here?*

She extends a hand, inviting. If I touch her skin, I fear I will disappear.

So again I run.

* * *

My mother died before you and I met, but I have one photo left—of when Laura (my ex-wife), Tara (just a toddler then), and I visited her in the hospital. She smiled brighter than all of us, even faded and tired from chemo.

"How can you smile," I demanded, when Laura took Tara out of the room to feed her.

"Why shouldn't I?" my mother responded, squeezing my hand. "I'm going on a new adventure."

"Don't," I whispered. "Please, Mom."

"Honey...I want to tell you a secret."

I pressed her hand against my cheek, hiding my face. She must have felt the tears.

"My third heart is a ship," my mother said. "A beautiful sailboat painted like the sunset. I'm undocking and mastering the rigging. I'm going to sail past the universe and see things never before imagined."

My shoulders shook harder. She pulled my head down against her side and stroked my hair like she did when I was small.

"I named my sailboat *Morgan*," she said. "Because I'll always be with you."

* * *

You sent me a selfie of you and Tara the night before the world ended. You were in a chic little café, Tara with an oversized mug of hot chocolate, you with your black coffee. You both made faces at the camera.

I was too tired to reply. So I just...deleted the text and pretended I'd never received it.

It was the last picture I could have had of you.

* * *

The rain rumbles towards me. The wall never ends. The ants and spiders follow in geometric patterns, their exoskeletons shifting through the light spectrum and the color wheels I remember from high school art class.

(Are you on the other side? How can I find you?)

The woman watches, her hair coiled like wet leaves about her shoulders.

My knuckles clang like bells when I punch the wall. If you and Tara are behind this wall, I will find a way over or around or through. Somehow. I keep your faces like a tattoo printed against my eyelids, every detail, from your crooked smile to the mole behind Tara's right ear.

I hope Laura is safe. We've always been good friends. When I find you, I'll look for her next. I will look for everyone.

The first drops of rain spatter near my feet. The ground evaporates where the water strikes.

The wall is endless. I don't have rope, or strength to climb.

I run again.

* * *

As a teenager I bound my breasts and wore baggy clothing and demanded people call me he, him, and sir. I cut my hair myself. I dated girls. I was a man.

In my twenties, when I met Laura, I was a woman. We married after college and two years into our marriage I told her I was once more a man. Our divorce was amicable; Laura never questioned my gender, merely said she preferred to be married to a woman who was always a woman. We remained friends.

When I met you, Shelby, I felt like neither. I felt ten again, confused because pronouns fit like jeans two sizes two small, pinching, not fitting all the way.

To you, it didn’t matter. You called me "they" like I asked, and I knew I would love you forever.

I can't lose you like this, a deleted selfie before the end of the world.

* * *

There is no break in the wall, no doors or windows or bridges. The higher I climb, the faster the wall arches up towards the red sky. I slide down, covered in ivy and stung by little poems like insect bites.

Shelby! Tara!

Ever silent, the woman watches.

I face her, shaking, exhaustion chewing at every muscle and bone. I sink to the ground. The rain is close again. I don't know how to go on. I don't know where you are.

I'm so sorry, Shelby. Keep Tara safe. (Can you hold her for me?)

I look up at the woman, defeat encroaching like the rain. I can't outrun her. *What do you want?* I whisper, wordless.

She offers her hand again, fingers curled like commas. In her palm is a tiny sailboat made of feather-edged paper, painted like the sunset.

* * *

"What's a heart, Baba?" Tara asked me as I read her a picture book one evening.

I tapped my chest. "It's where you keep all the hugs and kisses and love, like a big balloon that never pops."

Tara giggled. "My heart is as big as the balloon ride!" She stretched her arms as wide as she could. We'd floated up in hot air balloon the week before for your birthday, Shelby. Tara had never been so excited as when she looked out over the countryside and said we were as high as heaven.

"Yes, Boo," I told her. "That big."

* * *

I stare at the sailboat.

My mother smiles—I know her eyes now, beyond the sorrow. She has traveled universes...and she has come back.

And I know, then, why she's followed me.

Morgan is written on the sailboat's side.

My third heart is a compass. I feel it, the hands swinging towards a magnetic north I can't see. I pull it from my ribs, cupping it in both hands. You and Tara smile up at me, painted in photorealistic detail on the compass's face. Your heartbeat and Tara's hum in the compass's smooth, round shape.

I look my mother, at the boat in her hand—

At the rain that is erasing this world—

At the wall I cannot climb—

But perhaps, in a boat, I might sail over it to where you and Tara are, Shelby.

I take my mother's hand and feel the night wind in my face as the sail unfolds around me. She steers while I stand at the helm, compass in hand, guiding our course to find you.

SKILLS TO KEEP THE DEVIL IN HIS PLACE

Lia Swope Mitchell

1. Do Not Think About the Devil

This is like some kind of idiot savant shit, totally impossible and totally easy all at the same time. You have to hear everything else, see everything else. Know when to get distracted and where not to point your eyes. So when he's whispering in the corners, dancing around all fiery-sparkly and smelling like Drakkar Noir, only expensive—that's when you put on your headphones, turn up the volume and watch videos on your phone. And try not to think a single thought about the devil.

Because if you think about him, he's got a way in. He'll creep into your pupils, waft up your nose, croon through your earholes singing moody devil songs. From there, into your brain. I've seen it happen—it's happened to me. And then everything you see starts to look like temptation. An object, something to use or destroy. Then you're yelling at friends, telling lies, and stealing Mom's credit card to buy $200 jeans off the internet and who even knows where all this ends.

I try to stop, purify. Return the jeans, tell Mom everything. Maybe kneel down, beg God to take those bad thoughts away—if there's a devil, there must be a God, right? But this never works.

So it's best not to think about the devil at all. Really effective, if you can manage it. Take Julie, the new girl in study hall: she's deep in her *Autres Mondes* textbook, writing flash cards in pretty cursive. Meanwhile, the devil's bending his blood-red torso over hers, his long lips cooing around her name: *Julie Julie Julie.* She doesn't notice, doesn't feel a thing. Not even when he's wrapping his hairy arm around her waist, not even when he's got his tongue stretched out to tease her ear. That's when she sticks her hand up and says, "Miss Turner? May I be excused?"

Later, in French class, she's got the vocab down cold. So she was really concentrating. Like he wasn't even there.

Me, though, I can't do it. And believe me, I've spent hours on my knees. But God never answers. Mom just yells.

2. Do Not Talk About the Devil

Okay, say you're like me. Say you can't ignore him. Still, you can't tell anyone. They'll think you're crazy, they'll laugh. You can't blame them for getting defensive—nobody wants to hear they have a devil inside. So it's on you to protect other people if you can.

For example, here I am in the library and here's Julie with a pile of books about Africa or something. And the devil is here, too, all smooth dance moves, circling and swaying and looking for ways in. But with Julie, somehow, he can't do it. Like there's a barrier, a protective coating on her skin. Like that Bath Works vanilla stuff but better, less vomity-sweet.

What I want to know is where she gets that. How she does that. So I sit down all casual and say, "Hey, Julie."

"Hey, Rachel." Her smile opens up, all bright and hopeful. "I'm doing this geography presentation. What about you?"

"American history. I got this stupid paper."

She asks what it's about: women in the Civil War. Oh *cool*, have I seen *Gone with the Wind*?

And while she's telling me how much she loves Melanie and Scarlett, there's the devil doing Rhett Butler, his one eye heavy and knowing, that smirk around his lips. I'm trying so hard not to notice, to agree that yes, it's all about *sisterly* love and why do people always focus on romance but he keeps laughing at me so finally—

"How do you *do* it?"

Even her little frown is perky and nice. "Do what?"

"Ignore—"

He tells me go ahead, say his name, open my mouth and let him come in.

"Rachel?" Her eyes are soft cornflower blue, sky blue, angel blue. I can't do it, I can't break her seal and tell her he's there.

"Um... distractions." I take this big accidental breath and that's how he gets into me—like a fire down my throat, scorching my lungs, lighting through my bloodstream to my heart. Maybe a few seconds before the thudding slows. "You're always so organized. I really, like, *admire* that."

"Oh, well, it's all about priorities—"

I'm nodding and smiling and I can't see the devil anymore because he's in me.

She says how children in some countries don't even get an education. She is so *grateful*. She wants to give *back*.

"Pay it forward, right," I say. "You're such a fucking *saint*."

She flushes all perfect pink and I want to slap her, see my fingermarks printed on her idiot cheek.

"Oh, I never meant—"

"No, really. Those kids in Africa should just worship you. I mean, maybe they're starving or working in diamond mines or dying of Ebola or something but you, you're *studying*, you're like a *martyr*—"

Her eyes are Virgin Mary blue and so, so confused. I get up quick and leave, carry the devil out to my car where I sit the rest of the day, smoking cigarettes and staring at my phone, choking on the evil he's burnt on my breath.

3. Do Not Look the Devil in the Eye

It's my own fault, that's true, but I didn't know. I wasn't even afraid—we were both just waking. His face nestled on my other pillow, all scarred and twisted and red. His left eye was squinting at me, the other gone. Plucked out, maybe fighting some angel. I stared at him like he was an image on a screen, like he couldn't touch me even at that close range. After a second, the devil smiled.

See, it's not about meaning to, or choices. It doesn't seem evil, there in that calm moment, the last of your dream. More like inevitable. Like fate.

But instead, this Saturday, instead I wake up to my mother's head stuck inside my bedroom door. "Rachel? Honey?"

Another voice behind hers, higher and sweeter, offers to come back.

"No, she *should* get up," Mom answers. "It's almost noon."

"I'm up," I say. Wave an arm to quiet my critics, slap around for my phone. Four new messages. "Okay *god,* I'm up, I'm up."

"Your friend Julie's here," Mom says all snappish.

"Who?"

"Should I wait?" the sweet voice asks.

"No, uh... it's okay. Come on." I grab a hoodie off the floor and quickly assess the state of my room. No dirty dishes or anything, doesn't look too bad. Until Julie steps in, all shiny clean, like a doll fresh from her plastic box.

"I'll bring you girls coffee," Mom says. "And muffins. Julie, would you like a muffin?"

"I'd love a muffin, Mrs. Meyer," Julie answers as Mom turns. "Hi, Rachel."

"Hey. Look, I'm sorry, I musta forgot we made plans—"

"Oh no," she says. "We didn't have plans. I just—well, I thought maybe I could help you."

"Help me?" I thumb through Facebook on my phone. "Oh. That Civil War paper?"

Mom reappears with coffee and muffins, milk and sugar, the cloth napkins. She loves this shit, she'd wear a frilly apron if she had one. Julie gets a big smile but I get a frown for the phone, so I plug it into the charger.

"Thank you, Mrs. Meyer," Julie says. "Blueberry's my favorite."

Poor Mom looks flustered: politeness, for once. "Well, you girls call if you need anything else."

I dump two heaping spoonfuls of sugar into my mug, add milk. "Yeah, that paper, I haven't even started, so I dunno—"

"Not the paper," Julie says through muffin crumbs. She holds up a finger while she chews, takes a sip from her mug. "No, it's—well, it's about the devil."

I focus on my coffee, the steamy sweetness, the spoon swirling the sugar around. My phone buzzes but I don't even look.

"The thing is," she says, with such sincere blue eyes, "you're going about it all wrong."

4. Make a Place for the Devil

She could tell, she says, from my eyes. Watching the air around her, then totally down or away. He's been following her since, oh—almost a year ago.

"You learn to deal with it," she says. "To keep him quiet."

She can't answer any questions, like why her, or why me. If there's more than one, or how he manages to be everywhere if not, or any implications for humanity as a whole. If this is some kind of mass hallucination, like those girls way back in Salem. She doesn't know anything like that. Just how to manage, like, the day to day.

"What's in this closet?" she asks, polite fingers on the knob, then peeks behind the door. It's all my outgrown and out-of-season stuff, my violin and tennis racket, old books—

"Hey, it's Jenna Fantastic!" Julie squeals. "I watched that show every Saturday."

"And all her friends." Of course she watched it, we all did. "Nerds by day, superheroes by night, right?"

"Oh *cool*, you have the FantastiCar, too—well, maybe they can go up here?"

I let her arrange things while I peek at my phone. Last night's message from Trina: *beer+fire=yes!* Three more since then: first, Luke asks do I want a ride? Second: *That's what friends are fooooor...* Then a photo: Luke and Trina overexposed in headlights, shotgunning cans of Pabst. *Where R U?*

Finally, from Trina. *Bitch yr no fun,* plus three kisses. *What up?*

"Can I move these clothes?"

"Yeah, just a sec—"

Sry, i got aids or smpn, I text Trina, then go help Julie.

When we're done, boxes hide a square yard of space in back under the ceiling slant. Julie steals a pillow and plumps it on the floor, takes an empty box and draws a fat red pentagram on the bottom, sets a candle in the middle. We both squeeze in, half a butt each on the pillow. The little flame rises.

"It's easy to call him since he's already around," Julie says. Her white canvas sneakers glow bright and clean; her jeans have ironed-in creases down the front. Foil streaks sparkle in the Fantastics' neon hair. "You have to watch the candle, though. You don't wanna burn the house down—"

That's when the devil crawls in, muscles sliding along tendons and bones, stretching under leathery skin. He curls up like a big red dog, drops his head in Julie's lap. Her eyelashes flick downward. She sees him—I can see her seeing him. Her smile closes to a determined little pout. She lets her hand fall on his bald head, right between the horns. He leers. The points of his ears give a lewd wiggle.

"You can do your homework at the same time," she says. "Or watch TV or something."

"Okay, so... so you sit there and..."

The devil's nuzzling up under her beige sweater like a hungry puppy. She pulls it up, flashing the white of her belly. Under her ribcage there's a purple smudge like a hickey. His eye bulges as he goes in for the kiss.

"What? Oh, fuck no—"

"It doesn't hurt, really. You get used to it. And then—"

The devil's hand waves uncertainly, shiny-clawed, then lands on her breast. Kneads lightly. Like a kitten.

"—he'll leave you alone a while. And maybe the people around you, too."

In the candlelight Julie's face is golden, peaceful. A perfect blank. From beneath her sweater, I can hear a faint rhythmic suck.

5. Feed the Devil Daily

She's right, it doesn't hurt, there's no blood or anything. Just the circle of his lips all fever-wet, pulling on some invisible thread inside, a line that stretches from my belly through my chest, to some knot tied deep in my brain. And I sit and stare at that moist red skull, horns that crook and poke like fingers, as I let it happen.

Because I know what he does when he's not satisfied. I've seen it.

Like one of the first times. Me and Trina were out smoking by the dumpsters, and there he was. I pretended not to notice, because I knew Trina didn't. She was telling me about her English teacher, pretty hot for an old guy—like thirty? The devil's fangs were pricking into her neck, his arms twined around hers. She didn't see him, but I did. I saw his fingers creep into her mouth, then his whole hand, down to the wrist. Her mouth was moving like normal, her words falling out. But all garbled, nothing made sense. I stood with my cigarette burning down to my fingers, knowing I had to be crazy, as his arm slid into her throat, up to the elbow, to the shoulder, until he turned his head, gave me a wink and dove in headfirst—

I know how that sounds.

But if you're reading this, well, maybe you've been there. Maybe you've felt your skin crawling off your bones while you try to decide whether and when to start screaming at something nobody else sees, whether to give up now and admit you're fucking psychotic or wait and see how things play out. Maybe you know.

"What the fuck, Rach," Trina said. She looked fine. Pretty, with little curls of hair blowing around her face. Inside her slitted eyes, I could swear I saw a flame. "Did I grow another head or what?"

"Uh, no—" I dropped my cigarette, ground it into the gravel beneath my toe. Shook another one out of my pack. "I dunno, I got distracted."

"So what, am I, like, *boring* you?"

We'd had big fights before, all screaming and ugly tears. It was sort of like that, except this time we weren't drunk—we were just skipping third period. And she was the only one screaming. About what a stupid bitch I was and how Luke only fucked me that time out of pity and if I had any self-respect at all I'd drown myself in a toilet. I was still staring when she threw down her butt and left.

I've known Trina forever, is the thing. My best friend since the fifth grade. So I knew Trina wouldn't say that. I knew it wasn't her.

"Guess I was on the rag," she said later, like she barely remembered.

Same thing with my mom: that wink, that dive, and instead of a normal rotten teenager suddenly I was a shame, a curse, the wreck of her body and marriage and life. It happened with a couple teachers, other kids. Sometimes I was the one turned monster. Even if I knew better, it felt too good, too powerful—to see eyes go wide and cheeks go red, to say whatever shitty thing. Sometimes the truth, sometimes a lie. Whatever hurt worse.

In my lap the devil shifts, his eye flicking open. Almost done. Inside his pupil some part of me is burning.

"Why don't you ever talk to me," I say.

His mouth opens in a silent laugh, skeleton teeth gleaming from sharp points to the jagged gum line. His tongue waves around like a wine-stained, mesmerized snake.

I grab the candle and stumble out into my room, push the window open. The hickey on my belly itches. February air flows in, a damp chill that feels good after the devil's sweaty skin. With a cigarette stuck between my lips I lean out into the gray light, try to find the sun. But it's still winter. Up in the clouds there's nothing.

6. Make a Deal with the Devil

At least I knew not to talk about it, not like Julie. Granted, she had reason to think people would believe her, back in her old Catholic school. Her teachers invoked God and Satan on the regular, like the two of them were lurking around every corner, testing and tricking and watching to see how you dealt with all that temptation. So when the shadows of Julie's vision began to redden and solidify, when the devil became a real, present, dancing and flickering thing, of course it was strange, surreal, scary—but not without precedent.

Julie hinted, she thought casually, to a couple close

friends, tried to sound them out. "Do you think he could be, like, a real person? That you could see?" she asked at Sarah's sleepover. "Like, did you ever see anything like that, maybe?" But Sarah and Joy laughed and changed the subject, so Julie let it drop.

Instead, she went to her religion teacher, Sister Marie-Marguerite from Senegal. She seemed nice, spiritual, intelligent. Like she'd know what to do. Julie told her everything.

Sister Marie-Marguerite listened, her eyes behind thick glasses getting bigger, the line between her eyebrows getting deeper. She asked some weird questions: did Julie ever get migraines? Bad headaches? No... How did she get along with her family? Her friends? Fine, except... well, some arguments and one fight, but that was the devil, it wasn't Joy or Sarah, they didn't mean it.

Did she ever hear anything strange? Like voices? Or maybe smells? Did she have any other hallucinations?

Hallucinations—that meant crazy. Sister Marie-Marguerite thought she was crazy. Julie clammed up and decided she'd never say another word, just put up with things as best she could. The way I did.

But it was too late. God and Satan might be ever-present but you weren't supposed to actually *see* them, not ever. You *definitely* weren't supposed to see the devil possessing people, that was way too weird. Sister Marie-Marguerite called Julie's parents, who called a psychiatrist. A nice Catholic one, they said. And that was how everyone found out.

One Friday as Julie was leaving her appointment—fifty minutes of telling Dr. Kris that it was *real* and pills couldn't change things that were real, could they, so why should she take pills that made her feel funny—as she stood wiping tears and blowing her nose right in front of the *Sun Prairie Mental Health Clinic* sign, Andrea Lindquist from Julie's homeroom walked by, a tiny Pomeranian tottering along at her feet.

"Oh hi, Julie," she said, her voice rich with suppressed laughter.

The devil grinned at Julie, his long fingers scratching

behind Andrea's ears. "Oh hey," Julie faltered. "Um. Cute dog."

Cute dog, the devil mouthed, his face twisted up to mock Julie's: fake trembly smile, big sad eyes. *Cute dog cute dog oh isn't it cuuuuute—*

The Pomeranian burst into a furious yap, launching its fluffball body off the ground. Andrea caught it in her arms, where it twisted and panted with wrath. "Oh, Goofy—what's wrong, Goofy? God, it's like he's *possessed.*"

Again that rich, knowing laugh.

Thank goodness, Julie thought, that her mom drove up right then, so Andrea only dropped her dog and strolled onward. A little joke, was all.

Then it happened. Over the weekend, on Facebook. First Sarah, then Andrea and Joy, then all the usual selfies, funny faces and fake kisses, disappeared one by one, replaced by devils. The one from *Legend,* the ones from *Fantasia* and *Castlevania* and *Guitar Hero III, Hellboy,* the rabbit from *Donnie Darko*. Voldemort and Meryl Streep. Julie's newsfeed filled with red-tinted, pointy-browed sneers as they plastered her timeline with photos and videos, status updates about temperatures and torments in Hell, threats and greetings and obscene Google-translated Latin.

Just a joke.

For a second Julie watched an animated .gif of Linda Blair's head rotating over and over, that maniacal snarl with its soul stripped away. Then she hid the posts, changed her settings, unfollowed the devils—she'd follow them again later, she thought, when they turned back into friends. She shut the computer, swore she wouldn't look at Facebook again all weekend—though of course she did. The devils were still there. It was a big stupid joke and her friends would get tired of it soon.

On Monday, Sarah and Joy were clustered, giggling with Andrea, when Shannon Kossowitz called out, "Hey Julie, how was your weekend? Make any new *friends*?"

They were watching later, too, between geometry and lunch, when Julie felt a small shove from behind, just enough to trip her forward. When she turned from her locker to look, another little shove came from behind her, with it a giggling voice: *Sorry, the devil made me do it.* She whipped around again. But then everyone started pushing her from wherever she wasn't looking, their breathy giggles surrounding her, *the devil,* they said, *he made me,* voices swelling to laughter, unrecognizable. She slammed her locker shut and rushed to the bathroom, but from then on there were little shoves and giggles and balls of wadded paper bouncing off her head, "holy water" flung from little vials, and always, always the whispers following her: *It was the devil, the devil made me do it, he made me.*

It was all just a big stupid joke but it went on and on, for weeks, until one Wednesday, after a mostly uneventful morning—a few whispers and giggles, the new usual—Julie was hurrying to a safe-looking corner of the cafeteria when a jab in her crotch startled her lunch tray from her hands, her bowl of minestrone flying with a clatter and splash. “Let Jesus fuck you, let him fuck you,” said a gasping laugh, and Julie saw Tara Baker, a hefty tow-haired girl with a plastic crucifix in her hand. A nice girl, usually. But out of Tara’s pale eyes squinted points of red, a snaggle-toothed smile.

As soon as Julie opened her mouth the devil leapt. The spork in her hand twisted and snapped. She felt as though a barrier had melted; she felt as though her heart was on fire, like all this time she'd been weeping gasoline and now the flames were fed. Shades of fuschia developed across Tara's round cheeks. Julie twirled the broken spork in her fingers and started laughing. "What an excellent day for an exorcism," she said.

Tara began stuttering out an apology, but as soon as she opened her mouth Julie leapt.

She came back to herself with five girls scrabbling at her arms. Tara was sobbing and clutching a gouged forehead; the spork streaked blood across the white linoleum floor. Julie stopped struggling and started crying. She could barely remember the fight.

She spent her week of suspension numb, petrified, at the library. She did some research. That Saturday night after her parents had gone to bed, she locked her bedroom door, drew a pentagram on a box. Lit a candle. Waited.

The devil slid out from under her bed. His one eye glowed; his horns twisted over his pointed ears; his bald head glistened. Thick, curling fur darkened his torso. His grin was all yellow fangs and clot-colored gums.

Compared to Sarah and Joy and Andrea Lindquist? He didn't seem that bad.

"Okay," Julie said. "What exactly do you want?"

7. Learn the Devil's Ways

It's not our souls, it turns out. No. What he wants is the evil in people.

It has many luscious varieties, he told Julie. Many flavors. Deep ones, bright ones. Sour, acid, salty, sweet. Evil is his medium, his art. To see it, to evoke it—most of the time by slyly possessing, drawing out, and projecting what already lurks there. Unknown to his hosts. Most people do not sense his presence. Even those whose evil overruns its containment and rushes unseen through all the nerves and veins of the body, even they sometimes—often—do not feel him. Only in special cases, those who learn to see, who accept this special sight—

He doesn't speak exactly, not with his mouth. He thinks the words into your head and they circulate there, repeating like a pop song. What Julie whispers, I think I've heard it before.

He's a showoff, it's true. Normally he operates in secret, but give him an audience and he's a shameless ham. He'll expose secret thoughts, unravel the bonds of restraint, unchain the evil flowing through one person to another. He'll set off the most spectacular events, the most intimate destructions. He loves to perform, to impress. Appreciation has many forms. What humans call *shame, anger, sadness,* he simply considers a response. And he is addicted to the response. The way humans are addicted to food. He will do anything, just anything, to get it.

But he's willing to do this another way. If we permit.

In my mind's eye I can see his claws uncurl, a gentlemanly wave towards Julie's belly.

The seat of evil in the human body, he said, is the liver. Taken directly from a young person—for a young person's liver is fat with evil, untainted by years of experience or suffering—when offered freely, the flavor is perfect: deep yet delicate, light yet filling. It sates him utterly, for a while. He will seek nothing else.

On my belly the brown and purple ellipse of the devil's kiss is a smeared bruise. Behind it I can feel the line itching from my liver, through my heart, to my brain.

But now when I meet Trina in the cafeteria, my smile blossoms like Julie's does, big and open, full of affection. If only you knew, I want to say, the thing I do for you.

"Hey dopey," Trina laughs. "Did you fall in love?"

"I wish," I answer. Around us everyone's milling through the food line, slapping orange pizza triangles on plastic trays. Nice kids, probably. But if the devil gets in, then who knows. Just imagine what kind of evil might out. Look at danceline Kelly, poking at her salad—imagine her terrorizing babyfat freshmen into bulimia and cutting. Or Miguel, Mr. Future MBA with Wall Street domination penciled in for 2019—picture party drugs and date rape. Or picture sweet, vegan Freya, blowing up science labs.

Shuffling along behind Trina, I look at each one and think, I'm doing this for you. And for you. And you, and you.

Look at creepy Steve with the birdskull strung around his neck and Autopsy lyrics all over his notebooks. Harmless, probably. But maybe not. Maybe the evil in Steve is Columbine bad, Sandy Hook bad. The kind that blasts in Trenchcoat-Mafia-style and splatters cheerleaders across the basketball court.

I'm doing this for all of you.

Under my ribs, the sore spot breaks open. And beneath it, the itch.

"Hey, I gotta talk to Julie Rourke," I tell Trina. "We got this project."

"What is it, feeding the fucking children?" Trina says, and heads over toward Luke.

I squeeze past Steve into the corner and say, "Hey, Julie Fantastic, you saving the world today?"

For a second she's confused—we don't really talk much at

school. Then her smile engages, brightens, like the sun's come up inside. "Just this corner," she answers, watching me sit. "What about you, Rachel Fantastic?"

"Trying." I take a bite of my pizza. Together we look out over all these ordinary kids in their ordinary cafeteria. Voices bounce off the linoleum, hoots and calls, shimmers of laughter.

"Well, everything affects everything, right?" Julie says. "A butterfly flaps its wings and all that."

8. Do Not Trust the Devil

So you reach a certain status quo: you're allowing the devil to suck the evil out of your liver Tuesday, Thursday, and Saturday, around eight or nine p.m. while Mom's absorbed in TV drama. I pass the time—the long furry body pacified, vibrating with strange purrs—flipping around on YouTube or scrolling through clickbait lists of animated gifs. Staring at the Fantastics lined up on their shelf.

Once upon a time Jenna Fantastic was just some normal girl—nice, kinda nerdy, way into science and math. Until she and her three best friends (Jazzi, Jerri, and Jay) stayed late in chemistry lab and messed up their special energy drink experiment and kaboom, they became the Fantastics. Now at night they cruise around dressed like pop stars, using a mixture of psychokinesis, telepathy, chemistry, and geometry to save the world and solve crimes. Plus marketing dolls, t-shirts, and a whole line of promotional crap to the 8-to-11-year-old girl demographic, but whatever.

TV evil is so much simpler, so separate from everyday life. Kidnapping and robberies and piles of stolen jewels. They never show our kind of evil, not really. Jenna Fantastic never gets blackout drunk or wakes up next to Jay all sticky and unsure. Jerri and Jazzi don't talk shit behind her back. None of them shoplift or do drugs or puke beer in the FantastiCar.

All the ways we fuck up, the ways we fall apart. All this ordinary evil.

Julie and me, we got no demographic at all.

Julie fights evil while doing flashcards with the devil

Monday, Wednesday, and Friday, at exactly five p.m. She's saving the world and getting straight As, all at the same time.

Sundays she goes to church. No devil on Sundays.

At my place, Sundays are Mom's big cleaning day: wash the laundry! mop the floors! dust everything! Et cetera et cetera. She sticks her head in my room at eleven whether I'm awake or not, and tells me to do something about my disaster area *or else*. And I don't need her coming in and "organizing" my stuff, finding cigarette butts in the windowsill or my stupid homework covered in red pen. Or the cardboard altar in my closet.

So this particular Sunday I get up, open the window to the new spring air, hug the goose bumps on my arms. My mother's singing down in the basement, some Beatles song echoing through the vents. I feel good like I don't usually feel on Sundays, clean like there's no dirt in me. No hangover because I ditched Luke's party, ignored Trina's texts. Ignored also her posts about missing old friends, then friends who aren't really friends, then what is wrong with people?

LOL, of course. XOXO.

What's wrong? Nothing, really.

There's a scratch and a heat behind me. Inside an itch like a monster mosquito bite.

Except.

The closet door hangs quiet in its frame, closed, painted butter-yellow. Mom's still singing, folding the laundry while it's warm. I could go in for a few minutes. I mean, it's like totally revolting and all that—I mean, it's not like I *want* to—but I'm fighting evil, right? And I'm imagining the nauseating suck of his lips, lifting my hand to the doorknob, when the doorbell rings.

Mom tromps up and says hello, her voice bright and anxious. A lower one answers, minus the fake cheer.

"Maybe you girls need some coffee?" Mom asks. "Or muffins?"

"I'm good," Trina says, then, closer and louder: "Thanks." When I open my door she's at the top of the stairs, wearing Luke's Hot Chip t-shirt, old mascara smudged around her eyes.

"The party was lame." She flops onto my bed next to the

open window. "I thought you were like dead or something. What's up with you lately, anyway?"

"Nothing—God, hang on—"

Mom's started singing again, so I quick-scroll through Trina's Facebook likes to find her music. Sleater Kinney, okay. In my pause she lights a cigarette, blows a mouthful of smoke out the window.

"Are you still pissed about Luke?"

"No, *god*," I snap. Why would I be mad, just because he dumped me and moons over her? "That was like forever ago."

"You're so lying." She digs in her bag for her buzzing phone. "Wait up, I gotta..."

Somehow the closet door's cracked open. Maybe I'm imagining it, maybe I feel it more than hear it: a slow, deliberate scratch on the wooden frame. In between my shoulder blades, this vibrating itch.

Not now, I think, banging the door closed. *I can't deal with you now*.

"I told Luke to come up," Trina says. "You're not mad, right, so what do you care?"

"What? I'm like barely even *dressed*—"

"Oh come *on*." Downstairs I hear heavy boy's feet stomping upstairs, and there's Luke hesitating in the doorway, his smile one-sided, half-shy. His eyes, clear amber, that know me and don't want me.

"Hey Rach," he says. "Everything okay?"

No, I'm not mad. I'm over it, totally. Done.

The closet door blows open untouched. On the threshold Jenna Fantastic lies face down, stick arms and legs all awkward akimbo. It's dark as a throat inside, one red point of light shining out. A slow laugh breathes from the shadows. The itch in my liver's swelling, I can feel it, the surface cracking like a rusty scab.

Luke's saying something, Trina's saying something, and what's wrong, why am I acting so weird lately, staying home all the time, hanging out with that Jesus freak—

But I don't care. All I can feel is this weeping infection. All

I want is to get clean. And what am I doing, anyway, and where am I going, what's in the closet, Rach, what are you—hey—wait, *Rachel?*

The door slams shut. In the dark there's a howling embrace, a flavor rich and rotten flowing through my whole body. Out there let my friends fight, let the sun shine and the world fall aside, because in here, staring into the devil's left eye, this is where I purify.

9. Secure Allies Against the Devil

Tuesday's one of those random spring days when everyone sort of wakes up blinking and remembers what sunshine feels like. Kids scatter across the dead brown grass, clump around picnic tables. Julie's frowning and looking around, but the nearest ears are covered in fat headphones, the nearest eyes glued to tiny screens. Nobody hears me when I say we need to quit.

"Wait, why now?" she asks. "What happened?"

I try to tell her, but the truth is I barely remember. I know I went in the closet, leaving Trina and Luke to ask through the door what the hell I was doing, was this like symbolic or was I really hiding from them or what. I didn't answer. Luke thought they should leave me alone if that's what I wanted, but Trina said the whole thing was completely messed up and no way was she leaving. After fifteen minutes of debate, Trina opened the closet, found me knocked out on the floor, and screamed (she says) like a fucking banshee.

That woke me up, but of course it also freaked out my mother. So I spent the rest of the day in Urgent Care getting needlefuls of blood sucked out of my arm, peeing in a cup to prove I'm not pregnant or a junkie. "She's little anemic, maybe," was what the doctor decided after four hours of waiting and tests. "Eat more spinach. Get more rest."

Julie's shaking her head with this weird expression, like she forgot to finish smiling halfway through. "But that doesn't make sense, it's not a physical thing, so—"

"What if it *is*? Like a drug or something. Like sometimes I even *want* to. Do you—Julie, do you ever feel like you want to?"

She doesn't answer. A breeze flows between us, cool on my cheeks.

"And it hurts—right where he, you know—don't you feel that?"

One of Julie's hands rises, asking me to wait. There's a long silence. I want to fill it, I want to light a cigarette, I want to check my phone, see if Trina's texted. But now Julie's hiding her face, her forehead showing hot pink between her little hands so smooth and clean.

"Oh hey," I say, totally awkward. "Listen. We can do this, okay? I got a plan."

"How?" Julie chokes out. *"How* exactly do you get rid of the devil? That's *impossible*—and then won't everything be like before, and I can't *deal* with that again, I won't—"

"We can't go on like this, either," I tell her. "Because whatever he's taking? I think it's something we need."

She gasps a couple times, lets out a long sigh. A few deep and measured breaths. Her hands drop to clutch her belly, her mark, the kiss that makes a hole in her, keeps other evils away. Her voice comes small and mournful from her side-turned face.

"He's my only friend," she says.

"No." I grab her arm to make her look, give her a shake and let go. "Hey. Julie Fantastic. No, he's not."

10. Eat the Devil Raw

Privacy's the main thing, and Luke owes me, so when I asked to use his place *(what 4?—Satanic ritual LOL)* he couldn't say no. Too many nosy parents at me and Julie's houses, but Luke's basement is practically his own apartment. A kinda musty, ugly apartment with hand-me-down furniture and fake-wood-paneled walls. But private.

"What if you're wrong?"

All week long Julie's been asking me that. And *where* did I read about this, *how* do I know, and what *if*, so many *what ifs* I can't possibly answer.

All I answer is I need her. She has to trust me. And

anyway, I'm pretty sure the method isn't so important. It's the action, the intention, our willingness to go through with it. At least, that's what I'm saying, to her and me both.

"You ready?"

We're sitting cross-legged on the floor with our tacky cardboard altar between us. Underneath it we have a Bible (her idea) and Mom's butcher knife (mine). On top, the candle. Julie's eyes shine big and afraid, her lips pushed out and fretful, like she might cry. But she doesn't say no. I flick my lighter, touch it to the wick.

The flame rises in a long yellow line, settles to a waver. Strings of Christmas lights loop around the ceiling; Twin Shadow dances across a poster on the wall. Upstairs Luke and Trina are playing video games. I can hear her loud laugh, Luke swearing, the crash of explosions and screeching tires.

Thirty seconds pass, maybe less. Maybe forever.

He's in the shadows first, filling the corners, the cracks between wall panels. In dark hollows under the couch, in the wrinkles of Luke's sheets. Even without a body, he's there, lurking, observing, assessing our positions.

He has to be hungry, is the thing. He always is.

Are we assembled here to parley?

The devil's voice grinds along the edge of my mind, through layers of distortion, like some ancient monster rising from the sea. Neither of us answer.

Girls, girls. Is this how friends act?

He can probably read our minds anyway. I try to smother the doubt, because what's important is that me and Julie believe, and if I can do it, she can. Maybe. I think.

Are we not friends? Do we not trust each other? he whispers, still invisible but so close I can feel hot breath on my ear. *My girls. I give you purity. Freedom. And in return ask only for a taste. Is that not fair?*

Julie twists around, searching, then jumps a little in her skin at something I can't feel, stares at something I can't see.

Julie. Do you remember?

She shakes her head hard, like a little kid refusing

vegetables.

I expected this from Rachel, he says. *How could we trust her? She doesn't even trust her friends.*

"But that's not true," I exclaim. I grab Julie's shoulder, but her eyes are focused somewhere on the wall. "You know that's not—"

Remember, Julie. What it's like to be alone. Remember the evil rotting inside you. Running through your veins, sweating through your skin. Remember the shame. The hate.

"Yes," she answers. Her voice is tiny and choked; her fingers curl around her belly. I can feel it, too, the same vacuum, the itch that fills her eyes. Like a knife rusting under my ribs, a stab wound blackening with age. "I remember."

But all may be forgiven among friends. These words aren't for me; I have to strain to make them out. *Julie. Let me forgive. And I will let you forget.*

With a deep breath and a stretch, Julie pulls her t-shirt over her head. Her skin is bright as fire under her pink cotton bra, but his mark still stains her ribs.

The devil draws together into a body, solid shadows with claws and fangs spread out like snares. Julie leans back, opens her arms. And he flows between them. Her arm falls around his shoulders, her fingers in his fur. Her lips are moving, the words barely audible—*our father,* she's saying. Some prayer I never knew. Then her arm shifts, tightens, locks into a bar around his neck. His face smashes sideways, his lips snarling empty and black.

She's still strong. Still counting on me.

This is how friends act: I plunge the butcher knife into the devil's waist, push it down hard to open a big flap there. The flesh hangs empty for a second then fills, pouring hot liquid black. Pain's squealing through my brain, flaming through the hollows of my bones—but it's not my pain and I need the cut wider. I need a hole. Julie's still holding him for me, her other fist clenching a horn. I stab in again, carve out a chunk. And in the gaping void of his torso, I can feel it already, I can taste it, smell—I don't even pause before I shove my hands inside and grab hold of his liver.

The devil's howl is a garbled shriek of laughter inside my head.

I stretch the liver out, cut off a handful. It shivers like black Jell-O with a deep purple glow. The devil's long teeth bare in a skull's lost scream, his eye wide open and blazing like a spotlight.

"Julie, come on." I shove some liver between her lips. "Here, quick—"

She tastes, swallows, makes this huge grimace through her tears. I eat a piece, too. The flavor's like anise and molasses, mixed with the oldest, gamiest, and most congealed and burnt blood. After I swallow, this burst of pine tar and sugar. I slice off another piece, halve it and give one chunk to Julie. Close my eyes and get ready for the next bite.

The silence hits me. No pain, no scream, no words, just the quiet ticks and sighs of a hot water heater. Julie's hurried breath, a gulp for control. Real human voices, murmuring upstairs.

"Rachel?" Julie says. We're alone. She's sitting up and she's smiling, sniffling but definitely smiling. Her eyes shine at me, a red flicker deep inside.

"Yeah?"

"We should finish it."

The liver's still there, a messy purple-black blob staining the cardboard altar. I divide it as best I can, transfer one sloppy double handful to her. It drips and slips as she catches it, takes a big bite. Starts laughing.

"It's so awful," she says. "Oh my goodness, it's so gross."

We're both laughing our asses off when Trina and Luke come downstairs to see what the hell's going on, what are we doing, are we okay. They see Julie in her bra, both of us lying on the floor, our mouths and hands all smeared with black liver and blood.

We're fine, we say, and laugh harder.

I make them both try it. I tell them what it is, but they don't believe me. They think we've gone crazy, or it's some weird joke. But I don't care. I think it protects them anyway.

11. Always Keep the Devil in Your Sights

Maybe you can't see the devil. That's good.

But maybe someday you will. Maybe someday you'll be surrounded, trapped, doing everything you can not to see the devil do his dance for you. Maybe he'll drag your evil out of you, out of your friends and family, lay it out like some giant spider web to wrap you up and choke your whole life away.

Or maybe you can feel it in your liver, that hot acid itch expanding through your guts like a cancer, boiling your good intentions away.

That's why I wrote this whole stupid thing. For people like you.

I'm not pretending we have answers. But this is what we did, Julie and me. Now we can see it, smell it, taste it: find the devil in people, feel the explosions coming, isolate the bombs. Oh, we're vulnerable like everyone else, got our share of evil like everyone else. Maybe a little extra. But now at least we're in control.

But if you have questions, if you want to know more, come find us. I'm usually out smoking by the dumpster during lunch and after school, and unless she's at her church group, Julie's usually with me. We look like the others, mostly. Like Trina and Luke, like everyone else. But you'll recognize us. You'll know. We're the ones with the devil in our eyes, black holes like cigarette burns on the inside of our hearts.

Number One Personal Hitler

Jeff Hemenway

Dr. Francis Waxmann invented time travel in the summer of 2075. It broke the universe some sixty years earlier.

* * *

...rubber bands tied to rubber bands tied to rubber bands tied to rubber bands tied to...

* * *

Sitting in my room, at my desk, a fortress of textbooks in a semicircle around me, depleted paper coffee cups scattered like dead soldiers. I think it was nighttime. Jake's stuff was in piles across the floor, but only on his side of the room. His was a methodical sort of disorganization; he always knew where everything was. My side of the room was fastidiously neat, but I could never find a damned thing. Yin and yang. I don't think these things are accidental.

The portal opened behind me with a little gasp and I turned, nerves honed lancet-sharp by caffeine. The portal floated there, a sucking lamprey-mouth in reality, swirls of color licking the edges. Waxmann stood on the other side, a squat little man with interestingly parted hair. One hand held a smartphone-sized square of electronics, the other a gleaming silver pistol.

That hole in the universe in the foreground, the black O of a gun muzzle in the midground, Waxmann's flat gray eyes in the distance. Portals nested in portals.

The third edition of *Principles of Piezoelectrics* was sailing through the air before I even knew I'd snatched it up and flung it, and Waxmann stumbled towards the portal, through it, hand first. An alligator snap of noise and there was a severed hand on the floor, still clutching the smartphone.

From somewhere in the house, Jake shouted: *Hey, is everything cool back there?*

* * *

When you discover time travel, the first thing you do is kill Hitler.

Hitler isn't a person, though. Hitler is an idea. Hitler is the worst thing that ever existed, the evilest of all evils. In the first century, Hitler was the Roman emperor Nero. Four hundred years later, Hitler was Attila the Hun. Another millennium down the road and Hitler was Tomás de Torquemada.

In the year 2075, Hitler was a man named Clancy Rosemont. I don't know what he did, exactly how many lives he destroyed; the doctor's notes were vague and it's hard to Google someone who won't be born for seven years. What I know is that Rosemont was, at one point, the evilest of all evils. Right before a portal opened up in his bathroom and Waxmann put a bullet in his skull.

And then what? Hitler is dead, what do you do next?

You go down the list of history's greatest monsters. Man by man, execution by execution.

Actual Hitler was number five on the list. I was number four.

* * *

The bullet slammed through the portal, shimmering as it passed, wisps of another reality leaching through in its wake. It struck the belt this time. Bullseye. Jake dropped to the floor, gasping, clutching at his throat. The hole in space collapsed, but

I thought I saw him look up for one moment. Maybe he saw me. Maybe he understood. Or maybe he just chalked it up as a near-death hallucination.

* * *

Imagine you draw a dot on a top, then set it spinning. Put it on carousel. Put the top and the carousel on a bigger carousel. Now fire the whole mess out of cannon and try to map the motion of that original dot. What you have is a simplified version of what you're doing right now as you fly through space, whizzing about the Earth, around the sun, around the galaxy, cutting through a space that's been expanding at near the speed of light for fourteen billion years. Now try mapping it through time, down to the nanometer, down to the picosecond. You'll need a computer more powerful than anything on modern-day Earth by a couple orders of magnitudes.

Or you can make do with Doc Waxmann's smartphone.

It also plays Tetris.

* * *

My own personal Hitler was Jake's suicide. We were inseparable growing up, sharing a room even when Mom's financial situation improved enough that we could've each had our own. We spent long summers blasting cans with our BB guns, learning to read lips so we could hold silent conversations during church. Wrestling in the living room until Mom told us to knock it off already, then waiting until she left so we could do it some more, only quiet and sneaky-like.

I followed Jake to college, but something had happened after he left. In those two years between his high-school graduation and mine, we never really saw one another. We talked on the phone less and less frequently. He went from darkly sarcastic and coolly cynical to just dark, and just cynical, never laughing anymore, never smiling. After I arrived at the university, I lived with him for another eighteen months, sharing a room again. I thought he'd just lost his sense of humor, as though laughter was something you outgrew, like afternoon cartoons, or accidental erections during homeroom.

I came home one day and found him hanging by his neck in the doorway of our shared walk-in closet, my tidy piles on his left, his clutter on the right, and the exclamation mark of his body driving right between the two. He'd used a belt. The body was still warm.

I don't know what my Number Two Hitler would've been. You can really only fathom one Hitler at a time. Maybe Dad walking out on us when we were still little. Maybe Queensrÿche breaking up.

* * *

Time travel wasn't so much time travel as alternate-reality generation. Think *Back to the Future*. Think Biff Tannen and sports almanacs. Making new timelines spontaneously, everything a copy of a copy of a copy. Hitler's there one moment, and then he never existed, and suddenly the universe has to patch the hole.

There was something about wormholes, too, something about quantum, something about Many Worlds. Doc Waxmann's digital logbook wasn't annotated, but I doubt I could have deciphered the references even if it had been.

The smartphone actually *was* a smartphone. A modified one, little patches of electronics soldered to it, a few custom apps in its inventory. The app for generating a stable, localized wormhole connecting our universe to a spontaneously-generated alternate universe was called *Timehole v2.71.* I thought it was a pretty good name.

The logbook started with technobabble about how the whole thing worked. Musings on the schematics of the room-sized machine that would generate the portals, musings on how the construction was proceeding.

Eventually, Waxmann ran his first trial. It involved a sandwich. The sandwich did not fare well. There would be many more trials.

I opened the first portal accidentally. Flopped in the chair in my room, the side Jake had once occupied still empty. The fourth edition of *Introduction to Kinematics* that I'd hurled at Waxmann was still splayed on the floor. I poked at the icons on the touchscreen just to see what they did; the classic arcade games were largely intact, but most buttons did nothing but flash dejected *Network Not Found* messages.

A tap on the Timehole icon, though, a few half-read screens of text and a hiss of air—and I was staring at the back of my head through a fist-sized hole in reality.

* * *

A portal can stay open for a maximum of twelve seconds. A portal collapses if an object of excessive momentum passes through it. There were rules—of course there were rules, there are always rules. Some made sense, others were arcane declarations like MAXDIAM_100 and MINDIST_25 and PORTFIX_3 that I understood somewhere between very little and not at all.

When Waxmann successfully murdered his Number One Hitler, he took a lot of notes and drank a lot of alcohol. The first secret, he wrote, was finding that perfect point in spacetime and placing a portal *right there*, right at some pivotal moment in history. Say, in a certain bathroom in a certain hotel. Say, three months and two days and five hours and seventeen minutes and 53.1823 seconds before your target is going to initiate a sequence of events that kills twenty million people. The smartphone did most of the heavy lifting as far as that went; the magic box in Waxmann's lab did the rest.

The second secret was probably very important, but it had been typed by someone very drunk. I refuse to judge, though. I got drunk, too, the first time I killed my own Number One personal Hitler. And the second time, and the third time.

Some Hitlers just won't stay dead.

* * *

On my inaugural mission, I opened a portal six inches away from Jake's face, three seconds after he'd kicked out the chair. Bulging eyes, fat tongue swelling in his mouth, yellow snot bubbling from his nostril. He saw me, but I don't know if he *saw* me. I don't know if anyone in that position sees much of anything.

Twelve seconds later, the portal snapped shut, and I didn't touch the smartphone for a few hours. I just sat there in the pre-dawn light in my half-cluttered room, a bunch of books and some leftover pizza on my desk, a bottle of Smirnoff in one sweaty fist, Waxmann's severed hand rotting in the corner.

My next attempt landed the portal two minutes pre-death, a few feet off to the side, and I screamed the full twelve seconds before realizing that sound didn't travel through the portal. After the portal closed I screamed at the room, screamed at Jake, screamed at Waxmann's stupid, rancid fist.

That didn't accomplish much, either.

* * *

Doc Waxmann's second assassination went down more easily, and he was ostensibly sober during the post-game. A major change in the timeline, the untimely death of a genocidal mass murderer—it slams into you pretty hard. Black-out hard. When he woke up, he had new memories. He had all the old ones too, but the old ones were like a movie you'd watched a million times. You can recite all the lines and visualize all the plot points, but it's just this story you heard. It's just make-believe.

Once upon a time, a very bad man killed a lot of people, and everyone lived unhappily ever after. Roll credits.

* * *

Jake's gun was stashed in our closet, three feet away from where he killed himself. I was a pretty good shot; I split the belt just as he kicked out the chair. As the bullet sucked the portal closed behind it, I could see him tumble to the floor, and I knew past-me would get to him in time, no way could he rig up the belt again before past-me showed up.

I waited for the sledgehammer crash of my reality being overwritten, but it was really more of a flyswatter.

Once upon a time, a very sad man tried to hang himself with a belt. It didn't work out very well. So he used his gun.

* * *

How bad do things have to get before non-existence is the best possible solution?

After you've sat in a room for couple of days, not eating, not bathing, trying to reverse a suicide that happened six months ago, you ask yourself all kinds of questions.

How long is the battery life on this smart-phone thing, anyway?

How does this gadget still *work* when the actual time machine doesn't even occupy the same universe?

Is that really Jake I hear talking in the next room, or is it a phantom, or a memory, or something else entirely?

* * *

Eventually it came down to timing. Wait until he's already hanging-dangling-strangling and then *BLAM*, sever the belt, and now he's stunned. Can't get to the gun, can't get to the pills, just enough time for past-me to arrive and call 911, get Jake to a hospital where they can patch him up, good as new.

And they all lived happily ever after, roll credits.

For certain definitions of *ever*.

For certain definitions of *after*.

* * *

By the time he knocked off Hitler Number Three, Waxmann was a pro. One trip back, bang, wait for the shockwave of alternate history, off to the pub for a rum-and-Rogers, whatever that was.

He'd been wrong about the true nature of spacetime, he wrote. It *wasn't* copies of copies of copies, there was no spontaneous generation of alternate realities, and how monstrously silly of him to suppose otherwise.

Everything was already there, see, every possible timeline weaving through the multiverse in an infinity of infinitely-long strands. The magic box just created a link from one possible universe to another. Shoelaces tied to shoelaces tied to shoelaces.

Also, he wrote: Very important! Utmost and paramount! The links are permanent. The wormholes close, but they never *close*-close. They persist, like scars. Too close together and they get tangled. They choke the life out of reality, making kinks, tears. Travel back to the same time twice, and who knows what might happen?

I didn't know this at the outset. I didn't read this bit until after.

For certain definitions of *after*.

* * *

Never gaze into the abyss, for the abyss might also gaze into you. And it might be wearing your face. And it might be aiming a pistol.

Again.

And again.

* * *

The hardest part was visualizing how the smartphone had come into my hands. When Waxmann will/would/had

Rube-Goldberged his device into my lap, what would that look like, from the outside? A remote control stretching back through the hole it had just opened in the cosmos, connected to the magic box across space and time, reality twining around itself. Like someone trying to pull themselves through their own belly button.

* * *

Waxmann never realized that the portals were less like shoelaces and more like rubber bands.

I only know this because I heard it from future-me, but then future-me told me a lot of things. Things I couldn't hear, but I could read on future-me's lips. I could see future-me pleading with me from some other when.

Future-me was the one who suggested one final portal, right in the temporal center of the whole mess. Throw up one last portal right in the middle of when-where and watch it snap all the other portals, make it like it had never happened, and everything springs back to normal. Put it up right in between Jake kicking out the chair and Jake's heart pumping out its final beat.

Jake was sitting across the room when future-me mouthed this plan to me from inside the portal. Jake in his chair, cramming for some final. Or Jake wasn't there and never had been. There and not there, done and undone, everything shimmery and feather-edged.

The Jake who survived sometimes smiled, sometimes joked. We sometimes had fun. And sometimes he told me I should never have saved him at all, that he wished it had all stopped fast at the end of a leather belt. Maybe these were all the same Jake, but maybe some were different. With an infinity of Jakes, at least some of them must be happy.

Do this, future-me had said, or it all falls apart. The multiverse collapses on itself. Reality will not just cease to exist, it will never have been at all.

Somewhere, somewhen, there will still be a Jake, and we will be together, and we will be happy. We'll get married, have families, have barbecues and family get-togethers, laughing over beers or wine coolers or rums-and-Rogers.

Even if I never see any of that, it doesn't mean it's not out there.

* * *

The bullet tore through my jaw. If I look closely, I can see a tooth embedded in the sheetrock on the far wall, a fleck of white in a mess of strawberry jam.

This final-me appeared just as I was about to key in one last portal, fingers hovering over a screen that was dimmer than it had been three/five/seventy days ago. Waxmann's hand was black with ants.

I stared at future-me through the portal, barely visible in some preternatural dimness. I stared at the gun future-me was pointing, black or maybe chrome or maybe slate gray.

You can't do this, he mouthed from across time.

I have to, I mouthed back. Just this one last portal. If I don't, everything ends. Everything ceases to exist. If I don't do this, there won't be anything left.

I know, he said.

As he spoke, I noticed that something was very wrong on his side of the hole. Angles were off. Things seeped and shifted. I could see both his face and the back of his head at the same time, like a Mercator projection.

He fired, and half my face disappeared in a crimson spray.

* * *

My finger still floats above an Enter key specked with dots of gore.

How bad do things have to get before non-existence becomes the best possible solution?

I guess I'll find out.

Spirit Tasting List for Ridley House, April 2016

Rachael Acks

To Mr. T. H., happy birthday.

Welcome, honored guest, to Ridley House; the acquisition of this charming 18th-century Palladian Revival villa has been something of a coup for our club and we are beyond pleased to present a wide array of tastes for your pleasure, if for a limited time. Take a moment to enjoy the grounds, particularly the stately elms with their attendant garlands of Spanish moss, and the mist rising from the ponds and nearby irrigation canals.

Before proceeding, we respectfully remind you to check the condition of your crystal spirit glass; it should be free of all cracks, chips, or blemishes to be able to properly capture and concentrate energies. Please take advantage of the sanitizer provided at the door, which will remove any lingering ectoplasm. Should your spirit glass develop an imperfection during the course of your meal, new ones will be available for purchase at a reasonable rate.

This menu will address the spirits in recommended tasting order for maximum piquancy, though our guests are of course welcome to explore the experience however they might like.

FIRST TASTE: FRONT PARLOR

The manifestation may be found over the lightly stained floorboards where the house's pianoforte once rested. Warm flavors of charred wood and cloves harmonize over a dark mineral undertone that hints at a long history of violence perpetrated upon others. Sharp spiciness bursts upon the tongue, representing the surprise at the moment of death, a grace note of the unexpected. Note the floral scent that lingers after you've enjoyed your taste, the way it changes and enhances the preceding flavor.

Our historian believes this manifestation to be Martha Ridley, matriarch of the family, who was murdered in 1919 by a burglar, according to police records. A cane belonging to her has been brought down from the house's attic, the smooth polish on the handle and the multitude of microscopic cracks throughout the shaft indicating vigorous use.

SECOND TASTE: KITCHEN PANTRY

Open the antique ice box to find our next manifestation in the darkened interior, which is far too small to contain the full body of an adult man. To the discerning nose, the metallic hints of blood and salt linger even to this day, contained in the scraps of stained rope that sit at the bottom of the box. This spirit is redolent of leather, woodsmoke, and high-grade tobacco, decadently masculine. An acrid taste lingers, as of burnt leaves in the autumn, an echo of more drawn-out agonies, overlaid with a sweetness of hothouse flowers, familiar from the first taste.

This ice box is believed to be the last resting place of handyman Edward Smith, thought to have left the employ of the Ridleys in April of 1917 after the declaration of war on Germany, intent on joining the army. Records show that he never made it to the recruitment office. A picture recovered from a trunk in the attic shows him to be an uncommonly attractive young man, posing unselfconsciously with an ax before the trees.

THIRD AND FOURTH TASTE: ELM TREE

Outside the kitchen stands one of the manor's larger trees. Under its strongest branch you will find a manifestation redolent with gunpowder, gin, and orange peel, the strong relic of a man cut down in his prime. The flavor is, sadly, somewhat muddled with a cacophony of metallics unthinkingly inculcated at time of death. If you hold your glass to the moon, you'll catch a hint of the olive drab color that had become the staple of army uniforms during World War I.

A few steps away the second manifestation waits, a much more subtle mix of greenery, ocean salt, and the delightfully domestic sweetness of bread. Fascinatingly, the orange peel of taste #3 carries over to #4, linking the two inextricably together. This subtlety is almost overwhelmed by a contrasting burst of bright mint and dark truffle, clarity and despair that make for a decadent, almost chocolatey finish—violence turned inward.

Taste #3 has been identified as Corporal Jeremiah Green, from archived picture postcards of his lynching on May 12, 1921. He had returned home for leave and was accused of assault by Elizabeth Ridley (daughter of Martha), despite having never before been on the Ridley House grounds. Taste #4 is thought to be where her brother Nathaniel Ridley committed suicide three days later, by means of Corporal Green's service pistol. Rumor has it he had been planning to leave Ridley House within the week, departing for New York City—with Corporal Green.

INTERLUDE

On your way to the final taste, we encourage you to stop by the vegetable garden, study, and nursery. The manifestations in these areas are not well-defined enough to offer the sort of experience we prefer for our guests, but will whet the appetite and sharpen the senses. In the nursery, see how many distinct presences you might find; our most experienced sommeliers have caught between seven and nine, not quite overwhelmed by the sweetness of hothouse flowers.

FIFTH TASTE: BEDROOM

A fitting end to the evening, this manifestation is the reason for our limited run at the Ridley house; not anchored by the dark chords of abrupt or violent death, we expect it to be fully consumed within the month. Strongly sweet and floral with satisfaction to the point of being almost cloying; seek below the surface to find the bitterness of quinine, the spicy heat of foxglove, and lingering almond.

This is the known manifestation of Elizabeth Ridley, deceased due to heart failure in 1992 at the age of 90. She was born in Ridley House and is never known to have left the grounds, though she found local fame by cultivating hothouse orchids. Drink deeply and you may hear her reported final words whispered in an incongruously young voice: "We are the same, you and I, but I enjoyed my feast while you have only the dregs."

Now We've Lost

Natalia Theodoridou

The war is over, we hear. We've lost. We look at each other in the dark. What does this mean? We've lost so much already. What is it we've lost now?

One after the other, we go outside. The sky is draped like a shroud over the town. The sun behind ash and smoke. From our houses. From our fields. Our gardens. A bird hangs in the air, undecided. Can birds still fly now we've lost the war?

The foreign boys who are stationed outside have heard they won the war. They drink wine. They fire their guns. They laugh, the victors. Horsed, they circle us. They hoot and jeer. The victors. The stallions. Last night they were weeping at our feet in the dark.

* * *

The boys are gone. It's just us now. Women. Girls. Every morning, we step out of what remains of our houses and collect the rubble in piles on the street. I used to grow chrysanthemums in my garden. Now it's sown with cigarettes and shards of glass. The victors' seeds. I wonder what will grow.

At night we retreat inside. I check on the little mummy that lives in the dark room in the back. Will it stop breathing now we've lost the war? I kneel by its side and watch its chest rise and fall, rise and fall, until I'm lost to sleep.

I dream of wedding rings. They come out of my belly button, dozens and dozens of wedding rings. I spread them out on the floor and search for my own, but I can't find it. Then, I remember; it was one of the foreign boys, long ago. After he was finished, he took the ring off my finger. As payment, he said.

* * *

We've piled the rubble high, gathered everything we can use: bricks and stones, cement, window frames and planks and metal rods. We stand by our piles and wait for someone to come and build everything back up. Not because we can't do it ourselves, no. But if no one comes back, what would be the point?

The glass in my yard is still gleaming beneath the soil. It's yet to bloom.

* * *

The man comes early one morning. His khakis are worn and dusty. They hang off him, too large for his frame, or his frame diminished from wearing them for too long. We don't know him. Is he a victor? Is he one of our own? He seems our age. His hair is black and sleek like a crow's feathers. His features slender, his fingers long and thin.

He starts picking my pile of rubble apart. He loads the stones on his back, the planks, the rods. He kneels by my house's crumbling wall while I look on. He nods at me. We don't exchange any words. Do we even speak the same language? He mixes dirt with water for my wall. My glass garden catches the dim light of the sun.

At night, I pull him inside. He's cut his hands on the glass. I clean them with water and soap. His skin is soft. I want to kiss it. Do we still kiss now we've lost the war? He cups my face in his palms. I trace the gentle outline of his chin, the beautiful angle of his cheekbones.

I take him to the back room, show him the mummy in its bed. Its breathing forever the same. "It's been here a long time," I say. "Ever since they took my son." He looks at me, but I don't know if he understands. "If you don't mind it, you can stay," I add.

When he slips under the covers with me, khakis shed and grime washed off, his body is warm and smooth and supple. His body like mine. We don't make a sound. All I can hear is the mummy's breath in the dark.

Later, I dream of crow's feathers and silk.

* * *

Months pass, but no others come to our town. We finish fixing my house, and together with the other women we rebuild the rest. The women ply him with gifts of whatever they can spare, but he accepts none. I fear they'll find out how unlike other men he is when they touch his slender arms, when they stand too close to him, peering at his long neck, his beardless, stubbleless chin. But nobody says anything. They smile when they see him coming home to me every night. Are they bitter? Are they lonely? Do we get to feel lonely now we've lost the war?

* * *

Soon, we marry. There's no priest. No rings either. The women stand us one next to the other, shoulder to shoulder, same frame, same height. They rain flowers on our heads and wash our feet with cool milk. "You're wife and husband now," they say. "Kiss." We still kiss, after all. The women cheer. They hug each other. Bitter. Happy. There are blades of grass sprouting amidst the glass in my yard. My man smiles, but he doesn't speak.

Nobody wishes us children. "For all we've lost, there's true joy here," they say.

Back at the house, the mummy is still breathing. Despite all the joy.

* * *

My man, he lets his hair grow out. He ties it into a ponytail when he goes outside to chop wood. I watch him from the door, how he swings his axe up and down. My man. He grunts every time he brings the axe down on a log. He hasn't spoken a word in all the time we've been together. I wonder what his voice would sound like. He sees me and dries his brow, a solemn look on his face.

Later, I find him standing over the mummy, trying to smother it with a pillow. He's crying. I touch his shoulder and slowly take the pillow from his hands. His hair cascades down his back, darker than ever.

"It doesn't work that way, love," I tell him.

At night, I offer to braid his hair like I do mine. He lets me.

"Speak to me," I plead.

We lie in the dark, the mummy's soft breathing droning on, lulling us to sleep.

* * *

My man's voice is deep, it turns out, like a river.

He never speaks to me, but he starts singing one night when we press our bodies together in bed. He sings all night long. Melodies I've never heard before, in a language I don't understand. It makes me think of the boys, the victors, how they cheered and laughed all those years ago.

In the morning, I lay my head on the mummy's bed, check if its chest is still moving. When he sees me, my man answers with a song of drawn-out vowels and sharp turns that cut like glass.

The mummy breathes in slowly, then exhales before the song ends.

AUTHORS

Megan Arkenberg lives in Northern California, where she is pursing a Ph.D. in English literature. Her work has appeared in *Asimov's, Lightspeed, Nightmare*, Ellen Datlow's *Best Horror of the Year*, and dozens of other places. She was recently the nonfiction editor for *Nightmare*'s Queers Destroy Horror! special issue; she also procrastinates by editing the fantasy e-zine *Mirror Dance*. Megan tweets @meganarkenberg and blogs sporadically at blog.meganarkenberg.com.

Kay Chronister 's fiction has appeared in Beneath Ceaseless Skies and Clarkesworld. She lives in Seattle with her miniature dachshund, Victor Hugo.

Kostas Ikonomopoulos was born in Athens in 1976. He studied in Greece and the UK. Over the years, he has worked in education, development, trading & outsourcing, gaming and publishing, in Europe, South Africa, China and SE Asia. He recently published a non-fiction book about ruined and neglected sites of cultural significance in Singapore, where he has been living for the past five years.

Michael McGlade is an Irish writer with almost sixty short stories in journals such as Dark Moon Digest, Perihelion, Voluted Tales, SQ Mag, and the forthcoming Night Lights anthology by Geminid Publishing. He holds a master's degree in English and Creative Writing from the Seamus Heaney Centre, Queen's University, Ireland. Represented by Isobel Dixon of the Blake Friedmann Literary Agency. Find out the latest news and views from him on McGladeWriting.com.

Jessica May Lin recently returned to the San Francisco Bay Area after moonlighting as a nightclub pole dancer for a year in Beijing, China, and is now completing her last year at UC Berkeley. Her fiction has appeared in or is forthcoming in Chiral Mad 3, Nature, Daily Science Fiction, and others. Her nonfiction stories have been published in the Chinese-language edition of the New York Times. Visit her website at jessicamaylin.com.

Sarah Brooks grew up just down the road from Blackpool, then ran away to China, Japan and Italy. She wrote her PhD on Chinese ghost stories, and now lives in Leeds, where she teaches East Asian Studies. She is a graduate of the 2012 Clarion West Writers' Workshop, and has had work published in *Interzone, Strange Horizons,* and *Unlikely Story.*

Rachael K. Jones grew up in various cities across Europe and North America, picked up (and mostly forgot) six languages, an addiction to running, and a couple degrees. Now she writes speculative fiction in Athens, Georgia, where she lives with her husband. Her work has appeared or is forthcoming in a variety of venues, including *Lightspeed, Accessing the Future, Strange Horizons, Escape Pod, Crossed Genres,* and *Daily Science Fiction.* She is an editor, a SFWA member, and a secret android. Follow her on Twitter @RachaelKJones.

Gwendolyn Kiste is a speculative fiction writer based in Pennsylvania. Her work has appeared in Nightmare Magazine, Flash Fiction Online, LampLight, and Three-Lobed Burning Eye Magazine as well as Flame Tree Publishing's Chilling Horror Short Stories anthology. She currently resides on an abandoned horse farm with her husband, two cats, and not nearly enough ghosts. You can find her online at www.gwendolynkiste.com and on Twitter (@GwendolynKiste).

Arkady Martine is a speculative fiction writer and, as Dr. AnnaLinden Weller, a Byzantine historian. In both roles she writes about border politics, rhetorical propaganda, and liminal spaces. She was a student at Viable Paradise XVII. Arkady grew up in New York City and currently lives in Uppsala, Sweden. Find her online at arkadymartine.wordpress.com or on Twitter as @ArkadyMartine.

Bentley A. Reese is a fiction writer and English student at UW-Madison. He enjoys writing genre fiction of all kinds with a particular fondness for horror and sci-fi. Fresh on the publishing scene, Bentley's work was recently featured in the 2015 Edition of Midwest Prairie Review as well as Encounters Magazine. Drop him an email atbareese@wisc.edu.

Rich Larson was born in West Africa, has studied in Rhode Island and worked in Spain, and at 23 now writes from Edmonton, Alberta. His short work has been nominated for the Theodore Sturgeon and appears in multiple Year's Best anthologies, as well as in magazines such as Asimov's, Analog, Clarkesworld, F&SF, Interzone, Strange Horizons, Lightspeed and Apex. Find him at richwlarson.tumblr.com.

AJ Fitzwater is a meat-suit wearing dragon who lives between the cracks of Christchurch, New Zealand. A graduate of Clarion 2014, they were awarded the Sir Julius Vogel Award 2015 for Best New Talent. Their work has appeared in such venues of repute as *Beneath Ceaseless Skies, Andromeda Spaceways Inflight Magazine, Crossed Genres Magazine, Scigentasy, Betwixt,* Lethe Press' *Heiresses of Russ 2014*, Twelfth Planet Press' *Letters to Tiptree*, and others. Daily brain fluff can be found on Twitter @AJFitzwater.

Rachael Acks (now Alex Acks) is a writer, geologist, and dapper AF.
They're a proud Angry Robot with their novel *Hunger Makes the Wolf* forthcoming in March 2017. They've written for Six to Start and been published in Strange Horizons, Lightspeed, Daily Science Fiction, and more. Alex lives in Denver with their two furry little bastards, where they twirl their mustache, watch movies, and bicycle. For more information, see http://www.rachaelacks.com.

Nicasio Andres Reed is a Filipino-American writer and poet whose work has appeared in Comma Press, Queers Destroy

Science Fiction, Strange Horizons, Liminality, Inkscrawl and Beyond: the Queer Sci-Fi and Fantasy Comics Anthology. A member of the Queer Asian SF/F/H Illuminati, Nicasio currently resides in Madison, WI. Find him on Twitter @NicasioSilang.

K.L. Morris earned her M.F.A. from Lesley University in 2013. Her work has appeared in *The Flexible Persona* and *Body Parts Magazine: A Journal of Horror and Erotica*. She spends most of her time writing, walking her dog, and ignoring her husband in order to write. When no one's around, she writes inside of a tent with a large glass of wine. When people are around, she writes inside of a tent with a large glass of wine and the door zipped shut. She's neither as broody nor as introspective as she presents herself. Connect with her on Twitter @KareMoreIs. She blogs at www.thewritinggeek.com.

Avi Naftali moonlights as a fiction writer, composer, and sort-of essayist. He grew up in Los Angeles and currently works a nine-to-five in New York. He writes the Artichoke letters of the onionandartichoke blog, which can be found at onionandartichoke.wordpress.com.

Natalia Theodoridou is a media & cultural studies scholar, a dramaturge, and a writer of strange stories. Her work has appeared in *Clarkesworld, The Kenyon Review Online, sub-Q, Interfictions*, and elsewhere. Find out more at her website (www.natalia-theodoridou.com), or come say hi @natalia_theodor on Twitter.

Fran Wilde's work includes the Andre Norton and Compton Crook Award-winning, and Nebula Award-nominated, novel *Updraft* (Tor, 2015), the upcoming novel *Cloudbound* (Tor, 2016), and the novella "The Jewel and Her Lapidary," (Tor.com publishing). Her short stories also appear in Asimov's, Tor.com, Beneath Ceaseless Skies, Uncanny, and Nature. She writes for publications including The Washington Post, Tor.com,

Clarkesworld, iO9.com, and GeekMom.com. You can find her on twitter @fran_wilde, and at franwilde.net.

Lora Gray is a native of Northeast Ohio where they currently reside with their husband and a freakishly smart cat named Cecil. A 2016 graduate of Clarion West, Lora's work has most recently appeared in *Flash Fiction Online* and *Strange Horizons*. When they aren't writing, Lora works as an illustrator and dance instructor.

Ryan Row lives in Oakland California with a beautiful and mysterious woman. His work has been previously published, or is forthcoming, in *Bayou Magazine, Daily Science Fiction, The Sierra Nevada Review*, and elsewhere. He is a winner of The Writers of the Future Award and holds a B.A. in Creative Writing from San Francisco State University. You can find him online at ryanrow.com.

A. Merc Rustad is a queer non-binary writer and filmmaker who lives in the Midwest United States. Favorite things include: robots, dinosaurs, monsters, and tea — most of which are present in their work to some degree. Their stories have appeared in *Lightspeed, Fireside Fiction, Daily Science Fiction, Escape Pod, Mothership Zeta,* and *InterGalactic Medicine Show*, as well as the anthology *The Best American Science Fiction and Fantasy 2015*. Merc has considered making their tagline "The Robot Who Makes People Cry With Their Stories." In addition to breaking readers' hearts, Merc likes to play video games, watch movies, read comics, and wear awesome hats. You can find Merc on Twitter @Merc_Rustad or their website: http://amercrustad.com.

Lia Swope Mitchell was once a teenager who was way into creative writing and learning French. Today she is a writer, translator, editorial assistant at Univocal Publishing, and PhD candidate in French literature at the University of Minnesota. So, basically the same. She lives in Minneapolis. Find her online at liaswopemitchell.com.

By day, Jeff Hemenway analyzes data for the state of California. By night, he still analyzes data, but he doesn't get paid for it and people ask him to please stop. Somewhere in there, he finds the time to write. His work has appeared previously in such venues as Daily Science Fiction and in the award-nominated horror anthology, Dark Visions.

Shimmer

Shimmer aspires to publish excellent fiction across lines of race, income, nationality, ethnicity, gender, sexual orientation, age, geography, and culture, and encourages submissions of diverse stories from diverse authors. This includes, but is not limited to: people of color, LBGTQIA, women, the impoverished, the elderly, and those with disabilities. We encourage authors of all backgrounds to write stories that include characters and settings as diverse and wondrous as the people and places of the world we live in. Every story sent to us should be well-researched, respectful, and conscientious.

Shimmer publishes every other month, and can be found online at www.shimmerzine.com. Subscribers allow us to keep doing what we do. $15 gets you six issues, delivered straight to your email inbox—or, that of a friend. *Shimmer* makes a perfect gift for the short fiction lover in your life!

Made in the USA
Charleston, SC
24 January 2017